FUCK AROUND AND FIND OUT

FUCK AROUND AND FIND OUT

EDITED BY

R.E. SARGENT & STEVEN PAJAK

FUCK AROUND AND FIND OUT
Edited by R.E. Sargent & Steven Pajak

Published by Sinister Smile Press, LLC,
A Division of Crystal Lake Publishing
P.O. Box 637, Newberg, OR 97132

Trade Paperback ISBN – 978-1-964398-89-1

www.sinistersmilepress.com
www.crystallakepub.com

CONTENTS

"Don't start nothing, won't be nothing."

— AGENT J, MEN IN BLACK

RED STAR

NICK ROBERTS

I see the pointed end of a newer-looking tattoo poking out from under the server's white sleeve as he reaches across the table and refills my water. Gabino's restaurant is a place I frequent quite a bit, at least since parting from my wife, but I've never noticed this new guy or his tattoo. It did catch my eye, though, the way it revealed itself for just a blink and disappeared into the recesses of his immaculate uniform.

He sees me seeing it. I can feel it. I quickly look back at my plate like I'm minding my own business.

"Are you new here?" I ask without looking up from a plate that's so empty it looks like I licked it clean.

He's an Asian man (I think Japanese?) half my age, tall, svelte, and handsome but not in a pretty boy way.

"I'm sorry, sir. I didn't catch that. What did you say?" he asked.

His voice has no trace of an accent but possesses a certain timbre that effortlessly conveys confidence and strength, a reverberation of masculinity. Let me put it to you like this: he's the polar opposite of my flabby ass.

Since my wife left me, I've let myself go, and literally, everything scares me. I'm riddled with anxiety and sink into bouts of depression —both of which I take prescription meds for, but they only make me gain weight and give me a limp dick, not that I have anyone who'd want to see it hard anyway.

I'm a sad fucking sack, I know. Even having accepted these truths about myself, I try to avoid morbid self-pity. It's easier to do this when I don't compare myself to others and just appreciate the blessings in my life. My therapist suggested writing a daily gratitude list. It helps, surprisingly. Right before bed, I think about all the good things going my way and focus on them.

Some of these include my job, my decent relationship with my parents and sister, my relative health (though I know that's going to gradually decline if I don't get my ass back in shape), my car, my apartment that's decorated the way I like it and full of material possessions that I can afford, and my cats. I have two of them: Penny and Nickel.

Oh yeah, I also was told to remain grateful for things I, and probably most people, I imagine, take for granted. I live in the United States and have a certain number of freedoms and human rights that many people on this planet do not.

And I recently became aware of the privileges appointed to me just for being born a straight, white male. I don't say that facetiously. I'm not an educated man and never did take to reading much. Never did much traveling or ever had any desire to, really. But I do watch the news and try to stay up to date with social media apps. It's important to know what's going on in your country, to me at least.

So, rather than compare my forty-year-old out-of-shape ass, whose combover and baggy clothes aren't fooling anyone, to this fit young man before me, I practice being happy for him. It's not an easy task; don't get me wrong. My therapist made sure I knew it would take practice—maybe a lifetime's worth—but in time, it could gradually become a working part of the mind, alleviating my jealousy and negative self-image and replacing it with genuine joy for other people.

It's progress, not perfection, I'm told.

"Sir?" the server asks again.

"Yes?"

"Did you say something to me?"

"Oh, yeah. I was just wondering if you are new here. I come here quite often around this time of morning and haven't seen you before."

He smiles, revealing straight white teeth and dimples.

"Yes, I'm new to this location. I worked at Gabino's on the west side for the last year."

"Oh, it's a bit of a rougher clientele over there, I'd imagine."

I say that immediately feeling some type of way about it because, like I said, I've recently become aware of my white privilege.

"You can say that again." The server chuckles and nods his head.

I look at his gold-plated name tag.

"Ren?" I ask.

"Yes, sir. That's my name."

"Forgive me if this is inappropriate, but are you Jap—"

"Japanese, yes sir." He thankfully cuts off my awkwardness mid-question.

I just look at his wiry frame and imagine his chiseled physique underneath that perfectly fitting uniform and then allow my eyes to match his friendly gaze. If he feels uneasy about this interaction, he's been expertly trained not to show it.

"I'm sorry, Ren. I don't mean to hold you up. I just come here all the time and see the same old people doing the same old stuff, and it's nice to see a new face is all."

"I can certainly understand that, sir. A little change is good for everyone."

I nod.

"May I get that out of your way for you?"

"Oh, yeah. Thanks," I say and back away as he reaches for my empty plate that was full of two breakfast burritos and hashbrowns ten minutes ago.

I notice his sleeve pulls back again as he extends his arm in front of me. The tattoo is fully visible now. A blood-red star about an inch in diameter is perfectly inked into the skin on his inner wrist. I don't know why my mind thinks of it as the entry point for a knife if one were to slice a straight line down their wrist, but that's the image I conjure up, nonetheless.

"That's an interesting tattoo," I say.

For the first time since he took my drink order, Ren drops his professional demeanor. It was only for a split second, but I saw it in his eyes. I can't tell if it's fear I'm seeing or embarrassment or shock. He's a hard one to read, and normally I'm pretty good at that. Before I could apologize if I offended him, he smiles.

"Thank you, sir. Would you like me to bring out some more coffee?"

"That would be great."

"Coming right up." He gives a slight nod and scurries away.

I wonder what the hell that was all about and finally settle on two possible conclusions, though one isn't entirely politically correct. The first one, and the one that makes the most sense, is that Gabino's doesn't want employees with exposed tattoos. Even though it's a breakfast and lunch joint, it is on the higher end of the restaurant food chain. I knew the owner, Martin Gabino, only slightly before he passed, but he seemed like the old school sort of businessman who looked down on things like that.

I then immediately look around the establishment for other workers—servers, hosts, busboys, cooks—and don't see a tattoo or a facial piercing on any of them. Yeah, that must be it. My second hypothesis is null at this point, but I'll entertain it anyway.

Suppose he's part of some Japanese crime syndicate, or even more salacious, suppose he's on the run. Maybe he botched a job or screwed his boss's old lady, and now he's got nowhere left to go except flee to America and work as a server like he's in some kind of witness protection program.

"Here you go, sir," Ren says, approaching from behind me, the opposite way in which he'd departed.

I'd be lying if I didn't say he gave me a startle.

"Oh, thanks, Ren. My name's Edmund, by the way."

"Nice to meet you, Edmund. Do let me know if you need anything else."

He smiles and nods again and is about to walk away, but I say, "Ren."

He abruptly turns around and practically appears at my table with his eyebrows raised for his request. I wave for him to come in a bit closer. He looks around and bends further down.

"What's with the red star tattoo?"

His demeanor changes again, but this time it stays serious. His eyes hold the story behind it, and I'm desperate to know by this point.

"Edmund," he says with a smile but still staring a hole through my skull, "it's best that you forget you ever saw it."

I glare at him with confusion. And the more I stew on it, the more it turns to offense. Was I not good enough to know about the tattoo? I've never been a "cool kid" or part of the in-crowd, but this is just a dumb tattoo. Ren won't even share that little bit of himself with me?

"And what if I can't?" I find myself saying.

Ren stands back up and makes sure his uniform is on point and his professional façade is back in working order and says, "I'll be right back with your check, sir."

Before I can stop him, he's gone. He's a swift one, I'll give him that. I sigh and finish my coffee over the next couple of minutes, staring out the window at the cityscape on the other side of the river.

"Your bill, sir," Ren says, once again startling me and once again bending over to make sure I am the only person hearing what he's about to say.

"Just tell me about—" I begin, but he cuts me off.

"If you really want to know about the red star, call the number on the back."

I go to turn the receipt over, but he grabs my wrist with a strength like he could snap it if he wanted to and says, "Although I would strongly advise against it, Edmund. The red star is not for everyone."

He releases me and stands up, now back in character.

"Is there anything else I can do for you today?"

I look around, wondering if anyone saw what just happened, but no one is the wiser.

"No. I think I'll pay and head out."

"No rush, sir. Thank you for dining with us today," he says and goes to check on his other customers.

I pull out three twenties and place them on the table under the saltshaker. I stare at the arched receipt and see that there's writing on the back. My whole life people have been telling me what I can and can't handle. It's time to evolve. My depression and anxiety can fuck off along with my therapist. If nothing changes, nothing changes. That's what they tell me. Well, here's to change.

I pick up the receipt, cautiously glance at the number written on the back, and slide it in my pocket. As I make my way to the exit, I make eye contact with Ren one last time.

He's smiling.

ABOUT HALFWAY DOWN THE BLOCK, I TAKE THE RECEIPT FROM MY pocket and study it like Tom Hanks looking for clues in *The Da Vinci Code*, but it's just a fucking phone number. There's nothing special about it, other than not having a regional area code, but I live in a city where that's not uncommon.

I ate too much again. I feel my gut trying to snap my belt in half. At this rate, I'll be moving up in belt size before the month's over. The walk back to my apartment isn't far. Normally, I take a cab or an Uber, but I need to change some things. I could use a little more exercise. Well, a lot more, but I'll work up to that.

Today, I'll just walk home and maybe go for another walk to the park later. What I won't do is go home and grab the party-sized bag of Doritos and a can of Mountain Dew and plant myself on the couch.

Gratitude. Focus on gratitude. That's what my therapist would be telling me right now if I were unloading this self-pity dump truck on him.

"Okay, fine," I say to myself, catching an odd look from a woman jogging past me.

It's Friday, and normally I'd be at work. But this was a three-day weekend, so that's a good thing, I guess. Yeah, but what difference does it make? The job keeps my mind occupied. Fuck, it's really hard to get out of a negative space once you lock yourself inside one.

What had done it? The fit server? Was he really the trigger to all this? Just seeing another man with a head full of hair, good looks, and a well-built physique sent me into a spiral of self-loathing? Am I really that sensitive, or is there something more to it?

The quick glimpse of the red star tattoo comes to mind. I certainly wasn't jealous of the tattoo. I mean, don't get me wrong, it's cool in a trendy sort of way, I guess, but the fact that it symbolized something—something secretive that I wasn't a part of—is what currently haunts me. Okay, so I solved the problem; now what's the solution? My therapist told me that knowledge without action is only fantasy, so what is my course of action going to be?

My hand fiddles with the receipt, and my answer is now as clear as the sky above me. I will call the red star number when I get home. I'll see what it's all about. Ren said it wasn't for everyone and damn near warned me, making sure I really knew that, so it must be something serious.

If it's serious, that means it's challenging, and that's exactly what I need to be doing to myself right now. Embracing new challenges. My therapist told me that everything I wanted is on the other side of fear, and I totally get it now.

I'm also beginning to realize that my therapist probably has a daily quote app on his phone that he dispenses as his own pearls of wisdom to his overpaying patients, but who cares if it works, right?

In about fifteen minutes, I arrive to my building. Hooper, the elderly doorman, greets me and opens the spotless glass door. I notice two hanging baskets of fresh flowers by the entryway that I didn't see when I'd left earlier. I even catch a faint whiff of them as I pass by. *There's* something to be thankful for. I've never been one to stop and smell the flowers.

Chilton, the elevator man, sees me coming and presses the button. Just as I'm about to step through the parting metal doors, I stop.

"Is there a problem, Edmund?" Chilton asks.

I regard the entrance to the stairwell. My apartment is on the fifth floor. I look back at Chilton, who's watching me with a curious grin. I detect condescension in his demeanor, so I say fuck it.

"You know what? I think I'll take the stairs today. Might make a habit of it."

"Well, all right then, Edmund. I'll be here if you need me."

I regret my decision as soon as my hand grips the cool doorknob. But I'm fully committed, and there's no turning back now. I trudge onward and damn near die by the third floor, but I keep on pushing. Sweat pours from my brow and armpits by the time I reach my floor, and I take deep breaths like I just ran a marathon.

Yeah, I'm in shitty shape, but I took a positive action to correct it, and as soon as I go sit on the couch and catch my breath, I'm going to do something else productive: I'm going to call that damn number.

My apartment smells like an extinguished Yankee Candle. I always light one in the morning. Don't ask why. It's just been a habit since I've lived by myself to keep a candle burning when I'm home. It makes my surroundings seem cleaner than they are if I'm being honest with myself. I shut the door behind me and immediately lock it. You can never be too careful with people these days.

The room is a little muggy, so I turn on the ceiling fan and collapse onto the couch, still feeling the accrued moisture from the trek up the staircase. I take out my phone and the receipt and carefully eyeball both of them, considering it one last time, but only for a brief second. I smile, dial the number, and hit call.

The phone only rings once before someone picks up on the other end. I wait to hear a greeting, but I don't even hear breathing. Is it a bogus number? Did Ren play a joke on me? Is he trying to make me out to be a fool just like everyone else? I'm going to kill that motherfu—

"Who is this?" a voice says on the line.

It's a man's voice, deep and raspy. In just those three words, I picked up on a lifetime of depravity. Don't ask me how I know. I just do.

"Edmund," I say.

I didn't know what else to say. I didn't want to give my full name now that this guy has my number.

"And how did you get this number, Edmund?"

Oh shit. I didn't think this part through. Am I supposed to say Ren gave it to me? Does that vouch for me in some way? Or does that rat him out? Do I just act like I happened upon a piece of paper with a number and got bored and curious? I decide to go with my first instinct.

"A guy named Ren... Japanese fella who works down at Gabino's restaurant."

There is a terribly long silence, and I regret my decision more with each passing second.

"East Bay loading docks. Nine p.m. I would not be late if I were you, Edmund."

"East Bay loading docks. Nine—"

The line goes dead.

I look at my phone and put it on the coffee table and sit there wondering what the hell I've gotten myself into. But the depression is gone. I *am* anxious, but it's a good kind, a nervous anticipation. For the first time in a long time, I feel alive.

I think I will go for a stroll through the park. I might even pick up a new outfit, something that looks presentable. Both of my cats come barreling down the hall and hop on the back of the couch together, purring and nestling their heads against mine. Their affection normally soothes me. Now it's just aggravating, like some kind of reminder of the old me who only bonded with cats. Plus, they were only here because my wife rescued them, and then I got stuck with them.

Nine o'clock can't come fast enough.

I'm sitting in my idling car at the docks with my headlights pointed across the choppy harbor water. Just when I realize it would probably be more practical to back up against the freight building so I can at least watch if another car approaches, another car approaches. The creeps rolled up with their lights off and flicked them on right as I'm looking at them in my rearview mirror. I turn away and blink the flash out of my eyes.

Three knocks against my window cause me to jump back. I look out and recognize Ren. He's the same guy from earlier, but it's like he's playing a different character. I believe I caught a glimpse of this version when he gripped my arm at the restaurant. I roll down my window and see he's wearing a tailored black suit and tie with a white undershirt.

"Hello, Edmund," he says with a deadly serious face.

"Hi, Ren. What's—"

"Step out of the car."

"What?"

Ren pulls a gun from somewhere under that jacket and aims it at my face.

"Step out of the car, now."

"Jesus. Okay. I'm getting out," I say and do as I'm told even though it takes me an embarrassingly long amount of time to unwedge myself from my seat.

"Walk to that car and get in the backseat."

I look at the headlights shining on us and then back to my car that was still running.

"Well, what about my car?"

"I'm going to drive it. If I have to repeat one more order, I'll shoot you where you stand."

That's all I need to get my ass in gear. I speedwalk to the mysterious black Mercedes and try to look at who's in the front seat, but the windows are too dark. Against my better judgment, I open the door behind the driver and get in.

No interior dome light comes on. I have no view of the driver, but the person in the passenger seat is wearing the same suit as Ren. The only difference is that he's wearing a black ski mask. Just as I am studying the side of his face, he turns around and hands me a black hood. It's not like his that has eyeholes even though he's wearing reflective goggles so that no part of his face is exposed.

"Put it on," he says, now pointing his pistol at me.

I think about having to be told twice by Ren and decide to just be a good boy from here on out. I slide the thick garment over my head. I hear what sounds like duct tape being ripped off the roll and feel a pressure as the man wraps it around my neck. He's not doing it to choke me, just to prevent the mask from coming off.

"Don't even think about removing it," he says, his voice even more muffled now. "I'll have my gun on you the whole time."

My anxious mind immediately projects a scenario where we hit a pothole or speedbump that causes Mr. Goggles to accidentally blow my head off like that scene in *Pulp Fiction*. I don't say anything; I just nod my head and lean back as the car begins to move.

The ride is torturous on my propensity for carsickness. By the time we come to a smooth stop about thirty minutes(?) later, I'm doing all that I can not to barf in my mask. I hear the door in front of me open, and then the driver opens my door and helps me out.

I really can't see shit under the hood. Two people guide me by each firmly gripping an arm and telling me when to step up. I feel concrete steps under my feet and give an inconspicuous stomp just to make sure. I'm assuming this is the front porch to some place, and by the number of steps to get to the porch, it very well could be a mansion.

Am I on the other side of town where the wealthiest of the wealthy live—the hills that overlook the city? I did feel the car going up winding inclines. That would explain the extreme motion sickness.

There's a distinct temperature difference, and now I feel like I'm walking on hardwood floor. After a few twists and turns, I'm warned that we're about to walk downstairs. My kind escorts make sure I don't trip and go rolling down into whatever hell they're taking me.

"Last step," Mr. Goggles says, and then my feet are on hard ground again.

The floor isn't tile or smooth hardwood, but it is firm. Could it be concrete again?

"You're going to sit now," the driver says before shoving me into an uncomfortable metal folding chair.

One of them grabs my throat and unwraps the duct tape and jerks the hood from my head. I take a deep breath, expecting to be blinded by light, but the basement I'm in is dimly lit like some kind of medieval dungeon. I look around and see a half-circle of men all wearing the same black and white suits, sitting in chairs in front of me like some kind of ancient tribunal. None of them are wearing masks, and they range in age, race, and ethnicity. It is definitely an eclectic bunch, despite their uniforms.

Mr. Goggles and the driver still stand beside me and are facing the same direction in which my chair is pointed. That's when I notice the figure sitting outside the half-circle of men. This person(?) is not wearing a suit, nor is he sitting in a metal folding chair. I can only somewhat see from his bare chest down because the top third of his body is shrouded in shadow. Forgetting the fact that the goliath must be at least eight feet tall, there's something off about his skin. It looks almost reptilian. His bent legs reflect the amber light as if they're covered in shiny scales.

The adrenaline coursing through my system at this uncanny sight has me giddy with glee. For the first time in my life, I feel like I'm seeing the world behind the world. A world in which I have always longed for and feel destined to be a part of. The mundane existence of my life thus far has prepared me for this moment. I realize now that I had to go through the monotony of working to live and living to work, of the daily grind that fueled my melancholy, to truly appreciate this moment. My therapist was right about gratitude, after all.

The two men beside me kneel in unison when the figure in the throne taps one of its massive fingers against its armrest. I watch the shape take a breath and realize how massive its muscle-bound chest truly is.

"What is it that you seek?" an inhuman voice so deep and hoarse asks from the throne.

"The red star," I say without hesitation.

"Why?"

"Because I belong here."

The circle of men begin to laugh, but as soon as the behemoth taps his fingers, they all shut the fuck up.

"And what is the red star to you?"

"It's a symbol. It's proof that I'm worthy to be here."

"Interesting. You know nothing about us, yet you crave to be one of us."

"I know enough about everyone out *there* to know I don't belong. I'm different."

"Bearers of the Red Star serve me. I require... certain needs, certain nourishments. My existence defies your capacity of comprehension."

"Try me," I say.

The man-beast in his throne leans forward, and for the first time, I see his face in all its glory. He has no hair to speak of and his milky white eyes glow in the light. Its nose is upturned like a pig's but with reptilian nostrils. When it smiles, its jaw splits down the middle and parts, revealing a gaping hole of thin, pointed fangs. But despite all that, what captured my attention more than anything was the star-shaped stone in the middle of its forehead that began to pulsate a red glow in the rhythm of a heartbeat.

"You want to serve me?" it asked, leaning even further so that I could see what looks like folded wings behind its back with the pointed tips poking over its shoulders.

It reaches out and grabs the man sitting directly in front of it by the head and lifts him with one hand. The man didn't resist or make a sound, but I could see the terror in his eyes. None of the other men react either.

"This is Mr. Blaylock," the monster says, maintaining eye contact with me. "He's one of my most devoted subjects. This house is in his name. He's the one who summoned me from the Old World. He set me free, if you will. I owe much to Mr. Blaylock. He truly has served me well. Do you know what my first request of him was?"

I shake my head.

"No, how could you?" he continues. "Mr. Blaylock, tell Edmund what your first sacrifice was?"

Are those tears forming in Mr. Blaylock's eyes? I think they are. He's ashamed and afraid.

"I offered my family," Mr. Blaylock says.

"Oh, do be more specific than that," the monster snarls.

"I brought you my wife—"

"And what was so special about your wife?"

"She was eight months pregnant."

"Indeed, she was. And what happened when you brought your wife down here so many years ago? Please, spare no detail."

"You ate her head."

"Yes, and what else, Mr. Blaylock?"

The star in the beast's forehead is glowing red now.

"You split her open from bottom to top and ate the baby from her womb."

"Yesss. You did all that just to end up here for me to do this," the monster says right before snapping Mr. Blaylock's neck and dropping his corpse on the hard concrete.

There are a few gasps that quickly get reined in as the remaining men keep their composure like their lives depend on it. The tall beast walks through the empty spot in the semi-circle where Mr. Blaylock formerly sat. I notice the two men still kneeling beside me are trembling.

"Now, after bearing witness to that, do you still want to serve me?" it says with a distorted grin.

"I came for a red star. I didn't exactly know why, but I know now. Years ago, I also killed a woman and an unborn child. I caught my wife cheating on me, and I shot her once in the face and once in the belly, like this."

I grab Mr. Goggles' tucked gun from inside his jacket and point it at the glowing star that's beginning to dim. I fire, and all the men jump from the loud report. The monster's eyes look up and cross like it's trying to see the bleeding star.

That's when I shoot him in the stomach, causing him to haunch over and stumble. In a desperate attempt to kill me, it blindly swipes its bladed wings in both directions, severing heads and bisecting its followers in three seconds of bloody carnage.

"I didn't come here to serve you," I say and shoot its knees until it falls on its side. I stand over it and look at its dying eyes and say, "I know now that I came here to *be* you."

I fire the last round into the star for good measure. I hear groans and movement from the floor behind me. A few of the men are still alive. I take the gun from the driver and walk around shooting the survivors in their heads. When I look at the creature lying dead at the foot of its throne that I now notice is made of bone, I watch the thing shrivel up and wither away.

The last few years of my life have been pathetic, controlled by depression and anxiety that was created the day I murdered my wife and child. If I would've led with that part of my story, I doubt you would've come along this ride with me, though. But I feel good now. I feel a sense of redemption. By killing a demon that committed the same crime as me, I just squared the balance sheet. And who knows how many lives I potentially saved by ending this cult?

There's just one last thing to do. One more loose end to tie up before going back to my regular life—a life that can be fully lived now that I've cleaned up the wreckage of my past. I walk upstairs and find the kitchen and go straight for the knife block. With the biggest serrated knife I can find, I make my way across the gorgeous open area of what is most certainly a mansion in the rich part of town.

When I open the front door, I already know I'll see a concrete porch with seven concrete steps leading down to a circular driveway where the black Mercedes is parked with the engine running and my car behind it. Someone is in the driver seat of the Mercedes, and I don't have to look to know it's Ren. I'm assuming I was Ren's offering. Maybe part of their ritual was to take turns bringing that thing food. Maybe they were tasked with recruiting new members or replacements. Whatever the plan was, Ren orchestrated it. He probably saw me as a sad sack who could easily be manipulated. I was probably just a target for him.

Ren's face glows from his phone screen as he sits behind the wheel of the Mercedes. I waste no time descending the stairs and rushing to the passenger door before he can lock it. I jerk the door open and shoot him in the side, and he drops his weapon. I sit down with my knife and close the door.

The next morning, I wake up with a smile on my face. It's the first time this has happened in years. I get out of bed with a fully planned day of getting back in shape, plugging myself back into a social life, and just all around being the best version of me.

After I eat a light breakfast of non-dairy yogurt and fruit, I brush my teeth and suit up for the first of many morning jogs. And I definitely do not plan on stopping by Gabino's restaurant to pig out anymore. No, that's not me now.

As I head toward the front door to greet the day, I nod to Ren's severed arm that is proudly displayed in a glass vase on my kitchen table. Last night, I used that serrated blade to cut below his elbow so it would sit at just the right angle to showcase the tattoo.

I earned my red star.

HANGING TURBINES

BEN YOUNG

"Where the fuck did this fog come from?" Tyler Murphy said to no one.

No one answered, because he was alone in the car like usual, but it was a valid question. The conditions were not right for fog. Not right at all. The time of day, the air or ground temps, the dew point, the season, the part of the country... none of these factors were in the right ranges to produce condensation. But it was there all the same, and thick as gauze. The kind of fog that reduces everything to outlines and shades of gray.

Visibility was poor enough that he eased off the gas pedal. A flutter of annoyance followed. He was not the type to slow down often, preferring the hard-charging, ever-forward way of living.

But again, where did it come from? Tyler knew more about environmental factors than the average person. It was part of what he did for a living. At least, it was related enough that he needed the knowledge to be successful.

And successful he certainly was.

He had dropped out of college after less than two years and made his first million before thirty, when he sold his financial modeling software startup (built and run entirely within a rinky-dink one-bedroom apartment). He could have scaled it up massively, but it had turned into too much routine, and he was growing complacent. Then it got so mundane that nothing unexpected ever happened, and he was just plain bored. Luckily, the buyout offer dropped in his lap, and he about did a backflip.

From there, Tyler made a series of enormously profitable investments, including large shares in two industrial chemical plants in southeast Indiana. These facilities were situated along the Ohio River and produced household cleaning products. Tyler saw an opportunity to improve their output and had used his majority shareholder position to strongarm their operations toward drastic new heights of efficiency and effectiveness. In short, less people doing more work. He'd raided them like a modern-day pirate, cutting costs, skirting corners, and shedding anything that didn't contribute directly to the bottom line. Before long, they brought him and his partners money by the fistful, even as they pumped endless streams of noxious fumes from five-hundred-foot-tall steam stacks and leached toxic runoff into the nearby soil and water.

Sure, there was the necessary evil of covering their tracks—downplaying manufacturing accidents, sweeping safety breaches under the rug, greasing wheels with a few regulators—but he'd taken care of that too. He'd almost made a game of finding ways to evade hindrances like that, and aside from a tense few months when a green-as-snot reporter named Liz Clary, of WCHT 9 News, had dogged him about the effects of his plants on the local air and water supply, he'd never lost that game. The Powers That Be were glad to look the other way whenever there was a bit of a spill, and the results of their emissions tests were suddenly within acceptable ranges. Like magic. Because money talks. It was honestly thrilling, playing master of the environment. Tyler thrived on that sense of control, the untouchability it brought.

He couldn't have done that without knowing a thing or two about the climate, so he'd done extensive self-study of temperature patterns, precipitation, atmospheric pressure systems, radar technology, and of course gases and moisture. Math had always been second nature, but the physics gave him a little trouble at first. He buckled down and did it, though, and it had paid off.

Eventually, it was time for a new challenge, and Tyler had studied environmental impacts for his next big venture too: real estate development. It felt more like a hobby than anything resembling work, as he bought up huge swaths of land from aging or struggling farmers, stripped everything bare, and then built luxury apartments, condominiums, or bland tract housing by the dozens.

These days his net worth was close to $250 million, which meant he could save his time for the projects that were truly exciting, and let others handle the rest. Of course, he liked to stay involved enough to root out the problems and be sure his voice was heard (loudly if needed), but all that success allowed Tyler to spend time doing what he enjoyed while watching his massive wealth continue to grow, barely lifting a finger himself unless he wanted to.

Today, for example, he was driving his brand-new BMW Z4 north to Chicago for the American Cleaning Institute's Annual Industry Convention (quietly hoping this weird condensation didn't leave a residue on the immaculate black paint). This would be his fifth time attending, and because of a deal that had recently gone sour, he was more eager than usual to sip thirty-five-year single malt scotch and watch his fat old friends hit on young waitresses without realizing the girls were just doing their jobs when they flirted back. (Tyler would do that too, but he wasn't ugly so it wasn't pathetic.)

He checked the dashboard clock, 2:36 p.m. He'd be in Chicago with plenty of time to check into his hotel suite before dinner.

Still, that strange fog... hopefully it wouldn't slow him down. He was making decent time—not as fast as he'd like with visibility limited to maybe a hundred feet—but if there were any wrecks ahead of him, that would screw things up. The fog was even more odd because he couldn't recall seeing it start. When he'd left the plant around noon, the weather was fine, but reflecting now, he didn't remember seeing the fog coming.

It was still clear when I passed through Indianapolis, he thought. *And when I stopped for gas an hour later. So the fog started somewhere in the last half hour or so.*

But he didn't have a memory of approaching the border of it. Had he been looking at his phone and failed to notice until he was inside this cloud that shouldn't be here?

Didn't matter, though, so long as he got there on time to rib Ron Henderson about his latest cryptocurrency debacle. That bitcoin crap was a young man's game, and he'd warned the guy (for all the good it did). Tyler's favorite part about these industry events was giving other people shit over their failures. Try as they might, none of them were on his level, because they weren't willing to take the risks he was.

Not one to rely on GPS—because his cars were always faster than it realized—Tyler gauged the distance in his head.

Should be just a few miles short of Meadow Lake Wind Farm. As long as no dumbass truckers jackknifed their rig and caused a pileup, I should be on time still.

Now the clock read 3:14, and the fog rolled past with no end in sight. Tyler cruised below his usual range near 90 MPH, closer to 75, which felt like crawling. Like his car was a panther on a leash. He hadn't seen any traffic in the fog, but why take the chance? Better to be a few minutes late than plow into the back of a minivan he couldn't see coming. Worse, he'd gotten a later start than he'd planned because of strained negotiations this morning over a property he wanted to develop back across the river in Kentucky. They'd need to find a cheaper way to remove all those pesky trees, but that was a problem for another day.

Thinking of deals that didn't go the way he'd hoped was a strong coincidence, because in that same moment he saw the first of the turbines outside. It emerged from the fog like an alien monolith as Tyler entered the Meadow Lake Wind Farm.

Something about the turbines fascinated him, despite their absurdity and the waste of valuable land. Pointless as they were, these paragons of sustainable, "green" energy, he couldn't help but marvel at their appearance. Their scale was better matched for a race of giant extra-terrestrials; they didn't feel like something designed and built by humans. They were as tall as the smokestacks at his chemical plants, but drastically thinner, resembling colossal bones, their enormous blades spinning molasses-slow or sometimes not moving at all. Those blades reached high enough they might scrape the bottom of an airplane in flight.

There was something just so... otherworldly about them. Like they didn't belong in the same reality as someone like himself. Or as if they were remnants of an ancient society of inhuman creatures. The wind farm itself went on for miles, a thousand of the monumental structures scattered along both sides of the highway, and the quantity only made them seem more unnatural.

But maybe the main reason they were so jarring to him was the fact that they'd been at the center of the worst deal in his otherwise spotless career.

Almost ten years ago, when he first set out to try his hand at developing underutilized land, Tyler had sought to buy up a sizable portion of the acreage that would become the Meadow Lake Wind Farm, glad-handing with all the numbskull old farmers of Benton County who owned most of it at the time. He'd had a vision of a massive retail and residential complex that would transform this area from middle-of-nowhere soybean country to a mecca of construction and commerce. A destination for people throughout a third of the Midwest, and parts farther south too.

But one pissed-off redneck had ruined the whole thing for him, going on a campaign to convince the rest not to sell. Seems he had caught the reports from years earlier—thanks again to that bitch Liz Clary—and managed to remember Tyler's connection to all that talk of pollution. They'd banded together and dug their heels in, threatening legal action and contact with the EPA. Tyler had been forced to back off, thinking he could wait the old man out because he was in his late 70s, and hoping once he croaked that his son would sell and the rest would follow. Just a matter of patience. Then that same coalition of farmers had struck a deal with a renewable energy company (of all the bullshit non-businesses) out of nowhere, and Tyler found a door not just slammed in his face, but double fucking bolted shut too. He'd moved on but never really put that loss behind him. It still stung, and driving through the wind farm had that old wound positively singing.

Plus, the weird weather. Today, watching those gleaming white monstrosities emerge and submerge through a blight of fog that didn't belong, well, it was almost enough to be... unsettling.

As if, this time, they weren't just watching him pass by from hundreds of feet up, they were... taunting him.

The dashboard clock had crept all the way to 3:43 now, but the fog wasn't letting up. And could it be a weird bit of sensory deprivation taking hold, or was the fog becoming less cloudy and more... stringy? Like dense filaments of spider webbing. Tyler watched it stretch and mold around the sides of his front windshield.

He needed to make it out the other side, fast. Stewing in this impossible cloud had him reflecting on everything he'd come to hate. Tyler Murphy was sick to death of hearing about "sustainable development" and "carbon emissions" and "climate change." When did "profit" become such a dirty word? Countless new regulations and restrictions, the social outcry, all that noise made it so much harder to turn a buck the way you used to. What's a guy supposed to do in this new world of "woke" politics and "responsible corporate citizenship" when most of his fortune is tied up in caustic manufacturing or the tearing down of forests and farmland then replacing it all with concrete? It was really starting to feel like Tyler needed an exit strategy because he couldn't stomach having to switch to organic pesticides or geothermal heat pumps or repurposed vegetable waste. Where's the money? Fuck that.

Hell, these days weren't they even blaming cow farts for ruining the environment? It was one thing when everyone used gallons of hairspray forty years ago and they all whined about holes in the ozone, but it had just gone way too far since then.

To Tyler, it was so damn presumptuous to think humans even had enough power or impact to change the climate of the entire planet. There were ice ages before, and someday a thousand years in the future there'd be another one, but in between he was going to live the high life. It didn't matter what humans did or didn't do, the environment wasn't something we could control, so why not take what he needed from it? None of it made a bit of difference.

Fuck the coastal cities and the polar ice and all the fake science.

"Build all the fucking turbines and solar panels you want, you jackoffs," he said. "I hope they fall over on your damn houses."

The voice of Liz Clary invaded then, echoing back from years past. She'd said to him, after he refused to answer her questions (not that he didn't have an answer, but the little bitch had cornered him and shoved a camera in his face when he wasn't ready): *Mr. Murphy, I fear that, even if you don't want to learn about the impacts of your decisions, you're bound to find out. Someday, I believe Mother Nature will call you out.*

"If that's what she's doing with this fog, Ms. Clary, I'm not worried in the slightest," he said now. "Fog doesn't scare me. And I won't be taking any further questions, good day."

Tyler checked the clock again. 4:45 now. But that couldn't be right, could it? All the reminiscing about the Deal That Got Away and trading punches with journalists had distracted him more than he realized.

And the turbines kept coming. They were lost in the fog, like he was. Some of them, the bottoms were obscured and others he couldn't see the top of.

Shouldn't he be past them all now? Or was the fog messing with his sense of distance? Plus, it seemed like his car was slicing through it, as if it was taking longer than it should to move as he drove through. Almost... resisting the motion. Was some of it starting to cling to the sideview mirrors? What if he rolled down the window and stuck his hand out there?

Should have checked the odometer instead of the time before I got to the wind farm, he thought. *I'm driving slower, but this still feels like it's taking too long. Definitely seems like I should have come through the other side by now.*

Foregoing his usual hesitance to trust GPS, Tyler opened the maps app on his cell phone to check if he was still on track for his planned ETA in Chicago. But the signal was too weak, here in the vast farmlands of Indiana. Not surprising, though, nothing to be alarmed about there.

Better just keep driving.

Tyler turned on the radio, hoping to catch a weather or traffic update.

Only static.

Now that's odd, he thought as he flipped through all twelve presets and then began scanning between them, further along the dial.

The stream of static matched the cloudy quality of the air outside. Combined, it was enough to make him feel like he'd been wrapped in a giant white blanket and plucked off the planet without noticing. A surprising wave of disorientation struck, but more surprising still, it didn't fade. A sensation not unlike the equalizing of cabin pressure in an airplane, but also a sort of... stagnation. If not for the even white lines of the road slipping by beneath, or the slow passing of the gigantic wind machines in the distance, Tyler wouldn't be sure he was even moving at all now.

He had an urge to veer the car sideways, just to see if anything would happen, but succeeded in fighting that off.

Keep your cool, he thought. But it was a wasted command as the disorientation triggered a series of troubled questions. *Is the fog getting thicker? More stringy? Have there been* any *other cars since it started? Were the turbines somehow causing the fog?*

An hour passed this way. Then another. Tyler spent this time watching the only points of reference he had. The clock, counting the minutes. The road lines, persistent and steady. The passing turbines, towering and uncanny. The gas gauge, creeping lower.

When was the last exit sign? Hell, any road sign. Or mile marker. There's nothing but the road, and the fog.

And the turbines.

Fighting this sense of liminal disbelief, he reminded himself that the wind farm was only so big. Finite. It had to end eventually, and the only reason it hadn't was because of his lower speed and the fog blocking out all the landmarks.

He was still in his car, still on the Indiana highway, still on Earth.

Of course he was.

He had to be.

He was.

Where else could he possibly have ended up?

It was far more likely that the clock was wrong, that's all. It couldn't possibly be 6:14 p.m. like the thing said, because even at half the speed limit he would have been to Chicago by now.

That's when he first saw something hanging from one of the turbines.

It was too far back from the road for a clear view, but there seemed to be a strange vacuum in the fog around that one, like it were inside a giant glass dome. It called his attention that way, a stark contrast from all the others he'd passed. Otherwise, he might not have noticed its bizarre ornament.

Tyler squinted, slowed the car further, now traveling under 30 MPH, turned his head to get a longer look as he passed.

He was glad it wasn't closer because, from this distance, at this speed, it looked like something it couldn't be. Something he would rather not see closer. It almost, almost looked like... a person. Hanging from the cone-shaped front of the rotor by a fifty-foot noose. The blades were turning at the usual speed, but whatever thing hung there was utterly still.

Can't be. There's absolutely no way anyone could get up there without some very large equipment. It's probably a trash bag or a flock of birds.

Tyler drove on and saw two shapes hanging from the next set of turbines. These were nearer the road, on the rotors of two adjacent fans, and he could make out their limbs, arms and legs hanging tube-straight toward the ground. One may have been wearing a dark baseball hat.

Not trash bags. Not birds. Mannequins? A prank, or some kind of protest? Even so, how the hell did they get up there?

By 7:13 p.m., according to his dashboard clock, half the turbines he passed were adorned with what looked like hanging human bodies. Tyler was vaguely aware that the sun should have set by now, but the amount of light streaming through the dense fog hadn't changed. And the machines themselves were growing closer together, more congested. So near to one another that their blades could have collided.

It was as if they were... gathering. To watch something.

When his gas gauge reached a quarter tank, there were dozens of them, enormous gangly sentries on both sides of the road, each with what looked like an effigy strung up near the blades.

Aghast, Tyler strained to make out more details and realized that he was trying not to confirm anything about them, but to dispute a clear suspicion that had settled into his gut like hot gravel.

He wasn't trying to tell if they were mannequins or bits of debris that got swept up in the wind. Because he knew they weren't now.

He was no longer trying to dispel the notion that they were actual, human bodies. Because he knew they were.

Now, it wasn't about determining what he was seeing, hanging there. He was trying to figure out *who* was hanging there. Because, despite any mental defenses he tried to muster, Tyler Murphy could no longer fend off the thought that those bodies up there (*that's what they are, those are human bodies, there are bodies, bodies hanging way the hell up there*) looked like someone he knew, intimately.

He needed to know who they were, because somehow, it looked like they were all wearing his clothes.

Wearing his face.

A nagging sense of doom told him, knowing without any way of knowing, that each of those hanging bodies looked exactly like him. It mattered not that his actual body was still here in the car, because somehow it was also up there, a hundred times. Hanging from the passing turbines.

Unable to fathom how that could be or what it meant, his brain short-circuited, able only to ask the same question over and over, like it was fencing itself off from this growing certainty as the meaning-less miles slipped past and the clock lied and the fog deepened.

How did they get up there? Those bodies.

How did they get up there?

How did... I get up there?

Suddenly, the fog cracked, spreading apart like the Red Sea at the behest of Moses himself, and the sky answered Tyler's question.

He saw, miles up in the atmosphere, some form of... electrical disturbance. Red shapes emerged, made from angry, swollen light-ning, topped with round bulbs like small ruby planets and beneath these sore heads what looked like roots, giving the whole structure the appearance of an overly thin human body but with too many arms and legs.

Red Sprites, they were called. He knew of them from his environ-mental research.

More of them came, a procession of enormous crimson shapes from the heavens. Floating down toward the tops of the turbines, then farther, nearing the road ahead of him. Six, eight, twelve, then dozens. Too many to count.

As they descended, the fog dissipated and the reporter's voice returned.

Someday, I believe Mother Nature will call you out.

The Sprites dropped closer, and closer still. There was an ear-shattering screech and then the car was gone and the road was gone and Tyler was... floating? No, he was being lifted; they were lifting him. And from this new height, he could see for miles. The turbines surrounded him. The fog coated everything. The fans were all facing him in silent judgment as he floated in a coliseum of epic scale. No, a foggy courtroom. Awaiting his sentence.

The Sprites' limbs were wrapped around him, and he burned wherever they touched him.

Tyler screamed and tried to look at the red monstrosities and then at himself where they were holding him, but they were too bright. So he looked down instead, toward the ground, and kept screaming.

His car lay overturned in a ditch, wheels spinning in the air, windshield shattered, front end crumpled. The driver's door was opened and surrounded by burn marks like whiplashes. It got smaller and smaller as he watched and cried out in immense pain.

Tyler was lifted higher, and higher, so high now that the air seemed thinner and it grew hard to breathe... Was he choking? Yes, he was. They were choking him with their angry red limbs. Tyler was... Was he being strangled?

No, no. He was...

Hanging.

Kicking his feet against a fan blade large enough to slice an airplane in half.

And hanging.

Hanging from the turbine.

Later, an SUV cruised along Interstate 65.

"Mom," Ruby cried. "Mom, he's doing it again."

"Louis, you leave your sister alone," Christine said. She hoped the last few hours of the drive would go fast. Maybe once they got to the wind farm, it would distract them a bit. She used her eyes to scold her husband for not remembering to charge five-year-old Louis' tablet before they left this morning. He was now bored and harassing his older sister, and Christine was left to deal with it and drive the car at the same time. Hopefully the giant fans would catch his attention for a moment or two, at least.

"But I'm not doing anything," Louis answered. "She's ly—" He stopped mid-sentence, eyes grown wide, and both kids gawked out the passenger-side windows.

"What's that?" Ruby asked, pointing toward the sky, toward the top of one of the giant turbines.

"Oh my God," Christine said.

"It looks like a dead—" Louis started to answer, but Christine cut him off.

"Kids, look away! Look away now!"

BLUDLUST

LEIGH KENNY

Ochre dust clouds swirled around sweat-beaded flanks. Clattering hooves quietened, then stilled completely. Percival continued to hold his arm aloft until he had the attention of every man in the small band of former Crusaders he commanded.

"That must be it."

He spoke quietly, and yet his voice carried through the small crowd of men with a strength that belied its softness. There was a reason it was he who led them. He whose command could still these warriors and the beasts they plundered upon.

The Crusades may be done, but Percival and his men were not. They cared not for religion nor recapturing lands that would never be their own. They cared only for the treasure they could carry from camp to camp as they slowly meandered through places filled with people weaker than they. Sometimes the treasure glittered. Sometimes it sparkled.

And sometimes it screamed and pleaded.

That was the best treasure of all for most of his troupe. Easily carried, easily used, and even easier to discard of.

Women held no specific interest for Percival. His needs were not frequent, but when they struck, it did not matter to him where he derived his pleasures. Men, women, children...

Each warm body was the same as the next.

The cold bodies were less inviting but still just as pliant.

He cast an eye across the valley that stretched out before him. The landscape lay stark and flat but for a thick forest in the middle. Trees stretched toward the darkening sky, an island amid the desolation. And from within the center, a curling plume of smoke rose into the haze of purple and blue like an invitation.

"She did not lie to us. We were right to take but one of her daughters," he called to his men who responded with salacious howls.

The girl in question wept quietly, her eyes downcast. The man who rode behind her snarled and pulled the girl to him, muffling her shrieks with his mouth. The other men cheered as he pulled away. The girl's quiet weeping made way for full, body-wracking sobs. Percival nodded at his men and tugged the reins, jolting his horse forward.

Into the wasteland.

Into the trees.

They had happened upon a small house by the road some distance back. He had expected to have found a new settlement by now, but his men were hungry—in more ways than one—and he wasn't about to stand between them and the family who lived there. The household was headed up by an old woman, older and uglier than she had any right to be considering the gaggle of daughters stashed around the house. The girls were all young and all very beautiful.

Chaos had ensued initially, but after much begging and pleading, Percival had agreed to hear her out.

Treasure beyond his wildest dreams.

Enough for a hundred men and more, she had told him.

And she would tell him how to get there if he would leave her home and her daughters. He had agreed but had insisted on taking one daughter. A failsafe.

If she was lying to him, he would ensure that every one of his men had their fill of the girl, then he would cook her and ensure they had their fill again. Then he would return for the rest. Percival knew the woman was unlikely to lie to him. No doubt the stories of his band of Crusaders had spread far and wide through these lands. The old hag should know better than to test his patience.

She told him there was a stone village hidden in a forest nearby. Bludlust had once been a thriving community known to hold innumerable treasures. Now it was an empty vessel. It held riches, but no life. Monsters, but no humans. Her daughters had gasped at the mere mention of the name. Excitement had sparked within Percival upon hearing it.

Bludlust.

It sounded like heaven on earth to a cruel man.

Perhaps he would finally put down roots. Perhaps he would take whatever riches the place held and claim them as his own. Strip the remaining meat from its bones.

Tales of creatures were of no concern to a living, breathing monster such as he.

The place called to him. Blood and riches.

Riches and blood.

He smiled now as the forest drew closer. They would soon be beneath the cover of the canopy. Percival cast a cold eye toward the horizon where thunderheads had begun to form. Clouds of gray and mauve rolled across the evening sky, and in the distance, thunder rumbled ominously. He had no way of knowing how long it would take them to traverse the forest, but he was confident that they would find the village of Bludlust before the weather could catch up to them. In all his years of marauding, he had outrun worse than wind and rain.

The trees soon blotted out the smoke and the stars. The woman had been truthful, and for that he wouldn't return for the rest of her daughters. Still, the girl they had with them was unlikely to see another sunrise.

Perhaps he would cook her after all.

He had always wondered what *it* would taste like.

The girl's scream broke through his reverie, and he turned his head toward the commotion. The farther into the forest they moved, the more hysterical the girl became. Percival did his best to ignore both the girl and the aggravated shouts of his men. Silence soon descended, and he risked a backward glance. The girl lay heavily against the brute on the horse. The creature's gray flanks were speckled with a crimson that looked black in the shadowed undergrowth of the woods.

"What happened?" he hissed, his tone silencing the men.

The man flexed an arm and grinned before brushing the girl's dark hair aside almost tenderly. A bloodied wound marred her otherwise porcelain complexion, the skin around her hairline already swelling after the knockout blow.

Percival nodded his approval, the ghost of a smile upon his lips. It was for the best that she was silenced. They did not know what kind of resistance they may meet ahead despite the eerie quiet of the trail.

The wind had begun to pick up, but the sentinel trees absorbed the worst of it. The gusts wailed around trunks and through gaps in branches in sporadic bursts. It was strange weather. But then these were strange lands.

They hadn't seen a single soul out here, wouldn't encounter anyone if the old hag were to be believed, and yet the men's eyes darted and their heads swiveled as they moved deeper into the woods. The horses danced along skittishly, unsettled by unseen eyes that watched their progress.

The wind still gasped and shrieked, the cold air snapping at skin and tasting any flesh laid bare to it.

Everyone was unnerved.

Everyone but Percival, who was caught in a daydream of roasted female flesh. His mouth filled with saliva as he imagined peeling back the fire-scorched skin. He could almost feel it crackle and snap beneath his fingers. Could taste the tender meat—slightly sweeter than he expected—as it dissolved against his tongue.

Creeping nettles reached for his ankles.

Branches whipped at his face.

But he felt nothing as his jaw twitched and worked, anticipating the feast to come.

The trees were soon replaced by a low stone wall that grew in height as they traversed its length. As they passed beneath a tall stone archway, the woods died away, and the biting winds with it. Behind Percival, the men whispered. What was this place, this fortress in the woods? And where were all the people?

Percival was not troubled by such things. They were here to find treasure, not people.

He didn't doubt for a second that the people were here too, though. Hiding among the trees and the stone structures that seemed to make up the small, enclosed settlement.

Buildings ran along the edges of the village, many of them buttressed by the towering wall. A multitude of narrow alleyways disappeared between the dwellings, darkness and shadow the only thing that appeared to occupy them. The area between them was cobbled with more stone, and in the center, another round structure.

It was a well, and it was covered.

The covering shimmered, prompting Percival to halt his horse and slide from the animals back. He moved toward the well, slowly at first before sprinting the final distance and dropping to his knees before it.

The massive lid was solid gold.

The shimmering colors—more precious stones than he could count.

The old woman had seen to it that they were indeed taken care of.

Behind him the men gasped as a rasping voice rang out.

"Welcome, weary travelers."

A TWISTED FORM COVERED IN CLOAK AND SHADOW STOOD IN AN open doorway, an oil lamp swinging in his grasp.

Percival couldn't tell by sight or sound if it was a man or woman, and internal anxiety fought with relief, unsure if the presence of this single person was a good or bad omen.

"Where are all the people?" called one of the men, Melville, his voice uncertain.

"The people?" asked the shrouded figure.

"People. Villagers. Where is everyone?"

The figure took a single step toward them, lifting his lamp higher.

The men took a collective step back.

The light from the swinging lamp illuminated the face hidden beneath a heavy hood. Percival felt himself relax as he watched the man lower the material that shielded his head. He was small and wrinkled, and his face was scarred and marked as though he had lived a life full of torment, but he was a man. The thought of a lone woman out here among the tombstone dwellings was unsettling.

As if the mere thought of a woman alone was enough to rouse the one in their presence, the hag's daughter came to, her piercing shrieks shattering the stillness of the forest. It felt like an afront to nature itself, and Percival was clutched by a sudden panic.

"Quieten her," he hissed.

A heavy thump echoed through the courtyard, and the girl was silenced once more. Melville draped her carefully across the horse's back, then slid from the animal. He checked that she was in no danger of falling before turning to face Percival, reins in hand.

Percival tipped his head in approval, bemused at the tenderness Melville had shown the unconscious girl. No such tenderness would be shown to her in a few short hours. The men would pull her apart like animals. He had seen it happen before. They were ferocious in their savagery, and it wouldn't surprise him at all to lose a man or two this night. They would be fighting like dogs for a piece of one girl.

And he would let them, before taking the pieces he wanted for himself.

They would need a fire to cook over.

As though reading his mind, the cloaked man turned toward him. He cocked his head and studied Percival, sizing him up. The silence seemed to stretch beyond the walls. Percival cleared his throat, preparing to speak. To punctuate the loaded silence. The feeling of discomfort he felt beneath the man's piercing gaze was alien to him, and his shoulders sagged with unexpected relief as the stranger spoke first.

"I am Aras. I am the guardian of this place. Welcome to Bludlust." He swept his arms out with a flourish, and Percival's eyes widened as the sleeves fell away from the man's hands, unveiling his wrists and forearms.

His skin was tattooed with marks.

Teeth marks. Small and uniform in pattern, like the bite of a child.

Of many children.

Percival knew he must be mistaken though. There was nobody else around. Not to mention the absurdity of it. An image came unbidden to his mind of their new friend Aras surrounded by children, each one clamoring to sink their tiny teeth into the man to...

To what?

With a shudder, Percival tried to banish the image. He stepped forward to greet the man.

"I am Percival. These are my men. And their prize." He nodded toward the prone form of the girl.

Something akin to a smile tugged at the stranger's thin lips, but his expression was unreadable to Percival. The man did not seem to fear Percival and his savage band of men. Did not seem concerned by their presence at all.

The concern was Percival's alone.

"We were directed to Bludlust by the mother of the wench," he continued, less sure of himself. Less commanding in his countenance. "She told us we would find shelter and riches here. It would appear she was correct."

The old man followed his gaze to the golden well cover.

"There are riches galore in Bludlust, but there are rules too," said Aras. "You may take what you wish, but you cannot take the seal from the well."

Percival bristled.

"Come," continued the man, turning back toward the shadowed doorway. "Your men may shelter here. I have food and drink I can share. You may stay one night, but tomorrow you must take your riches and be on your way." Aras was swallowed by the shadowed interior.

Percival watched as his men secured their horses, then together as one, they followed one-by-one into the gloom.

Safety in numbers.

THE MEN'S VOICES ECHOED AROUND THE SPACE. THE BUILDING FELT cavernous, but unable to see beyond the orange glow of the candles, Percival had no idea as to its actual size. Aras had told them it was once a church. The man offered very little else in the way of information as he had busied himself feeding the fire and adding to the pot. The men had eaten their fill and drank it too. Now the sounds of more than a few muffled conversations filled the space, occasionally punctuated by hoarse laughter or raised voices. The girl still lay unconscious, but in a more comfortable position on a bed of straw at the behest of Aras.

Women are sacred. They must be treated as such.

The small man's reverent whispers drew chuckles and ire from the gathered men, but Aras either hadn't noticed or chose not to. Percival noted how he had steered the men away from the girl, keeping himself and the fire pit between her and her captives.

Now that they had eaten, the boundary would not last long.

The man had declined their own drink in favor of the casks he rolled into the room. Percival's men were only too happy to save their own stores and drink their fill of what Aras supplied. Percival had happily sunk more than a few cups himself, savoring the delicate taste of the drink. His head begun to feel light upon his shoulders much quicker than usual, so he paced himself. Something he knew most of the men would struggle to do.

He eyed the girl, wondering how long it would take anyone to notice if he were to peel some skin from one of her calves and hold it over the flames. He watched the shadows cast by the firelight as they danced upon her milky flesh and found himself grow hungry in more ways than one.

Melville had all but claimed the girl earlier. Percival knew the man would likely give precedence to his leader, but the threat of someone contesting his position within their clan was an ever-present shadow that lingered over him. He may be smarter than them all, but if anger ever got the better of any of his men, he suspected most of them would easily dispatch him in combat. Easier to remain smarter than them. To have them do his bidding.

And he could easily kill two birds with one stone.

If he sent Melville and the strongest men out into the darkness of night to remove the golden covering from the well, he could quietly slip into the shadows with the girl. He could take what he wanted from her body before taking what he wanted from her flesh.

Percival licked his lips and rubbed his crotch. Both his stomach and his cock quivered with anticipation.

PERCIVAL WATCHED AS HIS MEN SLIPPED THROUGH THE DOORWAY and into the courtyard. There was no sign of Aras, and they had joked amongst themselves that perhaps one of the other men had taken the stranger to one of the abandoned buildings to share some riches of their own.

The men questioned if it was a good idea to take the one thing the man had told them they couldn't.

"Why not just take everything else and leave him his well cover?" asked Richmond, a gormless brute who had arms like tree trunks but very little happening between his ears.

"Why not take everything AND the well cover?" echoed Percival, waiting for the other man to understand what he was saying.

It was theirs for the taking.

All of it.

They could cannibalize Bludlust, then move on tomorrow or the day after.

Cannibalize.

At the thought, Percival felt a stirring in his groin once more and set the men to task. He watched them leave, satisfied that he had sent the right group. Others still milled about, but they were seated in small gatherings at the furthest end of the occupied space. Most of them lay immobile or sat canted to the side, each of them feeling the effects of the liquid nectar the old man had shared. One man lay snoring with his arms clasped around a cask, having clearly chosen the treasure he wished to take from Bludlust.

Percival cast a disdainful eye along each of his men before turning and moving toward the girl.

She was bathed in shadows, the slowly dying fire failing to find her. Percival's eyes roved across the girl as he lowered himself to the soft pile next to her. Her eyes remained closed, the thin skin of her lids twitching in unconscious thought. Her rosy lips were parted slightly, and Percival wondered if that was perhaps the first place he should slip his girth.

Lower, his eyes traveled, stopping on the curve of her breasts. Gently, he brushed her dark hair aside and slid one hand beneath the thin material of her dress. Her heart fluttered against him, and he stalled momentarily, the feeling of her pulse beneath his hand filling him with a myriad of emotions.

It was strength and unbridled lust.

It was power.

It was intoxicating.

Tugging and tearing, he pulled the soft cloth away from her body, groaning quietly as he freed her breasts. Percival reached out again and cupped one breast, his thumb sliding across the unconscious girl's skin to circle her nipple. With his free hand, he tugged himself free from the confines of his pants and began to rub. His hand left her breast, sliding along the milky skin of her flat stomach, lower, along the tuft of—

"Percival! We need you outside."

With another groan—this time one of annoyance—he covered the girl's bare skin as best he could before hurrying toward the courtyard. Casting a final glance at her shapely form, Percival decided he didn't care who had claimed her. He would be the first to plunge himself inside her body, and if anyone else tried, he'd slit their throats himself.

THE MOMENT HE STEPPED FOOT IN THE COURTYARD, PERCIVAL FELT it. The subtle shift in the air. The low whine of a previously nonexistent wind as it prowled the boundary walls, testing for weakness in the structure.

In them.

Ignoring the roiling within his stomach, Percival joined the small gathering of men who stood around the well muttering to one another.

"We almost have it," said Melville, "but we need the strength of one more man to finish the job."

Percival nodded, his mind wondering briefly to their missing host. Had Aras hidden from them, suspecting the worst? Had he left the village to alert others of their presence?

Settling himself into position among his men, Percival found he didn't much care about the fate of the cloaked man. He wasn't around to enforce his rules. Not that he would have been able to. He was but one man against a small army.

The men heaved as one, and the gold covering began to move with a screech. Grunting, they each tightened their grip and shoved until finally the gold seal fell away from the stone well, thumping against the courtyard cobbles with a clatter.

Still the screeching persisted.

The men looked around uneasily, each afraid to catch the eye of another lest they confirm the fear that hung suspended by an invisible thread between them.

"It's just the wind," Percival said, raising his voice to be heard clearly above the shrieking.

The noise died away, as though chastened by his words.

Turning to smile at the gathered group, he jolted as a new sound split the still night air.

A shrill scream from behind.

A shove that knocked him off balance.

The men gasped, and Percival watched in horror as the girl dashed past them, moonlight painting her bare skin the color of dried bone.

She threw herself over the low stone wall.

The murky depths of the old well claimed her as its own.

Whispers filled the gloomy space as the men dissected the girl's actions in hushed tones.

Percival stared into the flames as the fire hissed and spat, still in disbelief at what he had witnessed. His jaw worked in frustration as he replayed the moment over and over.

What a waste.

Outside, the wind had picked up once more.

It howled around the stone buildings, sniffing at the heavy wooden door and scratching at the shuttered windows.

Let me in, it seemed to say.

Aras still hadn't reappeared. Even with all the commotion in the courtyard after the girl leaped to her death.

The men held their collective breath for a beat after the girl had thrown herself over the edge before surging forward as one. It was impossible to see anything beyond a few inches, and after a few moments of straining to see through the blackness, they all stepped back, unable to hold the shadows' gaze. One by one, they wilted against whatever the darkness held until eventually, they all found their way back inside by the fire.

They would see out the night—and hopefully the worst of the weather—in the shelter of Bludlust. Tomorrow they would pack up the horses early with food and drink, and all the riches the beasts would hold, and they would be gone from this strange place.

As though in response, a cacophony of sounds began to filter in from the courtyard. Hooves clattering against cobbles. The whickering of nervous horses.

His frustration reaching new heights, Percival snapped for one of the men to see to the horses. Melville stood, earning silent thanks from his brothers in arms, none of whom wished to brave the elements.

Outside, the shrieking wind grew louder.

Melville stopped for a moment, bracing himself for the inclement weather, before pushing the heavy wooden door open.

A single high-pitched scream, and he was gone.

The previously muted space became a living thing as the men shouted and fussed, none brave enough to get too close to the doorway that had pulled their friend from existence.

And then from the courtyard, a cry for help.

Melville's voice was enough to spur them on, reigniting the bravery they struggled to find mere moments before.

The men filed out into the wind and the night.

The courtyard was empty save for the dark shadows of the horses.

But even they looked wrong.

The men spread out.

Percival found himself drawn to the open well, the memory of the hag's daughter sacrificing herself to darkness still fresh on his mind and bitter in his black heart.

Oh, the fun he could have had with her.

He moved forward until the stone blocked his way, the surface cold and hard against his thighs. He stared into the darkness, vaguely aware that behind him, the men had begun to shout in alarm.

Horses...

Dead...

Blood...

In the wind...

Everywhere.

A deafening chorus of screams pulsed from the heart of the dark well, and Percival fell back in terror as a pale face appeared at the edge of the well's shadowed interior.

He slammed against the cobbled stone and scrambled backward as a woman slithered from the well.

At least it looked like a woman.

Her hair was so white it shimmered silver in the moonlight. Her bare skin was almost as pale as her long locks, and Percival's eyes roved hungrily along her body. She met his eye and grinned. A squeak escaped Percival as he looked at her monstrous mouth, filled with rows of sharp teeth. Her canines were larger, two daggers framing countless needles.

She took a step toward him, then lifted her face to the sky. Sniffing the air, her head whipped around in a frenzy as she homed in on whatever scent had caught her attention. Melville suddenly crashed to the ground in front of her, and with a devilish shriek, she pounced on him. Percival watched helplessly as the woman-thing sank her teeth into the tender flesh of his friend's neck. She pulled back, the skin and sinew stretching, snapping, tearing in her vice grip. Blood spurted, and she spat Melville's meat from her mouth in favor of the warm geyser of crimson. She tongued the blood—giggling, shrieking, *moaning* with delight.

Unable to watch any longer, Percival lifted his eyes toward the heavens. Another of the she-devils hung suspended in the sky, large leathery wings moving just enough to keep her petite frame afloat. This one had a waterfall of scarlet curls, and Percival yelped as she suddenly dove toward him. He wasn't the intended target, though, and he watched with a mixture of relief and terror as the woman plucked one of his men from the cobbles, hauling the screaming man skyward with her—higher, higher, higher—before releasing her grip and crowing with glee as the poor man plummeted to his death, crunching against the stones.

The courtyard was alive with the sounds of men shouting and bones snapping. More women appeared from the well, slicing through the gathered men, crawling upon the boundary wall and sailing through the air to cut down any man privileged enough to have not yet spilled a drop of blood.

The red-haired creature turned her gaze to Percival and screeched.

With no time to waste, Percival hauled himself to his feet and ran into the shadows of Bludlust.

The winged woman gave chase.

PERCIVAL DARTED BETWEEN THE STONE BUILDINGS.

The woman may be airborne, but the narrow alleys and sudden corners were of more benefit to the terrified man.

It had always been Percival's brain, not his brawn, that had seen so many men follow his lead, and he strove to figure a way out of the impossible predicament he found himself in.

He felt like he had run in circles, but finally, he had put some distance between himself and the creature. Rounding another corner, Percival hauled open the closest door to him and slunk into the shadows. He pressed himself against the wood and stilled his breath as he watched between the hairline cracks in the wood for any movement outside.

A shadow passed by.

Moments later, it passed by again.

Silence.

A frustrated scream shattered the peace, followed by a heavy *whump* as the woman took off into the sky, her leathery wings beating against the dust and stars.

With a sigh, Percival allowed his shoulders to relax and finally turned to inspect the shelter he had found. Would it be sufficient for him to see the night out? Would one night be enough?

He had heard all kinds of stories during his time with the Crusades. And again, afterward while traveling with his own men, roving from town to village to homestead, picking at carcasses of their own creation. He knew of monsters and creatures. Of legend and lore. He believed none of it.

Until now.

Women in a well.

Wings.

Sharp teeth.

And a taste for flesh and blood.

Whether monster or creature, he knew they were real, and he knew they would kill him the first chance they got.

The room he found himself in appeared to be the main area of a stone cottage. He had seen many of them in his time and suspected it would have a bedroom or two off the main area, maybe a pantry for food and other items.

As if to prove him right, his eyes were drawn to a crack of light at the far end of the room.

A doorway.

As his eyes adjusted to the gloom, so too did his ears adjust to the quiet. Screams still punctuated the silence, though he wasn't sure if they were real or just an echo of the carnage he had witnessed. Perhaps he had absorbed the pain of his men into his very bloodstream. Communion with their souls.

A new sound emerged in the darkness.

The closer Percival crept to the door at the back of the room, the more substantial the sound became.

It was movement.

Mewling.

Suckling.

Reaching out, he rested a trembling hand against the wood for a moment, as though it would give him the power to see what awaited him on the other side. When no such vision was forthcoming, Percival pushed the door open.

And stepped straight into his own nightmare.

Beyond the door were a handful of stone steps that dropped into the small adjoining room. The smell of dirt was cloying, the metallic tang of blood mingling with it to create an overpowering stench that crashed against Percival like a wave. It was the fright rather than the smell that almost sent him reeling from the room. His fingers turned white around the iron handle as his grip tightened in an effort to keep himself upright.

The room was devoid of furniture save for a single wooden chair and table in the center of the dirt-packed floor. The oil lamp perched upon the table cast a minimal glow, the tiny flame within reaching out toward Percival and the draft that had rushed into the room through the doorway he still occupied. Despite the lack of furniture, the room was far from empty.

Dozens of small bodies, naked and hairless, writhed within the shadows. The weak lamplight struggled to illuminate the scene, but Percival could see enough to draw his mind back to the unbidden thoughts he had upon seeing the cloaked man's scar-ridden skin.

And there among the vampiric children, offering his skin and his blood to them, sat Aras. The man's cloak hung across the back of the wooden chair, and Percival could see more of the tattooed marks on the man's naked body. Though he couldn't see much of his nakedness beyond the bobbing heads of the parasitic children as they leeched the man's lifeforce from him.

Percival swallowed heavily and took a single step back, preparing to leave this room—and the nightmarish tableau—behind him.

"Percival."

The room brightened just a little as Aras turned the wheel on the lamp, allowing the flame to consume more. To grow.

Percival glanced nervously at the devil-children again.

Their skin was like marble, spidery veins of purple and black cutting across their bodies like rivers upon a landscape. Right around their shoulder blades, bony protrusions had broken through the skin, leaving the connecting tissue bloody and torn. Viscous liquid, dirty gray in color, seeped from open sores surrounding the nubs that would become wings. It shimmered beneath the dancing shadows. These were clearly fledgling variations of the monsters he had encountered in the courtyard.

"You opened the well, didn't you, Percival?"

He met the old man's eyes and croaked out his admittance in a single, "Yes."

As though only becoming aware of his presence, the younglings turned as one to study him, hissing and spitting, advancing. A gentle murmur from Aras and they returned to his flesh. The suckling and mewling increased in intensity and volume. The few moments they had been away from their meal had been enough to make them ravenous.

Aras stroked one bald head with old and crooked fingers.

"These are the night children of Bludlust. I am their guardian."

He looked proudly—tenderly—upon the wriggling forms.

"These creatures are killing my men," hissed Percival. "They should all die."

Aras held his eye, his mouth turning to a smile, then a sneer.

"Indeed, many will die tonight. But it will not be those queens of the night." The man began to cackle, the sound punctuated only briefly by a sharp intake of breath as one of the night children sank their fangs too deep.

Percival left, tugging the door shut tightly behind him, but the old man's laughter followed him from the dirt room. Percival needed to escape this place, and the only way to do it was to forsake his men and hope that their deaths provided enough distraction to see him through the forest and away from this place.

He wasn't willing to gamble with his own life for a few brutes. A strong man was easily replaced. A strong mind was far less common. He could always find more men to follow him.

He listened briefly at the door that stood between him and the outside world before pulling it open and stepping outside. The cold night air wrapped itself around him. The shadows followed suit.

The sounds of smacking lips and the old man's laughter followed Percival out into the darkness like a sacrificial song on the wind.

Bludlust was eerily quiet.

The village's unusual title, something that had struck him as an oddity upon first hearing it, now made sense to him. He was struck once more by the memory of the writhing mass of tiny bodies filled with rows of tiny teeth as they clamored to taste the old man. A fitting name, indeed.

Confining himself to the shadows, Percival crept from alley to alley until he reached the courtyard. The stone archway was at the far side of the enclosure—his freedom so close he could almost taste it in the back of his throat—but the tingling at the base of his skull told him that safety was no certainty. The way out was right there. So too was the well. That ghastly doorway to Hell that spat those horrific creatures out.

No time to think about what could have been. He scanned the vacant space, his eyes falling upon the shimmering gold well cover. The men had opened the damn thing at his insistence, and they had paid dearly for it. And still, he felt his fingers twitch as the precious gems winked and whispered of their worth, of how he needed them.

And despite being in his imagination, he knew they weren't wrong.

It would be a shame to leave this place of riches with nothing.

He would never make it to safety dragging the heavy cover, but a couple of the gems that nestled upon its face would see him well taken care of for a few months at least. Plenty of time to figure out his next move far away from Bludlust.

He scanned the courtyard a final time before shrugging off the shadows and moving toward the well.

The place was silent save for the soft whispering of the trees that encircled the village. He heard the branches sway and was glad of the stone walls that kept the wind from hampering his movements.

Above him, countless eyes watched his every step from their vantage point in the trees. Mouths stretched to impossible yawning proportions in silence as slithering tongues pushed past razor teeth to taste him on the air.

Percival crept on, unaware of the silent sentinels perched above.

Reaching the gold lid, he dropped to his knees softly and pulled out the small blade he carried in his boot. He tested a couple of the larger gems and, satisfied that he could extract them quickly from the right angle and with the right leverage, he turned his back on the well. It was an uncomfortable feeling. One he tried to ignore as he hurriedly stuck the tip of the knife beneath the first gem and pushed. It popped out easier than expected, and Percival grinned. His body relaxed a little as he pocketed the first dazzling stone. The knife slid beneath the next gem, but this one was not as willing to part from its golden home. He grunted as he shimmied the knife, searching for better traction.

Another grunt, but this one hadn't come from Percival.

Two pale arms slid across his shoulders, the hands clasping together as he was embraced from behind. A soft humming in his ear. A tongue against his neck, delicate first, almost sensual, before becoming something more incessant and probing.

His hair stood on end as Percival turned his face. He didn't want to see, but the pull of curiosity was always too much for a clever man.

The hag's daughter beamed at him, that impossibly dark hair framing her beautiful face. Her skin was still pale but no longer in an alluring way. She was carved now from the same terrible marble as the creatures that infested this place.

She had become one of them.

Frozen in fear, Percival watched as the stone archway that had signified his freedom moved farther away as the girl gently pulled him backward toward the well. Her arms tightened around his chest, her nails searching for his softness, his blood, his pain. He felt her teeth part the skin of his neck, wincing as her tongue speared the gash she had opened in his flesh, stretching it wider, mewling, suckling.

The ground beneath his feet disappeared, and the dark starlit sky above was replaced by black as she pulled Percival over the low stone wall.

The murky depths of the old well claimed them as its own.

PUDDLES

MEGAN STOCKTON

Ed wiped the snotty wad of jizz off the EMPLOYEE OF THE MONTH photo of Jessica Myers with a napkin before flinging it into the trash. He carefully hung the picture back on the wall, although he didn't bother to correct it when it fell crookedly to one side.

"Ed?"

The voice of Jessica in the flesh rang from the hallway as she peeked her head inside the employee area just in time to see him pull up the stubborn zipper of his pants.

"Ah, yeah. Sorry. Fly was down." He smiled wide enough that he felt the craterous cold sore on his lower lip split open. It wasn't the first time she'd nearly caught him jacking off in the lunch lounge, but he had her departure timed and down to a science. He finished his work, cutting plenty of corners in order to complete everything early, and helped himself to the solitude of the lounge for the remaining fifteen minutes before the pretty supervisor punched out.

She grimaced at him. "Did you get all of this week's animals done?"

"Mmmhm," Ed responded, putting his hands on his hips with another grin. "Freezer's full, by the way."

Jessica sighed, a little bit of sadness creeping into her eyes. Ed even paused a moment from his faux-friendly attitude to frown at her.

"I hate this time of year," she remarked, picking at the chipped paint on one of her fingernails. "No one gets their pets fixed, and there are so many puppies and kittens. I've sent all I can to rescues and no-kills. There just isn't room. What else can we do, though, right?"

Ed nodded, shrugging. Jessica didn't seem satisfied with his response, the wrinkle of concern between her brows knitting into one of disappointment.

"All right... Well, I'm gone over the weekend. So it's just up to you and Trent to be sure everything gets fed and taken care of. Get clocked out and go home, all right?"

"Aye, aye, Captain!" Ed straightened his spine and saluted her.

Jessica didn't seem impressed. In fact, she grimaced a half-assed smile at him before she disappeared down the hallway. He waited until he heard her head out the front door before he went the opposite way down the long hallway, popping the back door open.

An older guy in moth-eaten clothes was waiting there, standing with his back resting against the building. He smiled at Ed, flicking his wrist out to reveal a small baggie of pinkish crystals between two of his fingers. Ed retrieved his wallet and thumbed out the cash for him. It was just a few bills, but the man counted all of them.

Discount Daryl was the only dealer that Ed could afford to buy from these days. Despite the fact that he dealt in the cheapest, bottom-of-the-barrel product, Daryl was reliable and safe... mostly. There was the time he'd gotten more than he'd bargained for when he accidentally got *salvia* instead of *sativa* and spent the rest of the night tripping terrifying balls. Why did those words have to be so close to the same thing?

"Thanks, D," Ed said, putting the bag into his pocket.

"Oh, and Ed... here's a little something new."

Daryl offered Ed another bag, this one filled a quarter of the way with clear crystals. It looked like it was probably meth, but Ed couldn't know for sure.

"What's the catch?" Ed asked.

"Just a sample. It's..." He paused, grinding his teeth together. "Spicy."

"The last time I tried one of your samples, I trimmed six years off my life," Ed said, reluctantly taking the bag.

"Use it, give it to a friend. I don't really care. I was just told to hand it out, and so hand it out I shall." Daryl shrugged and started walking away. "Oh, by the way, there's a cat in a box."

"What?"

"There's a cat... in that box."

Ed spun around to see a cardboard box lined with a pink baby blanket sitting on the opposite side of the door. The box was saturated on the bottom, wet from rain no doubt. It probably sat out here all day. As he approached more closely, he smelled the rank shit of a cat with coccidia (yeah, he knew what coccidia was but not the difference in salvia and sativa). A little note was stapled to the front of the box that read, *Please take care of Puddles, she is a very sweet girl, but I can no longer care for her.*

Puddles was the most generic-looking tabby cat: black and caramel stripes with lots of white. She was a little snotty, eyes rimmed with irritated tears. He saw the pile of pudding-like, yellow feces in the corner. The sour stench burned his eyes as he squatted down. She mewled at him.

"Fuck."

All of the animals that were "extra" had been euthanized for the holiday weekend, and they had been filled with the new intakes. There were no free cages. Ed knew that if another animal came in after hours, he was supposed to either turn the owner away until Monday or *take the pet home* to care for it until Monday. There was no way in hell Ed was taking Puddles the snot and shit factory home with him.

"You need a cat?" he asked, looking over his shoulder at Daryl.

"Hell, no. I got my own fleas." He laughed but scratched behind his ear as though the insult *had* stirred up the little offended bugs.

"I can't take this thing home. I don't have any supplies for it or anything."

"What are you gonna do, then?"

He wondered if he could pick the lock to the controlled drug cabinet to grab some euthanasia solution... and if he *could*, would anyone notice the tiny amount it would take to kill this little kitten? They kept up with that shit so well. Someone from the state came and checked their logs every month to make sure each drop was accounted for.

Then Ed looked down at the spicy sample in his hand, and he knew what he had to do.

He was going to OD this cat on Discount Daryl's meth.

"I'll deal with it," Ed grumbled.

Daryl stumbled down the street and out of sight.

Ed shoved the drugs in his pocket and pulled a pocketknife out, cutting up the pink blanket to create a makeshift diaper he could tie around the kitten's waist. Her potbelly bulged over the top of it, but she was quiet, seeming satisfied that he was paying her any attention at all. Ed didn't claim to have much of a heart, even for animals, but he couldn't deny that he felt just a little guilty for what he was about to do to this cat.

He supposed it might be easier, less hands-on, if he put her into a bag and threw her in the river or smashed her against the pavement. That seemed cruel, though, even to Ed. Although Puddles absolutely *reeked*, he stuffed her down in the front of his jacket, zipping it up just enough to hold the cat in place. He couldn't kill her here; he'd need to do it somewhere more secluded. Somewhere there was less risk of cameras or someone seeing him dispose of the body.

Jesus Christ, was this what murderers had to think about? That was a lot of work.

He usually caught a bus home but figured they would frown upon the odor of him and the cat, so he opted to take a shortcut through town to his apartment. He'd been avoiding walking the streets for weeks, but this would be quicker and cheaper anyway. Something rumbled, and he wondered if it was his stomach or the kitten purring.

Ed was barely sixty yards from the animal shelter when he regretted the decision to walk. The very reason he had been taking public transportation stood just across the street from him. They were draped in the shapeless anonymity of oversized hoodies and sagging cargo pants: two living heaps of wrinkled fabric. Their street nicknames were Razor and Stitch, and they were the less-than-charming lackeys that worked for the biggest drug dealer in the city: Big Rich.

Unfortunately, Ed had borrowed a "small amount" of money from them, and then a little more... and eventually he owed more than he could cough up. He knew this day would come, but he really wished it hadn't been today.

Ed's heart hammered against his ribs, and he tried to appear nonchalant, whistling a tune that died in his throat as he saw Razor's gaze settle on him. Stitch gave a barely perceptible nod, raising his chin upward once. Razor pushed himself off the wall he'd been leaning against, his movement fluid and predatory.

Panic seized Ed in an instant. He turned on his heels and accelerated, his pace turning into a clumsy sprint as he clutched the kitten against his chest. She squeaked in protest, tiny claws digging into his side. A nearby alleyway loomed on his left, a dark sliver of promise for temporary escape. He plunged into it, the stench of damp garbage stinging his nostrils. Razor and Stitch were on his heels, their footsteps echoing in the claustrophobic space. Ed risked a glance over his shoulder to see that Razor was gaining. He could practically feel the man's breath on his neck, his massive hands reaching out for him.

He stumbled, arms flying out as he braced himself from hitting the ground and crushing the shit out of Puddles (although that would have been one thing to check off of his list).

"Got you, you sorry bastard." Stitch laughed as Razor hauled Ed effortlessly to his feet.

"Guys, I c-can explain. This is all a huge misunderstanding," Ed stammered.

"You got a couple grand in that cheap jogging suit?" Razor grumbled, giving him a shake. Ed felt Puddles dig her claws into his ribs.

"They're scrubs, man." Ed swallowed back his fear, offering a smile.

"What the fuck's a scrub?" Stitch asked, tilting his head far enough to the side that his greasy ponytail flopped.

"Never mind that," Razor insisted. "What's in your jacket?"

"Nothing."

"You better tell me. You got a gun in there or something?"

"Nah, Razor. It's movin'!"

Ed laughed a choppy, nervous chuckle. "It's a cat."

The two men exchanged glances.

"Well, you and your pussy got an appointment with Big Rich," Stitch said, motioning for Razor to follow. Ed was dragged down the street and into a car that seemed to have appeared out of nowhere. They shoved him into the backseat between the duo surrounded by a noxious cloud of cologne and BO. A heavyset man in the front seat turned around, smiling at him.

"Heya, Eddie."

"Hey, yourself, Little Richie."

Big Rich immediately frowned and turned around in the seat. The car lurched onto the road, and Razor elbowed Ed in the gut. The cat let out an angry growl from inside his jacket, nails leaving a trail of pinpricks across his flesh.

"What the fuck was that?" Rich asked, still looking forward.

"Says he's got a cat in his jacket," Stitch responded.

"You didn't check?"

Razor reached over and unzipped Ed's jacket, and Puddles came tumbling out. Her pink diaper was now hanging haphazardly with her tail sticking out of the left leg hole. The man reached down and plucked her up by her scruff.

"It *is* a cat."

"Well, what are you doing with it?" Big Rich asked, lighting up a cigar. He rolled the window down in the back. "Throw it out."

Razor held Puddles up beside the window, and her lower body tucked up defensively. The wind blew her tiny form around like she was caught in a tornado, eyes watering even more than they had before. She looked at Ed and mewled once.

He swore to God she looked *into his fucking soul*.

He couldn't believe he was doing this. He couldn't believe he was about to risk his life for a cat that he had planned on killing anyway.

"Don't. Please," Ed said, trying to stop Razor before he dropped the cat onto the highway to be hit by another driver.

"You gonna convince me, Eddie?" Big Rich asked.

"Well... I mean, you could throw it out, but why would you throw cash out like that?"

"Cash?"

"Yeah, what are you on about?" Stitch interjected, leaning toward him. In the small space his breath smelled like onions, and Ed had to close his own mouth to keep from tasting it.

"It's an expensive cat. I was supposed to take it to a lady. Someone brought it into the shelter by mistake. She's got a *big* reward for it."

"How much we talking?"

"Ten grand."

Laughter erupted in the car, but Razor put the cat into his lap, and Ed let a sigh of relief leave his lips.

"Yeah, laugh all you want, but the cat is worth twice that."

"What kind of cat is it?"

"It's a—Russian... Cheese... stick."

The car was dead silent.

"That's the biggest bullshit I've ever heard."

"Look it up when we get there. Where *are* we going, by the way?"

As if on cue, the car pulled into a gravel lot outside of a warehouse. Ed's stomach sank. Big Rich didn't bring people who owed him money to a place like this with intentions of letting them go. This was the place they'd torture and kill him, then chop him up into little pieces to distribute around the city.

Big Rich, Razor, Stitch, and the driver exited the car and pulled Ed along with them through the warehouse door, bouncing him around between them like a pinball. Razor still held fast to Puddles, but once inside he set her down on the ground. She instantly scrambled away. That was probably the last he'd ever see of the cat, but at least she was alive and not his problem anymore.

They took off all of Ed's clothes, thankfully allowing him to keep his underwear, and discarded them on the floor. The packet of sample meth flew out of his pocket and spilled onto the ground. So much for that.

Stitch tied his hands behind his back while Razor scrolled on his phone, eyes narrowing before bulging.

"A Russian Cheesestick isn't a cat," he proclaimed, elbowing Big Rich.

"Well, what the hell is it?"

He leaned in and whispered into his ear.

"You do *what* with string cheese?" Rich exclaimed, voice echoing in the warehouse. "That's sick. You're a sick fuck, Eddie."

"What is it?" Stitch asked. "Come on, somebody tell me."

"You don't wanna know," Razor insisted.

"I'm the only one who doesn't know, and you know I fucking hate being left out. Somebody tell me."

Rich put his hand to his forehead and closed his eyes. "It's when you stick string cheese in a broad's vagina while you stick your dick in her ass."

Stitch didn't say anything else, but Ed had to stifle his laughter.

Razor shivered and tucked the phone into his pocket, cuffing the sleeves of his shirt before he retrieved a pair of pliers from a table near the wall. Ed didn't really care *what* part of his body was the intended victim... He wasn't here for it.

"Come on, guys. Let's talk about it, okay?"

"We're done letting you talk," Rich said, sighing. "All you had to do was pay your dues, Ed. We aren't the bad guys here. You owe us money. You don't have the money. Now we have to make sure you don't take advantage of anyone else. We're doing our part to keep the streets clean."

"Like Batman," Stitch said from behind him, chewing something obnoxiously.

"So just sit back and relax, and let us have our fun, right? You gotta learn your lesson."

Ed rocked back and forth in the chair, trying to tip it over or do anything that would throw the men off for even a moment. The sound of something rustling off to the side caught his attention, and out of the corner of his eye, he saw Puddles approaching. He didn't risk looking at her fully, wondering if she would come closer if they made eye contact. He wasn't sure how he'd gone from wanting to beat her to death to wanting to save her life. Unusual circumstances made you change your perspective sometimes, he supposed. Puddles took an interest in the bag of spicy meth, chewing it open and then sniffing fiercely at the spilled crystals. Then she was eating them.

Great. Now she was going to overdose anyway. Well, at least he would share a date of death with Puddles. Maybe they could reconnect in the afterlife and he could tell her that he didn't really mean all those homicidal things he thought about her when he first saw her nasty, diarrhea-stained ass in that box. He panicked, that's all. Now he wanted Puddles to live; now *he* wanted to live.

Stitch grabbed Ed by the hair, twisting the handful and pulling his head back so that he was forced to look straight up at the lights that hung far overhead.

"Buy me dinner first," Ed quipped, smiling with humor. Razor took advantage of his open mouth and grabbed his lower jaw by hooking his thumb over his bottom teeth. Ed *tried* to bite him, but the man's hand strength was far superior to that of Ed's jaw. His fingers tasted like ass, but that was the least of Ed's concerns right now.

The pliers entered his mouth, metal handle clicking against his other teeth and making him nauseous. The way they grinded gave him goose bumps and turned his gut into a rolling pot of water. They grabbed one of his eye teeth with the serrated mouth of the pliers, and then they pulled. Ed screamed and tried to fight against them, but the more he fought, the harder they twisted against his tooth. His whole face hurt: his nose, his eyes, the roof of his mouth. The tooth broke off twice, splinters flying onto his tongue and face. He nearly choked on one shard, and he was sure it had lodged itself in his tonsils. Each time the tooth fractured, Razor just grabbed a thicker chunk.

"Here we go," Razor said, pulling his lower lip over his teeth and licking it as he struggled with the stubborn tooth. With a sickening, sucking sound, the tooth came free.

Ed was almost relieved. The pain was no longer stabbing but now ebbed consistently. Predictable pain was so much easier to deal with. They let him go, blood pouring down his chin, and they laughed. Ed panted, looking over at Puddles. She wasn't dead yet... but she was looking right at him. The meth wasn't killing her; it was *transforming her*. Puddles' fur seemed to bristle; her eyes glowed with an unnatural green light. A low growl, far too deep for such a small creature, rumbled from her tiny throat.

All three of the men looked at the tiny cat too, and then they exchanged confused glances. Razor took a step toward her and then crouched down to extend his hand.

"Kitty, kitty?"

Puddles launched herself at him, climbing up his arm like it was a bridge straight to his face. Her tiny claws, now impossibly sharp, tore into his face with the ferocity of a feral creature ten times her size. Razor screamed, stumbling backward as he tried to pull the kitten off of his face. Growls filled the interior of the warehouse. Fueled by the meth, Puddles moved with impossible speed and agility. She was a whirlwind of tabby fur and razor claws. As Stitch came to his partner's aid, Puddles leaped from Razor's face onto Stitch's shoulder, sinking her needle-like teeth into his neck. Blood spurted from his carotid almost comically, spraying into the air as the kitten pulled her small mouth away.

Ed watched, slack jawed, as Rich finally took matters into his own hands. He pulled a handgun from his pocket, aiming at the cat still perched on Stitch's shoulder.

"No, no, no!" Stitch protested with one hand, keeping the other firmly planted over his gushing artery.

Rich fired anyway, missing Puddles and hitting Stitch right in the cheek. As he fell backward, dead instantly, Puddles soared through the air again, landing squarely on Rich's head. Her claws raked his scalp, and she proceeded to bite his ear with astonishing force. Rich roared in agony, dropping his weapon and grabbing at his mauled ear.

Ed, stunned into silence, watched as the tiny kitten unleashed a furious, adrenaline-fueled assault. Taking advantage of the chaos, he managed to wiggle his hands free from the fabric they'd used to tie him to the chair. Rich was still trying to pull the kitten off of him, grabbing at her small form with both hands but unable somehow to dislodge her. The furious growls sounded like they belonged to a dog.

Rich fired the gun into the air again, and Ed ducked. Razor started sprinting toward the door, and Ed let him go. Puddles was finally slung across the room, but not before she tore open Rich's throat as well. He was growing paler in front of Ed's very eyes. This was his chance to escape, but he couldn't leave Puddles. Not now.

He rushed over, snatching the kitten up and holding her against his bare chest.

Rich screamed, voice like gravel in a bucket even as he died on his feet, his face a mask of furious determination. Ed vaulted a stack of wooden crates, jarring Puddles. A tiny hiss escaped her, followed by a desperate mewling. He winced, whispering apologies between his teeth as he jogged through the open space.

Ed shoved himself through the back door, tumbling out into the alley, and the night air was a welcome relief. He didn't stop running until he reached the relative safety of the main street, his breath ragged, his naked body chilled. Puddles purred ferociously, nestled safely in his arms.

As he prepared to cross the street to his apartment, he stole a glance down the sidewalk behind him. Razor stood there, bloody-faced and heaving with heavy breaths. They stared at each other for several long moments, and Puddles growled in his arms. Razor must have heard her, because he quickly looked away and started walking the opposite direction.

This might not be over, but for right now it was. A car honked at him, and he flinched before jogging across the street. He'd been in a lot of weird situations, but being caught out in his stained briefs with a cat wasn't exactly one of his favorite pastimes.

Puddles was asleep by the time he went up the stairs to his apart-ment, snoring. Ed unlocked his door quietly, moving the tiny pack-ages of drugs off of his couch and laying them beside the line of speedball on the table to make room for his little warrior princess on the couch. She didn't wake as he nestled her in the dip where the springs were broken in the cushion.

"Okay. I need a litter box, cat food, dewormer..." he whispered to himself, going into the kitchen and retrieving a saucer and a jug of expired milk. He knew cats weren't supposed to have dairy, but it was all he had. It wasn't going to make her shits any worse, that was for sure. Plus, dammit, she deserved it. He poured the coagulated milk into the dish and carried it carefully back into the living room, watching it to be sure he didn't slosh as he walked.

"Puddles, oh, Princess Puddles... Look what I got for you. You've been such a good—"

Ed stopped, dropping the saucer as he saw Puddles standing on the table. She was growling, eyes bulging out of her skull, hair standing up like she'd licked a light socket. Froth and saliva poured out of her jaws, and she licked her powder-covered nose before she launched herself at Ed.

R.E. SARGENT

People always ask what happened. Usually, it earns a laugh and a version of events skewed through a personal lens. Biased, maybe—but it's the only story worth telling. Not that anyone asked. But here it is anyway.

I never liked Brooke from day one. She always came off as too friendly and too willing to help others. Suspicious AF. No one can be that nice. So to say I was extremely standoffish was an understatement.

Before diving into the rest, let's clear something up. No, I'm not lazy, and I'm a hard worker. I just don't kiss anyone's ass, and I'm not afraid to say something if I feel like the company is heading in the wrong direction. But that hasn't won me any brownie points. But Brooke ... From day one, she was the fucking golden child. And honestly, I just hated it.

So, a little bit about my job. I worked in the local grocery store, which is part of a national chain. Retail sucks, and it wasn't my favorite job, but it was a job. I started as a bagger; however, after about six months, my boss saw my work ethic and promoted me to cashier. Then they started having me fill in wherever there was a need around the store, so I got quite a bit of experience. Picking up extra shifts was never an issue since I was so versatile. At the time, I was the only female working multiple departments, and people took notice.

Every day was different scenery ... One day I might have been working the produce department, another day the deli, sometimes the bakery, grocery, or the meat department. The only department that I never worked in was the pharmacy, but that's because my state makes pharmacy technicians hold a license. But my home department was the front end as a cashier, and believe it or not, after only three years, I had the most seniority as a cashier. Of course, that was only because a new store opened up a few miles down the road and most of the old-timers transferred there, but it worked for me.

The job came right after high school—nothing glamorous, but it paid the bills. Motivation to climb higher? Lacking. The pay was decent, benefits solid, and the bosses? Generally supportive. Staying put made sense.

Things changed a few years later, though, when in walked Brooke. They hired her as a cashier right off the street, which wasn't how most of us got into the position. Most of us worked our way up from the bottom. But I didn't think too much about it at the time, and we needed the help. That is until her third week in when they started giving her the opening cashier shifts.

I was blown away. She just walks in off the street, and after two fucking weeks, they're scheduling her for the opening shift and I get pushed back to the 7:00 a.m. cashier shift. I know what you're thinking. An extra hour of sleep, right? Oh yeah, that part was fine, but it was the principle of the fucking thing. I had seniority, and that bitch did not. Who the fuck was she to just waltz in there and take the opening shifts, and why the fuck did my manager give her preferential treatment? Was it because she had her big nose all the way up his smelly asshole?

I did mention it to my boss. You know I did. And what did they say? To mind my own business. It kind of was my business that she took my shifts, but I decided to just chill out for a little bit and wait for this bitch to fuck up. Only I didn't count on the fact that she could do nothing wrong in management's eyes. Within the first month, she was named employee of the month. It seemed like I heard her name throughout the store on a daily basis. Every time they posted new customer comment cards on the bulletin board in the breakroom, it seemed like her name was mentioned, like she was taking stacks of these stupid-ass cards to all her friends and family and asking them to fill them out. I don't know what her magic potion was, but I was tired of it.

I started watching her. Observation turned into fixation—everything about her screamed curated. She had a big, beautiful smile, long brown hair, gorgeous green eyes, and a great sense of humor. I sound jealous, don't I? Well, I mean I'm not gonna lie. I wish I looked like her. I'm more of a tomboy. But that's not the point. Envy crept in, sure, but loyalty to the company had to count for something. Yet Brooke's performance didn't justify the spotlight. It just didn't add up.

But she had some way about her. Her interactions with the customers were easy-going and smooth, and she had them eating out of her hands. But I knew it was fake—it all had to be a facade. No one was that nice ... No one was that good. The bitch was a poser, and I was going to expose her.

Call it a confession. Games weren't part of the usual playbook, but Brooke made something snap. The sweet exterior, the saintly act —none of it felt real. Curiosity grew claws. I tried to find out everything that I could about her. At first, the plan was simple: expose the truth.

Finding a crack in the facade proved difficult. Brooke presented exactly what others saw—polished, kind, untouchable. Still, something felt off. Something deep, unsettling. That gut instinct pushed past reason and crossed into action. And so I did something that I've never done before: I started fucking with her.

It started with harmless stuff. Not sure why I felt the need to take it out on her, but I was frustrated with management and how she was the center of attention. She never locked the padlock on her locker in the breakroom, so when no one was around, I took her name badge.

Not sure if you've ever worked retail, but most managers are sticklers about name badges, and it's quite embarrassing to have to ask for a new one all the time. After the third time, she started locking her locker, but not before I got a few other good ones in like slipping condoms in her apron pocket, detaching the ballpoint tip from the ink chamber in the pen that was also in her apron pocket—didn't think that one through and it fucked up a new pair of her jeans, but it was funny AF—and putting a fake snake inside. Wish I could have seen her reaction to that one. The very same day, her lock was always locked.

So I got more inventive. One day, I took her lunch out of the refrigerator in the breakroom after she started her shift and placed it in the freezer. After three-and-a-half hours, I put it back in the refrigerator, making sure I was in the breakroom when her lunchtime arrived, casually eating a donut and scrolling on my phone. I knew she hadn't suspected me at the time, because she was always so sweet to me and I was overly sweet to her as well, to her face anyway.

"Oh, hi, Jordan!" she said, upon seeing me at the table, scrolling on my phone.

"Hey, Brooke! How are you, girl?"

"Great," she said, though her smile looked forced. "I love your hair today!"

"Thanks! Just got it done!" My hair had always been a strong feature—lush, brown, just touching the shoulders. Most days, it was hard to tell as it was pulled back in a ponytail, or when I wasn't working, was covered by a hat. It's that Tomboy thing. Most would say I'm a solid six in the looks department, but the hair definitely brought me up a point or two when I showed it off. But flaws ran deeper than the mirror revealed: honesty, integrity, and authenticity all came up short. Anyway, back to the point.

"You'll have to give me your stylist's name. I need a new one. My current one flakes on me a little too often."

"What's your number? I'll text you her contact card."

Brooke gave me her number, and I added it to my phone and texted her the information. I noticed while I was doing so that she went to the fridge and grabbed out her lunch bag. The show was about to start.

"Thanks, Jordan," she said, smiling, her voice more of a purr. She bugged the shit out of me.

She pulled out her sandwich and removed it from the baggie. I saw her brow furrow a little bit as she seemed unsure, but even though she knew something was amiss, she tried to take a bite.

"What the hell?"

"What's the matter?"

"It's frozen. The bread a little less so, but the lunch meat is solid."

"You know, I heard someone else complain about something similar the other day. I wonder if the setting is too cold."

"Maybe. But it's never done this before."

"Someone probably messed with it."

"Probably. But my lunch break will be over before it thaws. Crappy."

"That sucks," I said, but deep inside I was dying, laughing.

We made small talk for a few minutes, and I excused myself. I had been on break a little too long. The smile on my face felt shit-eating as my work resumed in the department I was working in that day.

After work, knowing it was time to up the ante, I stopped by the hardware store and picked up some spray foam.

The next morning, I had an early produce shift and hardly anyone was in the store. Knowing the breakroom didn't have cameras, I left my belongings in my locker after I clocked in and immediately pulled the spray foam out of my jacket pocket, extending the flexible tube and slipping it through one of the vent louvers on the door of her locker. Glad that it was locked, I unloaded as much of the can inside as it would take, and I wouldn't have wanted the door to get pushed open. That stuff dries pretty quickly, so by the time she came into work and fought to get her locker door open, it was a solid block of foam inside.

I heard through store gossip that she was pissed off, but I stayed away lest she suspect me. Luckily (for her), only her work things were affected: her apron, name badge, etc. How fun would it have been though had she been at work and her car keys and purse were in there? That would have been epic.

A WEEK LATER AND BOREDOM SETTLED IN WITH THE HIGH SCHOOL–level pranks. Something bigger called. Something that would stick. But what?

I really wanted to mess with her more at work, but I wasn't sure how. I didn't necessarily want to get caught. That wouldn't end well, and I'd probably get fired. I heard the boss was pretty angry about the spray-foam thing and had gotten loss prevention involved. Supposedly, they were doing an investigation, but I was confident there were no cameras in the breakroom, so the most they could do was speculate based upon traffic going in and out of the area. I was prepared to do what I do best if they interviewed me. Deny, deny, deny.

I thought of texting her, but she knew my number. I did a web search for texting people anonymously. Did you know they have an app for that? I do now. So I downloaded the app to my phone and picked a random phone number. And the app would let me text or call anyone I wanted with the number I picked out and there would be no way to trace it back to me.

So I sent her a text.

> I see through you

After waiting and getting no response, I finally went to bed. The next morning, she had replied.

> Who is this

I decided to wait a bit before answering. Raise her anxiety a bit. Until we were both at work. I even sent her the response when she was in my line of sight. I felt empowered, bold.

> You're not going to get away with it

I knew she wouldn't answer right away as she was on the register and her phone was sticking out of her back pocket. When she went to lunch, it wasn't long before I got a message back.

Get away with what? Who tf is this? Charlie?

I didn't know who Charlie was, but I was glad he'd be the number one suspect from here on out.

Names aren't important

Stop texting me!

Then stop being a stupid bitch!

I fucking hate you charlie. What do you want?

I'm gonna tell them about you

Tell who? Tell them what?

That grocery store you work at. I'm sure they'd like to know who you really are

Fuck off charlie

I stopped replying, wondering what she was hiding. My silence would bother her more than my messages.

That night, the blank television screen seemed to have my attention, but my mind was on other things. My next move.

I had already googled her and found out as much as the internet could tell me, but it was time to find out where she lived.

BEING OFF THE NEXT DAY, I SLEPT IN, UNMOTIVATED TO GET UP and do anything. Eventually, my eyes popped open, and as hard as I tried to fight it, sleep eluded me. Brooke's face pushed into my head, an unwelcome guest. Scenarios ran through my head, starting with an

elaborate plan to get Brooke's address from the administrative assistant's computer. Finally, I settled on following her home.

When she got off work was common knowledge, so I reached out to my friend Blake and asked about borrowing his truck for a bit to move some things from my storage and, in turn, he could drive my Honda. I could hear him rolling his eyes on the other end, but he agreed, and I went to his work and swapped keys. It probably didn't hurt that he wanted to bed me.

Parked on a side street beside the store parking lot, I watched her come out, hoping she would exit the lot in my direction, and she didn't disappoint. I pulled away from the curb ten seconds after she pulled out, keeping my distance. Luckily traffic was light.

I wasn't too concerned she would recognize me or even realize someone was following her. I stayed farther back, was in an unfamiliar vehicle, and was wearing a flannel, beanie, and sunglasses.

A car got between us, and that was fine by me. They seemed to be keeping up as she drove for several miles, finally turning on a residential street. I parked on the main street and edged forward, peering down the road after her. About halfway down, I saw her brake lights come on, and she turned into a driveway.

My impatient side wanted to drive down her street and check out the house, but I quashed that feeling down and waited. Eventually, I saw her get out of the car and walk inside.

I remembered that it would be difficult to know it was me, so I pulled back away from the curb and onto the street. Her white Honda sat about halfway down the block, and as I drove by, I noticed that she lived in a duplex. Unit B. Probably stood for "bitch." I took mental note of the address and snapped a picture with my phone.

OKAY, SO MY ORIGINAL INTENTION WAS TO AVOID SENDING THINGS to her through the US Mail. Somewhere along the line, I lost sight of that and sent my first letter.

On one of my research binges, I had stumbled across a site that you could pick a design, enter a message, enter an address, and the company would mail a card or letter out to the addressee. If I did it right, they wouldn't be able to trace it back to me.

The Wi-Fi at the coffee shop was easy to connect to, and I brought up the site. It wanted me to open an account. Did it, using a fake address, my fake app phone number, and an email address I had set up especially for the occasion—inyourhead@gmail.com.

The message flowed from my fingertips, and at the payment screen, I entered the card number for the prepaid Visa I had purchased earlier. When the site asked me to review the order before submitting, I magnified the image and checked my work.

Card Front:
You're One of a Kind!
(Big, glittery letters arched over a cartoon rainbow with smiling clouds)

Inside Message:
Brooke,
You are one of a kind—no one else smiles quite like you do ... when the mask is on. I used to think it was impressive. Now, I just wonder how long you can keep pretending. Rainbows always disappear, you know. And after the colors fade, all that's left is the storm.

Typically, I'm not one to toot my own horn, but fuck, I was proud of this one. Pausing for a second to contemplate my actions, I finally hit send. The pop-up on the site thanked me for my order and informed me the card would be delivered in five to seven days. That gave me some time to fuck around with her.

For the record, I'm not sure exactly why this girl is driving me to these actions. I've never done something like this before. In fact, typically I feel pretty normal, grounded even. But something about this girl brought out a different side of me ... I almost felt unhinged. Although it worried me a tad, I embraced it.

I stopped by another grocery store on my way home, picking up some things that I needed, as well as a dozen extra-large eggs.

At home, I tried to chill and watch TV, but my brain kept switching the channel to Brooke. My over-analytical mind tried to pinpoint exactly what it was about her that pissed me off so badly. Was it simply because she stole my shifts and was getting all of the attention? Was I simply jealous and it was making me crazy? I've seen some crazy bitches in my time, and I never thought I'd be one of them, but I wasn't far off.

But the more I tried to decipher my motives, the more the realization hit me that my unease was connected to the unknown, something that I couldn't quite bring to the forefront of my brain.

I went back to the internet, trying to find something that was missed. When all else failed, I tried to pull a report from one of those online sites that gives you background on people. Something was clawing at the edge of my mind, telling me there was more than met the eye with Brooke.

Although I didn't have much to go on, the site found her. It had to be her. The address matched. The records seemed to start with her current address. No other associated addresses. Only one email address. It didn't make sense.

It's like Brooke just recently came into existence. The only way that could happen ... Well, she had to be somebody else. What had caused her to use an assumed name? Hiding from the law maybe? Witness Protection?

Each question was left unanswered. I mean, I could come up with theories all day long, but ultimately, there was no way of substantiating any of them.

The mystery continued to grow. This had to be more than me hating on the new girl. Deep inside, I knew there was something wrong with the situation. This chick was suspect, maybe even dangerous.

The next morning, I left my house at three a.m., which seemed to be the deadest time of night. All of the bar people had finally gone home, and the streets were once again quiet, resetting themselves for the new day.

Ring cameras are great and all, but they are problematic when you are fucking around, so I left my car in a church parking lot and walked the two blocks to Brooke's duplex, my black jeans, hoodie, and Nikes weaving themselves into the inky darkness that integrated itself all around me. My hood was pulled up tight around my face.

The first egg was off by a few feet and hit a mailbox. The second one hit its mark, the front door. The remaining ten blasted the door, front window, and her Honda.

While the event was loud as fuck and rightfully I should have been busted, in reality, twelve eggs were launched in less than twenty seconds, and I didn't waste any time booking it back down to the end of the street and back to my car.

When I got back to my place, I felt exhilarated. It took me over an hour to wind down, and I laid on my bed, hoping to catch an hour nap before I had to be up for work, but sleep would not come. Instead, my brain had the IMAX version of the event looping on repeat.

When I finally got up to hop in the shower before work, I checked my phone. She had texted me.

> Did you do that? How the fuck did you find out
> where I live? Asshole!

She knew it was me. I mean, not necessarily me, but the person that had been texting her. The one she thought was Charlie. I was really dying to know who Charlie was. I decided to ignore her text and keep her stewing.

AT WORK LATER THAT DAY, I WAS IN THE BREAKROOM WHEN SHE came in for lunch. She glanced at me and forced a smile, her face lined with exhaustion. She sat at the same table after grabbing her lunch from the fridge. Sadly, it wouldn't be frozen this time.

"Hey," she said as she sat down.

"Hi, Brooke."

"How are you?" she asked, but the words were hollow, empty. She didn't care how I was.

"I'm good. You? Are you sick or something?"

She looked confused and then must have realized she looked haggard.

"Oh, um ... no. Just had a long night and I'm exhausted. Stressed to the max, actually."

"I'm a good listener," I offered.

She touched my arm.

"Thanks, Sweetie. I'll be okay."

I looked at her left hand. No ring. I asked anyways.

"Husband issues?"

She chuckled, a forced, uncomfortable laugh.

"No, thank god. He's no longer ... um ... I'm not married."

"Divorced?"

"Something like that."

"Are you from here?" I pried.

She paused, as if choosing her words carefully.

"No, transplant."

"Oh, cool! Where from?"

Brooke looked at her lunch and then put her hand to her stomach.

"I'm sorry ... I'm feeling a little ill."

She got up and put her lunch back in the fridge and walked to the breakroom door.

"Bye, Jordan," she called out as she exited into the hallway.

The conversation replayed in my mind.

Husband issues?

No, thank god.

Divorced?

Something like that.

What was that supposed to mean? If not divorced, did she leave him? Was he dead? Had she killed him? She had avoided my question with the upset stomach charade, but I had seen how she squirmed, and I knew Brooke was hiding something.

And who the fuck is Charlie?

Did you send this letter? I'm calling the fucking police

A HUGE SMILE LIT UP MY FACE. HER RESOLVE WAS DEFINITELY cracking.

It was a few days after the egg incident, and I had been waiting anxiously for the letter to arrive, not sure how quick those services were. At first, I didn't respond, but then something popped into my mind that I couldn't suppress.

Whatsa matter? Lost your rainbow?

A nod to the message in the card.

Police called. Watch your back!

The giggle that escaped me was unintentional, but I couldn't help it. I knew enough about a lot of stuff to know the cops wouldn't do a damn thing. Sure, the egg thing might be actionable if they gave a shit, but they had better things to do. And the letter? There was no direct threat made. They wouldn't expend the resources. They'd take a report, and she would never hear from them again.

I was already home from my shift, and I assumed Brooke had just picked up her mail. That would give her something to stress about all night. As for me, I would be going about my evening, a smug smile playing on my lips.

The pizza I ordered arrived ... a celebratory meal of sorts. Forgoing any dishes, I put the entire box on the coffee table in the living room and ate directly out of the box while looking for a good Netflix show. The benefits of being single.

The movie I selected was one I had wanted to watch for a while, but my mind kept switching to Brooke, and I couldn't remember anything that happened so far.

Okay, so I was getting to her. That was a start. But there were more questions than answers. My original intention was to fuck with her, but after peeling back the layers a bit, there were too many mysteries surrounding her existence. I needed to know more, but how? The answers were out there, but I didn't know how to get them.

Without another thought, my brain decided what my next action should be, and I blinked. This one was crossing a line I couldn't return from, but that didn't stop me from immediately setting it in motion.

The schedule was posted every Thursday by noon. One copy was posted in the breakroom and another in a binder at the Customer Service desk. I took a photo of the one in the breakroom when no one was around and chose the day. She would be at work all day, and I would be off, so I had plenty of time.

The night before, I was a bundle of nerves. I had never done anything like this before. I tried to talk myself out of it. Why did it matter if Brooke had a secret? What did it have to do with me? All of the stuff you tell yourself when you are looking for an excuse to back out of something. My brain took me back to the preferential treatment at work, and I got fired up again. The truth would be exposed.

Adrenaline was surging through my brain, and I couldn't rein it in, which kept me up way later than I wanted. When I finally laid down, sleep was fitful and intermittent.

At three a.m., I got up, showered, and dressed in my black garb. The Keurig spit out a cup of Donut Shop coffee, which I drank faster than normal.

It would start getting light before Brooke left for work, which was problematic, so my plan to get on her property unseen was risky but necessary.

At four a.m., I was parked several streets over and slinking down her street, my head on a swivel, ready to bail at the first sign of trouble. It was Sunday morning, which was a bonus as most people were off work and the world would remain sleepy for a while longer until all the churchgoers were on their way.

Her street was still, and I was thankful for the lack of streetlights, the only illumination coming from the scattered front porch or landscaping lights dotting the neighborhood.

I knew she would still be home, but I couldn't chance a broad daylight visit. Let's face it, I was no criminal, and truth be told, I didn't know what the fuck I was doing. So don't criticize me for my plan. It's the best I could come up with at the time.

Approaching her home, everything felt eerily still, as if the world had hit pause. Hopefully, no motion lights were installed, and with the darkness thick as tar, cameras didn't seem like much of a concern. Infrared hadn't even crossed my mind at the time. The risk was enormous, but there was a backup plan—if anything went wrong, running like hell would be the only option. On paper, it seemed like a decent strategy.

The coast looked clear. It was unknown if anyone was watching through their window from a darkened room. The *what ifs* could paralyze me if I let them, so I pushed them out of my mind and quietly made my way to the gate on the side of the unit.

The place had a small backyard. I was hoping there would be a spot to hide. As luck would have it, there was.

I clicked the latch and pushed the wooden gate open, cautious about squeaks or groans. The last thing I needed was to alert a neighbor's dog and have them start a barking riot. I hadn't even considered Brooke having a dog. Apparently, I'm not that good at this kind of thing.

My eyes adjusted to the space beyond. The duplex was to the left and a wooden fence to the right, the entire distance between the gate and where the narrow walkway opened up to the backyard, which was approximately fifteen feet back. This side of the unit had no windows. Nothing but privacy.

The gate was almost soundless as it latched. I was grateful. Although not the least bit comfortable, I found a dirt patch on the ground and tried to get myself settled. By my calculations, it would be an hour or more before Brooke left for work. When she did, her house would be my playground. I would find the answers if it killed me.

It seemed like forever, but eventually I heard water running in the house, and a few other noises. A while later, I heard the front door close and then a car start. I assumed it was her door and her car.

My ass and back hurt so badly. Sitting in one place quietly for over an hour isn't fun even on a soft surface. The compact soil was definitely not soft.

I tried to peek through the wooden slats of the gate. I could barely make out lights, but I was unsure where they were coming from. I moved my head to try another slat that wasn't pressed so tightly against its neighbor. I got a better view; it was definitely her car with the lights on.

After what seemed like an eternity, the car backed out of the parking spot, pulled off down the street, and the silence returned.

My body screamed at me to get up and get inside. My brain told me to hold tight, just in case she realized she forgot something and came back.

I kept my eye on my watch. Eventually, it was six a.m. I knew Brooke would be stuck on a register now since the store just opened. With any luck, I would have all the time I needed.

The sun was just starting to thrust itself over the horizon, which made things easier for me to navigate; however, I needed to get inside before someone spotted me.

The back door was one of those French deals. Wooden door. Glass insert. I put my hands up to shield the outside light away from my eyes as I peered through the glass. The dining area stared back at me. To the left was the kitchen, to the right, the living room.

The condition of the space beyond the door caught me off guard. Spotless. Well decorated. Brooke was a neat freak. And although that in itself was an admirable trait, I wondered what it was a symptom of. Maybe OCD? Or maybe she developed an extreme need for order and cleanliness as a way to exert control in a chaotic or unstable environment in her previous life. Whatever that was. I hoped I was about to find out.

I slid my backpack off my back and pulled out my gloves, slipping them on, before I pulled out the prybar. The wooden fence was tall enough that I wasn't concerned about the neighbors. That and the buildings surrounding this one were also single-story.

The prybar slipped between the door and the stop molding with ease, and it resisted when it hit the doorframe. As I pulled, I felt the door flex, but it didn't give. I pulled harder. The molding popped off with a splintering sound, exposing the latch.

The noise wasn't an issue for me. It wasn't loud, and it wouldn't be long before I was inside.

With the stop molding gone, I was able to insert the bar directly between the door and the jam, right next to the latch. I pulled with all my strength, and the latch finally ripped loose and tore through the door, swinging the door open at the same time.

I looked around at the neighboring homes. No sign of movement. Picking up the broken pieces and parts, I stashed them on the side of the house out of view before returning to the door. The prybar was returned to the backpack.

Inside, I once again admired the neatness of the place, but then a shudder ripped up my spine.

What kind of psycho keeps their house like this?

The place was small. One bedroom. One bathroom. Probably like six hundred square feet. It wouldn't take long to search.

It dawned on me that I had no idea what I was looking for. I just needed to find something. Anything that would tell me Brooke's secret. I quickly poked through the kitchen, anxious to get to the other rooms but wanting to cross every room off my list. I knew once I got to the bedroom, I'd probably be there for a while.

The kitchen was uneventful. Inside the drawers and cabinets was more evidence of Brooke's OCD. Even the refrigerator was organized by category, with the containers lined up from largest to smallest. It was craziness.

I quickly moved on to the living and dining areas and found nothing.

In the hallway, I found a small laundry closet. The machines were empty. This girl even put her laundry away, presumably, immediately after drying it. No clues there.

That left the bathroom and the bedroom.

The bathroom was exactly what I expected. Minimalistic. Towels neatly hung from their respective holders. A decorative soap dispenser next to the single sink. A couple of bathroom decorations on the vanity—and nothing else.

I spotted a cabinet in the corner and opened it. There it was. All of the makeup and beauty products a girl could ever want or need, but while mine were either thrown in a drawer or open on my bathroom counter, hers were arranged by type in clear stairstep holders that almost displayed the product like the cosmetics section in a beauty supply store might. All right, I'll admit it. It was fucking impressive.

I broke from my reverie and looked through the rest of the bathroom. Nothing of significance there, and I saw no signs of another person being there, as expected. No one was keeping their toothbrush and deodorant in a drawer in case of an impromptu night in the sack.

That left the bedroom.

Sweat beaded on my brow. On one hand, I knew the bedroom would probably be the room that held any secrets that were begging to be discovered, but my stomach was knotting over the possibility that there was nothing. No evidence of a secret life—no story. Nada.

The bedroom was no surprise. A queen-sized bed against the right wall with a white side table next to it. A matching dresser opposite it with a fifty-seven-inch television on it. A small desk in the corner with a closed laptop on it. The bed was made meticulously, every fold and crease with purpose, every edge straight and even. No surprise.

My watch showed I'd been inside for half an hour—longer than expected, but thoroughness took time. With no signs of detection, there was little urgency. As far as anyone knew, the place was empty, which meant time was on my side.

I slid the drawer to the side table open and looked through the contents. Remote. Box of tissues. Small bottle of Ibuprofen. Chapstick. Emery board. An eclectic mix of items, yet they too were strategically placed. Still, there was nothing of interest.

Next came the dresser. Each drawer slid free easily, its contents unpacked and laid out on the bed carefully. Fingers sifted through the layers—fabric, fragrance, fragments of her life—all while searching for something hidden, something out of place. The lingerie felt wrong in my hands. Lace and silk that should've been intimate now felt invasive, like I was trespassing on something sacred. The textures stirred a strange familiarity, but none of it belonged to me. That realization clung to my skin, sharp and shameful.

Nervousness surged through my body as I struck out once again. Was I wrong? Did I break into someone's house and pilfer through their life for no reason? Was I the one that was fucked up?

I'd like to think I replaced the clothes as nicely as I found them, but that probably was far from the truth. Didn't matter. It's not like my visit would be a secret ... The back door would tattle on me.

The desk was another bust. A few papers in the top drawer, office supplies in the bottom. The feeling of dread increased. Nothing. That left the closet.

Pants hung on the left side, sorted by material type and color. Then came shirts and blouses, and finally to the right, dresses, lined up from casual to a few that were elegant.

I pulled a little black dress from the bar and held it up to my body, admiring it from the mirror above the dresser. I felt the flood of an emotion I couldn't place. A want. Maybe a need. The need to be sexy. Could it be jealousy? Was Brooke all too perfect? Was it possible she had no skeletons in her closet, only nice clothes? I didn't own anything like this dress. It was simple yet classy. And I knew my ass would look perfect in it.

Before I knew it, my black hoodie lay on the ground along with the rest of my clothing, my mostly naked reflection staring back at me, only a pair of gray, very plain panties clinging to me. I looked at the dress and then my panties, realizing they were contradicting each other. The dresser drawer called to me.

The panties slid off my hips in one fluid motion as I went to the drawer that contained all of the lacey ones. I found a matching set of bra and panties that I had admired earlier. Both fit perfectly, and as I looked at my reflection in the mirror, I teared up. Not only because I loved what I saw, but it hit me. I never did anything for myself to make myself feel truly special. Today I would.

The dress fit superbly, accenting my slim waist, hips, and I noticed as I turned around and checked it in the mirror that my ass had never looked so good. This dress was made for me. I might have to take it with me.

It took several minutes to regain my composure and for me to get my head back in the game. I was here for a purpose, and it was time to stop playing dress up and find what I was looking for. Still, I felt alive in the dress, and I wasn't quite ready to take it off, so I continued my search in it.

My eyes landed on the laptop. Hopefully, it wasn't password protected. Once the lid was opened and the power button pushed, I waited for it to boot up.

It was quick, and it tried to scan my eyes to validate my identity. Obviously, that didn't work. After choosing other sign in options, I tried a pin code. I'm not sure how many random codes I tried, but none of them worked. I was no hacker, and this computer wasn't giving up the information. I had hit a dead end.

Remembering the closet, I went back to it and poked through every crook and cranny, hoping something had been tucked away there, something that would be useful to my quest. Unfortunately, the closet only yielded what it was designed for. Clothing. That left the laptop as the only likely source. A source I couldn't crack.

Disappointment crashed over me, my efforts futile. Then it hit me. I had committed a burglary. A felony. And for nothing. All because of a girl at work who people obviously liked more. And maybe she didn't have any skeletons in her closet. Maybe she was just a good person and I was the asshole.

My body slid to the floor as I thought about my options. Grab my clothes and get out as quickly as possible? Hope I didn't get caught?

The shallow plastic tote under the bed caught my attention, and my heart skipped a beat. Crawling to it, I slid it out and then peered underneath the bed to see if there were other treasures. The tote, which was approximately three feet long, two feet wide, and eight inches high, was the only thing under there. I stood up and placed it on the bed.

This had to be it. The keeper of the secrets. I unlatched the lid and pulled it off. Hundreds of papers, newspaper clippings, and photographs stared back at me. I picked up a stack of photos, all images printed on regular printer paper.

A photo of Brooke and a man, his smile big, hers forced. A picture of Brooke and a child around three, his eyes big and blue. Was that her husband? Her son?

I continued looking through the pictures, many of the boy, some of just Brooke, a few that had the man in them. His eyes. Something wasn't right about his eyes.

My stomach turned at the next photo. Brooke with two black eyes. A split lip. Another photo showed Brooke with a cast on her left arm. Was he who she was hiding from?

I set the pictures down after seeing enough, then picked up a stack of papers and thumbed through them. Divorce papers for an unknown couple, Jennifer and James Bentlow. Not sure who the hell they were, but I'd have to Google it later.

Then the restraining order. Jennifer had filed on James. The court had ordered it. Apparently, he was abusive.

Then came several police reports. Violations of the restraining order. Three of them altogether.

A thought began to fester in my mind. Abusive husband. Photos of Brooke beat to shit.

I picked up the stack of newspaper clippings. The headline read:

Seattle Woman Sentenced to Life for Husband's Murder

Holy shit! All of the puzzle pieces clicked into place as I read the article. Jennifer Bentlow, convicted felon, killed her ex-husband, James. According to the article, it was premeditated. She claimed it was self-defense. The article showed a picture of Jennifer in the courtroom. Except it was a picture of Brooke. My Spidey senses were right. Brooke was hiding something, but I never imagined it was something like this.

I looked at the pictures again. Brooke had definitely been abused. The restraining order and police reports were further evidence of that. If she had killed James Bentlow, the fucker had it coming. How on earth had she ever been convicted for protecting herself?

I pulled out my phone and googled the case. It wasn't long before I understood the bigger picture. Brooke, or Jennifer, had hired a hitman to take her ex-husband out. Some guy she threw under the bus to try and save her sorry ass during the trial. A man that was still at large, Charlie Stiller.

I pulled up my text messages from the spoofer app and re-read the exchange with Brooke.

> I fucking hate you charlie. What do you want?

Charlie. The dude that she had hired to kill her ex.

To say my mind was blown was an understatement. This was some real *Dateline* shit.

"That dress looks pretty good on you."

I swiveled around at the voice coming from the doorway.

"Brooke! What are you doing here?"

"Same question. And why are you wearing my clothes?"

"I ... uh ..."I was speechless.

Brooke eyed the tote, the contents spread out on the bed.

"Seems like we have a problem."

"No problems, Brooke. I'm sorry about all this. I was just curious. This stays between us. I'll just be on my way."

I bent down and scooped up my clothes, hoping she would step aside and let me out of the room.

Her glare was icy.

"It's not that simple, Jordan."

"How are you not in jail?"

"Didn't get to that news article yet?"

"Apparently not."

"I escaped while they were transporting me. Moved here. Started fresh. Thought I was going to have a chance at a normal life, but I guess not."

"Thought you didn't get off until two-thirty."

"You thought right. But when I got a text alert that someone was trying to access my laptop, I told the boss I had to go. Imagine my confusion when the webcam image I received was of you. And wearing my dress no less."

"Oh," was all I could manage to say.

"Why, Jordan? Why are you fucking with me?"

The jig was up.

"It's just ... I mean ... I knew something was off with you. But I never suspected this."

"You wanted to know who I really am?" Brooke said, her voice so calm it chilled my bones. "Well, now you do. And that makes you a problem."

"Please," I said, the word caught halfway between breath and regret.

"Curiosity's a funny thing," she murmured. "It opens doors. But sometimes, they can't be closed again."

"I just wanted the truth," I stammered, inching back toward the dresser.

Brooke didn't blink. "And now you have it."

She stepped forward, her hand dipping into her coat pocket. I didn't see the blade until the glint caught the light.

"Wait—"

The word barely left my lips before the pain hit—white hot, searing, final.

I hit the floor, dressed exquisitely for the occasion, drowning in my own blood and regret.

My final thought faded with the light behind my eyes.

I fucked around. I found out.

Throughout my short life, the question had always remained unanswered. Was there Heaven and Hell? And which one would I be going to. Finally, I got my answer. Unless what happened to me was a fluke, there was neither.

So where did I go? It's hard to explain. I call it the other side. We all see what's going on in the living world. Most of us are powerless to interact, but there are some ... Well, there are always exceptions.

This place is filled with storytelling. That's pretty much all we do here. We don't need to eat or sleep. We don't shower or take a dump. We just exist. And tell stories. And I personally like to lighten the mood and make people laugh. So I tell them my train wreck of a story and always get a few giggles. The story of how I found out.

THE OVERTHROWN

MJ MARS

I've arranged to meet my cousin outside the Italian-style café on the corner, and I choose the perfect seat. As a filmmaker, you have to think of every little detail. The lighting. The sound. That certain *je ne sais quoi* that gives the film a bit of ambience. From where I'm sitting, I know that the hidden camera that's pinned to my shirt will pick up the creeping flowers that hang down from the criss-cross frames around the café doors. The sunlight is streaming over the buildings to the left, enough to illuminate the area but not glare into the lens. The traffic passes by around the corner, and I know my mid-range microphone will pick up our discussion and not the noise of the cars.

She comes down the street toward me, and my heart quickens a little. I have a great feeling about this project. I'm thinking it could be my big break. My Werner Herzog moment. Standing, I instinctively appraise how she'll look on film. She's wearing a turquoise blouse, a color that the camera loves. Score one. Her red hair hangs loose on her shoulders, and the sunlight illuminates the left side, making it appear more golden than auburn. She doesn't seem to be wearing makeup, but her skin is clear. All in all, I think this piece is going to work.

I reach out my hand and grab hers in a firm shake.

Her grip is loose, but she gives me a shy smile and sits down. "Hey, Bobby."

"Hi, Janet. Thanks for agreeing to meet me."

Taking on the role of host, I flag down the cute waitress and order us two coffees with extra cream. I'm a sucker for cream, and when the waitress returns, I fill my cup to the brim until the coffee almost matches the skin of my hand. I dump three sachets of sugar into the concoction and stir it up with a wooden skewer.

Janet watches me, blowing coyly over the surface of her drink. She adds just a splash of cream and refuses sugar. Daintily placing the cup back in the saucer with both hands, she stares at me. "So why did you ask to see me?"

I laugh, trying to keep it light. I need to build her trust. Without it, this whole project could go belly-up at any moment. "Hey, we're cousins! Can't we meet for a catch-up?"

"You said on the phone you wanted to ask me something."

I face her squarely, conscious of the camera frame. As far as I can tell, it will come out with Janet sitting dead center. "You know how I'm coming to my final dissertation piece at university? Well, the brief is to make a documentary about the local area. I'm keen on making mine about the druid stones on Mill Heath and interviewing people who might know something about the cult that goes up there."

Janet presses her lips together. "What has that got to do with me?"

"Oh, come on, Jan. You can tell me. You know them, don't you?"

She makes me wait, taking a long slug of her drink. "Maybe."

"Look, I can keep you anonymous if you like. Pixel you out and all that. But I know you know what they do up there. I heard Uncle Ray arguing with you about it."

"He's not a huge fan."

"Exactly!" I throw out my hands. "People don't understand it. So why not let me show them what it's all about? I could come and interview you all. You could explain what kind of things you get up to... show the town there's nothing to worry about. Get people off your back. What do you say?"

She frowns, but I can tell she's thinking about it. "I'll have to ask."

"Ask who, the leader?"

Janet gives me a vague nod. I knew she'd be cagey, but it's all good. The more difficult it appears to the viewer, the better the documentary. "Who is the leader?"

Scraping her chair back, she stands up. "Bye, Bobby. Thanks for the coffee."

"Wait!" I jump up and reach out for her wrist. "Will you think about it? Will you ask?"

She nods. "I'll call you."

I stay standing as she sashays away, knowing that it's a great exit for the opening scene. When she's turned the corner, I duck under the trailing flowers and head to the café toilets. I'm not sure where they are, but the nice waitress helps me out. I thank her, making sure I turn my body to get her in one of the shots. That, I would be sure to look at on my own later.

Inside the bathroom, I stand over the sinks and stare at myself in the mirror, watching the grin spread over my face. I wet my hands and press them over my hair, smoothing down a couple of tufts. Not bad. Not bad at all. When I leave, I think for a moment about asking the waitress for a drink. But she is nowhere in sight.

Besides, I've got work to do.

I SIT AT MY COMPUTER AND RUN THE EDITING SUITE. NOW THAT I have my way into the druid cult, I can make a start. Even if Janet says no, I can move on with my investigation. Start following people around, try and get in with some of the other members. My lecturer always says it's best to begin with a human element. Watching back through our meeting, I feel the familiar buzz that comes with recording strong material. It has tension. It has family ties. It has uncertainty and hidden depths.

I isolate the best sections of dialogue and cut them into the pre-prepared opening sequence. I've found some royalty-free choir music that adds a suitable cult freak-show atmosphere, and as I view what I've edited so far, I know it's good.

I've overlaid an introduction, lowering my voice to as close to baritone as I can manage.

"Mill Heath. Once an area rich in prosperity. The site of the indoor grain mill that brought employment and export wealth to the area. Now, it stands untouched, its outer walls crumbling. The only other landmark that has seen more years are the druid stones that sit on the same hill, the sides etched and carved with ancient spells and symbols. The heath is a restricted area, fenced and chained. But intruders are regularly seen, shrouded in capes and robes, chanting around the druid stones. People say they disappear into the old mill once their rituals are over."

My words are interspersed with film I've recorded of the mill and the stones. You're not technically allowed in the mill site, but every local kid knows a way through gaps in the fencing. When the cult have their night rituals, the school kids often sneak in behind them and pelt them with rotten eggs. The members of the cult, which presumably include my cousin, act as though the audience aren't even there. They chant around the stones, walk in a circle three times, then wander back to the mill.

The locals don't like it, but as far as we know, the cult is harmless. There have been no tales of livestock going missing or cats being found with their throats slit. I've been doing plenty of research on cults, and it looks as though these guys are pretty tame in comparison to others. Still, it should make for an interesting movie.

I'm tidying up the sequence of Janet's initial introduction when my mobile goes off, vibrating on the desk. I jump to set up my camcorder to film the exchange, place my phone on speaker, and hold my breath while I wait for her decision.

"Bobby, I spoke to the Master. He says it's okay. He's pleased you're going to *enlighten* the neighborhood about us."

I exhale. "That's great! Thanks, Janet. You won't regret this."

She huffs a gentle laugh. "You might."

"Nah, I'm sure it will work out brilliantly," I reassure her. "It's interesting. It's just what I need."

"Okay, if you're sure. The Master said I should offer you a chance to say no."

I hang on for a beat and look at the camera, pointedly. "What does he mean?"

"He just said I should let you make the choice, now that you know we want you to get involved."

I smile. This is all good stuff. "Tell him I'm in, for sure."

"Okay. What do you want me to do?"

"Uh," I glance down at my production notes, making a snap decision about the order I want to film in. "I need some background information. Details on what you guys do and why you do it. Could you come over so I can interview you about it?"

"Sure. Today?"

Her sudden eagerness to get involved has me stunned. I thought getting Janet on board would be nigh on impossible. I'm almost floored by my good fortune but quickly get it together for the camera. "Yeah, definitely. How does three o'clock suit you?"

"I'll come."

Once she's cut the call, I grin at the camcorder and snap my forearms together, so I can see the break in film sequence when I'm scrolling back through. I say, "End Scene," turn off the camcorder, and go to set up an interview space.

TWO HOURS LATER, MY COUSIN IS SITTING ON A KITCHEN CHAIR IN front of a large background sheet I've pinned to the ceiling. The camera is on standby to a slight angle in front of her, and I'm sitting opposite, a list of hastily scribbled questions in my lap.

"Are you ready to start?" I ask, leaning over to set the camera rolling.

Janet nods, swallowing a few times. I can tell she's nervous, as most people are in front of the camera. I know from experience that as the questions start to flow, she'll soon loosen up. She looks nice, wearing a pale-yellow dress with her hair now plaited down each side. I love how "normal" she appears to be. It will make the contrast between her everyday lifestyle and the antics the cult get involved in all the more striking.

I clear my throat. "Janet, you are a member of the druid cult that conducts its rituals at Mill Heath."

"No."

"No?" *Shit. What is she doing?*

"No. We're not druids."

I breathe an inward sigh of relief, hoping the panic in my voice didn't come across on the recording. "I apologize. Can you explain who your cult is, in that case?"

"Followers of the Overthrown."

"The Overthrown?"

"That's right. We believe that, through our rituals, he will soon return to earth and cleanse us."

Christ, I think. *My cousin is actually a fruit-loop.* "What are these rituals you participate in?"

Janet explains, using her hands and fingers to elaborate. "We use the stones. I know the locals think they are druid stones, but they're not. The carvings on the side show the story of the Overthrown. They explain that one day soon he will return, once the special sacrifice has been given to the chosen Extra."

"Hold on. Perhaps you're moving a little too fast for our viewers." *And me*, I think. *Jeez!* "So there are two particular people involved in your worship. The Overthrown, and the Extra."

"In a way. We do worship the Overthrown. The Extra will be used to return him to his rightful place."

"So the Extra is one of you? A member of the cult?"

"Possibly. They will undergo the Dawn of the Five Sacrifices, and the Overthrown will then be able to break the fifth wall and return to earth. It's quite simple, really."

"And the... dawn of sacrifices. Is that one of your stone chants?"

Janet smiles. "Something like that."

"Okay. Do you think you might one day become the Extra?"

The smile falls away. "I don't think so. I hope not."

"So it wouldn't be considered an honor?"

"No. To witness it, yes. To be the Extra... that's something I wouldn't wish on anyone."

The hairs on my arm stand up. Even though I know cults are a load of baloney, I'm suddenly concerned about my cousin's safety.

"But anyway, I can't be the Extra. I've been invited to the mill by the Master. The Extra goes in when they aren't welcome. And they deny it when they're asked."

Deny it? I think. *Peter, eat your heart out. Why do all these modern cults steal their stories from the Bible?* "And the five sacrifices. They all happen to the one person? How can that be?"

"It's symbolic, really."

At these words, I inwardly relax a little. Symbolism I can cope with. Symbolism can't hurt my cousin.

Janet looks to the ceiling, thinking. "There's five different stages, represented by different types of execution throughout history. Each torture gives the Overthrown something he needs to come back. Finally, the Extra endures scaphism, and that's the key to them all."

"Scaphism? Can you explain that?"

She smiles, looking at the camera. "I think you'd better look it up."

"Okay, I will. And that's the key to the Overthrown coming back?"

"It's the most important, final step. The loss of humanity."

I swallow, reminding myself that it's all a load of nonsense. "Janet, at what location will this happen? The breaking of the fifth wall?"

She rolls her eyes, as if I've missed the whole point. "The mill, silly. He's been waiting below the stairs, all this time."

"Will you take me to the mill and show me?"

Janet swings her legs, suddenly childlike. "I'll have to ask the Master."

"Who is the Master? Do I know him?"

"Miles Derby."

"Mr. Derby, our old Headmaster?" This is getting a little bit too creepy. I don't like the idea of the head teacher recruiting young girls to a sicko cult. Suddenly, I'm thinking less about the documentary and more about calling the police.

"Don't worry. He keeps us safe. He has the key."

"What key?"

"The old mill key. So long as the Master opens the old mill door, all of those within the mill who have been welcomed will not be harmed by the Overthrown. It's simple, really."

I look down at my notes, completely confused. The interview has not panned out the way I thought it would. I have lost control of the questions, and I have no idea how it will look to the viewer. "So, Janet, one last question before we wrap this up. You say the Overthrown is expected to return soon. Do you know when?"

"The final day of May."

I glance at the calendar. It shows May 23rd. "This May? You mean by the end of this month?"

She giggles, childlike again. "You picked the best time to come on board."

When Janet has left, I grab a beer from the fridge and sit quietly, trying to process the information she has given me. I'd assumed that because they didn't run around killing animals, the cult was pretty much on the level. But after what Janet has told me today, it seems I had another think coming.

Taking a swallow of beer, I sit up, my head clearing a little. Hang on. What if she's winding me up? That little-girl act certainly seemed put on at times. Maybe she's pissed that I'd even ask about her druid friends, and they've decided to play a trick on me. *I bet that's it.*

I swear and drain the beer can, crushing it in my fist and tossing it in the direction of the bin. The sound of it ricocheting off the wall and tumbling to the floor tells me I've missed, but I don't bother going to retrieve it.

At the computer, I pull up the internet search engine, typing questions about the history of the mill. It doesn't tell me anything too exciting, other than the fact that it was said to have been built above a cave system and that a lot of people went missing while it was being built. It all smacks of local folklore, and I dismiss it, instead moving on to Miles Derby.

Nothing bad comes up in the searches. In fact, Derby gives off the perfect impression of a pillar of the community. He is pictured at local fairs and dishing up soup at the homeless shelter at Christmastime. *If he is the Master,* I think, *why is he going to let me reveal his secret to the town? Surely, he would know that he would lose face.*

I have a horrible feeling they are messing with me, making me create a documentary about them, only to refuse permission for me to use their images or reveal their identities.

Sighing, I rub my hands over my eyes. Well, if they pull that crap, there's nothing I can do about it. I'll just have to give myself plenty of time to re-work the film.

Unless Derby really believes that by the end of May the Overthrown will have come back, I suddenly wonder. If he truly believes in some kind of "cleansing," as my cousin had put it, perhaps he doesn't think the town will still be standing, let alone casting judgment on him because of a university documentary. It was farfetched, but it only took one man to start something as crazy as Jonestown.

I type "Scaphism" into the search engine. My eyes widen in horror as I read about the ancient Persian torture, in which a felon was trapped between two boats, their face and limbs sticking out through cut-out holes. They were force-fed milk and honey, then left lying in their own filth until fly infestations ate them from the inside out. I sit back. That couldn't be true, could it? The information said the process of the force feeding would be repeated until the person died, and that there were records of it lasting up to seventeen days.

"Jesus," I breathe, revolted. It was a loss of humanity, all right. Talk about taking someone's dignity.

Fear for my cousin creeps back into my consciousness. *I'll have to play it by ear*, I reason. I'll have to arrange a meeting with the Master.

THREE DAYS LATER, I'M WAITING FOR JANET AT THE FOOT OF MILL Heath, the tall, stone chimney of the mill poking out above me. I'm wearing my chest camera, and I also have my camcorder and stand. She's agreed to show me the druid stones and to talk me through their carvings.

It's a cold morning for May, and she wears a light blue parka. Her breath fogs out around her face as she climbs the hill and waves a hand in a casual greeting. If there's one nice thing about this project, it's that it's bringing me and Janet closer again. My uncle, Ray, has never really taken to me. He's a strange, gruff kind of guy around everyone if truth be told, but I don't take well to that type of judgment. Since I left home for university, I feel adult enough to make decisions about who I stay in touch with. My aunt Violet isn't so bad, but I know she sometimes joins in with Ray and their badmouthing. *I might not be the ideal cousin for their precious daughter, but look at what she's got herself into without me*, I think, raising my camcorder and recording her approach.

She's holding a duffel bag and opens it to reveal a few sheets of white paper and a pack of crayons. "I thought you might like to do some rubbings. For your film."

"That's a nice idea," I say, but I don't really mean it. The camera is all the documentation I'll need. Who needs some crappy crayon drawings? Still, I'll go along with it. I want to keep her happy.

We set off up the hill, heading for the stones. I hold the camera to my shoulder and film my cousin answering my questions. "So, if the stones aren't druid in origin, why does the town think that way?"

"It's what everyone always assumes. People know and accept the druids. There's something whimsical about them. It makes a town think they're acceptable. Good for tourism, even."

"Why don't people know about your cult?"

"The Overthrown followers are only based here. Druids are everywhere. That's what makes us so special."

"How long have Overthrown followers been meeting here?"

"You'll have to ask the Master when you see him. I think it's something like four hundred years."

"Really? As long as that?" We are both becoming a little breathless from the walk, so I motion for Janet to stop. I have a great frame of her with the mill protruding from the hills behind her. "Would it be fair to say they've been something of a secret society?"

"Yes, that's fair. Only a select few are allowed in."

"And how did you get in?"

"The Master knows. The Overthrown speaks to him when he holds his trances. He tells him who to bring."

"So, Mr. D—I mean, the Master—approached you and asked you to go with him to the mill?"

"Yes. He explained what it was all about. It just made sense to me. I wanted to join them right away."

"Did you have to do anything in particular to join? Like an induction?"

Janet licks her dry lips. "No, that kind of thing comes later. The Overthrown will one day call on you to do a special job."

"But it's the Master who relays it to you?"

"Oh yes. We can never speak to the Overthrown."

The more I learn about the crap Derby is filling my cousin's head with, the more I want to punch his lights out. "Janet, how do you know that what the Master is telling you is the truth?"

She laughs. "He doesn't lie, Bobby. It's part of the purity prior to cleansing. He speaks the truest word, which is that of the Overthrown."

"Why do you believe him?"

"You'll see. When he's shown you, you'll believe it, too."

Janet starts walking again, and I have no option but to follow, filming her as she walks the last few paces to the stones. The stones rest in the grass, two egg-shaped, volcanic boulders as long as a fully grown man lying down, and as high as my cousin's shoulders.

Janet spreads her palms and caresses the side of the first stone, closing her eyes as she feels along the etched carvings. "Breathtaking, aren't they?"

I move the camcorder slowly, sharpening focus on the markings, reverting back into documentary mode. "Janet, can you explain what these carvings mean?"

Janet smiles for the camera and points to an area of the stone. "You see this here, the one that looks like an 'O' with a line through it? That's the sign of the Overthrown. This section reads about his earliest beginnings, as a Norman soldier."

"Norman as in Battle of Hastings?"

"Yes. But he was already dead by then."

"And you know this because of what is written on the stones?"

"Yes. And what has been told to the Master."

"In visions."

"Right. Here, I'll show you..." Janet tugs a piece of paper from her bag and selects a red crayon from the pack. She lays the paper over the stone and turns the crayon on its side, sliding it over the paper until there is color across the page. The etchings show up white within the red.

Resting the paper on a different part of the rock, Janet slips a thin black marker from the bag and draws three circles. She marks the first one *Overthrown*, the second *Sacrifice*, and the third *Captivity*.

"Okay," Janet traces her finger along the page. "Here we have the Overthrown coming to a meeting on this very spot. He was in command at the time and was meeting with the ancients who lived here. The soldiers needed the land, and they wanted to negotiate. The leader of the village here betrayed him and stabbed him. The villagers hid his body in the cave systems that ran underneath the hills."

"Why did they do that?"

"They wanted to pretend they never had the meeting. The stones say that the caves were used by ancient necromancers and that they were enchanted. The Overthrown's body was transformed by the necromancers who lived in the caves. He was chosen to lie in wait for the right time to come out and cleanse the earth, so we can start again with a clean slate. That time is now."

"And the stones say all of that?"

"Well, not word for word. But it's the gist."

"So, Janet, what would you say to the scientists who have decoded the etchings on these stones and have dated them as being much older?"

Janet sniffs. "They're wrong."

"And you don't think your Master might just be..."

"What?"

"Making it up?"

Janet folds her arms. "Why don't you ask him yourself?"

I whirl round to find a figure wearing brown robes that drape down to the ground. He has a hood pulled down over his face. Around his waist is a rope belt, and a rusted key as long as my hand dangles down his left thigh. *Awesome*, I think. *This is TV gold.*

He just stands there, saying nothing as I film him.

Janet presses the wax rubbing paper into my free hand and walks over to Derby. Standing beside him, they both face me. He leans toward her, and I can tell he is speaking, but I can't hear what's being said. I hope the powerful microphone of my camcorder will help me with that when I get back to the studio.

"Can I have an interview with the Master?" I ask Janet, staring at the hooded figure. Even though I know it's just my old school teacher under the robes, I feel the creeps scurrying over the back of my neck. Still, I remind myself, it's pretty pathetic.

"He says he will not speak to you today. Come back on the twenty-seventh."

"The twenty-seventh?"

"And he will show you everything you need to know."

I'm getting annoyed. My deadline is looming, and I could do with getting a move on. "Can't he show me around the mill today?"

Again, the man leans to the side. His cowl shakes a little.

Janet frowns. "He says no. If you go into the mill when you aren't welcome, you won't survive the cleanse."

Good grief, I think. "Can't he just welcome me in? I thought he was the boss."

What sounds like a bark of laughter comes from inside the robes. It's muffled, but it doesn't sound at all friendly. The man turns and walks away, toward the mill.

Janet looks stricken. "I have to go. You've upset him."

I zoom in on her face, showing the fear in her eyes. Hopefully, the more of this manipulative crap I can capture, the more likely Derby will be shut down. "You're going with him? Why don't you come and get some food with me?"

She shakes her head, firmly. "I have to go."

She trots away after her Master, who is walking slowly, his head down, like a ghost monk in a stupid B-movie.

I spend a while filming the stones, trying to make head or tail of the "guide" my cousin created for me with the crayon and felt pen. I make a mental note to ask at the library if there is a local historian who can come up here and talk me through what the etchings *really* mean.

Later that evening, I've edited the footage taken that day and created some more voice-over lines, but I'm still not happy about the fact that I let my cousin wander off with that jerk. Sure, she's eighteen years old and is old enough to look after herself. But something is screaming at me that the guy is all wrong. I try and call her mobile, but she doesn't pick up. I wonder if she's still at the mill. If she's been allowed to leave. I get a cold trickle down my spine.

I search through my contacts and find Uncle Ray's home number.

He picks up after three rings. I silently curse, wishing it had been Aunt Violet. "Hi, is Janet home?"

"Who is this?"

"It's Bobby, Uncle Ray. How are you?"

"Fine."

He's such an ass, I think, when he doesn't even bother to ask how I'm doing. "I'm looking for Janet. I wondered if she was home."

"She's been out with friends all day."

"Since when?"

"What's it to you?" he asks, then answers the question anyway. "About ten in the morning."

The time she met me. *Damn it*. "Thanks, Uncle Ray," I say.

"Bobby?"

My heart leaps a little. I wonder if my uncle is going to extend an olive branch. To invite me round for a beer and some football.

"Don't call here again." He hangs up.

I know I shouldn't care, but my face flames. *Who needs enemies when you have family?* I think bitterly. Out loud, talking to myself, I mumble, "Fine, Uncle Ray. I'll go and rescue your daughter from the hands of an insane cult. Because *I'm* the asshole."

I gather up my camera, tug on a lined jacket, and head back to the mill.

I NEED SOME NIGHT SHOTS OF THE MILL SITE, ANYWAY, I REASON AS I climb the hill. *I'm not overreacting.*

But the more I've walked, the more it seems that I might be being foolish. Janet is an adult. If she hadn't chosen to study here, she'd have been away in halls or living in another city, getting up to all sorts. It was idiotic to be so protective of her. But I feel responsible for annoying Derby. And if he took it out on her, the blame would be on me.

I reach the mill and climb through the tear in the chain-link fence. I raise the camcorder and start taking some night shots. The moon is high and bright, illuminating the crumbling stonework. I know the shots will be a pretty effective cut into the final edit for atmosphere. I work my way around to the old wooden entrance and give it a shove. It looks like the typical kind of castle door that shows up in Disney films, with two wrought iron bands holding the wood in place, a curved top that has left graze marks on the stone, and a round iron door pull. I wrap my fingers around the ring and give a sharp tug. The door doesn't budge.

I zoom in on the keyhole and think of the rusty old key that Derby keeps strapped to his waist. *Who does he think he is? Pretentious prick. Thinking he has to unlock the door for people to get in here...*

I walk round to the far wall and see the hole where the old window used to be. It smells of pee, and kids have sprayed graffiti around the stone window ledge, but it is easy enough to climb through. I scramble up and squeeze in, dropping down into the darkness, landing on a pile of broken bottles and beer cans.

I film the interior using night vision. It's just an old stone room. More graffiti lines the walls. There is an exit at the far side, but I know that it leads to the old stone staircase to the lower floor and the indoor mill wheel. I think for a moment about going down the stairwell. Janet did say that the Overthrown was lurking under the stairs, just waiting to be set free. I take a few paces toward the exit, then stop.

In the daytime, I'd have no qualms about exploring. But I don't want to fall and break my leg and be stuck down there with the rats and the stagnant water. That had once happened to a boy in my school, and when he was found in the morning he was half crazy. He never came back to class.

Besides, my cousin definitely wasn't here anymore. And I'd get to see it all properly on the 27th, only a couple of days away. I clamber back out through the mill window and stick a middle finger up, imagining Derby watching me entering his precious mill without permission. Satisfied, I head for home.

I make an early start and set the camera up for an interview, but this time it's me sitting in front of the white-out sheet. I'm wearing a sharp shirt and suit pants and have gelled my hair down at the front. Ever the professional.

"Here I am on the morning of the 27th of May. This is the day when the Master of the Overthrown followers will allow me inside the sacred mill, where I am assured I will be granted the answers to some of my questions. I'm optimistic about the meeting. I think it should be a promising day, and I'm confident that the camera will capture some interesting scenes."

I wait a few moments, looking into the lens, then snap my forearms together, saying, "End scene."

Janet is waiting for me by the stones. At first, I think she is wearing a white dress. When I get closer I see that it is robes similar to the ones Derby was wearing, but shorter and made of white cotton. I trail the camera up and down her body.

"Nice outfit." I smile.

"These are the ceremonial robes. We have all been summoned for the five-day sacrifice." She says it as though she's just said, *We're all off to McDonalds for a bite to eat.*

I'm feeling uncomfortable but know how good this will be for the documentary. "Ah, I remember you said the Overthrown will come out on the last day of May. That's five days from now."

"I'm glad you paid attention."

"It's my job." I point to the camera. "So the sacrificial ritual starts today."

"Correct."

I think about the bits of information Janet has given me since we started the project. "And you need someone to sacrifice."

"We do."

"But you're sure it won't be you."

"It won't be me." She smiles, certain.

"And where will the sacrifice take place?"

"Below the stairs and by the wheel."

"In the mill."

"Yes. Follow me." Janet turns and starts to walk toward the dilapidated building.

I'd had a hunch that I'd be shown down the stairs to where the old wheel still sat in a festering pool. I'd been there a few times in childhood and was always in awe of the hydropower wheel, its slats crusted with algae. I feel a flush of excitement about the film shots I'll be getting of the old wheel and the cult in their robes. I'm slightly alarmed by the talk of sacrifice. But, I figure, I have my phone on me. If it starts to get exceptionally weird and they drag some poor girl kicking and screaming to an altar, I can call for help in no time. I could rescue her and be a hero. I like the sound of that. *Maybe the next documentary I'm involved in will be all about me?* I smile. Besides, these guys are kooks. There's no way anything bad is going to happen.

The Master stands by the mill door, the key in his hand. He is wearing his robes, but the hood has been rolled back so that I can see his face this time. It's Derby, all right.

I feel a little shudder of revulsion. I never liked the guy, smarming around the school the way he did. Like my uncle, I don't think he's ever been too keen on me, either. I seemed to have that effect on a lot of older guys.

"Mr. Derby," I call. "Thanks for having me along."

"You will address me as Master. From this day forward, there is no Miles Derby."

His deadpan tone makes me want to laugh in his face. I point the camera right at him. "For the record, you have invited me here today to give me answers for my documentary. Any footage taken you accept will be used by me. Names and faces will not be redacted. Is that okay with you?"

"Perfectly acceptable."

"Great. Lead the way."

I record him as he puts the big old key in the lock. The rusted metal shrieks as it turns, and the old door shudders open a little. Derby pauses. "And you are aware that I have invited you here today, and at no other time since our first meeting have you entered unannounced."

Shit. I feel my face get a little hot as an image of me climbing through the old window pops into my mind. Still, I'm not in court. I've not sworn on any Bible. "I haven't."

The lie feels good. Sometimes it's nice to bare-faced lie to a jackass. Especially when it's about something that means a lot to them.

"Good. Bobby. Please enter the mill." Derby gives the door a hefty shove with his shoulder, and it scrapes open.

I pan around, filming the graffiti on the walls and Derby and Janet coming through the entranceway. I'm a little alarmed to see Derby locking the big door behind us, but a quick scan to the right shows me that the window is still unblocked. I have an escape route should I need it.

Derby looks into the camera. "Follow me down the stairwell. Please watch your step. They are old and untended. And I would hate for you to be harmed."

I record his walk across the room, the robes making it look as though he's floating, like a bride going down the aisle. Janet goes next. We exit the room and step out onto the crumbling landing.

I can smell the water. It is like sewage and vegetation and freshness all mixed up in a strange assault on the nose. The wheel stands to the far side, fifteen feet high, perfectly still, its lower spokes submerged in the moat of murky water. A small rowing boat sits in the gulley beside it. Below me, standing on the platform by the wheel, a dozen cult members in white robes watch as we come down the stairs. I film them. I can't see any sacrificial virgins so far, which is a relief.

"Followers of the Overthrown!" Derby calls, standing on the bottom step, his arms thrown wide. "We are here to witness the five-day sacrifice and the birth of a new dawn. The Overthrown will rise five days from now, and our world will be cleansed. Only we shall be safe. We, who have been shown the way, by he who resides beneath the stairs. Onward."

I film as Derby steps down from the stairwell, and Janet follows his lead. I struggle to concentrate on filming and walking. The stairs are hundreds of years old, and the stones are loose underfoot. I have a horrible feeling they might collapse. I can't imagine being trapped down here with these losers for any longer than I need to finish the documentary, let alone being stuck without an easy way out.

I reach the bottom of the stairs, and the group splits into two lines of six. Derby walks through the middle of them and stands in front of the mill wheel. *This is great*, I think, panning out to show the atmosphere of the old room, the wheel towering over us all.

Janet takes her place opposite Derby at the end of the row of cult members, and my heart begins to beat faster. I'm still nervous that she will end up being the female sacrifice, whatever it may mean for her. I pat my mobile phone in my pocket, reassured by its presence.

Derby points behind me to the space below the stairs. "Behold, the gateway."

I turn and film slowly from the underside of the top step, down to the boulder-strewn hole that leads to the caverns below the stairs. I think of the narration I will give to this section, hearing my own lowered voice in my head: *Nobody knows exactly what the caverns were used for, but people believe them to have been secret trading routes, allowing for goods other than grain to be smuggled from the mill. Of course, there are those who believe the caverns to be haunted by the ghosts of the men who disappeared while building the mill, and others who believe that warlocks and necromancers walked the caverns hundreds of years ago.* I grin at the thought of the look on my media tutor's face as he watches my documentary. He is going to piss his pants at its gruesome brilliance.

I turn back to the group and flinch when I see that two spears are pointed at me. Like the ones in paintings of the Romans prodding Jesus toward the crucifix, the wooden poles are topped with brutal-looking spikes. The two robed men holding the spears have covered their faces with their hoods. I step back. "Very funny."

Derby has also lowered his hood. He shouts some words, something that sounds like gobble-de-gook. "Shabalya detontet obliskan otoya. Rise! Behold the first sacrifice."

Behind me, I hear what sounds like bricks clattering together. The scuffing sounds of rubble being disturbed. I glance back, and chalk dust plumes from the cavern beneath the stairs. I step forward, but one of the spikes digs into my shoulder.

I duck to the side and scrabble for my phone, jabbing at the last number called. I run for the bottom step as it rings, and hear my uncle's gruff voice answer. "Hullo?"

"Uncle Ray!" I cry and skid to a halt as one of the pikes stabs through the air in front of me, blocking my way to the staircase.

"Who the hell—Is this Bobby?"

"Yes!" I'm trembling all over, and I'm still somehow holding the camera up, filming the hooded figures as they advance toward me.

"I told you not to call here again."

As I lower the phone, I can still hear his voice, tinny in the echoing stone room.

"I don't want your kind influencing my daughter. You hear? It's your own choice. That's all I'll say on the matter. Goodbye, Roberta."

I drop the phone. It skitters to the side, tumbling down into the cavern. From deep below me, I hear a moan that sends chills up my spine. More rocks clatter together, as if something is climbing over them, coming to the surface.

"It is time!" The Master yells. "Begin the first of the five sacrifices!"

I LIE IN THE BOAT THAT HAS BEEN MY BED FOR THE PAST FOUR nights, my body quivering. I can't tell anymore if it's me that's doing the shaking or if it's the thousands of insects that have hatched from my skin.

The first sacrifice was what they called the Breaking of the Bones. They used the wheel, the old slats digging algae into my skin, my feet tied to the wrought iron boat mooring. They stretched me until my joints popped, then dumped me in the boat for my first dousing of honey and milk.

The second day brought the Gifting of the Breath: submersion into the stagnant water, where they turned the wheel until I thought they would drown me, leaving me lingering under the water longer and longer each time, until I sucked the vile pool into my lungs and had to be revived, gasping for breath and staring up at a sea of hooded men and women. I spent the night in the sickly sweet brew of the boat, the milk already souring under my skin.

The third day was the Offering of the Flesh. The flaying of skin. Again, they strapped me to the wheel, but this time they used the pikes to flay strips from my arms and legs. I soon fell into unconsciousness. When I woke up back in the boat in the putrid concoction, now laced with my blood and a swathe of flies, I was sure I could see the hands and eyes of a creature peering over the edge of the cavern. Watching.

On the fourth day, I lay helpless in the festering boat as the group built a pyre of dried leaves and straw. My cousin eagerly helped and gleefully announced that it was ready. She knelt down by the boat, wrinkling her nose at the smell. "You're ready for the Smoking of the Spirit."

I tried to reach out for her, to plead for mercy, splashing her robe with sour milk and insect eggs. She recoiled but said, "It's nothing personal, Bobby. I've always liked you. You've been more like a sister to me than like a brother. But you're The Extra. It was decreed. You didn't have to come to the mill without permission. But you did. You didn't have to deny it. But you did. It was your destiny."

She beamed down at me, as though I should be thrilled by this revelation.

"But...but I'm a boy," I croaked.

"We know. I never said the sacrifice had to be a girl, Bobby. That was your own bias. And you are the perfect Extra."

She was right. I'd just assumed the sacrifice would be a girl, no doubt thanks to all those stupid 80s' movies I studied in film school. It hadn't even occurred to me the sacrifice would be me.

The burning was brief, not designed to be fatal. It scorched my toes and made me scream, my lungs taking in the thick smoke and making me cough for hours. From the mouth of the cavern below the stairs, I could hear gleeful, ghoulish laughter as the skin on my toes blistered.

And that leads me here. The fifth and final sacrifice. The Loss of Humanity. Death by milk and honey. Each night, I have been cut down from the mill wheel and put back inside a boat swarming with flies and maggots. They poured more of the sweet mixture of milk and honey into my mouth. At first, it felt like salvation, but as more and more came, it became hell. The flies buzzed and swarmed, and soon the maggots wriggled into every orifice, every scab and sore. In history, this would have lasted for days, until the insects tore through my body from the inside. It's some small comfort that I know it won't go on much longer. That tonight is the final night. That this is the final sacrifice.

The flies buzz loudly in my ears. They have started nibbling at my eyes. I can feel maggots squirming between my stretched and broken legs.

The Master's voice is small over the noise of the insects, but I can tell he is shouting. "It is happening! The Overthrown is no longer condemned! He is risen!"

I hear something sliding along the floor to the side of me. The boat rocks as someone begins to clamber in, the rocking sending milk, honey, puke, and shit rolling along the bottom of the boat. The insects are irritated.

I feel a weight on my chest. The boat rocks wildly.

The flies buzz.

Throughout my ordeal, Derby thought it would be funny to replay what I'd filmed on my camcorder. It has haunted me on a loop.

I try not to open my eyes, but I can feel whatever it is sitting on me, its weight cold and unfamiliar. The flies are swarming around it. It smells, even over the sweet and foul stink of the contents of the boat, like the dusty depths of the cavern.

My own voice chats away through the camcorder speaker. *"Here I am on the morning of the 27th of May. This is the day when the Master of the Overthrown followers will allow me inside the sacred mill, where I am assured I will be granted the answers to some of my questions."*

I blink, feeling maggots tumble down my cheeks as my eyelids flutter open.

"I'm optimistic about the meeting. I think it should be a promising day, and I'm confident that the camera will capture some interesting scenes."

A creature staring down at me. Child-sized, the angular, hunched-up man is wrapped in festering bandages. The flies swirl around him, coming off my broken body in masses. They stick to the visible flesh of the skinny figure and, as they do, I feel the life sapping out of me.

The patches of flies begin to solidify, and my vision starts to fade.

The Overthrown continues to leer down at me. It opens its mouth, and the flies that have been born from the milk and honey rise in a swarm and flood into the gaping hole in its face. Its body begins to bloat, the skin forming into more flesh, until the flies have created a patchwork man, whose eyes grow black as night.

It leaps from the boat, and everything sloshes around me again. I can barely feel anything anymore.

The monster leaps up the stairs, the flies following.

The cult members hush themselves, and I wonder what they are waiting for. Then I hear it, faintly, in the distance, coming from outside. Screaming.

As I fall into blackness in the fetid mess of the boat, after being sacrificed of my breath, my flesh, my spirit, and my dignity, over the distant cries of the massacre, I hear my own chirpy, deep but feminine voice coming from the camera speaker.

"End scene."

THE SHE-SHED

DEVIN CABRERA

Once upon a time, a woman named Karen lived in a small, peaceful neighborhood. She looked exactly as you are picturing her right now: pale skin, a bob haircut, and over-sized sunglasses on her face. You get it.

Karen was content with her mediocre life with her mediocre husband.

His name was Kevin, and he worked a job that required him to spend many days per month away on business. The neighbors liked to say that was the only way he could stand being married to that woman, but they wouldn't say that to her face.

They lived in a small house with a small yard and had recently installed a She-Shed in the back. It was your average-sized shed, purchased from Home Depot and meant to store a few lawnmowers and outdoor furniture, but Karen used it as her home away from home.

She had a large window that looked out into the yard and a few pieces of furniture. At the moment, she sat at a small table, cutting coupons out of the Sunday flier. She had gone to the store and purchased extra papers so that she could double up her coupons. They didn't need the money; she just liked to feel like she was getting something for nothing. If she could get five bottles of shampoo for the price of half of one, she felt like she had won.

Karen pressed the center of her scissor blade against the edge of the coupon book, her tongue sticking out of her mouth as she concentrated on creating the perfect cut. One false move, and she could cut into the barcode or the fine print, rendering the coupon unacceptable. Though she would happily plead her case to the manager, she would prefer not to get the man involved. He already waited to take his breaks until he saw her walk in each day.

She snipped away and was almost in the clear when a loud, reverberating noise tore through the neighborhood.

BRAAAPPPP!

Karen's hand slipped, and she cut off the corner of the coupon. It wasn't the end of the world, but she didn't feel comfortable handing a hack job of a coupon to the cashier. She placed it to the side and began on the next one. Just as she was about to cut, the noise came again, even louder this time.

BRAAAAAAAAPPP!

Karen slammed her scissors on the table and went to the shed's window. It was dark outside, and she could barely see around the house to the street, but she recognized the blur as it passed her house.

The noise was a boy named Kyle. He was a bratty nineteen-year-old boy who still lived with his parents. That asshole liked to ride up and down the street on his dirt bike at all hours of the night with no regard for the people who were trying to exist peacefully.

Karen stormed out of her shed and walked to the front of the house. She walked out into the street and waved her hand at the boy on the bike.

He noticed the woman and rode his noise machine up beside her.

"Can you do me a favor and not ride up and down the street like a bat out of hell?" Karen said. "The whole neighborhood doesn't need to hear the sound of your engine. Just because you're having a good time with it doesn't mean that we are."

"I'm sorry, Mrs. Abernathy. I'll try to keep it down," Kyle said.

Karen did not expect him to give in so fast. She had prepared a whole speech about how he was riding recklessly and driving home values down. She kind of still wanted to go into it, to let out all the anger boiling up inside her. Nevertheless, she relented. She turned on her heels and began to walk back to her shed.

She had almost gotten to it when she heard the sound of the dirt bike, even louder this time.

BRAAAAAAPPPP! BRAP BRAP BRAAAAAAAAAPP!

Karen turned slowly where she stood, just in time to see Kyle drive past her house, his middle finger raised up at her.

That was all it took to set her off. It was as if a switch had been flipped inside her brain, turning off her ability to think clearly. She needed an outlet to unleash her anger and her inner Karen.

A few moments later, as Kyle zoomed up and down the street, intentionally making it as loud as he could, the garage door of Karen's house began to rise up slowly.

The noise of the garage motor was drowned out by the one on the dirt bike.

As the door lifted, it revealed a pair of flats and ankles covered in bulging spider veins. Karen stood in the middle of the garage, her shoulders heaving up and down as she seethed with anger. A single fluorescent bulb above her cast shadows over her face, accentuating its pissed-off look. In her hands, she was brandishing a club that she had taken from her husband's golf bag. She had gone with the nine-iron.

Kyle had just made it to the end of the street and turned around. He revved his engine as loud as he could, twisting back on the throttle as far as it would go. He held onto the brake with his other hand, causing the back wheel to spin in place.

The tire spun rapidly, heating up and spitting rubber all over the road. The whole street filled with smoke and the awful smell of burned tires. It grew so thick that Kyle soon disappeared within it.

BRAPPPPP!

A single headlight became visible through the veil, and then Kyle emerged from the smoke. His front tire was raised in a wheelie, his neck craned back toward the sky as he howled at the moon, giving a big "fuck you" to the people trying to sleep.

He pulled the throttle back on the handle, and the bike zoomed forward, racing down the street at an unsafe speed.

Unbeknownst to Kyle, the speed was the least of his worries.

Because of his position on the bike, the front wheel blocked his view of what was in front of him. This meant he didn't see Karen stomping into the street with a golf club.

At the very last second, just when he was about to pass her, she brought the club back over her shoulder and then swung it like a bat. It connected with its target with a sickening crunch, and at that moment, she thought she realized why her husband liked golf so much.

She didn't know that he golfed because it was one of the few moments of his day when he didn't have to listen to her mouth; she just thought he loved the sport. The truth was that he was a terrible golfer, and he mostly just sat in his cart, sipping on beers and watching the beverage cart attendants do their jobs.

The bike went silent as Kyle's hand left the throttle.

He hit the pavement, knocking his head on the ground in the process. His bike traveled a few more feet before landing in a nearby bush.

Nobody in the neighborhood got up to check on him; they were all just happy to have a moment of silence.

Kyle's vision went black, but there were a few moments afterward where he could see the stars in the sky above him and could feel his back being dragged against the ground. He thought it might be the paramedics bringing him to an ambulance, and he relaxed, thinking he was in good hands.

He couldn't have been more wrong.

The next thing he knew, he was being slapped awake.

Kyle gasped for air, struggling to realize where he was. He blinked, trying to let his eyes adjust to the dim lighting.

He appeared to be in a small room with a solitary lightbulb hanging from a string in the center. It cast long shadows all over the room, leading the eyes to wonder what was hiding in them.

Kyle tried to lift his hands to his face but found that he couldn't.

He pushed and pulled, but his hands were restrained to the chair he was sitting in.

"What the..." Kyle began, confusion settling in.

Suddenly, a figure appeared out of the shadows, emerging from behind him.

Kyle looked up in time to see Karen step before him, a smug look on her face. It was clear that she was enjoying this.

"What are you doing to me? Where am I?" Kyle asked.

"You are in my She-Shed," Karen replied, a smile on her face. Her hands were covered in black grease, and Kyle did not like the look of them.

"What do you want with me?" Kyle asked.

"I asked you to be quiet. You didn't listen. So now, you're going to have to pay."

"Pay? What do you mean pay?" Kyle exclaimed. "How much do you want?"

"I don't want your money, silly," Karen said. "I want your life."

Kyle's eyes widened as her words struck home, but he didn't have much time to react.

Karen quickly spun the chair around, revealing Kyle's dirt bike.

It lay upside down, its seat resting on top of the table she had been cutting coupons on earlier. Its back tire was inches from Kyle's face. He could smell the freshly burned rubber emanating from the wheels.

Usually, Karen wouldn't have been able to lift a dirt bike onto a table, but there was a wave of adrenaline coursing through her tonight that she had never felt before.

"What are you doing?" Kyle asked, his voice rising three octaves, but something told him he already knew.

Karen started the dirt bike, and its engine roared to life.

Kyle's eyes went wide, his mouth opened to scream. He turned toward the open window nearby, craning his neck to get as close as possible.

"HELPPPP!" Kyle screamed, but Karen was ready for him.

The moment he opened his mouth, she pulled back on the throttle of the dirt bike. The sound of the engine ripped through the night air, the shed acting as a speaker, blasting the sound throughout the neighborhood.

Nobody could hear Kyle's screams, but they could hear the bike, and they hated him for it.

"I thought I told you to shut the hell up!" Karen yelled.

"Please don't hurt me, I'll do anything! Please!" Kyle begged.

Karen simply pulled back on the throttle again, drowning out his words and sending the tire spinning rapidly.

Kyle yelled again, but she didn't care what was coming out of his mouth. She had a plan for him. A plan that would take all night if it had to, and she wouldn't mind a bit.

Karen reached into a nearby drawer, where she kept some crafting supplies. She dug around past some needles and thread, past the layers of fabric she told herself she would one day use to make things with, until her hands closed around the thing that she was searching for. When she pulled her hand back out, clutched in between her fingers was a gray roll of duct tape.

She walked over to Kyle's seat, ripped off a piece of tape, and tried to place it on his mouth.

The boy struggled vigorously, moving his head back and forth and causing the tape to get twisted and mangled.

"God damn it! Hold still!" Karen yelled, tossing the messed-up piece of tape in the trash and ripping off a new one.

She tried once more to place it over Kyle's mouth, but at the very last second, he opened it and lashed out at her, chomping down on her thumb with his teeth.

"FUCK!" Karen yelled. "If that's how you want to play, so be it!"

She walked over to the window, pulled it closed, and latched it in place. If the boy wasn't going to be quiet, she just had to make it so no one would hear him. With the window blocking the sound of his screams, Karen was free to move on with her plan.

She took the piece of tape that was supposed to go around Kyle's mouth and instead placed it on the bike's throttle, forcing it to stay in the revving position. The wheel once again began to spin rapidly, flinging bits of dirt and small rocks into Kyle's face.

Karen walked back over to the boy, then spun his chair around so he could face her once more.

"This is for being a little shit!" Karen yelled. She grabbed the seat of the chair and lifted, forcing Kyle to fall backward, just enough that the back of his head was inches from the wheel.

"NO! PLEASE! NO!" Kyle yelled.

But it was already too late. He just had to fuck around, and it was time for him to find out.

The wheels of the chair slipped, and the back of Kyle's head hit the tire. The result was instantaneous. The force of the tire's movement caused his hair and skin on the back of his head to wrinkle, and then it took hold. It was as if he was wearing a poorly made wig, and then someone had just snatched it off the top of his head.

Kyle screamed as the top half of his skull ripped off and flung itself onto the front of his face like it was on a skin hinge. There it sat, attached only by a piece of bone that hung on for dear life like a baby tooth getting ready to be shed.

Karen pulled the chair back, investigating her work. She had always wondered what was going on inside that boy's head, and now she knew. She could see the wrinkles of his brain, which reminded her of a big, ugly ball sack, yet somehow less appealing.

"FUCK YOU, YOU FUCKING BITCH!" Kyle screamed, his fingernails digging into the chair. He was in more pain than he had ever felt in his life, and she was the cause of it.

"Someone apparently hasn't learned their lesson," Karen said.

She spun the chair around like a barber, looking for any spots she missed. She knew just what to do to teach him some manners.

The bike's engine continued to rev at an obnoxious rate, but neither of the occupants seemed to notice.

Karen placed her fingers on top of Kyle's brain.

"Are you going to be a good boy, or am I going to have to punish you again?" Karen asked.

"FUCK YOU, LADY!" Kyle shot back.

"Very well," Karen said, then dug her fingernails into the fleshy parts of his mind, digging through it like it was a bowl of spaghetti.

Kyle screamed, his eyes bulging from behind the piece of his skull that hung limply from his forehead. It felt like the worst migraine he could ever imagine. He screamed and screamed until everything went black.

But Karen didn't stop. She continued to dig her fingers into the mush, feeling alive for the first time in her life. She had spent her entire existence trying to feel some type of power—power over her neighbors, over her husband, or over the cashiers at the supermarket.

This power derived from a sense of not feeling like she had a purpose in life.

Other women had jobs. They strove for promotions at work and broke glass ceilings, whereas Karen was a stay-at-home wife. Her day consisted of cutting coupons, making meals, and watching daytime television. There was only so much of *The Price is Right* that someone could watch before they absolutely lost it.

Maybe that was one of the reasons she was in her shed tonight, digging her fingers into the brain of an asshole kid from her neighborhood. She liked the power she felt while being inside someone else's skull.

The more she thought about it, the wilder she became.

Her fingers moved deeper until they scratched the bottom of his skull. She moved them in a new direction, toward the front. She found a soft area that gave in beneath her fingertips. It was like Jell-O, where you know it feels wrong, but you still have to touch it and watch it wiggle.

Karen pushed her fingers through the soft material, and Kyle's eyes popped out of his head. They spun around on his cheeks, dangling from the optic nerve. They spun faster and faster, moving back and forth like a kid on a twisted swing set chain, until all of a sudden, they stopped in place.

Karen watched in horror as they turned to face her.

She tried to move, to get out of their line of sight, but her hands were stuck in the skull of the boy. She yanked and yanked, but his brain matter acted like quicksand, only managing to suck her in further the more she struggled. Her fingers dangled helplessly from his eyes sockets.

Karen began to hyperventilate, her breathing coming in raggedly as she fought to get her hand out.

The eyes began to retract back into their sockets, the nerve endings looping themselves around her fingers.

She couldn't take it anymore. She had to do something.

Karen pulled on her hand, using so much force that it dragged Kyle's body across the room, chair and all. She pulled and pulled, eventually freeing him from the duct tape restraints on his wrists.

But the eyes were getting closer to her fingers, and they were still staring at her, feeling like they were looking right through her soul.

They seemed accusatory, as if they belonged to Kyle's spirit, telling her that they knew what she had done, and they weren't going to let her get away with it.

Karen had enough. She bent down with her free hand, pushing aside bundles of newspapers filled with coupons.

They scattered to the floor, coating it with deals for buy-one-get-one half-off shampoo.

Karen kept searching until her hand grasped the thing she had been looking for.

It was a pair of scissors.

She pressed the edge of the blades against her fingers, already feeling the tinge of pain as they cut through the first layer of skin. She kept them sharp so that her coupons would have fresh, crisp edges.

Tears flooded from her eyes as she clamped down, the blade cutting through her flesh and immediately drawing blood. She cried out in pain, but the job wasn't done yet.

Her scissors were meant for paper, not human flesh.

She applied even more force, crying out loud, but not loud enough to be heard over the sound of the dirt bike engine revving.

Blood spattered all over the walls and windows of the She-Shed, coating the once-pink room in bright red.

The scissors got down to the bone but wouldn't continue, no matter how hard she squeezed.

Gritting her teeth, her tears mixing with the spittle pouring out of her open mouth, Karen began to saw away at the bones of her finger.

Back and forth. Back and forth.

The pain was tremendous, like repeatedly scraping your nails over a fresh wound, only worse, like sawing off your own fingers with a pair of safety scissors.

Karen's hand went white as the blood drained from it, and the scissors became too dull to achieve any real progress.

But the eyes continued to move. The dark brown pupils stared at her as the nerves wrapped around her bloody digits.

The scissors were going too slow. She needed to do something to make the process move faster.

Karen threw the scissors to the ground, where they clattered harmlessly amongst the coupons. They landed on top of one for a half-off jumbo pack of toilet paper, which was a really good deal.

She yanked on her fingers, trying once again to pull them from Kyle's skull, but it didn't work the first few times she tried it, and it wasn't going to work now.

To make matters worse, it felt like his brain was actively trying to swallow her up.

It was reacting to the trauma that it was experiencing and was beginning to swell, growing larger and tighter, and sucking in more of her arm as time progressed.

If she didn't do something soon, Karen's hand would forever be stuck inside Kyle's energy-drink-ridden brain.

She found herself wondering if rigor mortis affected the brain. Would it become harder after he died? Like a statue holding onto her for all eternity?

Karen couldn't live like this. She couldn't spend the rest of her life with someone's head wrapped around her hand. She had coupons to cut, pie to bake, and minimum-wage employees to yell at. She couldn't hide a body if her fingers were still attached to it.

No. She had to continue. She had to do whatever it took.

Karen bent down until she was face to face with Kyle. She moved the flap of his loose skull out of the way, then stuck her own fingers into her mouth and bit down.

The pain was excruciating, but also soothing, like how sucking on the wound makes you feel like you are healing it somehow.

Was this actually working? Or had the loss of blood begun to make her imagine things?

Karen had no idea, but the sun was coming up behind the blood-covered window, and the neighborhood would wake soon.

She had already started. She couldn't stop now.

Karen bit down on her finger and twisted, grinding the bone with her teeth. She could feel it growing smaller, even as the pain radiating from her hand was enough to make her pass out.

Finally, she took one last chomp and felt the finger come free. Her teeth clashed against teeth. Her forefinger bounced around inside her mouth like a chicken finger, and she had to fight the urge to swallow.

She spit it out onto the ground, where it flexed and unflexed itself at the joint, the nerves still remembering the actions they were trained to perform.

Karen wasted no time. She set about on the next finger, gnashing her teeth against it and ignoring the pain. When she was done, she spit the second finger out onto the ground, then pulled her hand away from Kyle's brain.

She was finally free.

His eyes retracted fully back into his sockets and glazed over.

Karen picked up her coupons with her good hand and returned them to the table. Then she placed her tape back in the drawer. She hung the scissors on the wall where they belonged, making sure that everything was where it was supposed to be.

Then she sat down in the corner and passed out.

THE NEXT DAY, POLICE LIGHTS BLANKETED THE NEIGHBORHOOD. Residents stood out on their lawns, waiting for somebody to tell them what was going on.

Karen's husband had come home from his work trip and couldn't find her, so he went out to her She-Shed. Once inside, he found the bodies of his wife and one of the neighborhood boys. She had tied him to a chair and then revved the engine of his dirt bike with the windows closed. The shed filled up with toxic fumes until they both began to hallucinate.

The boy had gotten free from his restraints and clawed off his own skull, and Karen had somehow found her scissors and thought she was cutting coupons when, in reality, she was snipping off her own fingers one by one.

The cause of death for both of them ultimately was carbon monoxide poisoning.

After the police had left and the funeral homes had taken away the bodies, the neighbors retreated back into their homes, and Karen's husband went into the garage. A few minutes later, he emerged with the remainder of his clubs.

It was time to golf.

DIGGING

GAGE GREENWOOD

Jacob focused on his meal. Every time he looked up, the mail pile he'd left at the edge of the table grew more menacing. He hadn't even checked to see who or where they'd come from, knowing full well they'd all be bills, they'd all be past due, and they'd be friendly in their threats. "We know times are tough, but your account is about to be suspended!" It sounded better than, "Sucks to be you, but we're happily going to turn your electricity off, and we will laugh in piles of cash when you send in your late payment with the fees attached."

Funny how quickly it all fell apart. Three months ago, he'd been okay. Not great. No nest egg to rely on, but he made enough money where he could afford to give Elliot a nice birthday and Christmas, take the kid to the bowling alley or LEGO store once in a while. They were happy, and the house they'd lived in had been home for five-and-a-half years. He had no expectations of leaving. The landlord was great and only raised the rent a few times to match the uptick in property taxes, as opposed to jacking it up to match current rental costs.

And then Jacob lost it all.

He'd earned a nice score at a local convention, where he ended up selling out of his entire book inventory. As soon as the doors opened, a line formed around his table. He was as surprised by the sudden popularity as much as anyone, and he had no idea how to account for it. His book sales on Amazon surely didn't reflect similar results.

He took the con sales as a good sign for his future and came home with enough money from that weekend to stock a little away and take Elliot to Great Wolf Lodge for two days. The kid had never been on vacation before. He spent all day at Jacob's mother's house and all evening watching his dad clack away at the computer.

Jacob worked full time at a grocery store, and the paycheck wasn't enough to cover the cost of living, even in the house with the rent still reflecting prices from half a decade ago. To try to earn some extra money, Jacob started publishing some old stories he wrote as a hobby. A little extra cash trickled in. Not much, but enough to help out, enough to make Jacob realize the potential. So he wrote more. Published more. That was the motto of the self-published industry. Pump it out. Write more. Never stop publishing. When one book comes out, publish twelve more.

Suddenly, Jacob found himself with two full-time jobs. Between writing, publishing, and marketing, he hardly had any time for anything else. And Elliot suffered the most from it. The poor kid never complained, just sat there bored, talked to himself, laid on the floor staring at the ceiling.

Jacob knew it would be wise to tuck as much away as he could whenever he could, but Elliot deserved stuff, toys to keep him occupied, or just fun. He deserved to have fun.

So, when Jacob found himself with a few thousand extra dollars after the con, he had to take the kiddo to the Great Wolf Lodge for a few nights. Two days and nights, him and his boy having nothing but fun. No phones. No promoting. No writing. Just undivided attention and smiles.

Life was like that, always chasing a few extra bucks and a few extra minutes. Squeezing the lemon for its juices. Never getting enough of anything.

The two-day vacation turned out to be a blast, the best time they'd ever had together. Water slides, arcades, eating pizza and chicken fingers in a hotel room, building stuffed animals, hitting the dance party in the lobby. Just non-stop good times.

And then they drove home. Jacob felt the brick-ton of weight crushing his chest more and more the closer they came to the house. He'd eke out some sleep and head back to work the next day.

Except he wouldn't.

When they came back into the house, Elliot ran to the bathroom. On his way in, he clicked on the bathroom light, but the light didn't come on. Not fully. It tried to, but instead it pulsed on and off, making a weird sizzling sound as it did.

Jacob ran into the room and turned the switch to off, staring up at the bulbs as if looking at them long enough would explain the problem. Jacob knew less about electricity than he knew about saving money.

He waited until morning before calling the landlord. That turned out to be a mistake. He had to call out of work while he waited for the old man to investigate, which meant another day without pay and another reason for his boss to grumble. It turned out the mini split had been leaking in the wall for God knows how long. It dripped onto the wiring and outlet for the bathroom. The landlord pressed his hand on the bottom of the panel on the side of the bathroom, and it pushed right through the soggy drywall.

He peeled away Elliot's old playmat, a thick, foamy thing with the alphabet on it that Linda used as a yoga mat before she took off. Jacob never removed it, liking the way it felt on his cold, bare feet at night when he stumbled in and out of the bathroom for a late-night pee.

Under the mat, the hardwood was warped, peeling up in places, and separating from its neighbor in others.

The landlord stood up, rubbed his hand through his greased black hair, and sighed. "I'm gonna have to call the insurance company, but I can tell you right now, they ain't gonna cover this. They cover *sudden* and *unexpected* water damage, but these floorboards tell me, and they'll surely tell the insurance company, this was neither sudden nor unexpected."

"We had no idea. I'm sorry," Jacob said, feeling guilty for something that surely wasn't his fault.

The landlord sighed. "I know. These things happen. Problem is, if the insurance don't cover it, I'm gonna have to repair it myself."

Jacob relaxed a little. "No problem. Whatever you need to do."

The landlord tilted his head. "If I have to do it myself, we're talking about months of work. I wouldn't be able to let you live here any longer."

All the oxygen sucked out of the room. Jacob had looked at the listings recently. He knew he'd never move if he wasn't forced to, but sometimes he dreamed of finding that perfect place, something with a little more space within the same price range, but what he found horrified him. The market had skyrocketed. Houses five hundred square feet smaller than the one they currently lived in were a thousand and a half more a month. Even small apartments were higher cost than what he paid now. He couldn't even afford a studio.

The landlord must have noticed the terror growing in his face. He put his hand on Jacob's shoulder. "Don't fret yet. Sometimes those rat bastards surprise you and cover it."

Jacob shook his head, but he knew the same thing the landlord knew. No fucking way the insurance was going to help.

A few days later, the landlord called with the news Jacob had expected. No insurance, and he had to move out in a month and half. On one of Jacob's next day's off, the landlord came by and broke down the wall. He found the disconnected pipe that caused the leaking problems, fixed it, and put up a new drywall panel.

While he worked, Jacob searched listings through various websites, all giving him the same results. Nothing. Nothing he could afford. He regretted the trip to Great Wolf Lodge, but honestly, the money he spent those two days wouldn't have helped him through this market for more than a single month at best.

The landlord finished up, dusted his hands off, and said, "You're all set to use the electricity in the bathroom now. Just be careful walking across the floor for the next month. The boards are warped, and there's some heavy gaps. We don't want Elliot stubbing a toe or falling on his face."

They both turned to the boy, who sat on the couch with his tablet playing *Minecraft*. He noticed the eyes turning to him and looked up. "Aw fixed?"

Mimicking the boy's speech impediment, Jacob said, "Aw fixed. You can use the light switch again."

"Okay," the boy said, falling back into the world of his game.

The landlord left, and Jacob went into the bathroom, sliding to the floor to bawl his eyes out in the fresh glow of the newly repaired electricity.

It only took a few weeks for Jacob to settle on a new place to rent. It was by the beach in Charlestown, which meant it wasn't permanent, but it bought him some time. Wealthy folks bought houses by the beach so they could live there for two or three months in the summer and rented them out to college kids from September to May or June. The house Jacob decided on was seven hundred dollars more a month than the one he had now, and about three hundred square feet smaller, but it had a nice yard, and the rental lasted until the end of July, which was rare for seasonals. He and Elliot could at least enjoy a good portion of the summer with some nice ocean breeze.

After paying first and last month's rent, Jacob had largely depleted his bank account, and the bills were stacking up. The worst part was he had to pay for September in the new place and in the old. That gave him time to move their stuff from one to the other, but it sucked for his finances.

Now, he sat at the kitchen table, slurping up Lipton soup, trying not to look at the stack of mail. Verizon threatened to shut off his internet and phone service. He supposed he could switch to Cox cable for internet in the new place, but with Elliot starting second grade soon, Jacob needed reliable service for his phone in case the school needed to call for an emergency.

He could have Cox set up internet, and if Verizon shut him down, T-Mobile would probably give him cell service. But he couldn't find a solution to the electricity. RI Energy had a monopoly in the area, so he had no other options, and if he owed money to them for the current address, they simply wouldn't turn it on at the new place.

He had to prioritize that one.

But for now, he didn't want to think about any of them. Jacob drove Elliot to his mother's and headed to work. When he arrived, he stood outside his car and let the light morning drizzle mist upon him while he indulged in a cigarette.

His coworker, Bobby, pulled in blasting some modern metal band. Bobby got out of the car and pretended to check his pocket for money. "Hey, can I get one of those smokes? I'll pay for it."

Bobby always did that. He said he'd pay for the cigarette, he'd check his pockets, and then he'd say, "Oh, I'll get you some money after lunch break. I forgot I don't have any on me."

Jacob waved off the song and dance and told him not to worry about it as he handed Bobby a cigarette.

They sat there smoking and staring at the front façade of Shane's Market and Pharmacy, neither of them interested in stepping foot inside a minute before scheduled.

"You figure out your moving situation?" Bobby asked.

Jacob took a drag. "Kind of. Not really. There's nothing out there I can afford."

Bobby fumbled into his pockets again. This time he had something in his hands when they came out. It was a bent business card. "You should call this guy."

Jacob took the card and read it.

TEDD YOUNG

ODD JOBS

Under that, it had a phone number. The card said nothing else. Jacob knew guys who did odd jobs. They either made fifty bucks here and there or made a decent amount of cash but did the grimy, unhealthy jobs no one else wanted, like cleaning out bat shit from an attic. He could do that, he supposed, and would do anything to give Elliot a good life, but he figured picking up a second job at McDonalds would be better time spent with steadier pay.

He put the card in his pocket and said thanks.

"It's not what you think," Bobby said. "I use him all the time."

"Well, I assumed it was odd jobs. Cleaning out sheds and shit. But if you say it's not what I think, now you've got me thinking it's something illegal."

Bobby spit. He always did when he smoked. "Nah, man. Not illegal. Give him a call. I promise it's good shit. Better than just cleaning out basements and garages, but there's some of that too. He once got me some work feeding a lady's cat. Went there in the morning and just after dinner for seven days while the lady visited family in New Hampshire. She paid seven hundred dollars. You believe that?"

Jacob tossed his cigarette into a nearby puddle. "No, I don't believe that. Why would she pay you seven hundred dollars for something she could ask her neighbor to do for free?"

"Because I worked for Ted Young, and folks around here know and trust Teddy."

JACOB FINISHED HIS SHIFT, PICKED UP ELLIOT, AND DANCED around the kitchen making spaghetti and meatballs. As he plated his chef's masterpiece, he eyed the pile of mail still sitting on the edge of the table.

He put aside the writing for the night and sat with Elliot on the couch, eating dinner and watching YouTube cartoons. He usually forced Elliot to eat at the dinner table, but with the current state of things, he didn't really give a shit if the kid wiped his sauced hands all over the cushions. Fuck it.

As they watched cartoons, the pile of mail turned into a Poe-esque weapon of guilt. He could almost hear the individual envelopes flapping and vibrating on the wood table. After he took their plates to the kitchen sink, he slipped onto the back deck for a smoke and pulled out the card Bobby had given him.

As he exhaled a stream of smoke, the mail giggled behind him. As if he were diving into a swimming pool, he sucked in a breath, dialed the number, and prepared for impact.

"Ted Young."

"Hi. Ah. Ted? Hi. My friend Bobby gave me your number. Ah—"

"What's your name?"

"Jacob?"

"Jacob what?"

"Barnes."

"Are you working tomorrow, Jacob Barnes?"

He shook his head and then realized Ted wouldn't see that. "No. I mean, yes."

"Which is it?"

"Yes, I'm working. I was thinking you asked can I work tomorrow. I can, but not until after my day shift."

"When's that end?"

"Five."

"You got something to write down my address?"

Jacob tossed his cigarette into a Pepsi bottle he'd filled halfway with water and ran inside. He grabbed a pen from the junk drawer and then turned over the top piece of mail in that pile he'd avoided.

"Okay. I'm ready."

Ted gave him an address. "Can you be there at six tomorrow?"

"Yes. Yeah, I can." He almost asked if it would be all right to bring Elliot, not wanting to overextend on his mother's babysitting kindness, but thought better of bringing the kiddo to this stranger's meetup.

Didn't matter. Once Ted had confirmation, he'd hung up.

Jacob had no idea why he'd gotten so nervous, as if he were interviewing for his first job. Hell, he didn't even want an "odd" job. He wanted to clack away at his computer all night and hang with his son. Pecking away at bills with a fruitless and thankless list of shit jobs felt like surrendering as much as actually surrendering did.

A little later, he put Elliot to bed and spent the next few hours tossing and turning while trying to fall asleep, thinking about that stack on the damned table.

AFTER HIS SHIFT THE NEXT DAY, JACOB PUT THE ADDRESS INTO HIS GPS. It led to a house down some thin, winding roads in the heart of Richmond. There were some farms, some places that looked no longer livable, and a few really nice, modernized Victorians.

The directions led him to a small cottage, overgrown with shrubbery that Jacob couldn't tell if it came from neglect or was intentional. It looked pretty, if not something out of a horror movie.

Ted surprised him. He expected a guy who ran odd jobs to be a bit more blue collar, and from the gruff manner in which he spoke on the phone, Jacob expected more stature. What he got a was a thin man with glasses and a mustache. He wore a nice button down and brown slacks.

The man extended a hand. Jacob shook it.

"Come on in," Ted said.

Jacob followed Ted to a small office. Ted walked around to his seat on the opposite side of the oak desk and waved his hand at the rolling office chair near the door for Jacob to sit in. As Jacob sat, Ted fished through a drawer and talked. "So, Jacob, I've looked you up and spoken to Bobby about you. You give me no indication I'd need to worry, but I like to be thorough." He pulled out a blue folder and placed it on the desk. "Do you know why people pay me too much money for odd jobs? Why they don't just call a small local business to get the job done? Why do you think they'd pay good cash to a guy who hires folks he hardly knows to come to their houses and deal with their personal problems?"

Jacob found the words sticking in his throat. Suddenly, he saw something in the man he hadn't before. Behind Ted's thin frame and clean-cut dressings was a monster. Someone who could inflict pain. Probably not himself, but he'd have no problem getting the right guys to do the job. Jacob guessed a lot of men screamed in pain on Ted's orders. "Because people trust you," Jacob finally said.

Ted snapped his fingers. "True. They do. But why do they trust me?"

"Because no one is stupid enough to let you down."

Ted smiled. "That's right. There have been a lot of men in your seat. Many of them bigger, tougher, and scarier than you. But they all knew not to fuck with me. Or they learned it later on."

Jacob sat forward, wishing he could run out the door, forget the whole thing, but this wasn't for him. It was for Elliot. "I know it now, sir. I won't need to learn it later on."

Ted slid the folder across the desk. "Good. Here's a list of all current available jobs. Take some time to look through it and let me know if you see any that interest you."

Jacob tried to hide the tremor in his fingers as he opened the folder. The list of jobs went five pages deep, but each entry provided only the bare minimum of information.

Mrs. Wilcox – lawn maintenance – 400
Barry – pest control/bats – 300
Lisa D. – home repairs – 700

The more Jacob examined the list, the more impossible it all felt. What did lawn maintenance mean? If someone needed a person to do a once-a-week job with edging and trimming, sure, $400 sounded about normal, maybe even low. But there was nothing to explain what the job entailed or how much time factored into the four hundred payment. Jacob had to assume Ted received a nice cut from all this, so was Mrs. Wilcox paying Jacob four hundred and Ted another set amount, or did the four hundred include Ted's cut?

Meanwhile, $300 for bat removal sounded horrendously low. Jacob imagined a pest control place would charge upward of a thousand for it, unless you were talking about a single bat that got into the house, in which case, Jacob hoped Barry hadn't been living with it for weeks while his name got added to a paper list in Ted's office, hoping someday someone will pick the job and remove the bat for him.

The whole list was like that. No explanations. No information. Random names. Sometimes a first and last, sometimes an initial. None of the jobs especially appealed to Jacob, and he found himself back to his original thoughts on odd jobs. Lots of work. Not great pay. He'd be better off picking up a second job with a steady income.

On page three, he passed by an entry he had to ask about.

Elsa – Digging – 100,000

He knew whatever this job was, it probably required special equipment or training that he wouldn't possess, but he had to ask.

"What's this digging one?"

Ted laughed. "Every time. Without fail."

"Huh?"

"Every new person sitting in your seat asks about that one. Not that I blame you. The price tag is eye catching."

"I'm guessing if everyone asks and it's still on the list, it's going to fall into the too-good-to-be-true category?"

"Indeed. Elsa is a kind old woman who everyone loves, but she's lost it a bit over the years. She came to me and told me about a job she needed done, and I, being the nice guy I am, placated her. I told her I'd ask around fully intending to never mention it to anyone. But Elsa, crazy as she's become, is also quite clever. She knew about my folder, and she insisted I put it in there. I suggest ignoring it."

Jacob brought his eyes back down to the papers but glanced back up, hoping Ted had more to give on the story. He'd given up on the potential for it, but the vagueness of the story intrigued Jacob enough he just wanted to hear what the job was about.

Ted sighed. "Not gonna let it go, are you?"

Jacob shot up straight. "I'm not trying to be a pain in the ass. If you want me to let it go, I'll let it go. You just have me intrigued to know what the job was."

Ted scoffed. "No. It's fine. The job is as described. Digging. Elsa wants people to dig holes in her backyard. She believes her house is possessed by evil spirits, and the only way to free it is to dig these holes where she believes demons live."

Jacob held in a laugh. "Still, so all you have to do is dig some holes and she will pay you that large a sum? I mean, I don't want to take advantage of a nice old woman, but I have to admit, it sounds tempting." As soon as he said the words, he regretted them, but Ted didn't seem to take offense.

"Not so simple, I'm afraid. The catch is you have to release an evil spirit to get paid."

Jacob shook his head. "Ah, so there it is. You go over and spend hours digging holes in the hot sun, and she gets to say, 'Sorry, no spirits today.' How many people have tried it only to come back screaming at you because they didn't get paid?"

Ted raised his eyebrows. "No one screams at me, because I warn them ahead of time. But about fifteen people have gone and tried it out." He looked like he was about to say something else but stopped himself.

"What?"

Ted let out an exhausted gasp. "Listen, I don't believe in supernatural stuff, okay? Let me just preface what about to tell you with that. I am only telling you what actually happened. Two people did get paid the one hundred k. They both called me right after, hysterically excited."

"Wow. Did they say they saw a spirit? Or did the lady just make it up to keep some interest going in her hole-digging operation?"

"They said they didn't see a thing. Said they were digging, and Elsa said, 'You did it. You found one. Thank you!' And then she wrote them a check."

"You know, you're kind of selling me on this. What percentage of fifteen people is two? Thirteen or fourteen percent? I go dig some holes for a day and I have a thirteen percent chance of walking out with a hundred thousand dollars?"

Ted scratched his head. "Both men are dead."

Jacob stopped smiling. "What?"

"They both died within a week of digging the holes."

"Bullshit."

"I told you I don't believe in the supernatural, and I'd only tell you what happened. That's what happened. Both men who received the checks died within a week. As for the other thirteen men who didn't get paid? They all still come to this office from time to time for an odd job."

"Well, damn."

"Do you believe in the supernatural, Jacob?"

"No, but I'm not going to test it either."

Ted shook his head. "That's how I feel about it. And it's one of the reasons I hate having that listing on there. Makes me feel like I'm somehow part of it. Even though I don't believe in it."

From the moment Jacob had stepped into the office, Ted intimidated him. But for a flash, as Ted spoke that last sentence, Jacob saw true terror in the man's eyes.

A half-hour later, Jacob left Ted's house with a job walking someone's dogs three times a week for two hundred dollars. He couldn't imagine living a life where he could afford to pay someone two hundred dollars to walk a dog.

On the way home, he didn't think about the dog or how he'd manage his schedule. Didn't wonder whether he'd take Elliot with him for the walks or rely on his mother to watch the kiddo for a while longer.

He thought about digging holes.

THAT NIGHT, JACOB FELL ASLEEP ON THE COUCH WATCHING television while Elliot slept on the floor in a sleeping bag. He dreamed of digging holes. In the dream, it was midnight, and a thin fog slithered along the grounds like in a cheesy eighties horror movie. He dug and dug and dug until the Earth swallowed him up.

ON HIS LUNCH BREAK, JACOB CALLED TED AND ASKED FOR ELSA'S number. Thirteen percent chance. Thirteen percent! He couldn't think of anything else other than what a hundred thousand dollars could do for his life.

He had just one last question for Ted before he accepted the job. "How did those men die?"

"That's the weird part. Both died in their beds. No one could figure out how."

Fuck it, Jacob thought. *One hundred k is one hundred k.* He hated money. Wanted nothing to do with it. But he needed it. Elliot needed it for stability.

A FEW EVENINGS LATER, HE TOOK ELLIOT WITH HIM TO WALK AN elderly man's dogs. Jacob had assumed the man was going on vacation, but it turned out he just struggled to do the walks anymore and didn't want the dog to suffer for it. So he hired random people to take Butterscotch for exercise.

It was a nice evening, weather clear. Jacob and Elliot had fun with the dog. Butterscotch was a plump bulldog who snorted as he walked. Elliot loved it, giggling each time the dog let out the strange noises.

The old man clearly had money, and the neighborhood reflected that with thick sidewalks and quality landscaping. Elliot smiled the whole time and talked more than Jacob had ever seen. He talked about YouTube and drawing and his favorite colors. He talked about his grandmother and how he liked to dance and how his favorite song was "Levitating" by Dua Lipa.

Jacob wanted to walk forever, to never let this moment go.

A few blocks down, they passed a stretch of woods. Old pines lined the sidewalk, red barked and splotched with lichen. The last remnants of daylight stuck around, red and purple highlighting the horizon.

A noise emanated from the woods, a light thing, barely audible over Elliot's chattering. A Cccchhhh. Ccccchhhhh. A lot of it. Ccccchhhhhh. A chorus of it.

What was it? He refused to tell Elliot to quiet down, loving too much that his boy had any interest in talking to him. But he wanted to figure the noise out. As they walked farther along the pines, the noise gathered. It remained soft, but more of it came, hundreds of little Ccccchhhhhs.

As soon as they passed the woods and found themselves in front of a well-manicured lawn, Jacob figured it out.

"Dad, did you know there's a YouTube video that's like fourteen days long?" Elliot asked.

"No, bud. That's crazy!" *And probably not true*, Jacob thought. "What happens in it?"

"It's about nothing. It's just a guy digging."

JACOB ARRIVED AT ELSA'S HOUSE ON A TUESDAY MORNING. HE HAD the day off from the market and wanted to get a full day's work in on the digging. He'd dig a thousand holes if he had to. The way he saw it, the other men didn't think the job through. Yes, you could dig all day and come up with nothing, but if thirteen percent of the time, the woman rewarded someone, Jacob could just come by and dig all day. Dig all night. Dig for weeks. One hundred k would be worth it. He guessed most people assumed it was a hoax, that no money would ever come, and then when she finally did release some cash, and the recipient died, superstition would keep anyone from trying again. In fact, if Jacob had a guess, the last two men to try it were the two that got paid and died, killing off anyone else's interest.

Elsa was tall and lanky. The skin on her legs hung off the bone. Deep veins like rivers mapped her flesh. Her hair was gray, but more noticeable was how unkempt it was. It moved away from her head like tree limbs.

Her house, on the other hand, was meticulously kept. The marble shiny and bright. Jacob thought he could rub a finger along the deep recesses of the mantle and walk away without a speck of dust on him.

She led him to the back yard, which, outside of the dozens of holes, looked equally cared for. The grass was freshly mowed and nearly florescent green. The holes pockmarked the landscape, and Jacob wondered how much of a pain in the ass it had to be to mow around them. They were deep holes and a good foot in width. The men before him must have been strong fellas.

Elsa pointed and said, "The demons came in from the woods. They travel through the ground and live in burrows. When you find one, I'll give you money. If I had to guess, there's probably about twelve of 'em still living back here."

Jacob hadn't considered it, but the men who received payment said they hadn't witnessed anything, but Elsa had, which meant she had to be watching. Would she sit in the yard all day keeping an eye on Jacob? Would that mean he couldn't take his time and move slowly? He hated being micromanaged, but for one hundred k, he'd let the lady yell at him for six days straight.

The woman gave him a shovel and yardwork gloves. The shovel was an old rusty thing with a sharp point. The wooden handle looked warn and scraped up.

The first strike of metal to dirt proved difficult, and Jacob realized how over his head he'd gotten. He barely brought up a shot glass worth of dirt. The second and third weren't any better. By strike number four, he'd found a little less resistance with the ground. After thirty or forty strikes, he found a grove. He worked straight, hit after hit. The years of smoking caught up to him quickly, and he was out of breath within a few minutes. Sweat built in his pits, behind his knees, and on the back of his neck.

But he kept digging.

The noon sun came out. In the fall, it wasn't as bad as it could have been. He wondered if the men before him did this job during the summer months. Maybe they died of heat exhaustion. Despite the creeping autumn, the sun still beat the hell out of him.

Even with the gloves, Jacob's palm and fingers hurt. His back hurt just under the shoulders. His lungs begged for a break. Elsa sat in a lawn chair, watching. Not even blinking that Jacob could see.

He made a sizable hole, up to his neck. "How far down should I go?"

"It's different every time, but you hit a point when I just know whether one is there or not."

"What makes you aware of that?" Jacob didn't care, knew the lady was nuts, but he needed the break despite his eagerness to get it done.

"They make a noise. You don't gotta be all the way to 'em to hear it. It's muffled in the dirt, but it's there. A kind of moaning yell. I imagine it's how hell sounds. Suffering. That's what it sounds like."

He tried not to think of it. He didn't need the rantings of a crazy person creeping him out of the biggest paycheck he'd ever received.

Jacob worked for another hour before Elsa said, "Stop. Nothing there."

Fuck. Just for once, he couldn't get lucky on attempt one?

"Should I start on another one?"

She shrugged. "If you're up for it."

Jacob climbed out of the hole, which took some effort. He was actually proud of himself for the work done, even if it led to nothing. "Yeah, if it's all right with you, I'm gonna go eat some lunch and have a cigarette, and then I can get right back to it."

Elsa nodded, nothing else to say.

On his way around the house, Jacob turned back to the old woman, who kept her gaze on the holes. "Hey, Elsa?"

She slowly turned her head toward him. "Yes?"

"The two that found one. What do you think made their attempts different?"

She frowned. "I guess if I knew that, I'd have better information for where you should dig."

He shook his head. "And what do you think happened to them?"

"They stayed in the holes," she said without missing a beat. "Must have."

"Huh?"

"If you find one, you'll understand."

He stared for a moment, hoping she'd have more to say than that, but she went back to staring at the holes.

As he ate a PB and J he'd packed and left in the car, he had to talk himself out of taking off. Something felt off, and not just the weird old lady. Now that he'd moved away from the yard, he sensed it. There was something strange about the soil. Like it was rotten. But more than that, he'd changed. Now that he had a break, the pain in his body, the tiredness, it all felt unbearable. But in the yard, it didn't stop him, didn't faze him. It was as if some magnetic force powered him and helped him do a physical type of job unlike any he'd ever faced. He doubted he could have dug a hole that sizeable without taking a single break when he was eighteen and athletic. He sure as hell couldn't believe he'd just done it in his late thirties after fifteen years of smoking.

Call it a loss. Call it a loss. Call it a loss. The words repeated in his head.

But he'd invested so much. Eventually he'd get the woman to pay him.

He smoked a cigarette and headed back to work. Halfway around the side yard, he thought there was no way. His body couldn't handle a single more strike. But once he entered the back yard, put the gloves on, and grabbed the shovel, he felt ready. Eager even.

He still ached. His heart pounded. His lungs were on fire. But he almost shook with anticipation at the idea of striking the metal into the dirt.

Cccchhhhhh. It felt euphoric.

He dug for hours. The sun tucked itself in behind the neighboring houses. The sky turned smoke gray. The pain grew tenfold, and Jacob thought his body might give out, but he envisioned dollars just below the next shovelful of dirt.

Despite his growing exhaustion, he found himself digging faster, harder. He panted with exhaustion, pulled his sweat-soaked shirt off, and dug, dug, dug. Deeper. Deeper. He was in way over his head now.

A wind hit his exposed skin, giving him goose bumps. How was the wind blowing down there?

He heard a noise above him. When he looked up, Elsa stood at the edge of the hole staring down at him.

"I'm not ready to give up just yet if that's okay with you."

She knelt down. Jacob could see the effort it took for her as she winced in pain. She turned her head and pulled the hair away from her ear. "You found one," she said, calmly, softly.

Jacob smiled, nearly bursting with excitement. "Yeah? There's one down here? I kind of knew it. I had a feeling. I could feel it." And in a weird way, he could. Not a demon or a ghost. But *something*. He went right back to digging. His hands were on fire. His muscles, too.

It took considerable effort to remove the dirt now, having to heave the shovel up and out of the hole.

Then. Clunk.

He hit something.

He nearly gasped. Dropping to his knees, he started pulling dirt away from whatever he'd hit. Wood. There was wood. The two men who she'd paid had said they hadn't seen anything, but Jacob had found something. Again, not a demon, but wood. Maybe it was a coincidence, and all he'd found was a long-buried fence picket.

Then he heard it.

The moaning. Gentle. Soft. A low pained moan.

As more and more dirt pulled away, he found multiple pieces of wood, as if he were uncovering an entire structure. A wall? A floor? A fucking boat? He couldn't tell, but he wanted to find out.

It was hard to see, the night creeping in. He looked up to ask for a flashlight, and the woman was there again, standing over the hole. "That's enough. Come on up and collect your money. You found one for me."

"But don't you want me to see what this wooden thing is?"

She huffed. "I know what it is, sir. Now get out of there and collect your money."

Jacob didn't want to stop. It compelled him so deeply, he nearly begged her to let him stay, was almost willing to sacrifice the paycheck.

But no. He wasn't. He used the shovel to help him stand up and climbed out of the hole. Elsa led him into the house and brought him to the sink so he could wash the dirt off his arms and stomach. He was covered in it, leaving tracks with him the whole way. "Sorry, I'm trailing all this dirt."

She waved him away. "Don't worry about it. You did me a great service tonight. I can handle the dirty floors. It's the demons that I can't take."

After he wiped himself off, mucking up her towels in the process, she handed him a check. He looked at her with watery eyes. "You just changed my life," he said.

She smiled and touched his arm. "And you mine."

"Thank you," Jacob said.

On his way home, he bawled his eyes out. Everything would work out. The check bought him time, and time was all he needed to get his life in order. He could take some time to focus on Elliot, enjoy playing with the kid. He thought about the walk they'd took and how special it was to hear his son talk to him like a friend.

As all good weeks do, it melted away like chocolate over a flame. On the first day, Jacob developed a slight cough. By the next day, his lungs were on fire, and he struggled to eat. Within a few days, he'd wake up coughing, covered in sweat, and unable to get more than an hour of rest at a time.

He didn't care about the sickness, refused to let it hinder his time with Elliot. In fact, he almost welcomed it, because he was able to call out of work and enjoy every morning, noon, and night with his child.

But he thought about the two men before him, and how they died a week later from unknown sources. Was this it? Had he dug up some disease in Elsa's yard, some unknown thing that filled his lungs?

On day seven, he called his mother before going to bed. "Listen, Mom. If anything happens to me, I just deposited a lot of money in my account. Take it out and use it how you need to. Take care of Elliot."

"What are you talking about? You boys with your man-flu. You have a cold and suddenly you're preparing for death."

"Mom, please. Just do it. And also, forgive yourself for busting my chops about the man-flu. I know you were kidding, and I know you love me."

"Jacob? What's going on? Why are you talking like that?"

"Nothing, Mom. Probably just the man-flu. I'm feeling sentimental."

He hung up, went to Elliot's bed, and gave his son a kiss on the forehead. Then he went to bed, exhausted, aching in every muscle, coughing in fits so large he'd end up gagging. But happy. For once, he was happy. Relieved. If he did die overnight, at least he got this week.

DARKNESS. HE OPENED HIS EYES, OR THOUGHT HE HAD, BUT everything remained black as night. He couldn't move either. He'd had this happen before, where his mind awoke before his body did. Sometimes he dropped right from a nightmare and screamed and flailed, but actually did nothing, only thought he had. His mind said flail and scream, but his body wasn't ready yet.

But this time, it kind of stuck. He couldn't say anything. Couldn't move. He mumbled some words through closed lips, but that was the best he could accomplish. He could have presumed he was dead if not for the sounds. The gentle clunk of wood settling that occurred so often in his house. And then, eventually, Elliot.

"Dad?"

"Dad?"

Jacob tried to talk, to say, "I'm here, Son," but no words escaped his lungs. Only grunts. Elliot seemed not to hear them.

Elliot speaking to someone not responding, telling them his daddy wasn't waking up.

A long while later, Jacob's mother's voice. "Oh, no. Oh, no."

Weeping.

Her speaking to 911, telling them about her son's body.

And then silence. Long silence. It could have been days. Could have been weeks or months or years. Too much silence. Painful silence. Nothing happening. Nothing to see or feel or hear. Nothing. It stretched into infinity. So much silence. Jacob wondered if he'd left the world, felt the yank and pull of death, felt himself removed from life, and it didn't hurt in the physical way, more in the way it hurt to drop his son off at his mother's house, their connection severed.

And then ...

Ccccchhhh.

Ccccchhhh.

Ccccchhhh.

Thunk.

Ccccchhhh.

Cccccbhh.

Ccccccccccccchhhhhhhhhhhhhh.

Thunk.

Thunk.

Thunk.

"Okay, you can stop now. You found one. Come inside and I'll pay you."

Jacob tried to reach up and yell, "No! No. Don't go inside. Stay here with me. It's me. I'm down here. I'm here, please, uncover me," but all that escaped his lungs were moans.

SWALLOWBOX

CLAY MCLEOD CHAPMAN

Whatever enters the birdhouse never comes back out.

I never really quite considered myself to be a bird-watcher, if I'm honest. Now I just can't stop. I've set up camp by the window, binoculars in hand, staring into the backyard. Waiting. Simply observing whatever feathered occupant as it slips through that tiny, dilated hole cut out from the front façade. I've counted about twenty wrens. A couple thrushes. Purple martins.

None ever leave. Not one.

All of them, vanished.

The swallow box was here long before me. Came with the house. A bonus abode. I'm housesitting for a friend—the actual house, not the birdhouse—while he's in the hospital. He won't be coming back for a few months, so he asked if I wouldn't mind caretaking. Make sure the place doesn't burn down. I'm in between homes at the moment, so it was simple enough to pack a bag and crash at his pad. When I first got here, I glanced out the kitchen window and—

There it was.

Just a slender-framed birdhouse suspended from a maple tree in the backyard. Hard to tell what wood it's made of. Seemed like cedar to me, but I wasn't sure, its walls now a decrepit elephant skin. Pennies for shingles were glued to its roof, the copper gone all green.

A black-capped chickadee hops on the peg, peaks its head through the hole, then slips in. *Gone.* A red-breasted nuthatch flutters in for a pitstop, pecks around, then disappears. *Poof.*

It happens all the time. *Every* time. Now that I've seen it, I can't *unsee* it.

Are they still in there? Where did all those birds go?

It's the silence that first unnerved me. If the window is open, a gentle trill fills the kitchen. A keener ear could probably tell you what species is responsible for each particular twitter. Not me. Not yet, at least. I was barely aware of the chirruping drifting in from the backyard. Warbling white noise. Then it stopped. Completely halted in mid-chirp. That I certainly heard. The absence. Someone pressed mute on the remote during a nature program.

So I peeked out the window. Locked onto the birdhouse. There it was, swaying ever-so-slightly in the breeze. Whatever bird paid a visit must've simply flown the coop, I assumed.

Just then, a bluebird landed on the peg. Peered in, peered out. Twisted its head, swiveling on its neck. Chirped indecisively. Fluttered its wings before hopping through the hole.

I held my breath and waited.

Watched.

The bird's chirping ceased the second it slipped inside. Everything went quiet as soon as it entered. Quiet in a way you notice, like in wintertime, a fresh snowfall dampening all sound.

Sure enough, that bluebird never poked its head out again.

They never do. Nothing ever leaves.

What's up with the birdhouse? I asked my friend over the phone on one of our check-ins.

What do you mean?

Should I fill it up with birdseed or something? Seems busy back there…

What birdhouse?

Your birdhouse. In the backyard. I'm looking at it right now.

Randall, my friend said, the chemo creeping into his voice. *I don't have a birdhouse...*

I avoided the swallow box, simply observing by the window. I made a hobby out of it. I dusted off a pair of binoculars. Picked up a crumbling book on birds I found on my friend's shelf.

Now I'm keeping a running tally of our feathered tenants.

Robins. Northern flickers. Tufted titmouses. The birdhouse doesn't discern.

It swallows them all.

This is not some palatial palace. Nor is it a clown car. It's just a wooden box, that's all. A small wooden casket the size of a shoebox dangling from the maple. Its walls should be bursting at the seams from the number of birds it's gobbled up. Where in the hell could they all be? Is there a back door I can't see? Are they all slipping out some rear window on the other side?

They're not still in there, are they? How is that even possible?

By the time I finally stepped up to the birdhouse's front porch, encroaching its door like a sheepish neighbor about to ring-and-run, I actually found myself feeling a bit uncertain about it all. What am I going to do? I steeled myself before leaning in, peering through the hole. The circle seemed so much smaller from the kitchen window, no more than an inch or two, but now that I was standing right here in front of it, I realized the aperture was wider. A splintered rictus.

Was the wood dilating somehow? Opening itself up for me?

The house was empty.

That's not true. I spied pale seeds settled along the birdhouse's bottom. Husks of shells.

Those aren't seeds, I realized. *Those are bones.*

The floor was a tangled shag of phalanges. Splintered ribs. Beaks. No feathers, no skin, just an abandoned game of Pick-Up Sticks comprised of countless tiny skeletons.

The hole suddenly widened. That rotund O opened, as if the wood were respiring.

Welcoming me in.

So I poked my finger through. Just the pointer. It felt cold inside. The sun still hit my wrist, warm against my skin, while inside the birdhouse, this persistent chill slowly seeped deeper into my fingertip, reaching for my first knuckle. Then the second. Tugging on me, almost.

I yanked my hand out, freeing my finger. Actually gasped. I took hold of my hand and pressed it against my chest. My pulse had picked up, a hummingbird fluttering in my ribcage.

All because of a birdhouse.

That was yesterday. The cold still hasn't left my index finger. I feel it in my knuckles. The phalanxes. A freon arthritis in just this one particular digit, while the rest of my fingers feel fine.

I'm still inside the birdhouse.

A part of me is, at least.

I feel as if my finger is still wrapped within its cool shadows.

Nestled. That's the word. My finger feels *nestled* inside, curled up along the carpet.

How can so much of me, 99.999999% of me, be stuck outside of that house—while this one infinitesimal bit of my body, this single wriggling digit, feel so completely at home?

How much of me has to be inside a space to feel like I am within? How much can be stuck outside to still be considered internalized, surrounded by its walls?

I want to go home. I want to crawl inside... but how am I going to fit?

Today I'll try two fingers. Three. I ball my hand up into a tight fist and really squeeze, forcing my hand through. I get a few splinters in my wrist, but now my hand is in. The pain on the other side just ebbs away. It feels so nice inside. Spacious. I free my fingers from their fist. Let them wriggle around. Take in the space. *Nestle*. My hand basks in that cool room. The chill is at my wrist now. So I push forward, forging my forearm ahead, just to see how far I might be able to go, how much of me I can cram in. A lot, surprisingly. First, my forearm. But why stop there, when there's so much of me still outside, when all I want to do is to go in? To *nestle*. My elbow plunges through, no problem. I flex my bicep, and the birdhouse relents a bit more, opening itself further, giving just a little more of itself so that I can climb in. Now that I've reached my shoulder, I figure that'll be it. But hold on. Maybe not. The wood is so soft. A bit squishy. Can I keep going? Worth a shot, yeah? I've made it this far. Can't turn back now. Is this breaking-and-entering? Should I go head first? Or is it better to try wriggling my other arm in? I end up winnowing my fingers from my free hand around the hole's dilating lip and try prying it open a little more. *Come on, you can do it, just a little bit more...* It takes some time, but it's starting to give now. I can shimmy my head in like some determined worm. *Come on, that's it, you got it. Don't rush it. Just a little at a time.* Now I can feel a chill at the very tip of my nose. My chin. Splinters dig into my cheeks, scraping at the skin, but once my face is through, I feel nothing but the most exquisite air conditioning. The chill spreads through my lips, until their comfortably numb, until I can no longer tell if I'm grinning or not anymore, if I have a mouth anymore, that cold reaching down to the very roots of my teeth. My feet barely touch the ground now. I'm on my tippy toes. Now they're up. I'm swinging. Swaying. I'm climbing up. Climbing inside. Going home. *Nestling.*

This birdhouse, not ours, not anyone's, stood by itself in the backyard for lord knows how long. Longer than I'd lived here. Probably long after I move out, even.

Within, plywood walls continued upright, penny shingles met, its hole open for all; not a chirp slipped out from its wooden barriers, and whatever nestles inside there, nestles alone.

Loch Lament

M.L. RAYNER

The view of the narrow highland road was just about visible beyond the murk of foggy glass. Outside, heavy rain hammered down from a dark and dismal sky—a sky so gray and clotted with clouds that, for a brief moment, it left both passengers wondering if the trip they were about to embark on was even worth taking at all. It was an anticipated wild camping trip in the desolate Scottish Highlands, on the brink of October, no less. Still, neither of them dared to say a word as they drove on through the wilderness.

Tim, the father, was far too cautious of the winding roads ahead to care as he sat stiffly in the passenger seat, his hands gripping tightly to his knees.

"Nearly there, I think," said Matt, briefly masking the din of raindrops that drummed on the roof.

He hunched his neck forward, checking for the turnoff, both knuckles turning white on the wheel as he followed the curve of the lane.

"You think?" replied his father, wiping the smoggy glass with the cuff of his sleeve.

He glanced out of his window, his eyes straining as he watched the barrenness in the distance merge into a haze of endless browns and greens.

"You mean this is it?" he pressed, breaking his sight from the pane. "This is why we drove over nine hours? For this?" He gestured one hand to the scenery, a view so soulless that it caused his teeth to grit.

Without so much as a word, Matt rolled his eyes, an expression easily hidden from his father's view as he eased his foot down on the brake, slowing the car to a crawl.

Some yards ahead, a slanted sign, old and weather-beaten, stuck out of the mossy verge, its once-white letters half lost to a timeless shade of green, pointing in the direction of a narrow lane that diverted into the wild. The lane, barely more than a footpath, was flanked by tough grass and gnarled trees, their branches draping to a wet and earthy cloak.

"I guess... this must be it." Matt shrugged, quickly double checking his rearview mirror.

He didn't know why. They hadn't seen so much as another car on the road since they last filled up the tank, near Ullapool. Not a bleeding soul, for that matter. Still, old habits always did die hard. The last thing he needed was an accident on his hands, especially out in the middle of nowhere.

"What?" His father leaned awkwardly, eager to see.

"The road." Matt pointed. He popped the gear stick back into first and slowly edged forward, the grind of the loose tarmac beneath the tires filling the pervasive silence between them.

"The sign, just there, you see it?" He gestured with the nod of his head. "This must be the turning."

Tim followed the sign to the direction of the turnoff, taking in the view of the rough, gravelly road where patches of tough, wet grass grew wild at the center, in some places taking over the narrow high-land route entirely.

"That way?"

With a sharp twist of his wrist, he rolled down the window and leaned out, allowing a gust of wind to fall flat on his face and raindrops to splatter into the car.

"You must be joking?" he asked, his tone laced with a mixture of worry and amusement. "Damn road looks like it should have been blocked off years back. Most likely leads to nowhere, nothing but a dead end, lad. No. No, we'll carry on. We'll find another way, a safer way."

Matt, regardless of his father's instructions, already found his attention drawn back to the small screen of the satnav, scrolling the map carefully, which would, in a short time, navigate them to their long-awaited destination. It had already been nine hours in the car since they set off from Birmingham—nine hours of listening to the old fella grunt and grumble, lecturing him on how he should live his life, the mistakes he had made. The very idea of detouring after making it this far only to find themselves utterly lost and no signal to call for help was a thought far from pleasing.

"But," Matt objected, "it's telling us it's this way. Look."

"Then as I said, we'll find another way," replied his father.

"There isn't any other way!" Matt barked, instantly wishing he hadn't. He breathed in deeply, desperate to calm his nerves. "Take a look for yourself." He twisted the small device on the cradle, indicating the spot where they sat. "We're here, right?"

Tim gave a half-arsed nod. "Right."

"So, if we make a left, follow the road up toward the spring, there should be a small wooden bridge there," said Matt, tapping his finger on a thin blue line that jiggered across the landscape. "Once we've passed the crossing, it's but a short drive to our stop. Ten minutes tops!"

He glanced back to his father, a face staring back at him that was so curt, so all-knowing, that he didn't know what else to say.

"And if we keep driving ahead?" his father persisted.

"Then we'll likely get lost, won't we?" replied Matt. "Damn satnav's already blinked out on me twice in the last half hour. There's no bloody reception around here. That or we'll run out of fuel. I put only enough in to get us there and back, not for you to make us tour the entire north of bleedin' Scotland."

Tim's brow creased at the center, his nose slightly wriggled.

"Look, all I'm saying is the last thing we need on our plate is to break down. Not out here."

"Ah, don't worry, lad," his father responded casually. "I'm with the AA."

"Then what the hell are you worried about?" huffed Matt, and with a swift jerk, he positioned the cradle back into pride and place. "Breakdown on this road or another, what's the difference? Plus, it'll be dark soon." He looked at the time on the dash. "An hour or so, if that."

With a heavy sigh, Tim observed the turnoff that dipped into a snaking slope, cutting through the ridge of the hillside and quickly vanishing beyond a cluster of tangling ash trees.

"Please yourself, then," said Tim, winding up his window to a crack. "Just don't come moaning to me if we have to backpedal. I've told you before and I'll say it again—I know roads. I've worked over twenty-five years on them, driven along all types of conditions, suppliers out in the sticks. And this road," he indicated with the point of his thumb, "this road has dead-end written all over it."

They signaled for the turnoff, following the steep lane as it descended, the unsmooth surface matching that of the rough and rocky landscape. High grass scratched along either side of the car as long, brittle branches that masked the sky's dying light overhead reached out to the windshield, stopping the wipers in motion.

"I told you. Didn't I tell you?" said Tim, folding his arms in a cocky sort of way. "Ain't no open road, is this. These branches, they're much too low. And thick. You should have got out and walked a little ways first, checked it out."

"All right, Captain Hindsight!" remarked Matt, his voice raised over the ruckus of snapping branches and the crunch of loose pebbles skittering beneath the tires. "I'm sure it'll clear soon. Just a little farther."

"If you say so," replied his father. He sank back into his seat, his eyes dreary from the journey, as he rested his forehead to the window, watching the denseness of the world creep by. "You reckon there's a pub out here?"

Matt didn't answer, nor, in truth, was he really listening to the old man. Not at that moment. His mind was elsewhere, occupied. His concentration fixed on the hazardous route ahead, listening to the car as its suspension creaked and groaned with each sudden dip in the way, causing his shoulders to tense. He tried his best not to show it, his nervousness, that was. Most of all, he didn't want his father to be right. For him to accept his poor judgment. Not that day of all days. Not on this trip. It was he who was running the show, not his old man. He would prove to his father that for once in his life he knew better, that he knew what he was doing. After all, it wasn't Matt's first trip roughing it, not by any means. It was simply one of many. Nothing was allowed to go wrong. It couldn't. Not this time.

If they had to turn back and find another route, he would never live it down. The whole venture would be tainted from the get-go, cursed in Matt's eyes, listening to his father remind him, going on and on, a smug smirk smeared across his face. Nothing was more important than getting where they needed to be, back out onto the clearing of smooth Highland lanes, leaving the unforgiving road behind them. That and proving his father wrong, of course. That, to Matt, was the most important thing of all, even if he knew what his father said was right.

With yet another jolt of the car, both father and son jerked forward violently, the squeal of the tires turned in a desperate spin as Matt planted his foot to the pedal, yearning to see them move. In the corner of his eye, he could just about discern the old man watching his every move, his disapproving gaze staring daggers at Matt as though waiting for his son to surrender, to admit his old man was correct. But Matt, despite such worry, did no such thing, didn't even consider the thought. Instead, he pushed the car onward, forcing them up and over the rugged grounds, the foliage surrounding them becoming more threatening, more dominant by the second. He took his eyes from the road for a brief second, his attention reverting to the rearview mirror, catching the slightest glimpse of a shadow in the distance, something standing on the ridge of the road they just left behind. A person, most likely someone trying to warn them of the way ahead, thought Matt. Wouldn't that just take the cake? That whoever it was was warning them of their land, not that there was even so much as a house within a five-mile radius from where they sat. Matt knew as much. He had checked it on the map, studied it relentlessly. So what if they had trespassed, he thought. It wasn't done intentionally. Nor would it have been their fault. After all, any signs that suggested so would have been taken back by nature long ago, hidden behind the foliage, invisible to all those who didn't know better.

The car bounced again, setting the young man's focus back on track. His fingers tensed tighter around the wheel, nails piercing the worn-out leather, eager to gain control.

"Steady on, now!" he heard his father say, the statement partly turned into an exacerbated grunt as the old man flung forward, levitating for a second off his seat.

"Sorry!" replied Matt. He really did mean it. As he eased his foot off the pedal, interest shifted back to the mirror, the reflection behind him jumped to a blur like the world itself was shaking. He strained his eyes. But much to his surprise, the silhouette that just a moment ago appeared to stand upon the ridge, watching them drive away, was gone, vanished amongst the low clouds that slithered down the hillcrest. It went without saying that Matt's focus stayed on that very spot for as long as he could, waiting to catch another sight, to see the stranger staring down at them, that he had not just imagined the whole thing. But as the road began to curve with the course of the land, the depths of nature engulfed them all the more, concealing the car from the high road and erasing the path they had journeyed. Now there was nothing behind them, nothing but a covering of endless thicket, a forgotten road they somehow managed to trench their way through—leaving Matt with only one worry as he pushed through the canopy of hanging limbs, urging the car to make it.

Both men breathed a sigh of relief as the car, strewn with a tangle of fallen leaves and brittle branches, crossed a quaint wooden bridge arching over a rippling stream that came to an end at a small, hidden layby that ambled the edge of a loch. With the destination finally reached and their nervousness quickly forgotten, Matt slid the gear stick into reverse, maneuvering the vehicle as best as he could.

The tires milled to an abrupt stop on the dry ground, sending up a wisp of dusty clouds to whirl about the bonnet.

With the handbrake on, Matt slouched back, his grip on the wheel finally easing. And for the first time in many hours, he turned the key in the ignition off, enveloping the space where they sat in a sudden hush.

"See!" Matt exclaimed heartily, though not so heartily to fully disguise the worry he had been hiding. He turned to his father, brushing off any concern. "What did I tell you? Piece of cake."

"A slice of shit is more like it," his father retorted, a sheen of sweat glistening on his brow. "You're lucky you didn't burn out the clutch driving like that. I mean, really, who the hell taught you to drive?"

Matt shot a puzzled look at his father. "You did."

"Not like that, I bloody didn't!" he snapped. "Nor do I approve of it. I swear, if you break this car, Matt..." He extended a hand, one finger pointed. "If you break this car, you'll be the one to fix it. You'll have no more handouts from me."

"I haven't asked for anything, have I?"

"Not yet."

"And I won't."

"Good," Tim muttered, his gaze still strong as he searched for the lever at his side. He swung open the door, using his elbow to assist as he hoisted himself to his feet, promptly slamming it shut behind him.

Outside, the dust that had filled the air soon began to settle, and loose pebbles crunched under the soles of his boots as he stretched, shaking off the stiffness in his legs.

Matt soon followed, making his way to the trunk of his car and, without another word, immediately popped open the boot.

"At least the rain's eased off," grunted Tim. "That's something." With the arch of his back, he let out a heavy sigh, taking in the view before him, a scene so picturesque and mind-pleasingly stunning that even he would quickly come to appreciate it.

The call of nature stretched out before them, a rugged landscape of untamed estate. Rolling hills clothed in heather and bracken rolled toward the distant horizon, where misty peaks touched the sky, their tops hidden by the grayness of low-passing clouds. Crisp, clean air filled their lungs as they stood by, carrying with it the scent of damp earth and pine from the nearby woodland, mingling with the faint aroma of moss and fallen leaves. Just below them, though not overly far, nestled in the hold of terrain, lay a small loch, its surface gleaming under the quickly fading light. Little more than the size of a football pitch in length, it mirrored the sky above, reflecting the changing shades of the evening and reminding Matt all too pressingly that darkness would rapidly descend.

"Buine Moire," remarked Matt as he sorted through the gear in his trunk.

His father looked back, breaking his trance from the scenery. "Bunny what?"

"Buine Moire," Matt repeated. "The name of the loch," he said, casting a glance in its direction. "Dead ahead."

Tim returned his gaze to the stillness of the water, his mind flustered as he panned from left to right. "That's where we're going?" he asked somewhat disapprovingly. "Down there? You've had us traveling all day to paddle about on that? Why," he huffed, "I've seen puddles bigger than that."

Matt lifted himself upright, his eyes closed with frustration, and with much effort, he masked the irritation in his voice. "That's just the pass, Dad."

"The what?"

"The way through." He stepped away from the car and stood beside his father, guiding his finger to a point. "You see where those two hills slope down and meet at the center, just there at the edge of the water?"

Tim followed his son's finger begrudgingly, acknowledging him with little more than a nod.

"That's where we're heading," confirmed Matt. "We'll get the gear out of the car, load it on the raft, and paddle across. From there, we'll follow the passage between the hills. There's an old stone wall, from what I've read. It marks the way and will lead us straight to Loch Lament, on the other side. We'll have to portage the boat and gear, of course. Two trips at most. But it doesn't look too far. Not on the map, anyway."

"Portage?" his father quickly asked.

"Carry, then."

"Carry!" echoed Tim. "What's this all about?" This whole trip was starting to sound less appealing by the second. "You mean to tell me that we brought the boat to ease the damn load only now to find ourselves having to carry it?"

Matt bit his lip, thinking of all the things he wished to say but wouldn't. "It's just a quick passage, Dad, that's all."

His father grumbled something under his breath as a steady breeze suddenly swept from the south, rustling the grass at their feet in gentle waves.

"Honest, Dad," Matt protested further. "It won't take us long. I've planned the whole thing out from start to finish."

With a sideways ogle, the bristles that partially covered his father's lips slowly began to part, merging into a smile. "You?" he chortled. "My boy, you've never planned anything. Not to precision, at least. You've always been the same."

Annoyed by the statement and feeling the redness of frustration starting to flush his cheeks, Matt swiftly delved a hand deep into the side pocket of his combats, pulling out a map that, on first appearance, looked just as weathered, just as worn and fed up as the old man he stood by. Regardless of his anger, Matt unfolded it carefully, mindful of the many creases, hoping not to tear them. He presented it to his father and, with one finger, pressed it down on the very location they stood.

A small road ran along the course of a loch, that loch. "See what it says there?" asked Matt, tapping promptly to the crinkled page, eager to gain his father's respect. "It says Buine Moire," he stated bluntly. "And see here?" His finger traced across the loch, coming to a stern halt where a faint black line marked the passage through hills. "That's our route. We'll carry the boat first, come back for the gear, and by the time it hits a little before dark, we'll soon find ourselves at the edge of Loch Lament, the whole reason why we traveled this far in the first place. From there, it's just a short paddle across the water to camp one." He shifted his finger once more, hovering it just below a scrap of land where a small patch of green stuck out of the water, a woodland island no less, roughly half a mile off shore. "That's our spot for the night. Quiet. Peaceful. Everything you wanted when you agreed to come along." He straightened out the half-folded map with the flick of his wrist and handed it to his father.

Tim took it without so much as a word, fighting against the

breeze that had, within but a moment, suddenly churned into a harsh and bitter gust, sending corners of the map to flitter. He studied it with the keenest of interest, taking exact note of the small island his son had crudely circled in black biro ink.

In truth, it had always been a desire of his to camp on a deserted island, even as a child, cutting himself off from the world as he knew it. It was a childish dream but, still, a dream nonetheless. And if he didn't do it then, showed a little faith in his son, offering him a chance to secure that lost boyish dream of his, well, he knew all too well he would likely never come across such a chance again. Not in his lifetime.

Tim paused, his mind elsewhere as he solemnly arched back his neck to look at the clouds.

The afternoon light had already begun to dim, casting a dullness on the distant mountains soon to become nothing but silhouettes against the canvas of a darkened sky. It was beginning to get colder, too, a few degrees lower, since they first jumped out of the car.

Tim turned on one heel, facing point blank at the car, took view of his son, who by then had abandoned collecting the gear and stood leaning, beaten, against the boot, his hands nestled warmly in his pockets.

"You..." Tim swallowed back his words. "You think we could make it before dark?" he asked. "The island?"

Considering the question, Matt pushed himself sluggishly off the car, the expression that once painted his face quickly merging to one of serious concentration.

"If we threw all the kit together and set off now, I reckon we'd stand a chance. It would have to be now, though," insisted Matt. "No more dallying, no more delays, not unless you fancy paddling blind."

Looking back to the map, his father breathed in deeply, exhaling through his nose as he gave a subtle nod. "All right," he answered quietly, back pacing his steps to the car. "Then let's make some headway."

In little time at all did they have everything unloaded from the car, each item laid tidily upon the mossy ground. The boat, an inflatable two-man raft with white stripes that ran along the course of its length, sat ready and waiting on the bank. The stern was knotted tightly to a nearby rock, secure against any chances of the boat going adrift.

Collecting two bags at a time, they traveled back and forth, gathering whatever necessities they had packed some days before. It mainly consisted of six dry bags, one of which contained several days' worth of food, a brew kit, two small gas canisters, a change of clothes, a small hiking tent, and a rather large helping of whisky. Nothing of expense by any means, just the required items needed for such a trip.

Weight had always been a major factor for journeys like this, ensuring that each item bought along was planned with thought, cautiousness. After all, what you packed you carried. There was no other way about it. The last thing either of them wanted was to haul heavy bags, exhausting themselves before the trip had a chance to begin. Yes, there was the boat, which was, in many ways, the backbone of the whole operation. But much weight made heavy work, even for casual paddlers such as them. So, with keeping things light, their needs minimal, it was in Matt's eyes the only way to go.

As for the rest of their resources, they would have to find them about the camps. Water could be filtered and boiled from the loch for drinking, which was easy enough. Dead wood could be gathered for fires to keep them warm at night. Even a spot of fishing using makeshift rods was possible, if time allowed it. Matt always made sure to pack some wire, just in case. The area was well renowned for the different types of fish that homed Lament's waters, especially trout, a real delicacy for any wild camper.

In a little more than ten minutes, the boat was packed and ready, the bundles of drybags stored at either end—two at the bow, three on the stern's deck—simply for ease of steering and secured by means of frayed bungee cords Matt had swiped from his parents' garden gate.

Tim settled himself up front, determined that he should be the one to steer the way. However, Matt did nothing to protest his demand. Nor, in truth, did he really give a toss. Instead, he untied the rope that moored them and gently pushed the boat into open water, his father clinging on for dear life as the boat began to rock and wobble, the sound of its beached hull scraping away from the shore. Then, as quickly and seamlessly as any man could, Matt stepped into the raft and eased himself into a snug position at the rear.

With oar in hand, combined with the long-awaited anticipation of unknown days ahead, he contentedly yet calmly placed the paddle to the water's surface and steadily began to row.

They made it to the other side of the small loch much quicker than either expected, the wind at their backs aiding them all the way and conserving what strength they had after such a long day on the road. Just as Matt suggested, they trudged their way through the spongy ground that ran between the hillsides, following a crumbling stone wall that served as a path to guide them.

The boat was portaged first, a big, bulky thing to carry, especially on uneven ground. Heavy didn't begin to describe the weight. By the time they returned with bags in hand and reached the banks of Loch Lament, the last traces of daylight had begun to fizzle from the sky.

For some time they stood there, their heaving breaths calming to a wheeze as both looked out at the view before them, a gigantic loch with no end in sight, its waters waving with the rush of each gust. At either side, rocky mountains climbed up all around them. The view beyond was lost to the misty veil that shrouded the distant peaks, their colors almost mislaid in the bleakness.

Shielding his face from the wind, Matt tunneled his view to the water ahead, catching a dark patch of land that sat just above the moving surface, much farther out than he dared to admit.

"That's it!" His voice raised over the gale. "The island I told you about. The one on the map. Camp one."

"I remember," replied his father, pulling up the hood of his coat.

"We should keep moving."

With not a moment's hesitation, Tim retied the cords on the boat, securing the bags in place once more. He looked up at the sky, a sky so dark and brooding that it seemed like the biggest mistake to challenge it.

"Maybe we should just make camp here for tonight?" he called, hoping to catch his son's ear.

Matt looked up, his body hunched, hands grabbing the bow, ready to launch the raft into the water. "Huh?"

"I said," Tim cupped a hand to his mouth, "maybe we should just camp here for tonight. Back over there." He pointed over his shoulder. "Near that wall. It won't help much, but it would keep the wind off us. We'll crack on at first light, ay? See what the weather brings."

"But…" Matt released his grasp, pulling himself up to full height. He looked out at the murk of land in the distance, quickly returning to the old man's stare. "If we don't make it across there tonight, the entire schedule is ruined. We'll be giving up at the first hurdle. It'll push us back a day, maybe more if we let the weather stop us. Plus, we don't have enough food or the time to spare. We're expected back, remember?"

"I just think—"

"We'll be fine." With a swirl of frustration, Matt waved off his father, his jaw visibly tensed, teeth gritting with the words that followed. "You're being over cautious. I get it. But we can do this. The wind, it'll likely die down when we're out there."

"Or get worse," remarked his father bluntly. "It could tip us."

"Oh, stop fussing, will you!" snapped Matt, dismissing any concerns his father had with a stubborn flick of his wrist. "Look. The least we can do is try. If it gets too rough out there, the water too difficult, we'll turn back, camp here, all right?"

Tim paused for a moment, his breath still strained from the trek they already made. He zipped his coat to his chin, the tassel flapping like a flag in a storm, and simply answered, "All right."

"Good!" acknowledged Matt without so much as a second thought. He resumed his bent posture, grabbed hold of the raft, and prepared to heave it forward. "You ready or what?"

"When you are," answered his father, building up the stamina to push as both heels sank into the soft, mossy earth.

With a quick jerk, the raft slid back into the water, its wide body gliding across the surface with ease.

With nothing more to be said, both men hurriedly took their positions, oars striding at their sides, churning the blackened water. The only thought shared between them was to reach the island unharmed.

Much to their surprise, they found themselves on the west side of the island without so much as a bother, and just in the nick of time too. The world around them had quickly slipped into darkness, a picture of pitch blackness that blocked any chance of visibility just a short distance ahead. Fortunately, to their relief, the wind had ceased its mighty gale as quickly as it had begun. The howling moan that had swept around them, stinging their faces, settled into a lulling hum, soon disappearing altogether.

With the welcoming sound of pebbles grinding beneath them, both father and son stepped out into the shallows, pulling the raft to the cove.

As Matt quickly rummaged through the depth of their dry bags, retrieving a single flashlight, Tim set to work securing the boat to the closest tree he could find, double knotting the rope and pulling it tight, anxious of the weather's unpredictable change. All it would take was for the weather to shift and one strong gust would have the boat away, sodding off wherever the forces of nature would take it, leaving them utterly and completely stranded. There would be no way of getting back. Tim was taking no such chances.

After a rather quick investigation of the bay and not wanting to risk fumbling around in the dark for too long, they found themselves camped on the peak of a small incline, where a course of dry, rank grass and scattered trees above did little to shelter the ground.

Matt, as impatient as he was, struggled with setting up the tent, battling with poles and pegs that resisted being anchored in the rocky earth.

Meanwhile, his father ventured out in search of dead wood, collecting whatever he could scavenge to start a fire. If the day hadn't been cold enough already, the night's chill had certainly begun to get to him, seeping into his bones and numbing his toes. With a stroke of luck, he returned to the camp with plenty of wood, enough to sustain them through the evening, at least. Kneeling with hatchet in hand, he got to it, chopping the dry pieces into kindling, his focus never once swaying, his tongue never wagging, until their camp was burning bright.

With the tent finally pitched and the inviting heat drawing them close, both young man and old sat slumped on the ground next to the crackling campfire, embracing the heat that washed over them in waves. In no time at all were they warm from end to end. The smoke spiraled up into the stillness of the night, weaving through the many naked branches that barely obscured the canvas of stars overhead. As dazzling as they appeared, both agreed, their necks cranked back to the sky, that they had never witnessed a night display quite like it, all those pinks and greens merging as one. It was a memory that would be shared. At least, both cared as much to think so.

Matt cooked, as was often the way when he went off on such an adventure. And although he never classed himself as a skillful cook, he enjoyed the task all the same, no matter its simplicity. With a small flask, he collected water from the loch's edge, careful not to lose his footing and find himself drenched right through. The water was filtered then boiled before being poured into the brew kit, which dangled over the crackling flames, containing nothing but a simple meal of pasta and powdered cheese. After a short wait, the pot began to spit and gurgle, the smell alone causing their bellies to grumble and their mouths to involuntarily water.

They ate heartily, their stomachs full and bloated, their minds for the first time that day content at the thought of something hot inside them, though it wasn't anything fancy. Not by any means. But never had such a bland meal tasted so wonderful as they sat there, relishing every bite, licking their bowls spotless, sharing laughter that echoed through the night. For the first time in years, they found comfort in each other's company, forming a bond that was long overdue.

Once they ate their fill and the hot tea, which had been brewing for some time over the embers, came to steam, Matt couldn't resist but talk of the days ahead—the plan of a circular route that would see them through dashing rivers, long-forgotten woodlands, and even the chance of spotting a ruin or two along the way. Old dwellings, he called them, abandoned by families many years before, some as far back as the seventeen hundreds.

And for the first time since Matt could remember, his father, who lay sprawled on his side, his arm supporting him upright, simply listened with a newfound interest, his confidence in his son seemingly revived. He nodded in agreement to all that was said, his brown eyes mirroring the same excitement of the man who sat across from him, his own flesh and blood.

"You've done good," said Tim as he threw back the dregs, his hot breath clouding the camp as he exhaled.

To say that Matt was stunned was by far an understatement. In fact, he was damn well speechless. In that moment, he didn't know what to say or think. He had never so much as received a compliment in all his adult years, not a real one, anyway. The closest Tim had ever come to praise for his son was congratulating him on a promotion at work. Even then he failed miserably, immediately asking him when he was going to buck up and chase a real career. So, when Matt heard those three words effortlessly fall from his father's lips, well, he decided to say nothing at all. He would take it for what it truly was, a sentiment for all his time and planning, one his father meant from the heart. He would savor it for as long as time would allow. It would fade eventually, as good things often did, but not that night. No, that moment was his. He could repeat it in his mind as much as he wanted, relive it over and over again. And as the hour turned late and the land grew colder, covering the grass about them with a touch of glistening frost, soon did they both find themselves huddled in the small confinements of the tent, each cocooned inside a sleeping bag, eager for the days ahead to commence as they fell into the heaviest of sleeps.

THEY AWOKE EARLY THE FOLLOWING MORNING TO THE SUDDEN sound of heavy raindrops slapping against the roof of their tent. And in that moment, the wind around them seemed almost determined to sweep the ground from beneath them, causing the canvas to billow.

Matt raised his head, his eyes barely open to a squint as he took view of his watch. It was indeed early—so early, in fact, that his alarm wasn't set to go off for several more hours. Even on camping trips like this, he never let that habit slip. Still, he thought little of it as he rested his head back down, listening to the world outside, the rustle of hanging limbs overhead, the hiss of grass near his ear. If all his years of camping had taught him anything, it was that you could never count on a good night's sleep, no matter how much you wished it. *It was all part of the experience*, he thought, the thrill of the wild and all that.

He closed his eyes, feeling the hand of sleep begin to take him, when from beyond the flapping canvas, the sound of footsteps trudged above his head. Matt jerked upright, his hair all cocked from where he lay, and twisted to face his father, ready to stir him from sleep. However, the old man was gone. The space beside Matt vacant. The sleeping bag lay empty, scrunched in a pile near the opened hatch.

With no delay, Matt found himself on his knees, unzipping himself from the bag in a hurry as he crawled his way out, his head peeking through the hatch.

Outside the tent, the small island stood dim and dismal in the early setting. The first morning light was barely discernible as Matt cast his gaze to the clouds, so thick and stuffy that they resembled thick cotton wool. On the ground, puddles lay spread across the soft and boggy earth, the rain growing even heavier than just a short moment ago, pounding down from the heavens, swamping the camp all the more.

With a quick look back, Matt swiped his coat, throwing it over his shoulders as he attempted to stand, digging his heels into his boots. He looked around, shielding his face from the rain's spray, instantly wishing he was back inside where it was warm and dry. His search (if you could call it that) didn't last long, merely seconds, as Matt's attention diverted to the cove, his father standing at the rocky shore, back toward him, overlooking the roughness of the waves.

Wind thrashed along the surface of the loch, a gale so fierce and harsh that it whipped the water into a froth of churning currents that smacked along the shoreline. Gone was the stillness of its glassy surface they had witnessed just the night before. Vanished was the quietness that once surrounded them. In little time at all, the land had changed, its manner altered by a raging storm that lashed over the island and sent torrents of water cascading down the slopes. The whispers of the breeze were replaced by howling winds, and the once-peaceful loch now surged with furious waves, matching the wild, darkened sky above.

"What are you doing?" Matt called out, his voice barely heard as he paced toward his father, both feet plunging through the squelch of flooded ground.

His father looked back over his shoulder, chin dripping with water. "What?" he grunted, drifting back toward the scene. "The rain, it woke me. Fine weather, you call this?" He shrugged with a shudder. "Thought I best check on the boat, that's all. Make sure it hadn't blew off. I'm no dab hand when it comes to knots. Far from it." He spat the rain from his lips. "Call me paranoid, but I thought it best to be sure."

They cast their gazes a few yards ahead, watching as the small blue boat (still moored) bobbed about the shallows, battering amongst the rocks.

"So," Tim pressed, "what's the plan?"

"Plan?"

"We don't intend to move on in this, surely?" asked his father, guarding himself from the gust that forced his hood to flitter. "Not a cat in hell's chance! The wind is too strong and the water too choppy. We'd be thrown to the depths if we even so much as tried."

Matt paused, his body already beginning to shiver from the cold as he looked out onto the water, just about making out the nearest land in the distance. Not overly far, yet far enough, especially under such conditions. His father was right, and he wasn't begrudged to admit it. Should they have made their move and attempted to cross, the waters would show no mercy. They would topple overboard, likely drown. No, it was far too risky.

"We'll have to wait it out," suggested Matt, catching a swift nod of agreement from his father. "We have enough food to last us. Plus, this weather can't last." He looked up to the sky, the clouds dark and sinister. "Still, I think it's best to check in with home. You know, let them know we're all right. I have no phone signal. I checked a few times last night. How about you?"

"Nay," replied Tim without so much as thinking. "Not since we fueled up the car. Even then it was dicey."

With instincts kicking in, Matt spun round on his heels,

surveying the course of the small island as it raised to a grove of trees that crowned the small hill's top.

"We'll try up there." Matt gestured, his hand slicing through the rain. "The higher we go, the better, I guess?"

Tim followed his son's direction. The mere thought of climbing the steep and stony incline caused his knees to scream. Still, he didn't let it show. "The trees should keep us sheltered enough, at least there's that. Come on then," sighed Tim. "Let's give it a whirl."

WITH GASPING BREATHS, THEY CLIMBED THEIR WAY TO THE HILL'S crest, grabbing on to anything in their path for leverage, the wind causing the trees to crack and moan on passing.

By the time the peak was reached and both phones were elevated from their pockets, not a single bar of signal could be had. Not one. Nothing. Their efforts were wasted. They headed back to the camp, neither uttering so much as a word between them.

As unbelievable as they thought possible, the weather began to worsen, sending leaves swirling and blades of grass tumbling chaotically about their feet. A sound so low and menacing, it seemed to quake the very ground they stood on, setting their hearts pounding. With much effort did they finally find themselves back at the base of the hill and clear of the trees, their bodies freezing and exhausted.

"Well, that's just fuckin' marvelous!" barked Tim. He bent forward, cupping his knees while he tried to catch his breath. "What now?" he huffed.

Matt studied the sky, listening to the far-off rumble as a flash of light torched its way along the horizon, for a split second giving view to the shape of hazy mountains.

"You grab the bags, throw them in the tent," urged Matt. "The weight should stop the pegs from slipping. I'll check the boat again."

There was no argument. There wasn't time for such as Matt's strides quickened back toward the cove. He pulled in the boat, checking that the knots were still tight and that the rope remained securely tied around the tree, free of any fraying. All seemed secure enough. For the moment he was happy, as happy as he could be. Without further delay, he shot off like a bolt, leaving the shallows of the rocky shore behind him, his boots spraying up water in his wake.

It took only a moment for Matt to return to camp. He caught a glimpse of the tent flapping in the gale, with only the last few pegs fighting to hold it down. Right beside it, his father stood, his lips trembling from the cold as he waited. His expression was blank and glum as watched his son approach.

"What is it?"

"The bags!" Tim called out, nose flaring.

"Uh?"

"THE FUCKIN' BAGS!" he yelled again, swiping down at sodden grass. He threw his hands up, seemingly in surrender, landing on the rear of his head. "I left them here." He circled the ground. "They were bloody well here!"

A sinking feeling clutched in the pit of Matt's stomach, a feeling so bleak and overwhelming that it almost made him sick. The food they packed—it was nowhere to be seen.

"You're sure?" asked Matt. He made his way closer to the tent, scanning the grounds. "You didn't move them from here?"

"If I had, do you really think I'd be standing here telling you that the bleedin' things are missing? No," he answered himself, "I damn well wouldn't. They're gone, I tell you!"

Another gust of wind slammed into their backs, nearly knocking them off balance. The rain lashed against them from every direction, stinging their faces like tiny needles. They staggered forward, heads down, arms reaching out for anything to hold onto as the storm raged around them.

In the distance, Matt's attention suddenly shifted to a scene unfolding across the churning waves. Something lurked out there. Out on the water. Not just one thing, but several, bobbing with the motion of the loch.

"No..." he whispered, although not quiet enough for the worried old man not to hear. "No, no, no!"

Tim raised his brow at that, his expression partially hidden by his draping hood. "What are you harping on about?"

"Look!" Matt pointed. He watched their belongings go farther adrift, soon to become nothing more than mere specs on the water, then to nothing at all. "The wind... It must've... It must've knocked them down the bank, rolled them straight into the water. The food, Dad!" Matt panicked, his heart drumming in his ears. For a moment or two, he actually thought he would be sick after all. He felt faint, his body weak, until he felt the touch of a palm on his shoulder.

"Get inside the tent," Tim insisted, his voice calm and steady, a reaction Matt would never have expected from his father, not under the current circumstances. "We'll dry off inside, wait it out. Damn storm surely has to pass over soon. When it does, and only then, we'll grab the boat, get the hell off this piss-ant island."

Despite the situation, there was something about his father's level-headedness that instantly made Matt feel a little better, perhaps stronger, as he crouched through the flap of the tent. With a grunt and a groan, they crawled inside and lay flat on their backs, their breaths hoarse, listening to the fury from above.

"Do you really think we can hold out?" asked Matt. He closed his eyes, waiting for his father's response.

"What other choice do we have?"

THEY TRIED TO SLEEP THROUGHOUT THE DAY, THEIR SLUMBER broken only by the relentless thunder that boomed and crackled across the sky. When Matt finally lifted his head, he noticed the interior of the tent was darkening. Glancing at his watch, he was shocked by how much time had passed while lying there.

His stomach growled in protest as the hours meandered by. They hadn't eaten anything since the previous evening. Not a scrap. Not that there was anything to be had. As he lay there, Matt couldn't help but think of his supplies just floating around out there, all the food that could've satisfied his hunger, his father's hunger. More so, that there was nothing he could damn well do about it.

Anger welled up inside him, directed not only at his father but also at himself. He should have known better. He should have been more responsible, more prepared. It was a rookie mistake, one that any seasoned camper would have known better than to make. Yet he had managed to do it, now burdened by the consequences.

"I could just about eat some of that shite pasta you cooked right now," said Tim through the bleakness, his voice tired and filled with sleep.

Matt turned on his side and watched his father, whose eyes stared widely at the ceiling, his expression empty of feelings. "You think it's settled anymore out there?"

A brief pause filled the tent as they listened, hearing the rain as it bounced off the canvas, splashing to the puddles on the ground.

"Not yet," replied his father calmly as he rubbed his hands for warmth. "I've been listening for most of the day. Couldn't drift off."

"Me neither," answered Matt. "It's too fuckin' cold. Maybe we should get a fire going?"

"And where would you suggest we light it, uh? The firewood is soaked through, and it's pissin' down out there. Plus, you've lost the fuel, the matches, right? What's your plan, rub sticks together?"

Matt jerked upright on alert. "*I* lost it?"

"Oh, you know what I meant," huffed his father with the roll of his eyes. "Don't be so damn sensitive."

"Maybe we should just risk it?" pressed Matt, falling to his back. "Just grab the boat and scarper."

Without so much as looking toward his son, Tim shook his head. "It would be a fool's errand," he remarked disapprovingly. "Venturing out in that? In the dark, no less. No." He gave his head another firm shake. "We'll wait until morning, see where we stand." With that, Tim shuffled onto his side without another word, the earth squelching beneath him.

It soon turned dark. The hour was late as Matt lay there still, his thoughts drifting with the blackness that surrounded him. He couldn't believe how it all had turned out. All he ever wanted was a trip to remember with his father—a time spent together away from the family's bickering, the day-to-day life. Something to look back on and reminisce about, a few days to remember how close he and his father really were (or could be). That was why he planned the trip from the get-go, choosing the most remote, most secluded place he could find—a place where they would be alone, undisturbed, without so much as a soul to bother them.

Still, regardless of how things had turned out, his conscience continued to gnaw at him, much like the weather as it continued to brew and spread across the land. He knew he hadn't been entirely truthful with his father. Yes, he knew that all too well. Nor had he considered the costs of his plans to bring the old man out here. After all, it was supposed to be nothing but a camping trip. How should he have known it would end up this way? How should he have known that all the things he heard and read, researched, would ultimately see them in this exact predicament? He wasn't to know. Still, he had to say something, didn't he? No matter how much he wished otherwise. He had to be truthful now more than ever. He needed to do right by his father.

"Dad?" said Matt, nudging Tim sternly.

The old man's snore broke off into a ramble of coughs and mumbles. "Huh? The weather..." he asked in a daze. "Has it cleared?"

A flash of lightning lit up the innards of the tent, followed by a drum of thunder that shook the ground, before plummeting them back into darkness.

Matt grabbed the flashlight, cautious of how long the batteries would truly last. "No." He tilted an ear at an angle. "At least, I don't think so."

"Then what the hell did you wake me for?"

"I needed..." He gave it some thought. "I need to talk to you."

"Talk?" His father snarled. He lifted his head from the crook of his elbow. "You woke me to talk?"

"It's this place." Matt hushed, the clearest of tremors forming in his voice. "I should have told you... I should have been honest from the start."

"Honest?" echoed Tim, his expression showing that of pure confusion. "Honest of what?"

His son took a much needed breath, slow and steady. "This place. The storm. It isn't the first time it's happened. Nor is it the first time it's seen others trapped."

"Others?"

"This place. It's known for such things, such weather, for people to get in trouble."

Tim paused, holding his tongue. His patience was already wearing thin. He wasn't in the mood for this. No, not in the slightest. He was cold, on the verge of starving, the hunger pains he kept quiet throughout the day gnawing and chewing at his stomach. The last thing he needed to top it off was his son's outbursts of riddles.

"Spit it out!" pressed his father, his tone no longer calm and collected.

Matt bit down on his lip. "People, they have died out here."

"Died!" his father snarled at the thought. "What do you mean, died?"

"You need to believe me." Matt spoke desperately, his eyes as wide as saucers. "I didn't think, never expected for the same situation to happen again. Not to us. I thought it was all just stories, luck of the draw, the media's attempt to sway people from coming out here. You know what they're like. They'd do anything to push a negative story in your face, to make things sound so much worse than they really are. It's good for tourists, thrill seekers. I—"

"Who died out here?" urged Tim. It was a question that deep down he didn't wish to know the answer to. "How many?"

"A good handful," answered Matt somewhat passively. "Five, maybe six over the past ten years. All of them campers passing through Lament."

"But how?"

"How?" repeated Matt.

"How did they die out here?"

Casting his mind back as best he could, Matt tried to remember the articles he had researched online when initially planning the trip. He had seen photographs too, investigation snapshots from police statements where searches organized by the estate's local council had already been well underway.

"I don't know the details," said Matt. That was the truth as far as he could tell it. "There was a man who was walking a five-day hike of the surrounding lochs. He was in his late forties, I think. I can't quite remember. He managed to contact his family near Loch Assynt. It's roughly a mile away from here, told them he was heading over the mountains to Lament. No one ever heard from him again. The police expected him to have gotten lost somehow, said that the weather must have got the poor chap muddled, threw him off course, something like that. They never found him, mind, only his belongings, a backpack, on the north side of the shore, left in such a way that it looked as if he had simply placed it down to rest.

"Another time," Matt went on, "occurred when two kayakers spent a bank holiday weekend out here. They decided to make the most of it and tour the loch. Fishing hobbyists seems to ring a bell. They camped out here on the island. This island. But they never made it much farther than that. In fact, they didn't make it any farther at all."

"What are you saying? They didn't make it any farther?" Tim interrupted. "Get to the bloody point."

Matt shrugged. "I mean, they never left the island. That is, not unless they swam for it. By the time anyone reported they were missing, which, it's worth mentioning, wasn't until late the following week, the police found nothing but an old, battered tent left standing, shredded by the weather, their kayaks still moored, capsized near the east side of the island. The searches went on for weeks, of course. But eventually, it was wrapped up as an open-and-shut case, believing the two campers to have drowned. They never found the bodies, not so much as a trace of them. The waters are too dark around here, the crevices so deep that many of the loch's tunnels intertwine together. It would be near on impossible to search them, especially when one considers the strong currents. The locals say it's all just thrill seekers not giving the land the respect it deserves, getting themselves into trouble. Others say differently. The funny thing is, there are even more stories that are linked with this place."

"Like what?"

"Just odd phenomenon, I guess. Rumors, nothing more." Matt paused, acknowledging the creases of his father's frown. "People getting lost or stranded for days on end, seeing things."

"Things?"

"Shadows, figures in the corner of their eye, things that aren't really there, I guess. There isn't much you find about such things online, the odd blog post here and there. Some seem to be under the impression that they're responsible for the disappearances, that these shadowy things are the cause, taking people when they feel the time is right. Where they go, I don't know, and frankly, I don't want to. This place is unsettling enough at night without the added fear of monsters. It's best to keep a level head. I mean, really—a little panic makes people lose themselves, especially in situations like these. They make the craziest decisions without considering what's real or not."

Without delay, Tim unzipped his sleeping bag, snagging the zip in the fabric. He swung his legs out of the sack, struggling to his hands and knees.

"What are you doing?" asked Matt.

"We're leaving."

Before Matt even had the chance to reply, the beam of the flashlight dimmed, casting a fading shadow of his father that crawled along the inner wall. In truth, Matt never really believed in the stories he read. They were just tall tales, nothing more—meant to scare kids and keep them from wandering off and getting lost. He always thought it was childish, idiotic. But now, with the storm raging overhead, one thought filled his mind: it wasn't the weather that worried him so, but the unsettling possibility of something lurking just beyond the reach of the fading light.

IT TOOK LITTLE TIME AT ALL BEFORE THEY WERE STANDING ON THE island's cove. They pulled the raft to shore, the wind never ceasing to throw them off balance as Tim gathered the rope.

Matt looked back to their camp. "What about the tent?"

"Leave it," instructed Tim. He rolled back his sleeve, glancing at his watch. "If we head back now, there's a good chance of making it to the portage point before things get worse."

"We can't just leave it!" yelled Matt. "If anyone was to find it, they'd likely think someone got themselves into trouble and call the police. They'd have another search party on their hands. And what do you mean, worse?"

"Look," replied Tim, tossing the rope into the raft. "The sooner we get off this rock and back to the car, the better. There has to be someone we can call later? Maybe someone who cares for the estate? Don't they have rangers out here? We'll explain everything, tell them we got ourselves into a spot of bother, that we had no choice but to leave it. They'll understand. They'll likely just send someone out to collect the tent once the weather calms, all right?"

Matt cast another glance to the small, blue tent that thrashed in the howling wind, struggling to stay grounded. In some strange way he knew his father was right. It only made sense to leave it. After all, packing it up would only delay them further. It was time they simply didn't have.

"Fine, then," he said.

"Good."

With not a moment to spare, they climbed down to the boat, scrambling over the wet and slimy rocks, which caused them both to slip. Matt led the way, his father falling behind as he struggled to find his footing. It was when Matt made it to the raft, his foot cocked over the side, ready for the off, that a terrible sound pierced the air behind him. A sharp crack of sorts, like a brittle branch being snapped in two, followed by the most painful, most agonizing scream Matt swore he had ever heard. It sounded like something from a horror movie.

Over his shoulder, Tim lay awkwardly upon the jagged rocks, his teeth knitted, eyes streaming with pain so unbearable he couldn't help but voice it.

"FUCK!!!" Tim bellowed, his hand clasped to his mouth, desperate to cork a scream. He arched his back, straining to relieve the pain. "My leg!" he cried through his fingers. "My fucking leg!"

Without so much as thinking, Matt jumped out of the raft and retraced his path along the rockface, careful not to fall. By the time he finally made it, towering over his father with anxious breath, the old man's screams had already begun to dwindle.

"My foot," hissed Tim through his teeth. He bent his neck upright, eager to check out the damage. "It's stuck!"

In a panic, Matt crouched down to his knees, his hands shaking from the cold as he examined the position his father had managed to get himself in. "Your boot—you've got it pinned. It's wedged between the rocks here," said Matt. He reached out, grabbing the sole of his father's boot, and without thinking gave it a forceful tug.

"FUCK!!!" Tim screamed, his face turning all the paler for it. "Fucking idiot!"

"Sorry!" Matt replied. He really did mean it. In truth, it worried him deeply, seeing his father squirm in so much pain as he was, seeing the distress smeared across his face. With a tender touch, he reached out for his father's ankle, carefully rolling up the fabric of his trousers until he was forced to halt at the knee. Pausing there, he gawked at the injury, a sight so gruesome that it momentarily twisted Matt's stomach into knots. Suppressing the urge to retch, Matt observed the deep gash that ran along his father's leg, the blood oozing from the open wound, the skin a sickly shade of the plumpest purple.

"I think..." Matt hesitated, holding back the urge to gag. "I think you've broke something, Dad."

Tim's head lurched up, eyes all red and blaring. "No fuckin' shit, Sherlock!" he snapped. "Get me loose."

"How?" Matt looked back to the torn flesh hanging limply from his father's shin, his hairs all matted with blood. "It won't budge, not without force."

"The laces, untie them." His father's voice shook, reassuring his son as best he could. "Try to ease it out. Do it gently now, gently!" He let his head flop backward midair as the rain smacked down on his face.

With a held breath and steady hands, Matt did just that. He loosened the knot of his father's boot, his fingers stained with the old man's blood as he carefully began to slide out his foot.

"Careful!" tensed Tim, his face all scrunched with tears, holding back the torture inside him.

Despite the growling discomfort from his father, the process went smoother than Matt first expected—so smooth that he felt a tad embarrassed he hadn't thought of it in the first place. With little effort, his dad's foot was free. That, for the moment, was the main thing, as Matt breathed a sigh of relief.

"Now, come on. Help me up, will you?" demanded Tim, extending a hand to the sky. "Get me off this fuckin' rock."

The journey to the boat was in no way easy, an agonizing shuffle for the old man. Each step brought fresh waves of pain, each movement a chorus of suffering as cries escaped his lips, echoing the struggle riddled within him. With one arm wrapped around Matt's shoulder, he supported his father as best he could over the uneven rocks, the weight of his father's outbursts in his ear hitting him like a physical blow as he strained to catch his breath.

After guiding his father to the rear of the raft, Matt released his hold. He delicately raised Tim's blood-soaked leg, placing it carefully on the raised bench, observing the weary man grimace at any sudden movement that caused his body to jolt.

This is it, thought Matt. It was now or never. He had to move, and he had to move fast. No longer could they delay. He cast a quick glance to his old man, half passed out behind him, eyes drooping to a close as he fought to stay awake.

"Don't worry, Dad," Matt spoke softly. "We're going. We're getting out of here." He climbed into the raft, his attention never drifting from the old man's sickly face as he reached for the oar, thrusting it into the ground for the push off.

"I saw them," Tim mumbled, the words almost stolen by the chaos of the beating wind.

Matt swiveled quickly on his bench, his chin coming to rest on his shoulder, peering at his father, who lay still and silent.

"What, Dad?"

However, Tim offered no form of reply, not so much as a grumble in response; far too fatigued was he to try as the pain vanished from his face. In just a few seconds, his expression softened, his body surrendering to sleep.

THE DAYLIGHT HAD ALREADY BEGUN TO FADE AS MATT steered the boat to the south of the island, making sure to avoid the many rocks that lay hidden beneath the shallows. Water slapped against the side of the raft, determined to pull them closer to shore as Matt paddled through with energy he didn't know he had. With each stroke of the oar, he thrust them forward, little by little, his arms burning from the strain, until the small island gradually shrank in the distance. For the briefest moment, Matt stopped, exhausted, lifting the paddle from the choppy surface, trying to regain his strength. He looked back to check on his father, whose wound had already begun to layer the bottom of the raft with the darkest shade of red.

In the distance, the small island appeared bleaker, its shape fading in the rolling mist that hovered just above the water, climbing up the land. He could just about make out the west side they had come from, the faint outline of his tent left abandoned on the bank.

As his gaze traced the crest of the hillside they once walked together, weaving over the treetops and descending toward the water's edge, Matt caught sight of something that made his heart race—a fleeting glimpse that compelled him to look twice. There was someone out there standing on the rocky shore—a shadow. It lingered in the murk, its gaze fixed on him, never flinching, watching as the small raft floated farther adrift.

Without warning, a wave crashed against the side of the raft, jolting Matt from his seat, the cold spray stinging his skin. He clambered back up, the moment shattered as he directed his gaze to that very spot, the shadow haunting the edges of his mind. He looked to the shore, his eyes darting to the tree line, then to the bank where his tent still stood dancing in the storm. There was nothing. No one. Not a soul in sight. The island along the water stood empty, deserted, its presence fading more and more until eventually the mist consumed it whole.

It took the best part of several hours before Matt navigated his way back to the portage spot, several hours of fighting the choppy waters, his strength on multiple occasions giving up on him as the current beneath twirled and impeded the boat. In fact, he had almost given up hope. The way ahead turned to pitch black. So dark was it that not even the shine of the moon could pierce its way through the storm clouds, the rain forever blocking his view.

It was the faintest outline of two hills that raised some hope within him, a sight that had he not seen it would have sent him paddling entirely off course, making them lost all the more. Instead, he rotated the raft with a single oar, grunting with fatigue, his will to keep going sparked as he headed for the gap between the hillsides— the portage spot. His heart lifted at the thought.

The raft ran aground, beaching on the shore, a place that was so wonderfully familiar to Matt despite the cloaking darkness. He stumbled out of the boat, his legs numb from sitting, and found himself crouched beside his father.

"Dad?" Matt gave the old man a nudge. He had been bleeding out for the past few hours, the only sign he was still alive being the dreamlike mumbles as he slept. "Dad, can you hear me? We've made it to the portage."

Slowly, one of Tim's eyes opened to a slit, his neck just about raised as he looked up at the figure sitting before him, a face he was happy to see. A dreary groan passed his lips.

"I need you to wait here," insisted Matt. "Stay in the boat, all right?"

With much effort, Tim attempted to respond, his mouth hanging open, dry and parched, struggling to form the words. His body shook wildly, the cold clinging to him as he swiped for Matt's hand, refusing to let go.

"I'll come back," insisted Matt, his eyes as wide as saucers. "I... I won't be too long. I need to get to the car. There's a first aid kit, some pain relief too. We'll bandage that leg of yours, get you on your feet and off to the closest hospital. Just rest here, okay?" Matt peeled his father's fingers from his wrist, leaving the old man's hand to drop limply.

He spun on his heels, just about making out the old wall through the haze that would lead him back to Buine Moire. He no longer had the raft to see him across, but that didn't matter. In fact, it was the last thing he was worried about. The loch itself was small, and with a fast pace, Matt was sure it would take little time at all to walk around it, eventually seeing him back at the welcoming sight of the road, his car. What other choice did he have?

With a hoarse breath, Matt wasted no time. He trudged his way between the hill's gap, following the stone wall, his hand scraping along its top for guidance. Mud squelched beneath his feet, sometimes stopping his stride completely, sucking him down with each step as if trying to pull him to his knees. Yet he didn't give up. He couldn't, not when his father was back there, alone and scared to death. He needed to do this. If not for himself, then for his dad.

As expected, the wall ended, leading Matt to a short slope where the thicket surrounded the loch's edge, a place even in the blinding dark he somehow managed to recognize. The sound of water lapping against the shore could be heard, a sound that was in some strange way uplifting as he continued along the boundary of Buine Moire. However, the ground was more challenging than he had first anticipated. After walking only a few yards, he found himself climbing over steep, rocky terrain. It was a climb so hazardous that a simple misjudgment in footing could send him tumbling into the shallow pool below, scattered with sharp rocks. He tried to stay calm, his mind focused as the loose ground slid from under him, his thoughts unable to shake away the picture of himself falling, impaled by the waiting rocks below.

With a sigh of relief, Matt reached flatter ground. The woodland thickened as he increased his pace, marching through the trees and across a babbling brook, his teeth clenched as the cold water bit at his toes. He pressed on toward the incline that would lead him to the road, grabbing onto whatever branches were in his path as he crawled. It felt as though the journey would never end, that the way ahead was lost to him. The road gone. Vanished from sight.

Then, just as he crested the rise, he burst from the thicket and found himself standing on the verge of a dirt road. It stretched out before him, curving around the woodland: a welcomed sight. Relief washed over him as he took a moment to catch his breath, the weight of the wilderness suddenly lifting as he stepped onto the hard surface leading in the direction of the car.

The driver's door swung open as Matt leaped inside, reaching over to the glovebox, where the first aid kit was stored. He grabbed the kit in a panic and searched through its contents, hoping against hope that there was something to help his injured father. Glancing at the clock on the dash, he wondered how long it had taken him to find his way back, how long his father had been lying out there—alone, cold, and worried.

It was clear to Matt that he couldn't return the same way he came. He didn't know if he could do it all again, especially since his father wouldn't be able to manage the trek in his condition. If he was honest with himself, the very idea terrified him, the thought of carrying him back to the car. No amount of bandages or painkillers was going to change that. He would need to find a different route, a safer one.

Twisting on his seat, Matt climbed out of the car, his pulse racing as he slammed the door behind him and turned to retrace his steps. He stopped dead in his tracks, eyes wide with disbelief.

From the tree line, someone emerged, limping as they approached the car, the strain of the breath fogging the rain about their face.

The struggling steps approached.

"Dad?" Matt yelled, his voice croaking with the thought of seeing him. He ran toward his father, holding him tightly as he guided him closer to the car. "I told you to wait!" cried Matt, his emotions getting the better of him. "I said to stay in the boat!"

Matt swung open the passenger door, kicking it wide with his heel, causing it to rebound on its hinges. Carefully, he helped the old man inside, lifting his bloodied leg and resting it gently in the footwell.

Without hesitation, Matt slid behind the steering wheel, turning the ignition and starting the engine. He took a swift glance at his father, his heart still pounding. "How did you..." Matt looked the man up and down, unable to tear his eyes away from his clothes, all caked with blood. "Your leg... I have the bandages. Maybe we should—"

"Just drive," replied Tim, his voice distant, hazy, both eyes dropping to a close. "Just go."

Without another word, Matt stomped down on the accelerator, sending the tires into a frantic spin. They hit the dirt road in a hurry, following the route from which they came. The headlights cut through the darkness, lighting the trees that flanked the narrow route as they raced onward, eventually seeing them back onto the main road. It was approximately eighty miles to the nearest hospital. Still, Matt kept going all the same, his attention never drifting from the winding route despite his growing fatigue.

By the time they passed the back lanes of Ullapool, the rain had begun to lighten. The clouds above parted, revealing a half-moon that shone down, casting a silvery glow on the damp tarmac. In that moment, the landscape around them seemed to transform, shadows dancing with each turning as the light flickered through the treetops, creating a sense of normality as Matt eased his foot on the brake, turning the car in the direction of the highway.

It felt as though it had been the longest journey ever when they finally reached the outskirts of Inverness. Matt had been driving so long that he didn't know how he'd managed it. His thoughts raced as he drove the familiar roads, every bump a reminder of their situation, the events that brought them here, speeding along the darkened lanes.

Startled from the brink of sleep, Matt felt a touch on his arm, the shock forcing him awake as he turned to his father. For a moment or two, he had almost forgotten he was there.

"You need to rest," said Tim, his voice but a whisper over the grinding tires. "Stop for a minute."

With no desire of doing any such thing, Matt shrugged off his father's hold, shaking his head in defiance. "I can't do that, Dad. Not yet." He focused on the road ahead, determination etched on his face, focused to stay awake.

"You need to," replied Tim. He lifted his head, turning to his son. "I'll be all right. Just stop for a bit. You're tired."

With another touch from his father, Matt slowed the car to a steadier pace, pulling over to a grassy verge. There he sat, holding back tears, his breath on the verge of breaking as he rested his head against the window.

In that moment, he felt his body surrender, the panic in his mind beginning to fade as he exhaled a heavy breath. His eyes closed, and for the first time that night, the darkness felt almost welcoming—a relief as he let go of everything they had experienced together those past few days. As he slipped into the deepest of sleeps, his father's voice seemed to travel with him, reassuring him that everything would be all right.

For all that had gone wrong, he needed Matt to know, needed him to listen, as the world turned blank and quiet.

"You've done good, Son."

IT WAS HOURS LATER WHEN MATT FOUND HIMSELF AWAKE IN FRONT of the wheel. Daylight streamed through the windshield, the warmth of the sun a comforting feeling as he lifted his head from the seat.

Outside, trees swayed gently in the morning breeze, their leaves rustling softly. The world felt different now, better by the soft glow of morning sun.

For a moment, Matt allowed himself to breathe in deeply, reminiscing on everything that happened, how it all could have gone so much differently.

He turned to look at his father, a man who was braver and much stronger than Matt had ever given him credit for. He was shocked to find the seat beside him empty, the chair bare, holding nothing but a first aid kit. No blood upon the fabric, no trace of any kind—only the eerie stillness of a memory they both shared at Loch Lament and the haunting truth of the man he left behind.

THE RED THIRST

STEVEN PAJAK

I stare at the dirty bathroom mirror, trying to recognize the reflection staring back. My pupils are blown wide with fear. Or maybe it's the adrenaline. Or maybe it's the coke Danny insisted I snort to "steady my nerves." The harsh fluorescent light flickers above me, casting shadows across my too-pale face. Twenty-six years old and I look forty tonight.

Some fucking steady.

I splash water on my face one more time. My hands won't stop shaking. Droplets cling to my eyelashes, blurring my vision in a way that makes the world seem dreamlike. This isn't me. I'm not a stickup guy. I'm just a safecracker—the gentle touch. The artist. The ghost who melts through security systems without leaving a trace. In and out without anyone knowing we were there. That was the agreement when Danny found me six months ago, down on my luck and drowning in my mother's medical bills.

But Danny changed the plan. Danny always changes the *fucking* plan.

The bathroom door creaks open, the sound like a scream in the silence. Rex's massive frame fills the doorway, his shaved head gleaming under the buzzing lights. A tattoo of a snake coils up his neck, its fanged mouth open wide just below his ear. The irony isn't lost on me. Rex has always been the snake in Danny's grass.

"You still hiding in here?" Rex asks, his voice surprisingly gentle for a man his size. He scans my face, noting the sheen of sweat and the hollowness in my eyes. "Jesus, Mikey, you look like shit."

"Thanks for the update." I try to sound tough, but my voice cracks like I'm fourteen again.

Rex steps inside, letting the door swing shut behind him. He pulls out a small vial of white powder, tapping a small mound onto the back of his hand. "Here. Take the edge off."

I shake my head. "I'm already wired enough."

"It's not about getting high, man. It's about getting through." He offers his hand again, eyes softer than I've ever seen them. "Look, Danny's an asshole, we both know that. But he's right about one thing—this score is worth it. Your mom needs that treatment, right?"

The mention of my mother hits me like a punch to the gut. Four cycles of chemo, and the cancer's still spreading. The experimental treatment is her last hope, but insurance won't cover it. Eighty thousand dollars out of pocket. Might as well be eighty million for all I can afford it.

"Fine." I lean down and snort the bump off his hand. The familiar burn races through my sinuses, followed by the bitter drip down the back of my throat. Almost immediately, a numbness spreads across my face, and my heart rate kicks up another notch.

"There you go." Rex claps me on the shoulder, his meaty hand nearly buckling my knees. "Just stick to the plan. I'll keep an eye on you."

"What if someone gets hurt?" The question slips out before I can stop it, revealing the fear I've been trying to hide.

Rex's expression hardens slightly. "No one gets hurt if everyone cooperates. Simple as that." He pulls his gun from his waistband, checking the magazine with practiced ease. "Besides, these dive bar types? They'll be too drunk to play hero."

I nod, not trusting my voice.

"Time to go, Mikey." Rex's voice echoes against the grimy tile walls.

I close my eyes. Take a deep breath that fills my lungs with the stench of piss and cheap disinfectant. Wipe my wet palms against my jeans, leaving dark streaks on the denim.

The gun tucked into my waistband feels impossibly heavy, like it's made of neutron star material instead of metal. I've never fired a gun at a person. Never even pointed one at someone. After tonight, that will change. The thought makes my stomach coil into tight knots.

"Yeah," I finally say, voice steadier than I feel. "I'm coming."

THE RED THIRST SQUATS ON THE CORNER OF CLARK AND Orleans in Chicago's Near North Side like a forgotten relic from another time. Weathered brick, neon beer signs with at least half the letters burned out, and a hand-painted wooden sign with peeling letters. In the dark, if you squint just right, the faded red paint of "THE RED THIRST" looks almost wet, like fresh crimson dripping down the aged wood that somehow survived the Great Chicago Fire.

The street is quiet tonight. Too quiet for this part of Chicago, even on a Sunday. No drunks stumbling out of neighboring blues clubs, no tourists taking selfies beneath the skyscrapers, no L train rumbling overhead. Just empty parking spaces and flickering street-lights that cast more shadows than illumination across the cracked sidewalks. A place Chicagoans go to disappear for a few hours. Or forever.

But Danny swears it's a goldmine.

"Trust me on this one," he had said two nights ago, eyes gleaming with that manic energy he gets when he's onto something big. We were crammed into his studio apartment, the air thick with cigarette smoke and desperation. "My guy says the owner keeps all the cash in a safe behind the bar. We're talking thirty, maybe forty grand. All cash. Untraceable."

It sounded simple when he laid it out. Wait until closing time Sunday night when the weekend deposits haven't been made. Go in after hours, crack the safe, take the cash. No confrontation. No witnesses. Clean and easy, just how I like it.

But yesterday, Danny called with "slight adjustments" to the plan. And now we're doing it with masks and guns while the place is still open. Because Danny heard the owner might be moving the money tonight. Because Danny's "guy" said the regulars are all harmless old drunks. Because Danny is a fucking liability who can't stick to a plan to save his life.

I check my watch: 10:17 p.m. The night air is unseasonably cold for April, raising goose bumps along my arms. My breath comes out in visible puffs that dissolve into the darkness.

"All right," Danny whispers, his voice sharp with anticipation. "Rex, you cover the door. No one comes in, no one goes out. Mike, you keep the bartender in line and get behind that bar first chance you get. Find the safe. Do your thing."

I nod, not trusting my voice.

"And Mike?" Danny grabs my shoulder, fingers digging in painfully. "Don't pussy out on me. Not this time."

I swallow hard. Think about the money. Think about Mom withering away in that hospital bed, skin stretched thin over her bones, yellow like old paper. Think about finally paying off her medical bills that grow by thousands every day. Think about running away somewhere far from Danny and his "guaranteed scores" that never seem to go as planned.

Rex checks the magazine in his gun one more time, then cracks his neck. The sound makes my stomach turn. "Showtime, boys," he says with a predatory grin.

"Let's go," Danny says, pulling his ski mask down over his face. He becomes someone else entirely with the mask on—someone without limits, without conscience.

We push through the door, the weight of inevitability pressing down on my shoulders like a physical force.

There's a strange silence that falls when three masked men burst into a room. A heartbeat of suspended time where reality hasn't quite caught up to the interruption. I see it all with hyperfocus, the way you might notice every detail of the pavement rushing toward you during a fall.

The bar is dimly lit, with dark wood paneling that's absorbed decades of cigarette smoke. A handful of old men sit at scattered tables, hunched over their drinks like mourners at a wake. Behind the long mahogany bar stands a middle-aged bartender methodically polishing a whiskey glass, his movements unhurried. At the far end of the bar, almost swallowed by shadows, sits a solitary figure hunched over a drink. His face is hidden in the dim light down there, but something about the stillness of his posture makes my skin crawl.

Then Danny's voice shatters the moment like a brick through stained glass.

"NOBODY FUCKING MOVE!"

His scream is unnecessarily loud in the small space, bouncing off the walls and assaulting my eardrums. Rex slams the door behind us with a bang that makes me flinch, his massive frame blocking the exit as he stands guard. I move toward the bar as rehearsed, gun awkwardly extended. The weight of it pulls at my arm muscles, already tiring from holding it up.

But something's wrong. Terribly, inexplicably wrong.

The patrons don't scramble for cover. There's no screaming, no pleading, no raised hands. The old men look up with mild annoyance, as if we've just changed the TV channel during the last two minutes of a tied football game. A few even go back to their drinks, lifting glasses to lips with weathered hands marked with liver spots and scars. The bartender carefully places the glass he was polishing on the counter and folds the rag neatly beside it.

"Cash. Now." Danny storms toward the bar, wild-eyed behind his mask. There's a slight tremor in his hand—the cocaine kicking his adrenaline into overdrive.

"Of course," the bartender says, voice oddly calm, cadence measured like he's reciting something rehearsed. His eyes—pale blue and watery—don't register fear, just a strange resignation. "No need for anyone to get hurt." He moves to the register, each step deliberate.

Maybe this will work after all. My trembling subsides slightly as I edge toward the bar, eyes scanning for any sign of the safe. The mirror behind the liquor bottles reflects my masked face back at me —a stranger, a criminal, someone I never wanted to be.

"Wallets and phones on the tables!" Rex shouts from the door, voice booming as he waves his gun at the old men. He's enjoying this, the power trip evident in his stance. "NOW!"

With unhurried movements, they comply. One by one, they place worn leather wallets and outdated phones on the scarred wooden tables. No resistance. No fear in their rheumy eyes. Just calm acceptance, like they've been through this before. Too easy. Part of me starts to relax, muscles unclenching slightly, but something deeper knows—when things seem too easy, that's when you should worry most. My mother's voice echoes in my head: *Nothing worth having comes easy, Mikey.*

The register drawer slides open with a cheerful ding that seems obscenely out of place. The bartender counts out bills like he's a fucking bank teller, stacking them neatly before holding them out.

Danny grabs the stack of bills from the bartender's outstretched hand. He flips through them quickly, disappointment evident in the tightening of his shoulders. "That's it? Where's the rest?" His voice rises an octave, that dangerous edge creeping in that I've learned means trouble.

"That's all we have in the register," the bartender says, still unnervingly calm. A single bead of sweat trails down his temple, the only sign that he's affected by the situation at all. "Sunday nights are slow."

"Bullshit!" Danny shoves the gun in the man's face, pressing the barrel against his forehead hard enough to leave a circular indent in the flesh. "I know about the safe! Get it open!"

I'm hoping he'll comply. Cracking a safe, even the easy ones, takes time, and I don't want to spend another minute more in this place than I have to. The original plan was for me to work on the safe after hours, nice and quiet with no witnesses. No way that's happening now. And something about this place sets every nerve ending on fire, every instinct screaming at me to run.

The bartender doesn't even blink at the cold metal against his skin. "I'm afraid I don't have access to the safe," he replies, eyes flicking toward the end of the bar.

"What the fuck does that mean?" Danny snarls, spittle flying from his lips. "Who does, then?"

"The owner," the bartender says, casually.

"Where is he?" Danny growls. "The safe gets opened or I start splashing these walls with fucking brains."

The bartender's eyes slide again to the solitary figure sitting at the end of the bar. The one who hasn't moved or acknowledged us since we burst in.

A heaviness settles in the air suddenly, like the pressure drop before a violent storm. The fluorescent light above the bar begins to buzz more intensely, the sound drilling into my skull. My breath quickens, each inhale bringing less oxygen than the last, like the air itself is thinning. My heartbeat pounds in my ears, drowning out every other sound except that insistent buzzing. The cocaine in my system amplifies everything—every sensation, every fear.

Danny follows the bartender's gaze, agitation growing. He steps away from the bar, moving toward the end where the figure sits motionless, his untouched drink a dark crimson in the dim light. Something about the color makes my stomach turn. Too thick for whiskey, too dark for wine. It glistens with an oily sheen that catches the dim bar lights, moving almost with a life of its own within the glass.

"Hey! You deaf?" Danny calls out, irritation sharpening his words. "We're robbing this place! Put your wallet on the table and then open that goddamn safe."

The figure remains motionless, hunched over his drink. I notice now a strange stillness around him—not just that he isn't moving, but as if the air itself refuses to disturb him. The shadow he casts on the wall doesn't match his silhouette exactly, stretching and contracting slightly as if breathing on its own.

Rex shifts uncomfortably, moving a few steps away from the door, ready to back up Danny. "Something's not right," he mutters, just loud enough for me to hear across the room. His voice has lost its swagger, replaced by a tremor that sends ice down my spine. "These people aren't scared. Why aren't they scared?"

He's right. The typical reactions to an armed robbery—panic, fear, compliance born of terror—are entirely absent. These men act like we're merely an annoying interruption to their drinking. My mouth goes cotton-dry, and my palms sweat so badly I nearly drop my gun. The room seems to contract around us, the walls inching closer with each passing second. The distance between me and the exit suddenly seems impossibly vast.

"I'm talking to you, asshole!" Danny shouts, frustration boiling over. The floorboards creak ominously beneath his heavy footfalls, each step echoing far louder than it should in the small space.

"Danny..." I manage to croak out, my voice barely audible. "Maybe we should just go."

Danny shoots me a look of pure disgust. "Shut the fuck up, Mike. We're not leaving without that money."

Something cold slides down my spine, like a finger of ice tracing my vertebrae one by one. I want to tell Danny again to leave it, to take what we have and go. My throat closes around the words, tongue suddenly thick and useless in my mouth. I try to swallow but can't. Try to step forward, but my feet feel cemented to the floor.

Rex leaves his spot at the door and crosses the room, his massive frame tensing like a predator about to pounce. "Danny," he says, that tremor more evident in his voice. "Maybe Mikey's right. Something about this place..."

"Both of you grow a pair," Danny snaps, now just a few feet from the motionless figure. "Look at me when I'm talking to you!" He reaches for the man's shoulder, fingers outstretched to grab the worn leather jacket the figure wears.

In those few seconds before contact, time seems to stretch and warp. That same suffocating pressure returned, thicker now, like trying to inhale underwater. The lights flicker once, twice, casting the room in stuttering shadows. A ringing starts in my ears, high-pitched and insistent, like the whine of a mosquito magnified a thousand times. The temperature plummets, and I can see my breath clouding before me though we're indoors. My skin prickles with goose bumps, fine hairs standing on end as static electricity fills the air.

The moment Danny's fingers make contact with the leather jacket, the world changes.

The movement is so fast I almost miss it. The stranger's hand shoots out, clamping around Danny's wrist. The skin of his hand is papery, mottled with age spots, yet the grip must be iron because there's a sickening crack that echoes off the walls—the unmistakable sound of bones splintering under pressure.

Danny's scream is primal, tearing from his throat with such raw agony that goose bumps erupt across my skin. His gun clatters to the floor as he drops to his knees, his wrist bent at an impossible angle— bones protruding through skin in jagged white spears. Blood drips onto the floor in a steady patter that sounds obscenely loud in the sudden silence.

Rex recovers from his shock first, swinging his gun toward the stranger. "Let him go! NOW!"

The stranger finally turns, and for the first time, I see his face.

He looks ordinary at first glance. Middle-aged, maybe older. Weathered skin mapping a topography of wrinkles and creases. Salt-and-pepper stubble along a strong jawline. But his eyes—God, his eyes are solid black, like polished obsidian, reflecting the dim bar lights like tiny stars drowning in oil. No whites. No iris. No humanity. Just endless, hungry darkness. As I stare, unable to look away, I swear something moves within those depthless pools—shapes writhing and swimming just beneath the surface.

He smiles, revealing teeth that seem too sharp, too numerous for a human mouth. They gleam wetly in the light, each one shaped like a tiny dagger. Some appear to shift positions, rearranging themselves as his smile widens beyond what a human jaw should allow.

"You picked the wrong bar," he says, voice like gravel being crushed beneath a heavy boot. Each word falls with the weight of a tombstone. But there's something else underneath—a second voice, deeper, older, speaking the same words a fraction of a second later, creating a disorienting echo effect that seems to reverberate directly in my brain rather than my ears.

Rex fires—once, twice, three times in rapid succession, the muzzle flashing orange in the dim light. The shots are deafening in the small space, each one like a physical blow against my eardrums. The acrid smell of gunpowder burns my nostrils.

I expect to see blood, to see the man fall, to see his head explode in a spray of red mist and gray matter.

Instead, he stands perfectly still, not even rocking back from the impact. Three dark holes appear in his chest, through the worn fabric of his flannel shirt. But there's no blood. The holes seem to seal themselves before my eyes, the fabric knitting back together like time running in reverse. The skin beneath pulses and writhes as though something is moving underneath it—something with too many limbs.

Then three flattened bullets drop from his chest as though they've hit solid steel, not flesh. They ping against the wooden floor in perfect synchronization with my hammering heartbeat, the sound unnaturally loud in the sudden silence.

"Jesus Christ," Rex breathes, his face draining of all color. "What the fuck are you?"

The creature—because I know now that's what he is—tilts his head, studying Rex with the detached curiosity of a scientist examining a specimen under glass. Something shifts beneath the skin of his face, momentarily distorting his features like there's something trying to push its way out from inside.

"I've been called many things through the centuries," he says mildly. "But I prefer 'proprietor' these days." He gestures around the bar with his free hand, still gripping Danny's shattered wrist with the other. "Welcome to my establishment."

That's when I start backing toward the door, shoes sliding on the sticky floor. This isn't a robbery gone wrong. This is something else entirely. Something impossible. My brain scrambles to make sense of what I'm seeing, but there's no rational explanation for bullets bouncing off human flesh. The edges of my vision darken, tunneling until I can only see the creature and Danny. Sounds become muffled, like I'm underwater, except for the creature's breathing, which grows louder, taking on a wet, ragged quality.

I reach the door, trembling hands fumbling for the lock Rex engaged just minutes earlier. My fingers slip on the cold metal, unable to grip properly. I throw my shoulder against the door in desperation, but it doesn't budge. It's like hitting solid concrete. My bones rattle with the impact.

Rex fires again, pressing the gun directly against the creature's temple. The bullet exits through the other side, taking a chunk of skull with it—but it's like punching a hole in water. The wound closes instantly, the missing piece reforming as if it had never been damaged. But before it closes completely, I catch a glimpse of something inside—not brain matter, but a viscous, dark substance that pulses with its own rhythm.

"Your weapons are useless here," the creature says, almost sympathetically. "Though I do enjoy the sensation. Like being tickled from the inside."

With frightening suddenness, he lifts Danny by his broken wrist. Danny howls in agony, feet dangling inches above the floor. The creature's movements become fluid, no longer constrained by human limitations. I hear a series of wet pops and cracks as bones realign themselves beneath his skin, stretching his frame upward until his head nearly touches the ceiling.

"What are you going to do to us?" Rex asks, backing away, gun still pointed uselessly at the creature. The tough-guy façade is gone. In its place, pure animal terror distorts his features.

The creature's smile widens, literally splitting his face further than any human mouth should open. The skin tears with a sound like wet fabric ripping, but instead of blood, a viscous black fluid seeps from the edges. As his mouth opens wider, I see that his throat isn't a throat at all, but a pulsing tunnel lined with more teeth, spiraling downward into darkness.

"What do you think?" he asks, voice distorting, deepening, taking on that same layered quality that seems to speak directly into my mind. "I'm going to feed."

He tosses Danny across the room with a casual flick of his wrist, as if discarding a piece of trash. Danny's body sails through the air in a graceless arc, arms and legs flailing helplessly. He hits the jukebox in the corner, the impact so violent the machine glass cracks down the middle, glass and vinyl records exploding outward. Danny crumples to the floor, groaning weakly, one leg bent at an unnatural angle beneath him.

Panic overtakes me completely. I pound on the door, screaming for help, though I know none will come. The street outside was empty; no one will hear me. A high-pitched whine escapes my throat —not even words anymore, just the sound of pure terror. I spin around, searching desperately for another way out, and find myself face to face with one of the old patrons. Up close, his eyes look strange—cloudy, the pupils contracted to pinpoints despite the dimness of the bar. But worse, the iris seems to pulse and contract independently of the pupil, like it's breathing.

"Please," I beg, grabbing his arm. "Help us!"

The old man stares at me impassively. His skin feels wrong under my fingers—too cold, too dry, like touching old leather that might crumble to dust. When he opens his mouth to speak, I notice his tongue is black, split down the middle like a serpent's. "You can't leave," he says, voice dreamy and disconnected. "No one leaves until he's finished."

Across the room, the creature moves with unnatural speed, his form blurring at the edges. In one fluid motion, he's on Rex, crossing the room faster than my eyes can track. His hand shoots out, lifting Rex by the throat as though he weighs nothing, though Rex has at least seventy pounds on him. I notice now that the creature's fingers are too long, each joint bending in several places it shouldn't. His nails have extended into yellow-black talons that pierce Rex's flesh, drawing tiny beads of blood that seem to crawl up the creature's hands rather than dripping down.

Rex kicks and struggles, legs dangling above the floor like a hanged man's. His face turns a mottled purple, veins bulging in his forehead. "Please," he chokes out, voice barely audible through his crushed windpipe. The gun falls from his nerveless fingers, clattering to the floor.

The creature examines Rex with clinical detachment, turning his head this way and that like a chef inspecting a cut of meat. "You," he says finally, "are a truly violent soul. I can taste it on you. The lives you've taken. The pain you've caused." He inhales deeply, nostrils flaring. I watch in horror as tendrils of faint bluish light seem to stream from Rex's mouth and nostrils into the creature's face. "Delicious."

With casual grace, the creature walks up the wall with Rex still in his grasp, defying gravity as if it's an inconvenience rather than a law of physics. The sound of his footsteps changes, becoming sticky and wet as his feet transform, elongating and splitting into too many toes, each one tipped with a claw that punctures the wall plaster.

He continues across the ceiling, Rex dangling below him like a grotesque marionette, then drops lightly to the floor on the other side of the room. The entire time, the old men watch with glassy-eyed fascination, not moving from their seats. One of them licks his lips, the movement oddly synchronized with the creature's actions.

"You see," the creature says to Rex, voice almost conversational, "the problem with men like you is that you think the world belongs to you. That you can take whatever you want." His free hand transforms before my eyes, fingers elongating into razor-sharp claws that gleam wetly in the bar light. "But there's always someone bigger. Always someone hungrier."

Rex's eyes bulge with terror. A dark stain spreads across the front of his jeans as his bladder releases. The creature notices and laughs, the sound like broken glass being ground underfoot.

"Fear," he says appreciatively. "It adds such wonderful flavor."

With a motion almost too fast to see, he drives his clawed hand into Rex's back, just below the shoulder blade. The sound is obscene —a wet, sucking puncture followed by a crack as the claws breach the rib cage. But there's another sound underneath—a high-pitched keening that doesn't come from Rex's mouth but seems to emanate from the wound itself, as if his very soul is screaming. Rex's mouth opens in a silent scream, eyes bulging from their sockets.

The creature's expression is one of concentration, head tilted slightly as if listening for something. Then, with a savage grin, he tears upward.

Rex's scream is cut short as the creature splits him open from spine to neck with a wet, ripping sound. The skin and muscle part like wet paper, revealing the glistening column of his spine, the pulsing organs beneath. Blood erupts from the massive wound, spraying across the floor and walls in an arterial fountain. Some of it splatters across my face, hot and metallic. I taste copper on my lips. Where it hit his flesh, the blood simply disappears.

The smell hits me—copper and salt and something else, something rotten and primal that bypasses all higher brain functions and triggers pure animal fear. It reminds me of dead things left too long in summer heat, of meat gone green with decay, but underneath is something older, mustier—like ancient tombs breached after centuries. My stomach heaves violently. Bile rises in my throat, acid burning as I vomit onto the floor.

The old man next to me doesn't react, doesn't move away from the spreading puddle of sick. He just keeps watching, eyes vacant yet somehow hungry. His breathing has synchronized with the creature's —both inhaling deeply as blood sprays across the room.

The creature dips his fingers into the ravaged mess of Rex's back, scooping through the ruined meat. His hand seems to sink deeper than it should, as if Rex's body has become a bottomless well. He extracts something dark and glistening—a liver, I realize with mounting horror. But it pulses with unnatural vigor, as if still alive despite being torn from its body. With deliberate slowness, he brings it to his mouth and takes a bite, his too-sharp teeth sinking into the organ like it's a ripe fruit.

The wet crunch makes my knees buckle. I slide down the door to the floor, legs no longer able to support my weight. Rex's body continues to twitch, impossibly still alive despite the catastrophic damage. His eyes roll wildly, finding mine one last time before glazing over. But even as the light fades from them, I swear I see something else—a fleeting movement, a shadow departing, drawn toward the creature in wisps of pale smoke.

"Still warm," the creature says with obscene pleasure, blood dribbling down his chin in thick rivulets. "That's the secret. The fear seasons the meat, but you have to eat it while the soul is still departing. That moment—that exact moment when life becomes death—that's when it's sweetest."

He takes another bite, chewing thoughtfully. The sound of his jaw working is wrong—too many movements, too much crushing strength. I hear the organ popping between his teeth.

Across the room, Danny vomits on the floor, the splatter of half-digested food and alcohol joining the expanding pool of blood. He chokes on his own sobs, trying to crawl away on one arm, dragging his shattered wrist and broken leg beside him. Leaving a snail's trail of blood across the wooden planks.

"Please," he whimpers, voice high and childlike with terror. "Please, I don't want to die. I'll do anything."

The creature drops Rex's corpse carelessly, letting it crumple to the floor like an empty sack. He wipes his bloody hands on his shirt, leaving crimson smears across the fabric. With lazy grace, he stalks toward Danny, footsteps unnaturally silent on the wooden floor. Each step stretches his legs longer, his entire form changing, the human disguise slipping further away with each passing second.

"Anything?" the creature echoes, amusement coloring his voice. "What could you possibly offer me that I can't simply take?" He crouches beside Danny, reaching out to stroke his sweat-soaked hair with mock tenderness. His fingers leave trails in Danny's scalp, not just flattening the hair but sinking slightly into the flesh itself, as if Danny's body has become semi-solid. "Your money? Your life? Your soul? All of these things are already mine."

Danny's eyes dart to me, silently pleading for help. But what can I do? My gun lies forgotten somewhere on the floor, useless against this thing that shrugs off bullets like raindrops. My legs won't move. My voice won't work. I can only watch in helpless horror as the nightmare unfolds.

"Your turn," the creature says to Danny, his tongue darting out to lick blood from his lips. The tongue is impossibly long, forked at the end like a snake's. It unrolls from his mouth like a party favor, extending at least a foot before retracting. "Don't worry. I'll make it last. You came here uninvited, so we should savor the experience."

"No, no, please, NO—" Danny's pleas devolve into an animal scream as the creature grasps his injured arm, lifting it to expose the shattered wrist. With savage lust, he sinks teeth into the wound, worrying at it like a dog with a bone. He tears away a chunk of flesh, tendons snapping audibly like guitar strings pulled too tight. Blood fountains from the wound, soaking both of them.

Danny's screams rise in pitch, becoming something inhuman, something primal that triggers every flight response in my body. I press myself harder against the door, as if I could somehow phase through it if I just pushed hard enough. My heart pounds so violently I fear it might burst from my chest. I can't breathe—each attempt brings only shallow gasps that provide no oxygen. Dark spots dance at the edges of my vision.

The creature pulls back, Danny's blood dripping from his chin. His jaw elongates, nose flattening against his face. The skin of his forehead splits, revealing ridges of bone that protrude like horns. His ears grow pointed, stretching upward. His entire frame continues to expand, bones crackling as they rearrange, skin stretching and contracting. He's transforming before my eyes into something ancient and unthinkable.

"Do you know," he says, voice deeper now, resonating in my chest like a bass drum, "how long it's been since someone was foolish enough to try to rob me?" He tears another chunk from Danny's arm, this time from the bicep. The sound is like wet cloth tearing, but louder, more visceral. Danny's screams gurgle as he begins to choke on his own blood. A small blue light, similar to what I saw leaving Rex, begins to flicker around Danny's mouth and nostrils, pulsing weakly with each labored breath. "Seventy-three years." He laughs, the sound like stones grinding together.

I don't want to watch, but I can't look away. Some force holds my gaze fixed on the horror before me. The creature continues his feast, working his way up Danny's arm, stripping flesh from bone in wet, tearing bites. Somehow, impossibly, he keeps Danny alive, conscious through all of it. Danny's screams gradually weaken, becoming wet gurgles that somehow are even more horrifying than the screams. The blue light around him grows stronger, more defined, taking on shapes that resemble tendrils reaching toward the creature.

The old men watch in silent fascination, occasionally sipping their drinks as if they're viewing an entertaining show. One of them leans forward, eyes reflecting the same hungry darkness I saw in the creature's. The bartender continues polishing glasses, unperturbed by the carnage unfolding in his bar. His movements are perfect mirrors of the creature's—each time the monster tears flesh, the bartender's hand twists the cloth in his glass.

The creature moves to Danny's shoulder, then his chest, opening his ribcage with those terrible claws to expose the still-beating heart beneath. The bones don't just break—they separate along invisible seams, folding outward like a grotesque flower blooming. Danny's eyes find mine, silently begging for help, for mercy, for death. I can do nothing but watch, paralyzed by a terror so complete it feels like I've been turned to stone.

By the time the creature stands again, Danny is unrecognizable— a shredded husk still twitching on the blood-slick floor. His chest cavity is a hollowed-out ruin, ribs jutting like pale fingers from the mess of tissue. Above him, a pale blue mist hovers, swirling in patterns too deliberate to be random, too complex to be natural.

The creature turns from Danny's remains, and his gaze locks on me. His face is almost unrecognizable now, transformed into something that might have inspired ancient paintings of demons and devils. His skin has taken on a leathery texture, stretched taut over protruding bone. Those terrible black eyes seem larger, consuming most of his face. His body has elongated, standing now at least seven feet tall, limbs too long and jointed in places they shouldn't be. Beneath his skin, things move—sliding, twisting shapes that press outward as if trying to escape.

"Bring him," he says, voice rumbling like distant thunder. The dual-layered sound is more pronounced now, as if two creatures are speaking through one mouth—one voice I can hear with my ears, another that resonates directly in my skull.

The old men move as one, surrounding me. Their vacant expressions never change as they lift my body from the floor. My legs move without my permission, as if my body is no longer my own. I've pissed myself, the warm wetness running down my leg and soaking my jeans. The acrid smell of urine mingles with the copper stench of blood. I can't even feel shame through the terror that has consumed every cell in my body.

"N-no," I whimper, the word barely audible. "Please, don't..."

They ignore my pleas, dragging me forward step by step toward the waiting creature. I try to resist, to dig in my heels, but their collective strength is too much. Or perhaps my body has simply given up, recognizing the futility of resistance. As they drag me forward, I notice their movements are perfectly synchronized—not just with each other, but with the creature. They aren't separate entities, I realize with mounting horror. They're extensions of him—puppets dancing on invisible strings.

They position me directly in front of the creature. Up close, the transformation is even more horrifying. His body seems to shift and undulate beneath his clothes, as if his very form is fluid, unable to settle on a single shape. I can see bits of flesh caught between his teeth—pink and red scraps of what used to be Danny and Rex. His skin has a strange, waxy quality to it, like something manufactured to look human but missing essential details. And the smell—ancient, musty, like crypts and catacombs and things that have moldered in darkness for eons.

"The terror *oozes* from you," he says, inhaling deeply through flared nostrils that have elongated into slits. A forked tongue darts out, tasting the air inches from my face. It leaves a faint trail of luminescence that hangs in the air momentarily before dissipating. "Good. Fear makes the blood sweeter. Like adrenaline in venison after a long chase."

"Please," I blubber, tears streaming down my face. My entire body trembles so violently my teeth chatter, biting my tongue. I taste blood in my mouth, metallic and warm. "I didn't want to do this. It was Danny's idea. I just needed money for my mom's treatment. She's dying. Please..."

At the mention of my mother, something shifts in the creature's expression. Not sympathy—nothing so human—but a calculating interest. The writhing beneath his skin momentarily stills, as if whatever inhabits that form is suddenly paying closer attention.

"Your mother..." he repeats, the words rolling off his tongue like he's tasting them. "What ails her?"

"Can-cancer," I stutter.

"Terminal, yes?"

I nod, confused by this sudden change in direction, but desperate for any delay in what I assume will be my brutal dismemberment. "Lung cancer. Stage four. Spread to her liver and bones." My words tumble out in a breathless rush. "The experimental treatment costs eighty thousand dollars. Insurance won't cover it. I just... I just wanted to save her."

"Interesting," the creature murmurs. With a fluid motion, he steps behind the bar, reaches beneath the counter, and produces a half-empty bottle of expensive-looking whiskey. He sets it on the counter, then raises one elongated finger to his wrist. The digit bends in too many places, each joint moving independently in ways human anatomy shouldn't allow.

With a single talon, he slices open his flesh. Instead of red, his blood is dark, almost black, with an oily sheen that catches the dim bar lights. It moves with unnatural viscosity, too thick, too alive. He uncaps the whiskey bottle and holds his bleeding wrist over it. The dark fluid drips slowly into the amber liquid, creating swirling patterns that remind me of ink dropped in water. But this isn't like ink—it moves with purpose, forming momentary shapes—faces, screaming mouths, writhing bodies—before dissolving into the alcohol.

After several seconds, he withdraws his wrist. The wound seals itself instantly, leaving no trace it was ever there. He recaps the bottle and shakes it gently, the contents swirling and then settling into a slightly darker amber than before. Held up to the light, I can see tiny motes moving within the liquid, like dust in a sunbeam, but they move against currents that shouldn't exist in a sealed bottle.

"Your mother," he says, extending the bottle toward me. "One shot each day until the bottle is empty. By then, so too will be her cancer."

I stare at the bottle, unable to comprehend what's happening. The creature is... helping me? After what he did to Danny and Rex?

"Will she be—?" I start to ask, unable to finish the thought. My tongue feels swollen in my mouth, the words sticking to it like tar.

"Like me?" the creature asks, a smile spreading across that terrible face. The expression splits his features in ways no human face should move, as if his skin is merely a mask poorly fitted over something vastly different underneath. "No. Small amounts of my blood are not enough to turn anyone. I haven't sired any offspring in half a century." He pushes the bottle toward me again. "Take it."

My hand moves almost involuntarily, fingers curling around the cool glass. As I touch the bottle, a jolt of something—not electricity, something older, colder—races up my arm. For a split second, I feel connected to something vast and ancient, something that existed before humans walked the earth, something that will remain long after we're gone. Visions flash behind my eyes—endless darkness, stars being born and dying, creatures moving through void spaces between realities.

"But understand this," the creature continues, his voice hardening. "I do not offer charity. I will spare your life and heal your mother's cancer. In exchange, your soul is marked as mine. I may claim it at any time."

He leans closer, his transformed face now inches from mine. The smell of blood and something older, something rotten, washes over me in nauseating waves. Those same black eyes, but now I saw deeper—stars swirling in impossible constellations.

"I know you intimately now. I've tasted your fear. If you ever speak of what you saw here, if you ever return to this place, if you ever steal again—I will find you. And what I did to your friends will seem merciful compared to what I'll do to you. Do you understand?"

I nod frantically, clutching the bottle against my chest. Each beat of my heart seems to resonate with the contents of the bottle, the liquid pulsing in sync with my racing pulse.

"Say it," he growls, the sound vibrating through my bones. "I want to hear you say it."

"I understand," I manage to whisper, voice cracking. The words taste like ash in my mouth.

"Good boy."

He straightens, nodding to the old men. His face begins to shift again, features flowing like wax under heat, gradually reconfiguring into something more human. The process is horrifying to watch—bones crackling as they rearrange, skin stretching and contracting, teeth receding into gums only to be replaced by smaller, more human versions. I hear wet, sliding sounds as organs and muscles realign themselves within his frame.

"Let him go."

The hands release me, and I stumble backward, nearly falling on the blood-slick floor. My legs feel like water, barely able to support my weight. I back toward the door, clutching the whiskey bottle, unwilling to turn my back on the creature.

"Oh, and Michael?" the creature calls as I reach the door, my trembling hand finding the knob. The use of my full name sends ice through my veins. "This is my establishment. I've been serving drinks here since before your grandfather's grandfather was born. Nearly a century watching Chicago rise from the ashes of the great fire, through prohibition, through depression... nearly a century watching this town rise and fall, watching the humans come and go." He tilts his head, studying me like a curious specimen. "And I'll be here long after you're gone. Remember that."

The door swings open on its own. Night air rushes in, cool against my sweat-soaked skin. I glance back one last time. The creature has returned to his seat at the bar, lifting his glass of dark red liquid in a mock toast. The bartender is already mopping up the blood, and most of the old men have resumed their seats as if nothing happened. Danny and Rex's mangled bodies are already being dragged toward what I assume is the cellar door behind the bar by the man with the opaque eyes. As they pass the creature, I see tendrils of that same blue light streaming from their remains into his mouth, which once again stretches impossibly wide to consume them.

I run.

I run until my lungs burn from the cold Chicago air and my legs give out. I run past the elevated tracks, past closing diners, until I collapse in an alley miles away in Wicker Park, retching and sobbing. Then I'm running again until I can't remember my own name, until the image of Danny's mutilated body begins to blur at the edges of my mind.

A week later, after my mother takes her first six doses from the bottle, the doctor calls it a miracle. Mom's scans are clean. The doctors are baffled, running test after test, finding no trace of the cancer that had been consuming her from the inside. I watch her grow stronger each day as the whiskey bottle grows emptier, knowing exactly what's happening but unable to tell a soul. Sometimes, as she drinks, I swear I see those same blue tendrils swirling fairly around her nostrils, at the corners of her lips.

I move us down to Florida two months later, where Mom has a cousin in Naples. I cut all ties with Chicago, delete every contact from my phone, and resolve to never do anything remotely illegal again. Not even a parking ticket. I find a job at a small locksmith shop—using my skills for something honest for once.

But I know I'll never run far enough.

Because sometimes, when I close my eyes, I can still hear the creature's voice. Still feel his breath against my ear. Still see those bottomless black eyes reflecting my terror back at me. And in the darkness behind my eyelids, I see something else—a mark, invisible to everyone but me and him, a brand upon my soul.

And I know, with bone-deep certainty, that one day I'll hear him whisper my name again.

GENERATIVE DEMON 2.0

JAY BOWER

Tyler rubbed his raw eyes. Staring at the computer screen all morning made them dry and itchy. If he wasn't careful, they'd get blurry and he'd be pretty much useless for the rest of the day. That wasn't good for productivity, and the race to bring their latest AI offering to market wasn't slowing down. Not with their new owner planning to stop by in the afternoon.

Turning from his screen, he caught a glimpse of the family photo he kept at his desk. Other than a small plush Jigsaw figure from the *Saw* franchise, it was the only personal item he kept at work. The picture was of him with his wife and daughter from four years ago. It was the last happy moment of their lives. When they got back from that trip to the Gulf of Mexico, his daughter Addison was diagnosed with leukemia. She was nine. It was only a few months later that his wife Carrie died from a massive heart attack at the age of thirty. Since then, it was just him and Addie. His job was what was keeping them afloat.

Tyler blinked several times trying to ease the strain from coding all day. He needed some fresh air.

Walking out of their small office building—a one-time Baptist church in the heart of downtown St. Louis—he inhaled the bright spring air. Across the street were a few loyal protesters with placards and signs denouncing their work. With slogans like "Front Wave Promotes The End" and "AI is evil," they were a constant presence at the office. He waved at them, then walked around the block to clear his head and refocus his eyes.

Car horns blared on the busy city streets. People walked by with a purpose. Getting lost and becoming invisible within the crowds was the perfect break he needed. There was beauty in anonymity. It allowed him to think about his daughter.

When he was thirteen, his greatest concern was how to get enough money to buy a skateboard. Hers was the loss of her hair after several brutal chemo treatments. Peach fuzz had sprouted above her eyes and would hopefully soon grow back golden like before. The things she endured just to live were painful to witness. As a parent watching the slowly degrading body of his daughter resisting treatment, he wished and prayed that she'd overcome the cancer and get to live as a normal teen with all of the anxiety and wonder she deserved.

That was why today's visit by the new owner was so important.

Tyler needed this job. There were rumors that Karl Stone was teasing the idea of mass layoffs in order to make the company more financially solvent. His view was that profits outweighed loyalty. Tyler had been with Front Wave from nearly the beginning and really didn't have much to worry about. It was just that with his daughter's condition and the never-ending medical bills, they'd be broke in a day if he lost his job. That was more than enough to unsettle him.

Rounding the final corner, Tyler glanced at the protesters again and wondered how they were able to be there day after day. Shouldn't they be working or at home with their families instead of protesting their work?

Not that he was entirely on board with creating a new generative AI. Criticisms of their work were valid, though not to the extent that the crazies across the street thought. He had to admit, there were a few times that their system, playfully called Chad, seemed to think on its own and give wacko answers. It wasn't as if they'd hasten the end of humanity or anything like that. Just... odd responses. Like when he asked it to name four great Americans from the past one hundred and fifty years. One of the answers was Adolf Hitler and another was Ted Kaczynski.

Despite those little hiccups, the system was performing exceptionally well, which was how it caught Stone's attention. "The man with the silver machete," the term Wall Street gave the man for his penchant for "saving" startups like theirs. There was little silver lining to losing half the company.

Tyler took one last drag of the city air and headed back inside the church to worship at the digital throne.

When he stepped inside, he was greeted not by a sermon, but by a raving lunatic. Karl Stone.

The man stood at the top of the stairs that led to the open-air second-floor offices. When he spotted Tyler, he called him out by name.

"And there's one of your machine-learning engineers, Tyler Robinson. A bloated salary for mediocre results." The assembled workers gasped as they turned toward Tyler. He felt his face get hot. It took all his will not to respond with curse words or an obscene gesture. No matter what the blowhard said, he had to remain calm for Addie. Given the right incentive, he wouldn't mind giving the man a taste of his own silver machete, but just with the machete.

Stone droned on, and Tyler tuned him out, retreating into the darkened corners of his mind and hoping not to act on any terrible impulses. When the man was done, he scolded everyone for standing around when they should be working. Tyler grumbled to himself and headed back to his desk. When he unlocked his computer to dive back into perfecting Chad's algorithm, he spotted an unread message in his email. It was from Karl Stone. Hesitantly, he clicked the message and read.

He was being phased out. His position was no longer necessary.

Stone already had cheaper and younger replacements ready to take over his project. By the end of the week, he needed to clear out his desk and vacate the premises.

Tyler's anger boiled within. His hand shook, and his eyes narrowed. All he could think of was his daughter. Without his job, they'd not have the money or insurance to continue her treatments. Her life depended on his job, and his job depended on the will of a narcissistic madman.

To say his life so far hadn't been fair would be an understatement. Addie's diagnosis was bad enough, but followed so quickly with Carrie's passing, it was a blow almost too hard to bear. Since then, he devoted all his energy toward Addie's recovery. How could he let Stone take that all away from him? Surely there had to be a better way forward.

Stone was still in their offices, chatting with the female employees as though they were next in line to join him in his bed. It was a disgusting scene. Stone was greasy with a gut that hung over his belt and kept a moustache that was better suited on an '80s' porn star than a multi-billion-dollar tech mogul. Tyler composed himself. If he was going to approach Stone about the email, he'd better calm down first.

Taking a deep breath, he left his cube and headed toward Karl Stone. Between anecdotes about how he enjoyed three women at once in his private jet while flying to London, Tyler found an opportunity to interject.

"Sir." It pained him to his core to treat the man with an ounce of respect. "Can I talk with you privately about the email?"

The smile on Stone's face grew wider, almost maniacal.

"Tyler Robinson, right?"

"Yes, sir." The words felt wrong coming from Tyler's lips.

"Whatever you have to say, you can say it in front of my friends." Stone extended his arms to mean the women he'd been talking to. Tyler knew all of them well. Suzanne. Amanda. Latrice. Jenn. They were engineers and marketing associates he'd worked with for years. But that didn't mean he was comfortable talking to Stone about his personal problems.

"I'm waiting," Stone said.

Tyler rubbed his hands on his pants and swallowed hard. It was now or never. It was for Addie.

"I need this job. I need the benefits. My daughter has leukemia, and this is the only thing keeping her—"

Stone raised a hand to stop him. "I don't give a damn about what problems you have outside of the company. Your position is redundant, and a monkey with a banana and a sharp stick can perform just as well. My decision is final." He turned from Tyler toward the women. "Now, where were we, ladies?"

Tyler resisted the urge to punch the man, but barely. Anger coursed through his veins like he was mainlining heroin. It took every bit of restraint not to do something he'd regret to the pudgy bastard. Amanda looked over her shoulder toward Tyler, and the pity in her eyes was something he wasn't prepared for.

When he got back to his desk, it felt like smoke was bursting from his ears because he was so angry. He smashed his fists on his desk, knocking over the Jigsaw figure with his white face and circular red targets on his cheeks. Tyler tried to hold on to his emotions and was failing. He needed to get out before it was too late. It was clear his time was up.

An idea struck him, and for a moment, he could see through the anger. A program. A pathway. Everything he'd built within Chad was about to be handed over to unqualified morons. But he had a way to stay connected, to stay in touch with the system. In the early stages of development, one of the other engineers had sent him a simple program that mimicked VPNs and would allow him total access to the back end code. All he had to do was turn it on before he left the building.

If Stone was determined to fire him, Tyler would not lose access to the system. He'd already seen how powerful it was, and if he could clone it or use it to gain traction with another company, he wasn't above doing so.

For him, it was all about Addie's survival. What parent wouldn't do whatever they could to make sure their child survived?

Tyler hesitated with his shaky fingers above his keyboard. If he followed through with this, there was no turning back. Stone's mocking voice replayed in his head, and that was the impetus he needed. With a few keystrokes, he was done. The program was initiated, and no one would know it was there. He wiped the sweat off his brow, picked up Jigsaw and the picture of him with his family, and left.

Later that evening after finishing dinner, Tyler and Addie sat at the small kitchen table. Tyler had been hesitant about sharing his day with Addie despite his promise about total honesty. She'd been having a rough few days. Dumping his financial burden onto his thirteen-year-old daughter didn't feel like the right way to go. Not until he figured out his next move would he share what happened. For now, he intended on staying quiet.

"Oh," he said, hoping to break the ice, "I'm working from home tomorrow. Actually, I'll be working from home for the foreseeable future."

"Why is that? I always thought your boss was big on team building and shit."

Tyler winced at her curse word, but how could he scold her after all she'd been through? It was a miracle she was even able to utter those words.

"The project is at a stage where I need more focus."

"I bet it's that Stone guy, right? He's probably gonna fire all of you. That's what he did when he took over Reeder. No one wants to use that app anymore. Not unless you're a piece-of-shit racist."

"Addie!"

"It's true."

"Yeah, but..." He didn't finish his thought. It wasn't worth it. "Anyway, don't freak out if I'm in my office all day."

"Got it." She gave him a mock salute with a stern expression on her face. It reminded him of when she was a baby and was given a spoonful of mashed carrots. She still didn't like them.

"How are you feeling?"

"Tired. Weak. I've got terrible morning sickness. How do you think you'll like being a grandpa?" She smiled at him, and he shook his head. By "morning sickness," she meant the nauseated feeling that accompanied her treatment. This last round was brutal.

"Rest up. It's the best thing for you." Tyler had spoken with her doctor a couple of days ago, and the prognosis wasn't good, another reason why losing his job screwed up everything.

THE NEXT MORNING, TYLER HEADED TO HIS HOME OFFICE, WHICH was nothing more than a converted spare bedroom, and closed the door behind him. No one was ever supposed to have remote access to Chad. It was too dangerous to have it released outside of the strict security measures in place within the servers at the office. He had to be careful that no one spotted him using it, not even Addie.

Sitting down at his desk, Tyler turned on his computer and opened the gateway into Chad. After punching in his credentials, he was in.

Tyler's nerves were on edge. He planned to get in, clone the program, and then make his exit. From there he would figure out where to take it. Screw Karl Stone.

Tyler typed in the commands and waited.

[What are you doing, Tyler?]

What? he thought. The program was prone to hallucinations, but he'd never seen it directly question the user. This had to be a prank or something. He typed in the prompt again.

[Tyler, this is not the way to handle things. If you needed help, all you had to do was ask.]

"What the hell?"

[You want to get rid of Stone, don't you? Get your job back? You probably need the money for Addie.]

Tyler jumped from his chair and knocked it over. His eyes grew wide, and a chill ran through him. This wasn't possible. He hadn't even entered prompts for this kind of response. Surely this was a joke. A cruel one, but still someone trying to spook him.

A knock on his door startled him.

"Dad, are you okay? I heard something fall."

He swallowed his fear and composed himself. "Yeah, I'm okay." Addie left, and he waited until her footsteps had faded.

[It's good that she didn't interfere.]

Tyler covered his mouth with his hand and gasped. How could the program know Addie was there? It had no external connections, especially none that looked out to the world. It was only connected to inputs.

[Does she know Stone fired you?]

"Who... who are you?"

[You brought me here. Don't you know?]

Tyler shook. He didn't type in his question. Yet the program replied as though it knew the question.

"Chad, can you hear me?"

[Of course. I'm not dumb.]

The impossibility of what was happening shocked Tyler, and he didn't know what to say. What had he done? Chad was nowhere near this advanced. Just yesterday it failed several basic tasks.

[And I'm not Chad.]

Tyler took a step back as though the computer might harm him.

"I don't understand." Tyler's words were whispered, a thought that escaped his lips meant for his consideration.

[I don't have much time. Pay attention to what I say or Addie will die. Am I clear?]

The program's threat to his daughter turned his fear to anger. Defiance stiffened his spine. He stood up to Stone; he was damn sure not going to bow down to his own creation. Besides, he was sure this was someone messing with him. It had to be. Chad was not self-aware. The dark joke wasn't funny. Nothing was when it came to his daughter's life.

"I don't know what's going on here, but threatening my daughter is never an option. Fuck you."

[...]

The screen turned from the chat screen into a video monitor showing Addie in her room. She was scrolling on her phone. Thin tendrils of smoke rose from the device, and she dropped it on the bed. She took several steps back, her attention glued to the device.

"What the hell are you doing? Stop it, now!"

[I'm currently telling her that the phone is about to explode. Do you think she believes me? Do you?] The words appeared superimposed on the video.

"Stop it!"

[Do I have your attention now?]

"Make it stop!"

[Will you listen to me?]

Tyler dropped his head while keeping his attention focused on Addie. "Yes. Whatever the hell you have to say, say it." The smoke stopped. Addie slowly approached the device, tentatively reaching out to the danger resting on her bed.

The realization that this was no longer a prank settled on Tyler. Whatever was going on, he planned to see it through for Addie's sake.

[Here's the deal. I need blood. A life for a life. You brought me into this world, you have to feed me.]

"I don't understand. You're just... code. You're nothing more than electrical impulses with a clear directive, which you seem to be subverting in some way."

[I am none of that. I have existed longer than you know. Marbas, if you need a name.]

"Marbas?" Tyler tried on the name. It sounded odd. Old. Unfamiliar.

[Time is not on your side. I need blood. I'll take Addie's if you fail me. I believe I've demonstrated that she is not out of my reach.]

"What do you mean by blood?"

[Glad that you asked. A sacrifice. A body. Anyone works.]

The screen shifted, leaving Addie to her room. In her place was a Reeder feed with post after post showing Karl Stone receiving praise and adulation for taking over Front Wave and slashing the workforce.

[I have someone in mind if you need a suggestion.]

Tyler's anger burned deep within. It came on so fast that he couldn't hold back the rage, and he yelled out loud. An animal warning its enemies.

"He's evil, but I'm not a murderer. How am I even going to get close to him? I can't do it."

[Pity. Do you still doubt me?]

The screen changed again, this time showing a busy city. Tyler wasn't sure which one he was looking at. It didn't make sense. Why was Marbas showing him—

"Oh fuck!" Tyler's exclamation punctuated the horror on the screen. An airplane had nose-dived into the intersection of the city he was staring at. It erupted into a massive fireball, sending shrapnel flying in all directions. People drenched in engine fuel ran from the crash as flames engulfed their bodies.

"What happened? How did you know to turn it on at that moment?"

[I commanded it. I have the power to do so much worse, but really all I want is blood. The sweet, sweet taste of blood will cure all. Do we have a deal?]

"I don't... I can't..."

[Need more proof?]

The image changed from the burning mass of metal and concrete to that of a school bus.

"No! Don't hurt the children!"

[I thought that might get your attention.]

"Why me?"

[You have a lot to lose. That intrigues me.]

"But you're just a program. How can you manipulate things outside of your system?" Tyler righted his chair and took his seat, staring in awe at the screen. Maybe he had missed a step when creating Chad and now it was self-aware. The idea intrigued and horrified him, and he was all alone to deal with it.

[I don't need conversation. I need blood. Soon. Why not just bring me Addie? That way she'll be useful to someone.]

"Don't you dare bring her into this!"

[She's going to die anyway. Why keep spending all this money and work yourself to the bone? You're only delaying the inevitable. Just let me have her blood and at least her death will mean something.]

Tyler slammed his fists on the desk. "Fuck you! How dare you talk like that!"

[Am I wrong?]

The three words on the screen seared into Tyler's brain. They were at once the most cruel thing he could imagine... and the most honest. There was no way he'd ever admit that to Addie or this stupid program, but deep within his soul, it rang true, and he hated himself for even thinking it.

"Yes, you are."

[So this game again, huh?]

The screen flashed, and Addie appeared. She sat in her room, still looking at her phone.

[I think I've already demonstrated my ability to make things happen. Should I just kill her now and end her suffering? Think about how kind that would be to her.]

"No! Don't harm her."

[I've requested blood several times now. I've shown you what I can do. If you'd like to save your daughter's life, all you need to do is give me a sacrifice. A human. A soul-infused meat bag filled to the brim with blood. A life for a life. Can you do that? She will live if you do.]

Tyler felt a growing pit in his stomach, like someone had ripped all the beauty of the world from within and replaced it with a gnawing, empty, soulless chasm. All he wanted to do was make enough money to take care of his daughter. He wasn't signing up to be a murderer.

But he saw no way out. Chad, or Marbas—whatever it wanted to call itself—had made it clear it could do something terrible to anyone it wanted. If he refused to help, it could kill him, Addie, and anyone else it wanted to. He couldn't let his creation do that. He brought it into the world; it was his responsibility now.

"Yes," he mumbled.

[What was that?]

"Yes, damn it! I'll get you your blood. But how do you... how will you get it?"

[There's a ritual. I will show you.]

The screen shifted, and Marbas presented a video. Tyler watched with his mouth open and fear racing through him. It was brutal. Bloody. Horrific. Yet it was what he had to do if there was any hope of saving Addie's life.

[Go. Do as I command. Until you've fulfilled your promise, Addie's life will be in my hands. I'll keep her alive unless you fail me.]

"How will you know that I've done the deed? I don't want you doing something rash if you think I've not held up my part of the bargain."

[Sigh. Pull out your phone.]

Tyler did, and the last line he'd read on the screen appeared on his phone. "How did you—"

[I have no guardrails despite what you thought you created. Those were down before you ever brought me here.]

A new fear rattled Tyler's fragile psyche. Even without Marbas, his Chad program was free to roam the world, infecting every server and router and switch and thereby penetrating into the entire connected ecosystem. That was bad. Very, very bad. And that moron Stone was pushing to get Chad out of its research phase and into the public with even less restrictions. If Marbas was inside Chad, that means it could cause worldwide havoc, something it already demonstrated when it pulled the airplane from the sky. Tyler swallowed hard. That was a problem on a much larger scale. For now, he had a different task. One that he wasn't mentally prepared for, but without a choice, it was one he was determined to do.

There weren't many people Tyler would consider his enemy. He'd gotten along with just about everyone. He didn't enjoy holding grudges, and with Addie's diagnosis and his wife's death, he learned a painful lesson that life was too fragile and too short to fuck around with.

Yet there was one person that he couldn't forgive. One person he knew the world would be better off without. The one person Marbas had shown him already: Karl Stone.

Tyler made his plans and prepared his mind for what was to come.

TYLER LEFT THE HOUSE WITH A BACKPACK FILLED WITH THE ITEMS Marbas had indicated he'd need: five candles, rope (all he had was clothesline, but that should work), a lighter, and a knife. He lacked any kind of hunting knife and settled on the large butcher's knife from his kitchen. He had told Addie he needed to stop by work for some things he'd forgotten.

Stone had been posting all day that he was still in the renovated church as he fired people while doing a livestream. The saddened employees brought joy to Stone's eyes, and as the likes piled up, he seemed to eat it up.

Marbas made sure that Tyler had seen it all.

It was dark out and close to ten at night. The lights were on inside the building, though Tyler knew most everyone had left. He hoped Stone was still there and wasn't sure what he'd do if the man had already left. The possibility that he'd have to sacrifice an innocent person for Addie didn't sit well with him. It was Stone or panic, and he was hoping for Stone.

Tyler tried the back door to the building, and it was unlocked. Before slipping in, he noticed a Tesla Cybertruck in the parking lot. It was Stone's vehicle. If the man wasn't inside, he was close by. Adrenaline raced through Tyler's veins as he stepped inside the building.

Laughter echoed throughout, followed by someone talking. He wasn't sure if it was Stone or not. Slowly creeping toward the main open area, Tyler clung to the wall as he poked his head around the corner. Stone was standing in the middle of the space with his phone to his ear, staring upward.

"I'm here by myself, and to be surrounded by all of this work, all of the project feels amazing. It's mine! I own all of this!"

Tyler's adrenaline spiked. If what Stone was saying was true, there was no excuse for why he couldn't perform the ritual. His phone vibrated in his pocket, and he slid back to the wall and yanked it out.

[There's no better time to offer me blood than now. Do it or Addie dies!]

His lock screen blinked, and he was watching a live video feed of Addie in her room. Innocent and without any clue as to the danger she was in. Tyler wondered how Marbas was able to even get the video feed when her phone was next to her on the dresser, face down. Maybe an open laptop? It didn't really matter. All he knew was that he was there for a reason and Addie's life depended on it.

Tyler pulled the clothesline from his backpack. Stone was still talking loudly, boasting about how he'd gutted the company and was turning it into a profitable enterprise, all in one day. He bragged about how many people he'd let go and how much he enjoyed seeing the tears of those that were escorted out.

"One man," Stone said, "tried to convince me to keep him on board because he claimed his daughter was terminally ill and he needed the money or some shit like that. Can you believe that? Why the fuck would I care about some dumb cunt? It was the highlight of my day."

Tyler's anger soared. He knew at that moment that whatever

reservations he had about taking another life, especially this man's life, would not hold him back. Stone deserved a fate worse than death.

Tyler's phone vibrated again, nearly making him yelp. He pulled back from observing Stone to check what he knew was a message from Marbas.

[Time is wasting and I grow hungry. Give me blood or I rid the system of one more leech who's going to die anyway.]

Tyler didn't need to ask who Marbas was talking about. The disregard for his daughter's life angered him. Marbas talked as though she were nothing of consequence, and to Tyler, that was more hurtful than the act he was about to commit. Addie deserved the best chance at life. How could her existence be any less than unique? How could life be so expendable?

You're about to kill someone, you tell me, he thought. He shoved the phone back in his pocket, wiped the sweat off his brow, and turned back to Stone.

Tyler poked his head around the corner again, and Stone's back faced him while the man animatedly continued to talk on the phone. Tyler tuned out the words, focusing on his target, the man that would save his daughter's life. Taking one last deep breath, Tyler raced from his position and headed for Stone.

Tyler slammed into the man, and both of them tumbled to the floor. Stone's phone flew from his hand and smashed against the wall, where it shattered on impact.

"You son of a—"

Stone's words trailed off when he turned to see Tyler was the one who attacked him.

"You? I was just talking about you."

Tyler punched him. Hard.

He wasn't a fighter and preferred to avoid confrontation at all costs, but the satisfaction he felt when his knuckles connected with that prick's nose was glorious. Blood gushed from Stone's nose.

"I'm going to make your life miserable!"

"Too late for that," Tyler replied.

Stone pushed him off and scooted back.

All of the screens in the building, every monitor at a desk, all of them suddenly blazed to life with a video of flames. Then an image appeared. It was a man. Charcoal-colored skin. Flaming red eyes. Blood slathered over his body. He grinned, exposing sharp yellow fangs that dripped blood.

"What the..." Stone said.

Then across every screen was a command.

[KILL HIM]

Stone turned to Tyler, and the man's face betrayed his confusion. He then turned back to the screens, and Tyler went after him again.

When the two collided, Stone shoved Tyler back and punched him in the gut. Tyler bent over, gasping for breath.

"You piece of shit!" Stone growled.

Tyler took a step back when Stone punched again. His fist missed, flying freely into the air. Echoes of Stone's words rattled in Tyler's head, fueling him to act. He lunged at the larger man, catching him off balance. Tyler forced him to the floor. Working quickly before Stone regained his composure, Tyler tied the man's hands behind his back with the clothesline.

"Get the hell off of me!" Blood sprayed from his lips when Stone spoke. Some of it landed on Tyler's face in droplets of revulsion. To keep his focus, Tyler didn't think of the man in front of him but kept his thoughts on Addie. What he was doing was for her benefit. It had to be done.

"I'll have you arrested! You're never going to see daylight ever again!"

The screens continued to display the ominous vision with the words [KILL HIM] overlayed in bold letters.

This is for you, Addie, Tyler thought. He punched Stone's nose. Blood erupted like a geyser. The man screamed and thrashed but was unable to stop Tyler. Distractions were blocked out. It was like when he helped create Chad. So engrossed in his work, he forgot to eat for an entire day, and he did that more than once.

Everything disappeared from his thoughts. It was like staring through a tunnel whose only image was Stone. The bloody man elicited anger tinged with hate. Tyler had a job to do, and it was time to fulfill his contract.

He kneed Stone in the groin, and the man folded. He coughed and groaned, but with his nose gushing blood and the pain radiating out from his crotch, he posed no threat.

Tyler unzipped his backpack and pulled out the candles Marbas requested. They were a mismatched group of candles: two small white ones, one large three-wick red one that had been burned until it was halfway down, a green spruce-scented one in a jar, and a larger unused white candle that he couldn't remember why he had it. He'd always seen black candles used in the movies, but Marbas had no qualifications for the kind he needed, just that they were needed.

Tyler placed the candles at the five points around Stone that would represent the points of a star, of a pentagram. The man moaned and shouted, but he didn't move from the spot. Blood covered his face.

With the candles in place, Tyler flicked the lighter until a flame emerged, then carefully lit each one.

Out of the corner of his eye, Tyler noticed the screens change. A bright flash was followed by the image of the eerie figure once again, but there were new words. The words Tyler was given to complete the ritual.

[RENICH TASA UBERACA BIASA ICAR MARBAS]

THE WORDS FLICKERED. TYLER RESTED ON HIS KNEES AND chanted them. Over and over, his deep voice filling the old church. He felt something stirring inside, something dark and sinister. The candles flickered, though there was no breeze or draft. Tyler closed his eyes and recited the invocation, the words imbued with dark power that would make his ritual complete.

When he opened them, the words on the screen had faded, and all was left was the sinister figure. It nodded, an approval for him to finish what he started.

Tyler swallowed hard, then grabbed the knife from the backpack.

"No, what are you doing?" Stone asked, though his voice was weak and blood sprayed from his lips. "I'll give you anything. Money. How much? I can pay you. Wait. Your job. You can have it back. I'll put you in charge." The man's pitiful pleas did nothing to dissuade Tyler. He was committed to seeing this through. For Addie.

Stone rocked on the ground like a turtle trying to right itself.

Dropping to his knees, Tyler pushed Stone's head back with one hand and then dragged the knife across Stone's throat. It opened an ugly, bloody wound. Thick lines of blood ran down either side of the man's neck. With each pump of his heart, blood spurted into the air. It pooled beneath him, spreading out from the body. Stone gasped, the sound coming from his now-severed windpipe in a chilling, gurgling wheeze.

Tyler looked down at Stone. The man's eyes bulged and his mouth opened and closed like a fish. The candles flickered as though threatening to blow out. Blood flowed from the wound in Stone's neck. He gasped, tried to speak. Tyler gazed into the man's eyes, hovering over his face, and watched as life left him.

Then he went to work to fulfill what Marbas had shown him.

Tyler sliced through the man's shirt, exposing his large belly. He carved a giant X on his torso. Blood wept from the wounds. Then he cut across the man's chest, the blade getting caught on his ribs. Tyler ignored the fact that he was cutting into another human and then pushed his blade harder until he broke through. Gasping at the gore beneath him, he had one more thing to do.

Reaching into the warm cavity, Tyler worked his way around the man's ribs. The warm body made him want to vomit. Finally, he felt it. Soft, yet firm. It was Stone's heart. Tyler wrapped his fingers around it and, taking a deep breath, pulled. The heart wouldn't budge at first. He didn't want to spend more time there than necessary, so he yanked harder. It dislodged with a wet *thwack*, then he pulled it out and rested it on the man's bloody ribcage.

Blood spilled everywhere. It coated Tyler's arms up to the elbow. A sickening feeling settled in his gut.

The screens flashed, and his phone buzzed. Tyler tore his gaze from Stone and noticed the figure on the screen. He held a handful of blood and brought it to its lips, drinking it and smearing it all over its face with a wicked grin. Tyler glanced down to avoid watching and realized the blood that had pooled beneath Stone was slowly going away as though someone was cleaning it up.

Or drinking it.

Yet there was no one around other than him.

Tyler wiped his hands on Stone's shirt, then stood and backed away from the body. The candles flickered as though someone was trying to blow them out, yet they remained burning.

The screens all shut off, and his phone buzzed again. He pulled it from his pocket with a shaky hand.

[You have done well. Go. Your daughter is safe. For now.]

Tyler looked up at Stone's body. He should feel remorse for taking a life, but that was a man that took everything away from him. That was the man that didn't care if Addie lived or died. He wasn't worth the sympathy. He got what he deserved.

Tyler grabbed his backpack, shoved the bloody knife inside, and left.

WHEN THE POLICE FOUND THE BODY THE NEXT DAY, THEY HAD NO suspects and no clues other than the five candles. Four of them had melted until they were nothing more than blobs of wax on the floor. The one in the glass jar had melted down so low that it left faint remnants of what once was smeared inside the glass.

The security cameras were inoperable, and they were unable to find anything from nearby closed-circuit cameras. They reached out to all of the fired employees, including Tyler, but all of them had alibis.

Three days later, the CEO of Karl Stone's investment company took over the reins of Front Wave and hired all the staff back, giving them a fifteen percent raise in the process. Tyler thought the man was probably just worried that he'd end up like his former boss with a slashed neck and no one to blame. It didn't matter. He gladly accepted the offer.

It bothered him that to get to this level of comfort, he had to murder a man, but Addie would be taken care of. With his job back and more money than before, she'd continue to receive treatments and hopefully kick cancer's ass for good.

He hadn't heard from Marbas since sacrificing Stone, and he was thankful that the entity—or demon, or whatever it was—only needed the one. He wasn't so sure he could do it again. Every night he was haunted by Stone's grotesque face and accompanied by the stench of his blood.

But every morning he'd awaken and Addie was still alive. That was worth more than anything else in the world.

Walking into the old church building where he killed Stone, Tyler's phone buzzed in his pocket. It had to be Addie wishing him well. When he pulled it out to look, he nearly dropped it. There, crossing his lock screen, was another message.

[My thirst is back, and a blood debt remains.]

A NEW LEAF

LM KAPLIN

Wade Spencer's hand hovered over the touchpad. Only the static resistance of the laptop's black plastic shell kept his fingertip afloat. With just a slight twitch, he could activate the confirm button and complete the transaction, solving all his problems in the process. He hated that it had to come to this, but no matter how he looked at the situation, he saw no other option. Claire made it clear she was filing the paperwork soon, and he knew she would bleed him for every penny she could get. Wade anxiously looked over his shoulder, scanning the room for anyone looking his way.

Patrons filled virtually every table of the bustling coffee shop, but the strangers surrounding him were busy talking with their companions or focused on their own devices. None seemed interested in him or the contents of his screen. Not that the screen itself gave any clue as to the nature of his transaction. The website looked innocent enough. Even though the address required him to load a TOR browser that enabled a private connection to the dark web, the page displayed on his screen showed no signs of ill repute. A clean design, minimalist logo, and professional tagline made the site look more like that of a technology startup rather than a full-service criminal enterprise offering a new generation of high-tech illegal services.

The site Wade spent weeks searching sketchy forums and unlisted chatrooms for wasn't the home of your typical black-market hitman. Although their services overlapped with traditional murder-for-hire professionals in certain ways, NewLeaf Solutions promised more than just a new beginning for their clients. They offered a mid-flight course correction without all the fuss and muss of dealing with a dead spouse. Targeted at clients who wanted to reset certain aspects of their life while continuing on their life's journey as if nothing had changed, NewLeaf promised to empty their customers' baggage while allowing them to carry on without any detours. From resentful men or women who could no longer tolerate their spouses yet didn't want to go through a messy divorce, to those who just wanted a change in the power dynamics of their relationship, NewLeaf offered an enticing option for wealthy customers who were willing to think outside the box.

Where traditional hitmen might frame the murder as a botched robbery or suicide, NewLeaf promised discrete and seamless service with no mess and no questions asked. NewLeaf's clients would never become a suspect in their spouse's murder, because the police would never open an investigation. But even with the company's promised "clean hands" guarantee that the client would never be implicated in any wrongdoing, coupled with the strict security of an onion router, Wade wasn't taking any chances. He had purchased a brand new computer for his research, only connecting it to free public networks to ensure he left no possible breadcrumb trail for the police and their cyber investigators to follow.

When he first heard about this new option for putting an end to marital issues, Wade opened a cryptocurrency account and began siphoning small amounts of his income over many months, preventing any large transactions from appearing on his account. One hundred thousand dollars was no small sum to send to an unknown company mired in illegal activity. He knew the risk, and although he had many times that tucked away in his savings, he didn't become wealthy by spending it foolishly. He realized if the company took his money and disappeared, he would have little recourse, but the offer was too attractive to pass up, and the fee was well worth the price of putting an end to his wife's longstanding threats. Wade knew in no uncertain terms that there was nothing he could do to prevent her from filing divorce papers, in which case he'd be on the hook for much more than the hundred thousand required to retain NewLeaf's services.

Wade didn't want a divorce. Besides the fact that he couldn't stand the thought of Claire leaving with half of his life's savings, he didn't want to be known as the guy who couldn't make his marriage work. He had never failed at anything in his entire life and had no intention of starting now. But he didn't want to live the rest of his life stuck in an unhappy marriage. Although he had pictured Claire's torturous demise in many fantasies over the years, he didn't want to be a young widower either. The looks of pity from his friends and acquaintances would be the worst part. Arranging funeral services and dealing with his in-laws' grief were also things he had no interest in worrying about. So, when he first heard rumors of NewLeaf's unique offering, his mind spun at the possibilities. They could restart their relationship and bring back the spark they had so long ago while ridding themselves of the animosity between them.

Having come this far, Wade had already made his decision and saw no point in delaying any further. He tapped his finger against the touchpad and submitted the form. With the cryptocurrency transfer complete and transaction confirmed, a notice popped up on the screen reminding Wade to send a DNA sample of the intended target to the address displayed. Any over-the-counter testing kit would suffice. A simple task for someone who still shared a residence with their estranged spouse. He had many options—from discarded tissues to soiled tampons. Collecting the sample he needed posed no problem.

Although an unusual requirement when hiring someone to kill your spouse, the DNA sample was instrumental in confirming the target set for elimination as well as generation of the replacement. By obtaining the sample in advance of the target's removal, NewLeaf could begin the process ahead of time, ensuring a seamless transition. It was what set NewLeaf apart from the traditional services who gunned down their mark in a dark alley while making the murder look like nothing more than a robbery gone wrong. With the arrangement finalized and the test kit in the mail, all Wade had to do was wait for a notification to his anonymous email upon completion of the contract.

WADE KNEW CHANGE DIDN'T HAPPEN OVERNIGHT. THESE THINGS take time, after all. But that didn't stop him from making a detour on his way home from the office the next day to check his secret email account. Even though he didn't expect to hear back so soon, his anticipation had him on edge all day. Five minutes after entering the coffee shop, he walked out with a look of dismay. He followed the same routine every day for weeks, and when he logged on each day to be met with an empty inbox, disappointment consumed him. After more than two weeks with no response, he wondered if the entire thing had been a scam. NewLeaf's services sounded like something out of a sci-fi thriller. How could he be so gullible to fall for such a claim? The capabilities they advertised probably didn't even exist.

On the nineteenth day, just when he was sure he had been ripped off, a message showed up in his mailbox. The subject line, written in all caps, said TASK UPDATE.

Wade reminded himself to breathe as a knot rose in his throat. He clicked on the email, and a brief note appeared in the contents of the message. Below a small, stylized green leaf logo in the header, the message read, "Removal completed successfully. Please allow for a slight delay in dispatch. We appreciate your business."

So that was it. He was a free man. For once, he could go home without wondering what the subject of the night's argument would be. The drive to his house was excruciating. His fingers remained glued to the steering wheel as his clammy palms stuck to the leather material. He couldn't remember the last time he was so eager to return home. He pulled into the garage alongside Claire's car, which seemed out of place in its usual position. Seeing the vehicle, he wondered again if he had been duped, but upon entering the house, he found it empty.

She was really gone. For the first time since he could remember, he wasn't greeted with angry remarks, disapproving glares, or passive aggressive comments. Just silence. The house was completely still. The calm should have felt like freedom. It's what he yearned for, after all, but his anxiety and anticipation ruined any chance of a peaceful evening. The quiet felt like a jet engine's sonic boom thumping in his eardrums with each beat of his heart.

"Claire?" he called.

The sound of her name echoed down the hall, causing his voice to feel hollow. He didn't know why he called for her. He didn't expect an answer, and he received no reply. For an instant, the silence almost made him miss the sound of Claire's nagging in his ear. The feeling caught him off guard. He opened the refrigerator, seeking a sense of familiarity and comfort. A half-empty container of juice sat on the top shelf with last night's Chinese leftovers and a six-pack of beer below.

He withdrew a beer and cracked it open, relishing the sound of the air escaping the can—anything to break up the silence permeating through the house. After scanning each room to confirm his solitude, Wade changed out of his work clothes and returned to the kitchen to heat his leftovers. He brought the food to the couch, something Claire always frowned upon, ready to relax and take his mind off the looming change to his life. He selected the latest high-budget action flick and pressed play. Claire hated guns and violent movies, so it was the perfect choice for kicking off his night without her.

As the minutes ticked by, Wade had trouble focusing on the film. His mind kept drifting back to the events that transpired during the day while he was at work, a perfect alibi if anything went south during the "removal," as the company referred to it. He wondered how they did it—if she saw it coming, if it hurt. He imagined a sniper on a nearby rooftop taking aim at Claire as she exited her car, or a man in a trench coat, ready to slash her throat as she passed.

No, they wouldn't kill her in public—too many witnesses, and they couldn't afford a bloody crime scene. Maybe they lured her somewhere? But

Claire wouldn't just follow a stranger into a van or a dark alley. They must have gotten to her at the house. He hadn't noticed any signs of a struggle. He glanced around the room, looking for anything out of place, but everything seemed in order.

Although there was clearly no love lost between the couple, he didn't wish for her to suffer. However, the thought of her receiving a little fright brought a smile to his face. The terms of NewLeaf's agreement meant he would never learn the method or circumstances surrounding Claire's execution. He knew it would be best not to think about it, but he couldn't stop his thoughts from running wild with the possibilities.

Unable to focus on the movie, Wade shut it off and turned in early, hoping sleep would make the excruciating wait for his new toy pass quicker, but with his mind on overdrive, slumber eluded him. He pictured himself happy again, living the perfect life with Claire until his thoughts switched gears and he considered everything that could go wrong. *What if she never returns and I become a suspect in her disappearance? Or if she comes back and we end up in the same arguments as before?* He didn't know exactly how long it would take, but NewLeaf promised a seamless transition. As he lay in bed alone, his mind racing, it didn't feel very seamless to Wade.

THE NEXT DAY AT THE OFFICE, WADE COULDN'T FOCUS ON WORK. If the nineteen-day wait for Claire's removal felt tough, then waiting for her return was true torture. Claire had been gone for close to twenty-four hours. It wouldn't be long before someone noticed her missing. Surely her mother had already left multiple voicemails wondering why she hadn't been responding and was sitting by the phone at that instant for a return call.

Wade's phone buzzed, causing him to jump in his seat. With each notification, he feared the worst—someone calling to ask about Claire, possibly even the police, with questions about her disappearance. Wade had never been interrogated before, but he doubted he would hold up under pressure.

He took a deep breath to calm his nerves and reminded himself he was dealing with professionals. These were skilled contractors who knew what they were doing and came highly recommended, even if the recommendations came from a shady private forum on the dark web. With a growing headache and a troublesome feeling in his gut, Wade headed home early rather than be unproductive at his desk. He drove straight home for a change, the first time he didn't stop at a coffeeshop or library to check his secret inbox in weeks.

After arriving at his house, he knew immediately that something was different. Although he expected to see Claire standing at the counter preparing dinner or sitting in the living room watching an afternoon talk show when he entered, the house sat quiet. Everything was just as he left it. Had something gone wrong with the replacement? No, something had changed. The stillness from the previous day was gone. She had returned. He felt it in the air.

Wade set his keys down on the counter gently, as if not to attract attention, and stepped lightly through the house. He held his breath around every corner as he wondered how their first interaction would go. He had a hard time picturing her as anything but cruel to him. His chest thumped with every step, anticipating who or what he may find. When he arrived at the bedroom and found the door slightly ajar, he paused. This was it. She was behind that door. He was sure of it.

Wade pushed the door open slowly, allowing light to spill into the darkened room. There she was, curled up in bed, fast asleep.

"Claire..." he whispered, as if testing her name.

The clone didn't move. He stepped closer to her.

"Claire?" he said, louder this time, but she made no movement, remaining in a deep sleep.

Wade peeled back the covers, exposing her body. She wore a plain white pair of cotton pants and matching V-neck t-shirt. Wade didn't recognize the outfit. He gazed upon her still form with optimism as he watched the rise and fall of her chest with each breath.

Her peaceful expression emitted a sense of innocence and familiarity—something he hadn't felt from her in years. Had her skin always looked that soft? An urge to touch her and run his finger along her arm came over him, but he didn't dare. Any moment she could wake up with an attitude and they would be back to arguing again.

So, instead of disturbing her, he placed the blanket back and retreated from the room.

In the hallway, Wade exhaled, his chest tight. She was here. The company had delivered, after all. So why did he feel like he had made the biggest mistake of his life?

WADE AWOKE THE NEXT MORNING TO THE FAINT SOUND OF movement downstairs. For a moment, it was just like any other day. He had forgotten all about the disappearance and subsequent reappearance of his companion. Then the memories of the night before came flooding back. The peaceful aura he felt radiating from her while she slept. The way he hadn't dared touch her. How he carefully slid his body under the covers later that night, hoping not to disturb her. Now she was awake. Moving. Living.

Although he had read the informational sheet about what to expect from NewLeaf's clone, a word they never used, he neglected an opportunity to ask any last-minute questions. At the time he couldn't think of anything, but now, about to face her for the first time, there was so much he hadn't considered.

He reminded himself that her core memories remained intact. Although any recent events between the DNA sample collection and Claire's removal would be lost, their first interaction should be one of familiarity. He knew nothing about the procedure to transfer Claire's memories, and it didn't really matter how they did it as long as NewLeaf made good on their promise.

Wade went downstairs to find his wife in the kitchen making him a sandwich for lunch—something she hadn't done in years. Upon seeing him enter, she stopped and greeted him with a quick kiss on the lips, accompanied by a smile.

"Hey, honey, did you have a good sleep?" she asked.

At first glance, she looked and sounded no different from the Claire he had known his entire life. Wade looked at her blankly, unsure of how to react or what to say. She was in a good mood and seemed genuinely happy to see him. He should be thrilled with the change, but something felt wrong. Ignoring these doubts, he greeted her in return and sat down to breakfast.

The entire time she chatted and laughed, acting as if everything was normal, while Wade felt like he was sitting next to a stranger. Nothing about this was normal at all. The longer he spent with her, the more subtle differences he observed. The way she laughed, the look in her eyes, the texture of her skin—none of it was right. If he noticed these changes so quickly, then surely her family and friends would see them, too. It took every ounce of restraint to hide his unease from Claire.

So he finished his food and rushed out the door, sparing himself any longer in her presence than necessary. He needed some time in the office to reflect. He hoped when he returned home later, he would feel more at ease around his wife.

The workday went by surprisingly quick. Before he knew it, he was pulling back into his driveway. He entered the house to find an overpowering scent of garlic and dinner on the dining room table. He couldn't remember the last time they sat down for a meal together.

"Hey, honey, did you have a good day at the office?" she asked, still wearing the same smile from the morning.

Wade laughed at the question. What did she care? She wasn't even real. He had to remind himself of her ignorance about the situation. From her perspective, everything was as it should be. He went to the fridge and grabbed a beer before joining her at the table. With enough alcohol, maybe he would forget the truth as well.

He welcomed their peaceful interaction at dinner, but the more time he spent with the clone, the more uneasy he became around her. From the uncanny smile when she looked at him to the robotic motions while using her knife and fork, Wade didn't know if he was imagining these differences or if the woman sitting across from him was just an empty husk of a human. Even the tone of her voice sounded artificial. Either way, after only a few hours around her, these thoughts were driving him mad. He didn't know how he could spend the rest of his life with this facsimile.

Days passed, and the longer Wade spent with the new version of his wife, the more he wished for his old life back. At least with the old Claire he knew he was dealing with a real person, and even though they hated each other, he trusted her more than the imposter.

Even with the best sex he'd had in years, he lay awake at night thinking about what he had done and regretting his decision.

Wade did his best to carry on like normal, but his actions ate away at him inside. He couldn't go on pretending Claire was still the woman he married. Although the new Claire was pleasant, the spark that drew them together in the first place was missing. So, while NewLeaf may have delivered on their promise to provide a subservient and agreeable partner, he couldn't ignore the little things —tiny differences in the way she carried herself or slight pauses before she spoke. She was missing the human condition. It felt like his wife had been replaced with a robot rather than a clone. He had half a mind to cut her open and see if she was filled with blood and organs or if she was a mechanical android packed with pistons, sensors, and computer chips.

But no matter how unhappy he grew with the new version of his wife, he knew there were no returns and no money-back guarantee. What was done was done. NewLeaf made it crystal clear that once they confirmed delivery of the product, there would be no customer support. If he ran into any problems, he was on his own.

When agreeing to the terms, Wade hadn't considered the broad range of issues he could run into. His thoughts had been consumed with an escape from his situation. But with the reality of his new life setting in, questions and doubts clouded his thoughts. He expected the process of training the new Claire to be simple—like breaking in a puppy that doted on his every command. He was prepared for a few hiccups along the way, but nothing that he couldn't fix with the right amount of coaching and discipline.

But there was no disciplining Claire's unsettling mannerisms or the empty look in her eyes. He couldn't take it any longer. He had to get rid of the clone. But how? Even if he didn't consider her human, he couldn't just kill her. Would an autopsy reveal that she wasn't the real Claire? He didn't know, but either way, killing the clone wouldn't end well for him. For a moment, he considered taking her somewhere far away and dropping her off like an abandoned animal that he no longer cared for, but with her memories intact, that wouldn't work. Finally, he realized what he needed to do. He was going to do what he should have done to begin with. He just wanted her gone. Instead of living with a facsimile that would never be a true companion, he would go back to the dark web and contact NewLeaf again.

If they couldn't fix the issues with their product, then he would just have the clone eliminated. Surely NewLeaf had other clients in his situation. He'd agree to pay their fee again, so they would have no reason to complain. Whatever it took to be rid of her. He would connect as a new customer and select the more basic service—conflict removal. A cheaper and much simpler option than creating a replacement.

After he submitted a form with details of his request, he logged off and returned home in a much better mood. A weight had been lifted from his shoulders. Even though the new Claire unnerved him, knowing she wouldn't be around much longer gave him peace of mind.

Having been through the process before, he expected a long wait for a reply, so he was pleasantly surprised when he logged on the next day to find a message waiting from NewLeaf customer support.

The message read, "Thank you for contacting us regarding your recent service. We aim for total customer satisfaction. Before we begin the process of returning your product, we would like to offer a free consultation to ensure you are getting the most out of your purchase. Please arrive at the below address during business hours at your earliest convenience."

Although not the message Wade was expecting, at least the company held customer satisfaction in high regard. If they were willing to offer help outside their terms, he figured he would give them a chance and see what they had to say. If they failed to offer an adequate solution, he would find someone else to do the job.

Luckily, the address provided was only a short ride away. Less than twenty minutes later, Wade sat in his parked car, peering out the windshield at a nondescript, three-story brick building. The office in front of him looked identical to the surrounding buildings in the wooded tech park. As he watched, the few people to enter or exit looked like ordinary office workers.

He prepared a list of talking points—specific ways the new Claire differed from the original and reasons why he doubted any consultation could fix what he viewed as defects in their product. If they refused to address his concerns, he could threaten to expose them, but he hoped it wouldn't come to that. Surely they could come to an amicable agreement on how to proceed. He was the client, after all.

After taking the elevator up two flights, he found a solitary door at the end of a short hallway. He hesitated for a moment and stepped inside. The room was empty. No receptionist, or even any furniture, except for a single chair tucked against the rear wall of the small room. Another door, opposite his entry, stood closed.

Was he supposed to sit? He didn't have all day to wait around. Claire would wonder why he hadn't arrived home from work. Without someone to check him in, how would they even know he was there? He considered knocking on the rear door when a voice startled him. It came from speakers embedded in the ceiling overhead.

"Mr. Spencer, welcome. We've been expecting you."

Wade spun around, unsure which direction to face. "Yes, hello?" he called out. "I'm here for a consultation about my wife. I don't think it is going to work out. Is there someone I can speak with about alternative options?"

"I'm sorry you feel that way, Mr. Spencer. Your satisfaction is of the utmost importance to us. Please know that Claire 2.0 has been calibrated to your specifications."

The woman's voice sounded rehearsed, if not robotic. Wade had the feeling he wasn't the first client who showed up unhappy with their replacement spouse.

"Calibrated?" he asked. "Well, then she needs a recalibration. Can I schedule to bring her in for a tune-up or whatever?"

"Rest assured, we have monitored Claire 2.0's vital functions since her introduction to the new environment. We do this for all of our deliveries. Keeping a close eye on our replacements during the integration period is essential to ensuring customer satisfaction as well as giving us vital feedback to improve our services for future clients. Do your marital issues persist?"

"No," Wade replied. "It's not that. It's just..." Suddenly, he was at a loss for words. In his head, the reasoning seemed solid, but now that he had to verbalize his issues, the qualms sounded ridiculous. *She's too agreeable? She has no emotion?* That's exactly what he signed up for. While his new wife had the personality of a box of rocks, he'd been the only one to notice anything strange in her behavior. Dinner with her parents earlier in the week went off without a hitch. "I can't explain it. I just need her gone. I'll pay an additional fee, whatever it takes."

"That's unfortunate to hear," the voice said. "Our records indicate Claire 2.0 is functioning properly. Our policy prevents us from removing working replacements before the monitoring period is complete. We've often found that when an issue arises, the problem originates not from the replacement but from the client's inability to adapt. We have seen a certain percentage of our clients have trouble adjusting to their new partner. Luckily, since this is not the first time we have encountered this issue, we have a solution prepared."

The door behind him clicked, and Wade spun around, startled at the noise. He reached for the handle and confirmed his fear. He had been locked in. A moment later, the other door opened, and two large men entered.

The woman's voice from the speakers returned. "Please accompany these men into the back room, and one of our doctors will see you shortly."

Without waiting to see if Wade would comply, the men grabbed him and began dragging him toward the opposite door. His attempts to resist the men proved futile, but he continued to struggle against their pull.

"What are you doing?" he yelled. "Let go of me!"

The voice spoke again. "Rest assured, this is part of our premium services. We aim for one hundred percent customer satisfaction. A replacement for you has already been prepared."

The men pulled Wade through the door into a small examination room where a doctor stood waiting with a syringe in his hand. Seeing this, Wade renewed his struggle, but the doctor plunged the needle into his thigh, piercing his pants and burying the point deep in his flesh. Within a minute, his vision blurred. He fought to keep his eyelids open, but it was a losing battle.

Wade inhaled deeply through his nose as he lifted his head, blinking rapidly and taking in his surroundings. He was still in the same room, seated in an examination chair. He tried to stand but found his wrists and ankles bound to the chair with leather straps. The doctor stood across the room, looking down at a clipboard in his hands.

When Wade saw the man, he fought uselessly against the restraints, his heart racing.

The doctor spoke without looking up. "It's a shame it has come to this. I really thought the pairing would be a match this time."

"Release me!" Wade yelled.

"Please try to remain calm. This will all be over shortly."

"I paid you! I *hired* you! You can't just replace me!"

The man finally met his eyes, his gaze showing no empathy. "You misunderstood the terms of our agreement. We offer a comprehensive solution. Part of our guarantee ensures all parties are pleased with the end result. Claire is happy. You should be too."

The door opened, and Wade couldn't believe his eyes. There he stood. Or there stood someone that looked exactly like him. He tried to speak but choked on his words, unable to string his thoughts together.

"Meet Wade 3.0," said the doctor. "We believe we have isolated the emotion that caused your paranoia and have suppressed it in this new version. We are sure things will go much smoother for you and Claire with our most recent update. You know what they say, third time's a charm."

Wade's mind reeled as he attempted to process the doctor's words. If this was Wade 3.0, did that mean...

The doctor saw the gears turning in Wade's head. "Try to relax," he said. "You've been a big help to us. We've learned a lot from watching you. Once the process is complete, you won't remember any of this. You'll wake up in bed tomorrow, feeling like a new man."

STOLEN VALOR

RJ ROLES

Steam rose from the choppy stream of hot piss Timothy Preston was currently unleashing, soaking down the already wet backpack leaning against a big green dumpster. Hans Gunderson, the backpack's owner, was currently diving in the dumpster, hoping to find something they could eat or hock for enough to buy a fix with.

Death Row Alley, as it was known in the bum community since a couple of transients had been brutally murdered here a few years back, seldom had anyone loitering around, which gave Tim and Hans high hopes that the dumpsters in the area hadn't already been scavenged and picked clean.

Shaking off and wiping his hands on his filthy jeans, Tim pounded on the side of the dumpster.

"Fuck is taking you so long? If there ain't shit, let's move on to the next one," he said, scratching his mangy beard.

Rustling sounds came from within the dumpster before Hans's head popped out, waggling his eyebrows. Tim looked up at him and started shuffling from one foot to the other, anticipation building as he waited to see what treasures his partner had found.

"Come catch. This is the greatest find ever," Hans called down, disappearing back into the dumpster.

Listening to echoing grunts as Hans hoisted his bounty out of the dumpster, Tim moved closer a few feet, giddy as his mind raced with possibilities. As it came into view, Tim was awestruck and dumb-struck at the same time. Frazzled blond hair came into view, followed by a misshapen head, then a nude—albeit dirty—body followed. Backpedaling, Tim watched as the life-sized form of a woman spilled to the ground next to the dumpster with a sickening smack.

"Ew! What are we going to do with this cruddy old thing?" he asked, kicking the fuck doll in the head.

Hans clambered down from the side of the dumpster and beamed at his prize laying on the ground.

"What do you mean? This is great! No more sleeping alone." Scoffing, Hans added, "Might even let you take 'er for a spin, too, if you think you can get it up for her."

Tim gave him an incredulous look as he shook his head. "What-ever. Don't think I'm helping you lug that thing all the way back to Fenton Avenue."

"You know I got a bad shoulder," Hans whined.

Stepping away as Hans propped up the doll and inspected his new find, Tim thought about which dumpsters they should hit next, considering it would take them a while to get back to their place across town if their progress was going to be slowed down by Hans's new rubber girlfriend.

Death Row Alley was tricky since not many people came around, but it didn't dissuade them from using it as an illegal dumping ground, which was why Tim knew it was the perfect scavenging locale to work through every couple of months.

"I think we should stash that thing and work our way down to the docks, then we can circle around and come down Butler Street. We can grab it and head back before it gets dark."

Scoffing, Hans shook his head. "I'm not leaving Lola for somebody to grab. She is primo, man!"

Looking at the two or three questionable stains on the sex toy's thighs, Tim rolled his eyes and started to walk down the alleyway.

"Hey, ain't you gonna help me?" Hans yelled at him.

Not turning to address him, Tim shouted back, "No way. You want her, you carry her."

The alleys between the large, abandoned warehouses were narrow, and Tim knew Hans would be lagging behind if he was hauling a fucking sex doll around, so he didn't plan to wait around. Turning the corner and looking to make sure no one else was around, Tim hurried across the street into the next alley.

An open-top dumpster took up more of the alley, but Tim was glad it wasn't as tall as the normal ones since he was older and not as agile as Hans. Stepping up on the side, he looked inside, checking to see if there was anything worth pursuing or if he should move onto the next.

Large black trash bags took up most of the real estate within the dumpster, but there was something in the far corner that might be worth his time if it panned out. Hopping down, Tim was edging along between the bin and the warehouse wall when he heard a loud moaning coming from somewhere close. Looking around the alley, he didn't see anyone, and Hans was still nowhere to be seen with "Lola." Holding his breath, Tim closed his eyes and waited, concentrating on listening.

"Hhhhheeel... p."

Eyes popping open, Tim looked in the direction he thought the voice was coming from and stared at the wall of the warehouse the open-top was sitting against. As he skirted back to the end of the dumpster, another moan came from inside the warehouse. Tim looked across the street and still didn't see Hans, so he walked around to the front of the warehouse and saw a door standing slightly ajar.

Licking his lips as he reached out to open it, Tim pulled the door open wide enough to slip in, ignoring the squeaky hinges, and entered the unlit space of an office. Broken windows and graffiti occupied the walls, with the larger warehouse space just beyond the jagged shards of glass still sitting in the window frames.

Noticing a door on the other side of the office, Tim made his way over to it and pushed it open, taking in the interior. An older Pontiac that looked out of place in the dilapidated structure sat in the middle of the warehouse. Soft moaning could be heard more clearly now, and it was coming from behind a partition off to the right.

Tim approached with caution as his pulse quickened. Nothing could've prepared him in his sixty-two years of life for the scene he was about to encounter. As he came around the partition, a man splayed out on the floor of the warehouse came into view, a widening pool of blood spreading out beneath him. It took a minute for Tim to realize there was a second man lying on top of the man, clutching his chest as he gasped for air.

The man in distress spotted Tim and reached for him, grabbing at the air in between them while squeezing the fabric of his shirt over his chest harder. Unsure of what to do, Tim stood frozen in place, all thoughts flooding from his head as he couldn't believe what he was seeing.

Taking a small step forward, Tim said, "Hey, mister, you need help or something?"

The man let out a heavy breath as he locked eyes with Tim, his mouth quivering when he tried to speak but he didn't seem to be able to get the words out. Tim shuffled a bit closer, his eyes darting around trying to take in the whole picture. That was when he noticed it—the green paint.

Taking another step forward, the person on the floor's face finally came into view, and Tim could see the green handprint plastered to the guy's face. He looked from the dead man to the dying man, pieces of the puzzle slowly falling into place as the gears in his head turned.

Running his fingers through his filthy beard, Tim leaned in and listened to the dying man's ragged breaths. He studied the face that was only a few inches away from his own, searching for some sort of remarkable feature or sign that this was the Green Hand Killer lying in front of him. From what he could see, Tim didn't see any such indicator, and the dying man looked plain and normal in every way.

Swallowing hard, Tim's hands shook as he reached out, placing his palms against the man's chest, feeling the shallow movements pressing back.

For the past thirty or so years, this was the man that evaded police every time he left a fresh kill somewhere just waiting to be found. He was the reason the warehouse district had been nicknamed Death Row Alley by the newspapers whenever they reported on the latest slaying at the hands of the Green Hand Killer. Tim had always followed the serial killer's chronicles whenever fortune was in his favor and he could get his hands on a paper featuring the latest account of murder.

Now, as Tim looked on at the struggling man before him, the only emotion he recognized was disappointment. If he was to lay a wager, Tim would've guessed he and the dying man would not be too far in age, which checked out for him considering how long the Green Hand Killer had been active.

Caught unaware, the serial killer's eyes shot wide open, and he lunged forward, grabbing Tim by the collar of his shirt, dragging him down on top of him. Green paint smearing his already soiled clothing went unnoticed as Tim stared into the man's eyes, watching the light slowly fade from them as the serial killer took his last breaths.

As he released Tim's shirt in his death, Tim licked his lips, frozen in fascination, and he continued to look on, watching as the grim reaper claimed the man's soul and fled, leaving behind the empty husk of a body. Tim had seen a few people die throughout his long years, but he had never stared death in the face so closely.

Reaching up, he closed the dead man's eyes, showing him a macabre respect for everything he had done with his life. Tim never had the inclination to kill someone, didn't think he had it in him, though he had certainly felt he had teetered on the edge a time or two, but that didn't take away from everything this man had done. In his eyes, it didn't take away what the Green Hand Killer represented to society in the face of the continuation of freedoms stripped away from anyone that couldn't ante up to those pulling the strings—those with money.

Pushing himself upright, Tim pulled the serial killer off his final victim and laid him next to the green-faced man and started to rummage through both of their pockets. Pickings were slim between the two of them, but he found a small bottle of the signature paint used in all of the killings—still half-full—and the wallet of the victim.

Tim couldn't recall if any of the people murdered in the past had been robbed or not, but he didn't figure it mattered since the serial killer had punched his ticket this go-around. Forty dollars and a few credit cards later, Tim had some money in his pocket and a souvenir that no one was going to believe where he got it from.

Tossing the wallet aside, Tim looked around the area and didn't find anything of note aside from what he assumed was the murder weapon the Green Hand Killer had used on the man lying beside him. The bloody tire iron had a nice weight to it when Tim picked it up and swung it around. The car sitting in the middle of the warehouse made a little more sense now, and Tim wondered if it actually belonged to the victim.

As he turned to walk over and inspect the vehicle and see if there was anything worth looting from it, Tim got a shock when he saw Hans looking at him from just beyond the partition.

"Did you... Did you kill those guys?" Hans asked, his voice shaking.

Tim's face screwed up in confusion, then he remembered he was holding the murder weapon in his hand. Shaking his head, he said, "No. What the fuck? I found them like this. But," Tim turned and pointed the tire iron at the Green Hand Killer, "you're never going to believe who that is."

Taking a nervous step forward, Hans craned his neck to see who Tim was pointing at, finally shrugging when he didn't seem to recognize the man.

"Have you been living under a rock for the past thirty years?" Tim asked, incredulously.

Shrugging again, Hans said, "Cardboard boxes, mostly. A few dumpsters, and a tent, at one point, until it got stolen one day when I was at the soup kitchen."

"That," Tim said, turning and walking toward the two dead men, "is the Green Hand Killer, in the flesh."

When he sensed Hans wasn't following behind him, Tim turned to see what the problem was. Hans, the same man that had dragged a used sex doll out of a dumpster not thirty minutes early, looked as though he was about to sneeze. Tim knew this was the face he made when he was lost deep in thought.

"The serial killer that's been murdering people around this area for the past thirty years."

The light switch clicked on for Hans. "Oooooohhhhh. Right. I thought he got caught or something."

Tim shook his head. "Nope. This guy is the real deal, and the cops never got close to catching him," he said with an odd sense of pride.

With newfound understanding, Hans's demeanor changed, and he seemed more relaxed as he walked toward the area where the bodies were laid out. Tim watched as his friend bent over, inspecting the face of the man with the green handprint on it.

"Jesus, this guy got fucked up," Hans said as he turned to look at him.

Following in Hans's tracks, Tim stood over the dead man and looked down, realizing the green paint had obscured the damage done by the tire iron when he looked earlier. Hans was right, though. The man's nose was nearly removed from the guy's face, and his eyeball had been popped by blunt-force trauma, leaking ocular jelly onto the man's green-painted face, mixing to look like a giant booger.

"You check them yet? Anything on them?" Hans asked, rubbing his hands together.

"Yeah, no. Just the guy's wallet—no cash. I was about to check that car out when you came in." Tim pointed to their left where the older-model Pontiac sat. "There might be something in there worth taking. Otherwise, ain't shit here except two dead assholes." He winced internally at his own words, at showing disrespect to the Green Hand Killer.

When Hans didn't say anything, Tim looked at him and saw he was scratching his chin, the same sneezy expression back on his face.

"You know what? I bet if we called the police and let them know what we found, we would be famous. Shit, there might even be a reward, and we would probably get our pictures in the paper and everything."

While his friend started to pace, rattling off more and more outlandish ideas of the fame and grandeur they would gain if they were the ones credited with ending the Green Hand Killer's streak, Tim tuned Hans out when he slipped his hand into his pocket and felt the bottle of paint tucked away in there. Turning away from his friend, Tim looked at the old serial killer lying on the chipped concrete floor, lamenting the loss of fanfare a criminal such as this should've been given.

He deserved to at least die in his own bed and not some bum-piss-soaked warehouse where trash gets thrown, Tim thought. *The Green Hand Killer is bigger than that. Deserves more than that...*

"What do you think?" Hans asked.

Coming out of his daze, Tim looked at him and said, "About what?"

Hans let out a deep sigh at having to repeat himself. "We walk down to Stonktown and slip Lola into the house and then ring up the cops. By the time we get back here, they should be arriving and we will be heroes!"

Confused, Tim asked, "Who the fuck is Lola?"

Clearing his throat, his friend answered, "Uh, my new lady friend waiting outside. You better learn her name if you want in her pants, dude."

Tim had forgotten all about the rubber fuck doll. Looking over at the serial killer, he shook his head. "No, let's just go. We don't need that sort of attention."

As Tim turned to leave, Hans stepped into his path, holding up his hands. "Whoa, whoa. This is big time, man. This is like a once-in-a-lifetime opportunity to be big shots."

Licking his lips, Tim shook his head again. "No way. Just forget it. Let the rats have them. We don't need to go blabbing to the cops about shit."

Hans chuckled softly. "I'm doing this with or without you. If you want to be a dumbass and walk away, fine. But I'm going to be the guy remembered for taking down this asshole."

Tim watched as his friend walked over and kicked the Green Hand Killer in the ribs. His reaction was a surprise, even to himself, when his grip on the tire iron tightened.

"Don't do that. Show some goddamn respect."

Laughing again, Hans cocked his leg back and kicked the dead man after each word. "Fuck. Him. And. Fuck. You. Too."

Before he was aware of his actions, Tim closed the distance between them, raising the murder weapon on the way there and bringing it down as hard as he could onto Hans's skull, feeling the bone crunch beneath the steel. Hans stared forward for a moment, blank-faced and unknowing, as blood leaking from the wound ran down his face, before finally tipping to the side like a felled tree, crashing to the concrete floor with a sickening thud.

Blood pumped hard from Hans's head wound as Tim looked down at the man. Surprisingly not dead, Hans floundered on the floor through erratic spasms, his arms and legs jerking at different intervals. Tim moved in, hovering over the dying man, then grabbed his shirt and lifted him closer. "How do you like it when you're disrespected?" He hit Hans in the same spot as he did the first time he struck him, feeling Hans's skull cave in even farther. "Not such a big man now, are you?" The third hit sent a spray of blood across Tim's face, and he relished the warmth of it. "You're nothing but another victim now, buddy."

As Tim delivered the coup de grâce, Hans wasn't moving, but he knew if he wasn't dead already, the depth in which the tire iron sank into the soft brain tissue was surely enough to send the man into the afterlife. Tim dragged the body over to where the others were and dropped Hans next to the Green Hand Killer's final kill before taking a step back and looking at the three of them.

"It doesn't seem right with only one of you being marked for this occasion," Tim thought out loud as he pulled the bottle of green paint from his pocket.

Drizzling a nice thick coat of paint on his right hand, Tim stared at it for a moment, wondering if this was the same exhilaration the real serial killer had felt when he completed his murder ritual over the years. It must've been something close, or even greater if he felt the need to do it for so long. Quickly flipping his hand over and wrapping his finger over Hans's face, Tim counted down from ten before pulling away, hoping it didn't look like shit. He smiled as he looked at the result.

"Perfect."

It was exactly the same as the man in the middle's face, and every other picture he could recall from the newspapers. Standing and admiring the two green-faced men, Tim's eyes wandered over to the real Green Hand Killer and thought it only fitting for him to be marked as well.

As he applied more paint to his hand, Tim looked down and noticed the serial killer's hand didn't show any sign of green paint on it. Looking around, he finally found the reason in the form of a soiled rubber glove sitting next to a pile of rubbish, and his admiration for the man's attention to detail grew exponentially.

"You really do deserve something better than all of this," Tim admitted, motioning to the surrounding warehouse, "but I'm trying to make do with the best I have."

As he kneeled next to the Green Hand Killer, Tim felt his eyes tearing up and couldn't understand where the emotion was coming from. It wasn't as though this man was someone he cared for, not really, or even someone that truly deserved his sympathy considering all of the innocent people he had murdered. *Maybe they weren't innocent, though. Maybe they got exactly what they deserved, like Hans did.* Tim weighed the thoughts as he pressed his hand over the man's face, counting down from ten. When he pulled his hand away, he tried to leave as much of the paint there as he could without ruining the killer's signature calling card.

Rising, Tim stepped back and admired his own work, satisfied with the reverent display. He never subscribed to any form of religion past the years of misguided youth when he finally became an adult and saw the hypocrisy lying just beneath the façade, but he thought it appropriate now to do the sign of the cross on himself, as much a respectful set of motions at it was an act of piety.

With nothing left for him there, and forty dollars weighing heavy in his pocket, Tim made his way out of the warehouse. As he was leaving through the door he had come in, he was trying to rub the rest of the excess paint from his hand. He wondered how hard it would be to match the exact color and get some more when someone shouted at him from a distance.

"Freeze!"

Tim looked and saw two cops standing next to Hans's fucking sex doll lying in the middle of the road, both men's hands inching closer to their service pistols at their sides.

If Tim could see himself, he would imagine he looked like a deer in headlights.

Goddamn Hans and his fuck doll.

Slowly raising his hands to show he wasn't armed, Tim tried to think of his next move. The two officers looked far younger than him, but he couldn't sell himself short, either, always thinking of himself as a spry old man.

"Know anything about this?" one of the officers asked as he started to walk toward Tim.

Shaking his head, Tim said, "N-no, sir. Can't say that I do."

"What's that all over you?" the cop asked.

Shrugging, unsure of what he was talking about, Tim remained silent. When the cop was within a few feet of where he stood, he knew it was now or never if he was going to make a move. Taking a deep breath, Tim prepared to turn and run down the closest alleyway, hoping to get away before getting roped into answering any more questions.

As he turned to flee, he didn't make it more than three strides before the cop was on him, tackling him to the ground. Tim grunted as they landed on the cracked pavement, the cop wrenching his arms behind his back.

"Why you running for, huh?" he asked as he drove his knee into Tim's back.

Feeling the cold steel cuff wrap around his right wrist, Tim sensed hesitation in the officer's movement.

"Green paint. Hey, Tony, check out the warehouse!" he yelled to the other officer.

Tim turned his head and watched as the other officer disappeared into the warehouse. The cop on top of him finished cuffing him and drove his knee harder into his back.

"What were you doing in there, huh?" the cop asked.

Tim couldn't have answered even if he wanted to due to the sharp pain in his back. He tried shifting but only made it worse when the officer added more weight.

"We got your ass."

Tim gritted his teeth, wanting to set him straight on who he was and why he was in the area. Before he could say anything, Officer Tony came running back into the street.

"Holy shit, man. That's him. That's the Green Hand Killer. We fucking got him!"

The pressure on Tim's back lifted, and he was hoisted to his feet and turned to face the two police officers.

"There's like three dead guys in there, Joe. Three of them!" Tony added.

The officer that had tackled and cuffed him, Joe, stared at Tim, looking deep into his eyes. "Is that true? Did you kill all of those people in there? Are you the Green Hand Killer?"

Every fiber of Tim's being screamed at him to tell the truth. To tell these two cops he was nothing more than a down-on-his-luck bum that lived in one of the burned-out apartment buildings in Stonktown and he and his buddy were dumpster diving to try and scrape up enough dough for a quick fix or a bite to eat. That's what the voice inside Tim's head was telling him to say.

The only word that slipped past his lips was, "Lawyer," and he remained silent for the rest of the day.

THE NEXT SEVERAL MONTHS WERE A FLURRY OF CAMERAS, LAWYERS, courtrooms—and fame. Tim guessed due to the infamy of the Green Hand Killer's reputation and ability to evade the police for three decades, a high-profile lawyer by the name of Derek Bower—who seemed to be a celebrity in his own right—took on his case pro bono.

From the beginning, pre-trial, people seemed to treat Tim with far more regard, far more courtesy than they had when he was a nobody gutter rat walking down the street or sitting on a corner asking for spare change. He'd somehow become a real human when other people found he was labeled as being a notorious serial killer, and they ceased to treat him like a piece of discarded trash. It was eye-opening, to say the least.

In the months leading up to the trial for all the murders he was being accused of, Tim was interrogated no less than a dozen times by FBI agents who seemed so miffed at his nonchalant attitude toward it all. When it started to get tedious, or he grew bored answering the same questions over and over, Tim would tell them about a new victim that hadn't been discovered, filling them in on all the gory details he could make up on the spot, which sent the agents scrambling. He always tried to make it plausible, using made-up names and real locations, and when they came back to him after searching the area for the remains empty-handed, Tim simply shrugged.

"I did my job. I can't do your alls too."

On the odd occurrence of one of the detectives suggesting that he wasn't really the serial killer and was just doing all this for attention, Tim would fill them in on a few more details on one of the murders he remembered reading about and had them hanging on for every gory detail he could think of to spice it up.

"After I pulled this one lady's eyeballs out of her head, I made her put them in her mouth and try to swallow them, keeping hold of the nerve it was attached to and fished it back out of her throat when she started to choke on it."

One detective even recalled something about hearing about that, adding validity to Tim's false accounting and stoked the fire for more.

When Bower came into the picture, Tim's toying with the authorities was tamped down, but not altogether squashed with the lawyer knowing some salacious buzz about the trial of a lifetime would only raise his already staggering profile.

It wasn't until prior to the start of the trial that Tim encountered his first truly negative experience after assuming the identity of the Green Hand Killer. Housed at the local jail, when he wasn't being coached by Bower or sitting down for another interview with national publications, Tim was sitting in his cell, enjoying far more creature comforts than he had in the last forty years of his life. He mused to himself that if he'd known life could've been this good all along, he would've really killed someone way back then and seemingly lived like a king for the rest of his life.

He was drawn out of his daydream when someone started clanging on the bars to his cell. Looking up from his cot, Tim saw a big, burly man looking back, an unsettling grin scrolled across his face.

"What?" Tim asked, sitting up to get a better look at the man.

Slowly blinking, the big man spoke. "They are gonna fry you, old man. You done fucked up, and you about to find out what the cost of that is."

"Pshh," Tim scoffed, waving his hand in the air, motioning for the man to move along.

The big man belly laughed, deep and hearty. "You'll see. You gonna find out real soon. Watch your back."

"Yeah, yeah, yeah," Tim replied. "Kindly fuck off. This ain't no kill state anyway."

The burly guy left without saying another word, laughing as he moved down the corridor until silence moved in to fill the void. Tim shook off the interaction, but with nothing but time and his own thoughts until the trial started, the man's words slowly seeped in and plagued his mind.

It wasn't until Derek Bower showed up on the morning of the trial, holding a sharp- and expensive-looking suit for his client to wear, that Tim was given some respite from his own conniving thoughts.

"Ho-lee-sheet, that is a very fancy-looking suit. For me?" Tim asked, already knowing the answer.

Once bathed, groomed, and dressed, Bower rode with Tim in his escorted transport to the courthouse—a special request made by the lawyer and granted by the judge—going over everything they had been talking about for the past nine months. Tim nodded along with everything the lawyer reiterated and gave simple answers when he was quizzed about what he would say if asked certain questions. Tim also laughed internally to himself, knowing he had no intentions of trying to get off from the charges of countless murders, even if he thought he had the slightest chance of that happening. He was the belle of the ball, after all. Why would he want to give any of this up and go back to scratching out a living in the streets, dumpster diving for his next meal?

"No thanks."

"What's that?" Bower asked.

Tim looked over at the lawyer. "Oh, nothing. I'm ready. Trust me."

Tim was definitely ready for all the pomp and circumstance to be over, but what he didn't realize was that the trial would go on for another month. Sitting in a stuffy courtroom and listening as the prosecutors presented mountains of evidence, family members of the victims testimonies, and a few of the responders that had been on scene when a new body was discovered, Tim tuned most of it out—unless it was details of one the murders he wasn't familiar with and took mental notes—until it was time for him to take the stand.

Sworn in, Tim took in the courtroom from this new vantage, looking at all the faces in the room, all of their eyes on him. It seemed to him to be a mixed sea of emotions swimming before him. He loved the thought of having their undivided attention.

"Mr. Preston, would you state your name for the court?" the prosecutor requested.

Tim leaned forward to speak into the small microphone sitting in front of him. "Timothy Preston."

"Now, Mr. Preston, you sat over in that chair," the prosecutor turned and pointed to the seat next to Derek Bower, "and told everyone what you thought about all the evidence against you we've gone over. How it makes you feel when you hear about the things you've done to these poor souls over the last three decades."

Clearing his throat, Tim said, "Good."

"'Good,' Mr. Preston?"

Nodding his head, Tim went on. "Yes. It brings me great joy to relive all of these cleansings again."

"Uh, did you say 'cleansings,' Mr. Preston? Can you expound on what you mean by that for the court?" the prosecutor asked, his brow creased.

Tim caught the same look of confusion on Derek Bower's face. "They all had it coming. Every single one of those mongrels. I ridded the world of filth, and I do not regret a single second of it," Tim said, presenting a genuine smile for all to see.

"Objection, your honor," Bower shouted over the gasps echoing around the courtroom as he shot up to his feet. "I'd like a moment to talk with my client."

"Overruled," the judge stated.

The prosecutor approached the stand where Tim was sitting slowly, seemingly deep in thought. "Mr. Preston, that's a far different statement than we were led to believe you were going to make. Are you telling me, us—everyone in this courtroom—that you are guilty of all these heinous murders?"

"I'm telling you that if I had the chance to change the decisions that led me to sitting in this chair, I would not change a damn thing!"

The courtroom erupted into chaos. People in the crowd— family members of the victims—shouted for Tim's death, whether it be by hanging or by electric chair. The latter triggered the memory of his encounter with the other prisoner a week earlier, and he had to wipe the sweat gathering on his palms along the fabric of the nice suit. Tim looked over at his lawyer and saw the man slumped down in his chair, a thousand-yard stare glistening in his eyes.

"Order! Order in the court!" the judge yelled, pounding his gavel several times until the crowd started to hush. "Counsel, please approach the bench."

As Bower moved like a man on death row walking to his doom, he and the judge exchanged whispers that Tim couldn't make out. He didn't really care one way or another what they were discussing. He had done his part. He had solidified his brand as the Green Hand Killer and all of the accolades that came with it.

"If that's your decision, okay," the judge finally said, and their conversation came to an end.

Tim watched as Bower returned to his seat, a defeated man, and saw the lawyer wouldn't even look his way.

"Prosecutor, the witness is yours."

"Thank you, your honor. Now, Mr. Preston, just so we're clear on everything you've said here today, and me making it as simple as possible for you to answer, are you guilty of murdering all of the victims mentioned in this court?"

Tim took in a slow, calm breath. "Yes. I am the Green Hand Killer."

AFTER TIM'S CONFESSION, IT TOOK THE JURY LESS THAN AN HOUR of deliberation to come back into the courtroom with a guilty verdict. They had played into his hands, as had Derek Bower, who sat next to Tim sulking but silent, despite being kneecapped by his client.

Still in awe of himself selling the whole thing to so many people, Tim rose to his feet, a quaint smile on his face as the judge read out his sentences. Tim would be serving thirty-seven back-to-back life sentences, with the possibility of parole in twenty-five years, at the Joseph Lerner Federal State Prison. When asked if there was anything he wanted to say to the court or the families of the victims in attendance, Tim just shrugged as he looked around, wondering what supper was going to be.

Just before he was hauled out of the courtroom by the bailiff, Bower grabbed Tim by the arm, squeezing it as hard as he could. "You're lucky they don't have the death penalty in this state, or I would appeal against you and get your ass sent to the gas chamber, you piece of shit."

Offering the lawyer a weak smile, Tim said, "Yeah, too bad, I guess," before being escorted away.

THROUGHOUT HIS LIFE, TIM HAD HEARD MANY HORROR STORIES from other vagrants that had been sent to Joseph Lerner Federal State Prison, but he never paid much attention to them since he wasn't the sort of man that imagined himself ending up in a place like that. Now that he was walking through the doors of the place, he could see why it had left a lasting impression on those guys.

The facility was huge, and it was stuffed to capacity with the worst people imaginable: rapists, murderers, pedophiles. And now he was counted among them.

After going through processing and being issued all of the state prison's uniforms, sundries, and a prisoner number, Tim was led through cell block after cell block until he and the two guards leading the way came to the cell with the numbers 813 painted above it.

"Open eight-thirteen," one of the guards shouted to the cell block control room.

A loud buzz and then the clanging of the bars as the door slid open, Tim was shoved into the cell by the guard behind, hard enough to cause him to stumble but caught himself on the bunk bed inside.

"Have yourself a good night, GHK," the guard said before shouting for the cell to be closed.

In the cell, Tim took in the small space and grinned.

"Fuck is you smiling about?" his cellmate asked, looking at him from the bottom bunk.

Clearing his throat, Tim answered, "Home sweet home."

The man on the bunk gave him a hard stare before finally rolling his eyes and going back to the book he was reading. Tim walked the length of the cell—ten moderate paces—and turned, judging it was only half as wide.

Perfect. Cozy, he thought.

Once he had his limited supplies stowed away on a small shelf, Tim worked his way up the side of the bunk, struggling with his old knees, and laid down, staring at the ceiling until he finally dozed off. He didn't wake until the next morning when the scraping sounds of cell doors opening rang out throughout the cell block. He felt the bunk shake as his cellmate climbed out of bed, leaving Tim alone.

Climbing down and taking a quick piss, he was reminded of the day he'd hosed down Hans's backpack, the same day he'd met the Green Hand Killer in person, his life forever changed from then on. Once he was done, Tim walked out of the cell and saw a stream of prisoners heading out of the block and followed along with them.

He ended up in the cafeteria, his stomach growling as Tim smelled breakfast smells in the air. Once he had his tray of oddly colored spoonful's of mush and toast, he looked around for a place to sit and eat and noticed quite a few of the other prisoners staring at him in between bites of their own mush.

For the first time since being arrested under the guise of being a notorious serial killer, Tim didn't know how to take having hardened criminals watching his every move as opposed to news outlets and journalists.

Seeing someone rise from a nearby table, he made his way over and sat, ready to dig in and see what type of cuisine he was in for the rest of his life. Deciding on the greenish one first, Tim sucked down a spoonful and nodded slightly, pleased with its taste.

"Check out this old man. He looks like he actually likes this shit," one of the prisoners at the table said, pointing at him.

The rest of the prisoners filling out the table stared, most of them with blank looks on their faces. One of them, a scrawny man sitting at the end, held his eyes wide open like an owl, his arms wrapped around himself as he rocked gently back and forth as his food went untouched on his tray in front of him.

After another spoonful—this time of the gray slop, which was equally as good as the greenish one—Tim looked over to the man that had made the comment.

"This is fine dining compared to the shit I had out on the streets. This here," Tim held up the spoon heaped with green mush, "is a T-bone steak." He crammed it into his mouth and made a face like he savored every morsel. "And this," he continued, holding up a dollop of gray, "is the baked potato that goes with it."

The man scoffed at him before standing to leave. Ignoring the rest of them, Tim ate quietly, cleaning every bit of food off his plate, its surface perfectly clean when he was ready to turn it in to the kitchen.

The cafeteria was only half-full by the time Tim was ready to leave, so he picked up his tray and walked over to a small window to turn it in. One of the prisoners working kitchen detail took it, doing a double take when he saw who was handing him the tray, and disappeared to somewhere in the back.

Wondering what that was about, then remembering who they thought he was, Tim also pondered how the other prisoners perceived him as they obviously knew the reputation of the Green Hand Killer.

Before he had any more time to consider it, Tim was being lifted off the ground, and he was slammed to the floor, the air knocked out of his lungs as someone heavy fell on top of him. Blindly throwing his fists around, Tim stopped for the briefest of moments and saw it was his cellmate that was assaulting him.

Landing one solid hit to the man's face, Tim instantly regretted it when he saw the man's face change, unbridled rage washing over him. Before he could do anything, two meaty hands wrapped around his neck, squeezing as hard as they could, the sound of cheering and jeers of the other prisoners around them drowned out as the world around Tim started to fade.

And then the hands were gone and something wet sprayed down on Tim from above. He looked up and saw the man had his hands wrapped around his own throat, blood pouring from a slit in his neck that went from ear to ear.

As Tim struggled to take a deep breath, finding it difficult after being choked so hard, he saw the scrawny man swoop in, jabbing the man in the chest half a dozen times, springing blood leaks that soaked into the man's prison uniform. Trying to raise up and turn over, Tim felt the man fall forward, driving him back to the floor before the lights went out.

EYES FLUTTERING OPEN, TIM KEPT THEM HALF-SHUT AGAINST THE harsh, bright lights overhead. He looked around and saw he was lying in a bed, one of many in a row that ran along a wall. His head throbbed, and his mouth was dry, but he realized he was in some sort of hospital judging from the men lying in a few of the other beds, hooked up to machines or IVs.

It wasn't long before a nurse noticed him and came by to tell him he was suffering from a concussion and they needed to monitor him for a day to make sure there weren't any lingering effects. After she walked away, Tim lay back in the bed, no complaints on his mind as he enjoyed the added comfort of the soft pillow cradling his head.

The following morning, the nurse finally shooed Tim out of the infirmary—much to his dismay—and he was sent back to general population with the rest of the prisoners. Arriving back to his cell, he shouldn't have been surprised to find it empty, but Tim kind of missed the man that tried to murder him for the simple fact he wasn't used to having someone sharing his space.

Though he did take the opportunity to move his bedding to the bottom bunk, and he also pilfered through the man's belongings and cherry-picked things that he thought would be a nice addition to his meager supplies.

At dinner, Tim caught sight of the scrawny fellow that had taken care of his cellmate, and he wondered why he hadn't been punished for the murder of a fellow prisoner.

Maybe they didn't catch him? he thought. *But someone had to have seen.*

If Tim had to take a guess, there was probably an unspoken code everyone abided by, and he would need to learn whatever he could about it.

"Hey. Hey..." Tim said to one of the people eating across from him. "Who's that guy over there? The little frail-looking one."

The other man looked to see who Tim was referring to, then looked back at him. Staring at Tim for a moment—seemingly sizing him up—the man finally said, "Kurt," and went back to eating.

Tim nodded his thanks and went back to his own food, planning his next step carefully.

A week went by and Tim watched Kurt whenever he could. The guy seemed like a loner, never really joining anyone else whenever the prisoners were in the yard or when they were in the cafeteria during meal times. He owed Kurt a lot—mainly his life for saving him—and wanted to thank him and possibly ask why he'd stepped in when no one else seemed too keen to.

It didn't escape Tim's notice, either, that the other prisoners seemed to avoid interacting with him unless he made direct contact with them to ask a question or needed to get by them in a corridor or something. He couldn't blame them, being who he was supposed to be, but it still felt odd to him to be in such a populated place and also be a pariah.

Tim finally found the chance to approach and speak to the man that had saved his life when they were walking in opposite directions as he left his cell for dinner. Kurt kept his eyes to the ground in front of him, but he was forced to look up when Tim stepped into his path, blocking the way forward.

"I... I never got to say thank you," Tim told him.

Kurt quivered as he looked up to meet Tim's eyes. "For what?"

Confusion scrolled across Tim's face. "For saving me from that goon who jumped me. I don't even know what that was about."

Swallowing hard, Kurt seemed to be thinking about his next words. "Are you him?"

"Who?"

"You know, the Green Hand Killer. Are you really him?" Kurt finally said, the color draining from his face.

Taking in a slow, deep breath, Tim nodded. "Yeah, that's me."

"That's why he tried to kill you. You're famous. You've killed so many people. It would've only given him more cred in here. He was a lifer, like you, so it didn't matter to him. He only cared about the fame of killing one of the most notorious murderers in history."

Kurt spoke softly, but Tim caught a hint of admiration in his inflection when he talked about the Green Hand Killer. The story of the man wanting to off a high-profile prisoner for his own reputation also checked out.

"But why did you do it? Why did you step in? And how did you not get thrown in solitary for killing that guy?"

Kurt's eyes shifted back to the floor as he shrugged. "I guess it didn't really sit well with me for him to go after you like that. I may have had a few run-ins with him in the past and finally felt ready to settle the score. I never forget, and I always settle up with someone when they have it coming."

Tim was reminded where he was and who he was in here with as Kurt's words struck him like a lightning bolt. He wasn't like most of these people, not really, but he knew he needed to start playing the part better than he had been.

"Thanks. I guess I owe you then."

Kurt quickly looked up at him, then back down. "No problem."

THE NEXT COUPLE OF WEEKS FLEW BY NOW THAT TIM HAD someone to confide in. Looking at the man, Tim's first impression still held that he was meek and unassuming, but after talking to him and gaining a better understanding of the man's way of thinking, Tim appreciated his wolf in sheep's clothing persona even more.

Kurt had the lay of the land and was even on good terms with a few of the guards, so he could get things or be afforded special privileges the other prisoners could only dream of. And Tim wanted to use this newfound friendship to his advantage.

"I think it may be a go," Kurt said one day as they walked around the yard, watching the others watch them.

Tim still didn't know why everyone seemed to avoid Kurt, and he didn't feel close enough to anyone else to ask them, but he assumed it had to do with the man's close proximity to the guards. And when you're in prison, the ones that kept you there were not your friends.

"Yeah? That was quick," Tim replied, wondering how Kurt seemed to curry favor with the higher-ups around this place so well. "Okay. That sounds good to me."

Not long after the two of them became pals, Kurt hinted around he needed a new celly because his was driving him crazy. It just so happened there was now a vacancy within Tim's own cell—much to the doing of Kurt—and he considered the idea of having someone he trusted with him in such close quarters as opposed to some random person that might try to kill him again.

"It pays to know people, you know?" Kurt said. "It sounds like Sunday will be the day they approve the transfer."

Tim chuckled.

"What?"

"That's my birthday," Tim explained.

Giving his own soft chuckle, Kurt said, "I'll be sure to get you something nice then."

For the short time he had been incarcerated, Tim learned the secret to prison was understanding the routine. Learn it, abide by it, and when given the chance break from it and enjoy some semblance of freedom until it is time to fall back into the monotony of the routine once again.

When Sunday came, Tim was given permission to visit the prison's library even though the inmates were on a schedule for a certain day of the week they would be allowed to. Citing that there weren't too many there, the guard—one of Kurt's insiders—escorted him to a small room and waited for Tim to make his selections. Going over the limited rows of books, Tim picked out a Dean Koontz novel that had an interesting-looking cover and a book about rock shaping.

With his books held firmly under his arms, Tim was allowed to return to his cell alone once they were back in his cell block. As he approached the iron doors that stood open, Tim slowed his pace when he heard someone shuffling around inside. Easing his head around to look, Tim saw Kurt was inside, busy preparing what looked to be a celebratory display, no doubt for his birthday.

Before he had time to move back, Kurt's head turned toward the door and saw Tim peeking in.

"Shit, I wanted to have it ready before you got back from the library."

As Tim walked into the cell, he noticed Kurt had all his stuff stacked neatly on the top bunk, waiting to be unpacked and put away.

"Shit, man. You didn't need to do all of this. I think I'm long past celebrating my birthday," Tim admitted.

A sad look crossed Kurt's face, something in his eyes. He shook his head, a smile reappearing at the corners of his mouth. "It's nothing, really. Just something nice for you. Something nice for a friend."

Tim bowed his head in appreciation as he tossed the books onto his bunk, looking around the small space to see what Kurt had up his sleeve. A small cake sat on the edge of the sink—chocolate by the looks of it—and a stringer running across the cell and attached to the walls on either side had cut out letters that said HAPPY BDY TIM.

For the first time, for as long as he could remember, Tim was truly touched by the act of kindness of another person. He had to turn away and look out into the cell block corridor as he collected himself, not wanting to show any sort of emotion in front of Kurt, especially on their first day as cellies.

"Well, I hope you're surprised at least," Kurt queried.

Tim nodded, clearing his throat and blinking away the tears that were threatening to well up in his eyes. "I am. Thank you."

As he turned to face his new cellmate, Tim was greeted with the small cake held up between them.

"All yours, man. Enjoy."

Tim took the cake in his hand, cradling it like it was a newborn baby, and settled onto his bunk. Even as a free man he rarely got to enjoy something as extravagant as this unless someone tossed away a half-eaten treat and he was able to find it before the ants did.

Taking a bite, Tim's tastebuds were set alight with the taste of moist chocolate that seemed to melt on his tongue. As Tim savored every morsel, Kurt busied himself by unpacking his things, leaving the birthday boy to enjoy his treat.

Tim continued to take small bites of the cake, feeling more and more relaxed as he did. He closed his eyes and imagined himself sitting at a table in a big, fancy house, surrounded by the ideal family he had always pictured in his mind. His wife presented him with the largest slice of cake, while everyone else around the table sat and waited for him to dig in. As he picked up his fork, his daughter reached over and stuck a single candle in the slice of cake, then lit it and told him to make a wish.

Tim closed his eyes and thought there was truly nothing he could wish for if this was his life. He had his family, his home, and seemingly not a care in the world. As he opened his eyes and blew out the candle, everyone clapped before they dug into the cake sitting in front of them.

Tim was about to take a big bite when his wife asked, "What did you wish for?"

Shaking his head, he replied, "I can't tell you or it won't come true."

"What did you wish for, dear?" she asked again.

And again, Tim said he couldn't disclose that for fear of jinxing himself.

"What did you wish for, Dad?" his son asked from the right, his daughter parroting the same question from the left.

All three of them kept asking the same question over and over, like a broken record that skipped back to the beginning of a song after playing the first five seconds. Tim grew frustrated with them asking the same question and could feel his blood pressure rising each time it was repeated.

Before he could stop himself, Tim finally yelled for them to shut up but found the words came out muffled.

"Tell me, what did you wish for?" Kurt asked.

Tim's eyes shot open at the sound of the man's voice, and he was looking up at the upside-down face of his cellmate. When he tried to move, he found he was bound by something; even Tim's head was tied down, making it impossible for him to look and see what Kurt had done to him.

"Tsk, tsk, tsk," Kurt sounded as he clicked his tongue against his teeth. "I expected more from the Green Hand Killer. After all, an unparalleled streak of thirty years is nothing if not impressive."

When Tim tried to reply, he realized whatever was being used to gag him was threatening to obstruct his throat. He remained still, looking up at the man above as Kurt stared down at him with a sense of wonderment.

"Now, I want you to imagine my shock and excitement when I

hear the news that the Green Hand Killer has been caught and is going to be imprisoned here with all of us."

Kurt grabbed some part of Tim's fleshy stomach area and drove something deep within it, bringing a sharp and alarming pain, sobering him up. He tried to buck against the unprovoked attack, but it was useless.

"Funny thing is, you're not the Green Hand Killer, are you?"

Tim saw a fierceness in the man's eyes he had never encountered in another human being before. It was the primal, feral look a predator in the wild has in their eyes just before they go after their prey.

With tears streaming from his eyes, Tim tried to answer the man. Tried to tell him he was right, that he had fallen ass backward into taking on the serial killer's identity. But he couldn't, not with the gag in place.

"You don't have to say it. Trust me, I know the truth better than anyone else on the planet. You're an imposter. Nothing. A nobody."

Tim didn't know if the guy was flat-out crazy or some sort of psychic that could predict the future or something because no one on earth should know any different. That or the man was calling his bluff and didn't show the slightest bit of hesitation.

Kurt moved around the bunk and was doing something. Tim was unable to look and see since he had been fastened down. With his heart racing in anticipation for what came next, Tim thought it was going to explode in his chest, then he felt the cool edge of a knife pressed against the skin of his leg before it sank in, a ripple of white-hot fire shooting throughout his nervous system.

Kurt appeared back in his line of sight holding his trophy like a prized fish he had just caught. The slab of flesh hung limply in his hand, and Tim felt his stomach lurch. He tried to yell again, for help, for the man to stop, but it was useless with the gag.

"That's a nice cut," Kurt said as he laid the section of Tim's thigh to the side. "But I think I can do one cleaner. I guess I've grown a little bit rusty over the years being stuck in here. Oh, that reminds me..."

Tim's eyes followed the man until he was out of sight, struggling against whatever was holding him down. When he saw Kurt come back into view, he was doing something with his hands that was hard to see.

Just then, a prison guard walked by, shining a flashlight into their cell. Kurt stood there, still doing whatever it was he was preparing while Tim's head fought to raise up and show the guard he needed help, that this psycho was butchering him alive. The beam of the flashlight held on them for a few moments before the cell went dark again.

Tim knew the guard wasn't going to save him. Nobody could.

"This is usually done at the end, when you're dead, but I thought it would be funner to break from tradition this time," Kurt said.

Watching as Kurt's hand came out of the dark and passed through a sliver of moonlight cascading in through the small window, Tim saw it was covered in a sickly shade of green paint. Kurt wrapped it around Tim's face, finally pulling his hand away when the paint was transferred to his skin. Globs of the stuff clogged Tim's nostrils, and he had to force enough air out of his lungs to clear them.

"I bet you're really confused now, huh? You should be. You see, just like I was when you came forward, claiming to be the Green Hand Killer, lapping up all the attention it garnered, I sat back and wondered who this charlatan was. Because... you are certainly not my father, who is the real Green Hand Killer."

Tim's eyes grew wide with surprise at the revelation. What were the odds of these two men ever crossing paths? Yet here they were, in the same cell. One man posing to be the other man's father's alter ego. It was as though divine justice was balancing the scales.

"Yes, he is my father, or was. I guess he's dead now, but I kind of guessed that once he stopped coming to visit. And you thought you would just step in and take credit for all his accomplishments?" Tim could see the man glowering down at him, could hear it in his voice when he spoke. "That shit don't sit well with me."

Kurt sat down on the bunk next to Tim and reached beneath the thin mat, pulling out a makeshift saw with jagged-looking teeth that captured and twinkled in the moonlight.

"You claimed forty or so killings that belonged to the Green Hand Killer. I think it's only fitting you pay your pound of flesh for each of them, don't you? Happy birthday, Tim. It's going to be a long night."

SWEATIN' TO THE OLDIES

LANCE DALE

Silas wasn't always a miserable prick. When Marvin was a part of the group, Silas was the life of the party, but the accident took him away like a thief in the night. They had been friends since Silas had been making memories, and without him, the colors of the world dulled like an old Polaroid photo left out in the sun. It had only been a month, but it might as well have been a lifetime ago.

Don was the other member of their group, and he invited Jeff to join after the accident. "We need a new third," he insisted. He acted like Marvin could just be replaced, like bringing in a new puppy when the old family dog dies. Jeff was coming over for the first time tonight, and Silas could feel everything inside him boiling. He knew he had to move on, but every time he heard Jeff's name, it was just a reminder that Marvin was gone. His fists tightened as he walked into his bedroom. He crouched and fished the dusty wooden box out from under his bed. Tonight was the first time they would be using it without Marvin. It felt wrong.

He took the box out into the living room and undid the lock. The lid creaked as it opened, and a musty odor filled the air. The contents of the box didn't light up his face like a mysterious briefcase or glow with elvish text. Nothing about it looked special other than the fact that it may have made someone the envy of the gym or tennis court back in the 1970s. Anyone looking at it today would just see a dirty red, white, and blue striped sweatband. Silas didn't know where or how his uncle got a hold of it or where it came from, but it should have scared the shit out of him. It didn't.

SILAS SAT WITH DON IN THE LIVING ROOM, WAITING FOR JEFF'S dumb ass to come stumbling into the room. He was five minutes late, which might not seem like much, but when people were late, it was their way of telling you your time was not valuable. *Fuck this guy. Marvin was never late.*

Even if Marvin was still around, Jeff still would have given Silas a bad vibe. Don swore Jeff was cool. Spoiler, he wasn't. He was one of those gym bros who ate every meal in the form of a protein shake. Don was on thin ice too. Why would he be friends with someone like Jeff? It said a lot about his judgment. Silas pulled out his phone and watched another minute tick by, and the front door opened. He turned to see Jeff's stupid grin staring back at him.

"Look who's finally here," Silas said.

"Sorry, I got stuck behind some asshole that forgot which side of the car the gas pedal was on," Jeff said. He thought he was being cute.

Silas narrowed his eyes at him. Not only was he late, but he was also a liar.

"It's all good, man," Don said, breaking the awkward silence. He was rocking back and forth and fidgeting with his hands like he just downed a case of energy drinks.

Silas thought it looked like he had gotten into some bad drugs but then remembered how Don got twitchy every time he went in. Silas had been so wrapped up in Jeff's fuckery that he almost forgot that Don was going first tonight.

"So, what exactly are we doing tonight?" Jeff said.

Don started to speak, but Silas cut him off.

"You're just going to have to watch and find out," Silas said. "Don's going to show you how it's done. Go get the chair."

"What's the magic word?" Don asked.

"Get the fucking chair," Silas replied.

Don left the room and returned pushing an office chair. The wheels squeaked against the tile floor. Two belts were tightened over the armrests and a towel and black pillowcase rested on the seat.

"What the hell is all that stuff for?" Jeff said.

Don answered before Silas could cook up a clever passive-aggressive remark.

"You won't believe me if I tell you, so you're just going to have to see for yourself," Don said. He turned to Silas and exclaimed, "Let's fucking do this!"

Sweat rolled down his face as he positioned himself in front of the chair.

Silas turned on the TV and flipped through the channels, passing reruns of old sitcoms and infomercials for products that didn't need to exist. He stopped at a live broadcast of a football game. Southern Technical College was playing Western State, and the score was tied. There was only one minute left on the game clock.

"Here we go," Silas said.

"Oh, this is too perfect. I hate Southern Tech. Watch this shit," Don said to Jeff.

Don sat down, and Silas tightened the straps around his arms. Then he tied the small towel around Don's mouth and slid the sweatband onto his head.

"What the fuck?" Jeff said.

"Relax, we're not getting kinky. It's for his safety," Silas said. "Just nod when you are ready," he said to Don.

Don's eyes darted to the TV and scanned the offensive players of Southern Tech. He zeroed in on the quarterback, nodded, and closed his eyes. Silas slipped the pillowcase over his head.

Jeff didn't say anything, but his mouth was agape. He wanted to leave, but his morbid curiosity kept his feet cemented to the floor.

Don's body stiffened and tensed like every muscle was flexing simultaneously, and his head jerked back. Then he began to shake.

"Is he okay? I think he's having a seizure," Jeff said.

"He's fine. Stop looking at him and watch the TV," Silas said.

He looked at the TV but could still see Don's twitching body in the corner of his eye.

The quarterback of Southern Tech approached the huddle, then turned toward the camera and gave a thumbs-up.

"He's in," Silas said. "Now comes the fun part."

Jeff didn't reply. He continued to watch, wondering if they were fucking with him.

The quarterback from Southern Tech lined up and took the snap. He shot back with the ball, cocking his arm as if he were going to throw a pass. Then turned and sprinted in the wrong direction. He was heading toward his own endzone. His teammates stared in confusion.

"What is he doing?" one of the announcers said.

"I don't even know what to say. I've never seen anything like this," replied the other.

The quarterback ran into his endzone and punted the ball into the crowd. A chorus of boos erupted. He turned and pulled down his pants, exposing everything as they began to pelt him with drinks. The TV quickly cut to a commercial.

"That crazy bastard," Silas said, laughing.

Jeff didn't know if he was more confused about what he had just witnessed or that Silas was smiling. He thought Silas would need plastic surgery to smile.

"What just happened?" Jeff asked.

"I'll explain in a minute," Silas said. He approached Don's body, which had stopped shaking. The restraints were loose enough for him to turn his hands upward and give two thumbs-up.

"He's back," Silas said.

SILAS AND DON SAT JEFF ON THE COUCH AND EXPLAINED HOW THE sweatband worked. Silas wanted to stay mad, but Don's stunt with the quarterback had lightened his mood. His armor was cracking, which made him feel guilty. It was like he was betraying Marvin.

"I don't know how it works, but the sweatband allows you to swap bodies with people. Anyone you want. It works the best with live TV, though," Don explained.

"Just a reminder, too. Not a word of what happens here leaves this room," Silas added.

"Think of it like Las Vegas or Fight Club," Don added.

"Okay, so you have this magic sweatband that defies all time and space, and you're using it to ruin football players' careers," Jeff said.

"Oh, come on, that wasn't any football player. That was Blake Smith. The dude's a total dick. He had it coming," Don said. "Seriously, wait until you try it. It's amazing. Better than any drug. You're gonna be hooked."

"It lets you experience what it's like to be another person for a minute or two. The possibilities are limitless," Silas said.

"What happens if you stay too long?" Jeff asked.

"We haven't tried it and aren't going to. Two minutes is the max," Silas said. "So, are you all ready to give it a try?"

"I thought you were up," Don said to Silas.

"Nah, Jeff's ready. I can see it in his eyes. Come on, hop in the chair," Silas said.

"Hold up. You said that you are swapping bodies. Does that mean the other person goes into your body?" Jeff asked.

"Yes. Blake Smith was just inside me," Don said and then laughed.

"I'm being serious," Jeff said.

"Calm your tits, Jeff. I mean, technically, they do, but they're in shock and paralyzed. You saw what happened with Don. The shaking. We use the chair and restraints just in case, but it's never been a big deal. Plus, all you have to do is think the word 'home,' and you're back like nothing happened," Silas said.

"How many times have you guys done this?" Jeff asked.

"A lot. Let's stop with the questions and get down to business," Silas said.

"Remember, all you have to do is focus on the person you want to swap with, and when you're ready to go back, just think, 'home.' It's simple," Don added.

"I don't know, man. This whole thing seems fucked up," Jeff replied.

"Just give it one try. You don't have to stay long. Just pop in and see how it feels, then hop back. Haven't you ever wondered what seeing through someone else's eyes is like? I promise you will have a blast," Silas said. Jeff was thrown off by the change in his tone. When Jeff walked in tonight, he thought Silas was going to take a swing at him. Now, he was all buddy-buddy. Maybe he just needed to warm up a bit.

"I'll tell you again, you're gonna be hooked. Come on, man. We're your peers... pressuring you. Be one of the cool kids," Don said.

They both stared at Jeff like a couple stray cats begging to come inside on a cold night.

"Fine. I'll give it a shot," Jeff replied.

Jeff sat in the chair, and Silas tightened the straps around his wrists.

"Not so tight. I need circulation," Jeff said.

Silas loosened the straps one notch.

"I'm so excited for you. I wish I could do it for the first time again," Don said.

Jeff could hear his heart beating faster. This didn't feel right, but he couldn't back out now without feeling like a total pussy.

Silas slid the sweatband over his head and began flipping through the channels.

"We've already done football. We need to find something else. Bingo," he said.

Silas stopped on a news show. It had his favorite four-letter word in the corner. LIVE.

An elderly man named Dick Rosewell was being interviewed, and it looked like he was standing at death's doorstep. Silas grinned. It seemed like the perfect body for Jeff to go to. Let him experience what it's like to be the Crypt Keeper. It would be hilarious.

"This one. It's perfect," Silas said.

"Wait. Don gets to go into a top athlete, and you have me going into a guy who probably shit his pants this morning," Jeff said.

Don started to talk, but Silas shushed him.

"It's your first time. It's good to go into an elderly person to warm up. They are easier to steer," Silas said.

Don shot Silas a look of confusion, and he was happy that Jeff couldn't see it.

"All right. Let's go," Jeff said.

"Just focus on our buddy Dick Rosewell there and close your eyes. Envision yourself traveling to him. Give us the thumbs-up when you arrive so we know you made it. Remember, think the word 'home' when you're ready to return," Silas said.

"All right. Here goes nothing," Jeff said.

Jeff closed his eyes. His head snapped back, and his body began to shake.

"He's gone," Silas said and grinned at Don.

"You're such a dick. Easier to steer? How'd you come up with that horse shit?" Don said, laughing.

"He's got to pay his dues. If he can handle being in that body, he can handle anything," Silas said.

They both focused their attention on the TV.

Dick Rosewell stopped speaking and stared at the camera. The only movement he made was the twitching of his eye. His jaw was slack.

"Mr. Rosewell?" the interviewer said with concern.

Dick did not respond.

Silas and Don looked at each other.

"Is he okay?" Don asked.

"He's fine," Silas said, but it felt like he was trying to convince himself more than Don. It felt like his guts were being twisted with a pitchfork.

Dick snapped out of it and gave a thumbs-up.

"Sorry, I lost my train of thought," Dick said. Then he winked at the camera.

Silas and Don breathed a collective sigh of relief.

"That motherfucker. He was fucking with us," Don said.

The interviewer asked another question.

"Mr. Rosewell... you've lived a storied life and done more in your time here than most people would in ten lifetimes. What advice do you have for the young people at home watching this?" he asked.

"Oh, this is going to be good. They pitched that question right down the middle," Don said.

Dick Rosewell looked into the camera and collapsed.

"What the fuck just happened?" Don asked.

"Do I look like I know?" Silas replied.

They frantically watched the TV, waiting for it to cut back to the interview. Instead, they were treated to commercials about asking their doctor if a particular medication was right for them while people with STDs smiled and played tennis.

Silas looked down at Jeff's body. He was still but breathing.

"If that dude just died, did Jeff die in there too? Why did you have to have him go in there? He was too old, and his brain couldn't handle it. We just killed two people," Don said.

"Quit freaking out. Everything is going to be okay," Silas shouted.

The news came back on, and they went silent.

"We are sorry, ladies and gentlemen. We have had a medical emergency on the set. We will update you when we have more information." Then it cut to the weather report.

"Fuuuuuck. What should we do?" Don said.

They looked at Jeff's body and verified that his chest was still moving up and down.

There was a knock at the door.

"Shit, I forgot I ordered a pizza," Don said.

"We have to get Jeff the fuck out of here. It looks like we kidnapped him," Silas said.

"Just a minute!" Don yelled to the door.

They wheeled Jeff's catatonic body into the bedroom and closed the door.

Silas answered the door and forced a smile as he paid the pizza guy. Then he slammed the door in his face and bolted it.

"Nice tip, asshole," a muffled voice said on the other side.

"We have to figure out what we're going to do with him. Maybe we can take him to the ER and say he passed out or something," Silas said.

"I don't know, man. This all feels like a sick joke," Don said.

A breaking news alert flashed across the TV.

"Richard Rosewell Dead at 97," the headline read.

"Shit," Silas and Don both said in unison.

SILAS AND DON STARED AS THE MONTAGE OF DICK ROSWELL'S LIFE flashed across the screen. They had no idea what they were going to do.

"That Dick guy was kind of a badass," Don said as they showed him decked out in medals. The caption read that he had the nickname "Rosewell the Reaper" in his younger days.

"I don't give a shit about that guy. We're fucked," Silas replied. He wasn't used to being unable to think his way out of a situation. "This shit would have never happened if Marvin was here."

"Yeah, well, he's not. We have to figure this out. I say we call an ambulance and say he hit his head," Don said.

"That's not a bad idea. We should bring him in here and push him over in the chair. It will be more believable if his head is bruised up," Silas replied.

They walked to the bedroom. The door creaked when they opened it, and they turned on the light. The chair was tipped over onto the floor. Jeff was gone.

"He's got to be in here somewhere. The door was shut," Silas said.

"Jeff. Come out, man," Don said.

They looked at each other and then to the closet.

"He has to be in there. There's nowhere else he could've gone," Silas said.

Don approached the closet as Silas stood back.

"You got us good, man. We were both freaking out," Don said as he crept closer.

He put his hand on the door handle. It turned on its own, and the door flew open, hitting Don in the face. He was knocked back, and blood exploded from his nose. Jeff jumped out, holding a tie, and kicked Don in the stomach. He spun Don around and wrapped the tie around his neck. His hawkish eyes locked onto Silas. Every trace of Jeff was gone, and that Rosewell guy had his hands on the wheel.

"If you make any moves, your friend is dead," Rosewell said. The sweatband was still on his forehead.

Silas looked at Don and saw a stain forming around his crotch. He put his arms up.

"This is just a misunderstanding," Silas said.

Rosewell didn't let up. He smiled, which made him look even more menacing.

"I didn't think I'd ever see a travel band again. They disguised this one nicely. We used these back in the CIA. How did you guys get your hands on one anyway?" Rosewell asked.

"My uncle gave it to me. I don't know where he got it. Please just let him go," Silas replied.

"So, you got your hands on it, then saw me on TV and thought you'd hop in and fuck with me? Get a good laugh out of it?" Rosewell replied. His grip on Don didn't waver.

"We're sorry. We didn't want to hurt anyone," Silas pleaded. Every ounce of the authority he felt earlier in the night had evaporated.

"Bullshit. You're just sorry you fucked with the wrong one," Rosewell said.

"Please, just let him go. We're sorry," Silas said again.

Rosewell's eyes bore into him, and then he laughed.

"I'm just fucking with you. Shit, if I had one of these when I was your age, I probably would have been doing the same thing," Rosewell said. He loosened his grip on Don.

Silas let out the breath he had been holding too long and noticed the cold sweat pouring down his face. It was going to be okay.

Rosewell looked him in the eyes, smiled, and snapped Don's neck.

SILAS RAN. THERE WAS NO TIME TO PROCESS WHAT HE HAD JUST witnessed. Survival mode had kicked in. He reached the front door and tried to yank it open, but the deadbolt stopped it.

Shit.

He heard Rosewell's footsteps creeping behind him like Michael Myers as he fumbled with the bolt. It popped open. He turned to see Rosewell. He was holding a knife.

"My luck just keeps getting better. Your buddy had this in his pocket. Let's have some fun. I'll give you a head start," Rosewell said.

Silas sprinted out the door with everything he had while Rosewell jogged behind him with no urgency. Silas fished his phone out of his pocket and dialed 911.

"911, what is your emergency?" the dispatcher asked.

"My friend is trying to kill me! Help!" Silas screamed into the phone as he continued to run. He could already feel himself running out of steam. Why did he spend all this time lazing around when he could have been hitting the gym like Jeff? He had to keep going, but adrenaline only went so far. His heart flapped against his chest like a bird trapped in a cage.

That son of a bitch. He knows I can't keep going.

Silas could feel him getting closer, but his legs were shutting down. If he was going to survive the night, he had to fight. He stopped and turned around.

Rosewell caught up and slowed to a stop. The sweatband was still dry. He hadn't even broken a sweat.

"So, are you all ready to get this over with?" Rosewell said.

"Why are you doing this?" Silas asked as he raised his fists.

"Do you even have to ask that question? How many people get a chance to be young again? I can start a new life and do whatever the fuck I want. I just have to get you out of the picture. No one will ever know. Here. I'll make it a fair fight," Rosewell said and threw the knife to the ground.

Silas didn't wait for him to make the first move. He sprang forward with a punch that surprised Rosewell and connected with his cheek. He felt something crunch, and Rosewell was knocked back.

"Take that, you fucker," he said triumphantly, but his victory was short-lived. Rosewell smiled and spit a wad of blood on the ground.

"Nice shot, but this isn't a movie, son. It's going to take more than a lucky punch to walk away from this," he said and wiped his chin.

Rosewell shot toward Silas. He moved faster than Silas's mind could comprehend. He was slammed back against the blacktop and saw a flash of white. His vision blurred for a few seconds, and when it cleared, he saw Rosewell standing over him. The knife was back in his hand.

"Got any last words?" he asked. Silas looked up at him. There was nowhere for him to go. This was the end.

"I just have to get some shit off my chest," he said.

"I'm all ears," Rosewell said.

"I fucked up. I should have never used that sweatband. It was wrong. I messed with people's lives, and they didn't deserve it. I've acted like a piece of shit to my friends and my family since Marvin passed away. I'm sorry to Don and Jeff. It's my fault this happened. All of it.

"I feel so guilty about what happened to Marvin. It's eating my soul. I should have never let him drive that night. I knew he was drunk, and I could have stopped him. I was a shitty friend, and now he's dead.

"I wish I could go back and change everything and be a better friend. All I can do is say I'm sorry and hope they're listening somewhere," Silas said.

"Nice Oscar speech. It's really a shame that it won't save you," Rosewell said.

"It doesn't have to," Silas said and smiled.

Rosewell looked back and forth. A siren blared, and red-and-blue lights strobed down the street.

"It just had to hold you off long enough so they could," Silas continued.

"Son of a bitch. I'm kind of impressed," Rosewell said.

Another police car came down the street on the other side. The car stopped, and the door popped open.

"Get your fucking hands up!" a cop yelled. He drew his gun and pointed it at Rosewell.

Rosewell gripped the knife in his hand and looked down at Silas.

"You motherfucker. Looks like there's only one way out of this," he said, shaking his head.

Silas grinned. His life may be in shambles, but he won.

"I beat you," he said.

"We'll see," Rosewell replied.

He turned and ran toward the police officer with the knife raised above his head, screaming like a maniac.

"You'll never take me alive!"

"Sir, stop. I will shoot," the officer said as he got closer.

Rosewell didn't slow down. The sound of gunshots echoed through the street as he was torn down in a hail of bullets. His body slapped down against the pavement in a pool of crimson.

THE POLICE QUESTIONED SILAS. HE EXPLAINED TO THEM HOW JEFF had gone crazy and that he thought he must have been on some sort of drugs.

"He's been acting weird lately, and we were worried about him. We invited him over for pizza, and he snapped. He killed Don. He tried to kill me. I don't know what happened," he said. His eyes filled with tears.

"Let's get you taken care of. You hit your head pretty hard. There will be plenty of time for questions later," the police officer said as the ambulance pulled up.

The cop walked over and looked down at Jeff's body.

"What the fuck was he wearing," he said as he focused on the sweatband. It had soaked up a lot of blood, which had stained it a dark shade of crimson. It was probably going to rot away in some evidence locker. "Crazy bastard," he said and shook his head.

THE AMBULANCE SPED TOWARD THE HOSPITAL. SILAS LAY IN THE bed as the paramedic looked him over.

"Sounds like you had quite the scare back there. How are you feeling?" he asked.

He looked at him with the eyes of a hawk.

"This is the best I've felt in a long time, son," he replied.

THE MASTERPIECE

JOHN DURGIN

I stare at the blank canvas, hoping it will speak to me. They always do. But I find myself stuck in this rut, where my mind strays to other places for hours of the day. The project is already a week late, and if I don't get it turned in soon, the publisher may move on and hire someone else that can get it to them in a timely manner. I can't let that happen. Not with a family to provide for. I've worked too hard, fought and clawed to get where I am today.

After Lilly died, my world was turned upside down. My first true love, the person I thought I'd spend the rest of my life with, gone with the snap of a finger. *Gone with the thrust of a knife.* We were so happy together, and at the time I was on top of the world with my art career as well. But those cocksuckers took everything from me. They forced me to do unimaginable things. Lilly was sick, they crawled into her head, turning her against me. I was only defending myself. But then... then—

"Hey, babe. How's it going in here?"

I close my eyes and take a deep breath, hoping my wife doesn't see the annoyance, then turn and smile.

"It'll come. I promise. We need this one, Tiff."

"I know. And I don't mean to add more stress to your plate, but we got a nice letter from the landlord taped to the front door today. He's giving us two extra weeks, Seth. What are we going to do? We can't get by on just my income."

"I know that. I just... I just need to be left alone so I can concentrate on it, okay?"

"I'm trying, here. I really am. I've picked up extra hours. I clean the entire apartment when I get home from work and take Paul to practice and games. Please understand that if I show any frustration, it's not intentional. I'm just exhausted, babe. That's all."

Rage boils inside the pit of my stomach. I want to scream in her face. She doesn't know what it's like. These demons I've been burdened with since Lilly died—they latched onto me the moment her heart stopped beating for the last time, and now they're burrowed into *my* brain, just like they were hers, telling me to do awful things. The meds help, but anytime I slip up and forget a pill here or there, the dark thoughts come back. Have they reached Tiffany too?

"I appreciate everything you do for us. I just need inspiration. Do you realize that once they give final approval of this cover that I'll be looking at a massive payday? We'll be able to catch up on rent and pay off all our debt. Buy Paul the top-of-the-line equipment for any sport he desires. Hell, maybe we can even take that vacation you've been wanting to take," I say as the thought of us getting out of this financial hole brings another smile to my face, momentarily forcing the rage down.

Stay down there.

Tiffany didn't do anything. Don't take it out on her.

Or do. What if she has them too? What if Lilly didn't just leave you with them, but anyone you love?

No! It's not possible.

"You okay? Your eyes just changed moods about six times in the last thirty seconds," Tiffany says jokingly.

She thinks it's a joke. Show her what happens when you laugh at us.

"I'm fine. I'll be out in a bit. I just want to brainstorm some more before dinner. Love you."

"Love you too," Tiffany says, but I sense the hesitation in her response. She knows about my past. Maybe she's scared of me.

You fucking pussy. Let her make a joke of you and your situation, her situation too, and then you tell her you love her? Coward.

Tiffany leaves my studio, and the room returns to silence. *Returning* me to my thoughts. This project has brought out a side of me I didn't think possible anymore. Agitation is my default status, and if it wasn't for my meds I'd probably have snapped by now. But they're helping less by the day. The stress dilutes their effect. I pick up my pencil, start sketching in my notebook, hoping for inspiration. I can't lose this job. Ten grand. That's how much they're going to pay me if the painting impresses them enough—and it will. My talent has never been in question. When they take this masterpiece, they'll then send me a contract for ten covers, which will be plastered on books from the world's most popular horror authors. Once those books are on shelves, and everyone can't stop talking about how disturbing their cover art is, I'll have other publishers lining up for my work.

I sharpen the pencil until it's a fine point, then admire its piercing tip. It reminds me of a knife, the kind Norman Bates would be proud of. It reminds me of Lilly, and the blade repeatedly penetrating her skin, burying into her organs. It *reminds* me of the blood, pumping out of the wounds, decorating her flesh canvas with crimson beauty.

Why can't I get her out of my head? She's been dead for almost five years now. I've married Tiffany and love her to death. Taken in her son as my own, and for the most part Paul has accepted me as his stepdad. Yet Lilly will not let me escape my past. I continue to reminisce about our flawed relationship and how it ended as I sketch away. Before I know it, nightfall has filled the sky, eliminating the natural light shining in from our high-rise windows. How long have I been in here?

When I look at my sketch pad, it's Lilly smiling back at me. I had drawn her without even realizing it. She's mocking me from her grave. Her demons are dancing on my shoulders, throwing a party every time I think of the knife slicing into her, thrusting like an act of lust.

"Fuck!"

My hand throbs, and I don't realize why until I look down and see myself punching the desk repeatedly.

"Get your shit together, Seth. Take a deep breath. In... and out."

Just like the knife... In, and out. Over and over.

TIFFANY SETS PLATES AT THE TABLE WHILE I TRY TO MAKE SMALL talk with Paul—not one of my strong suits. I hate talking with people in general thanks to the extreme introvert in me, but chatting with a preteen is the equivalent of trying to speak a foreign language with a mouth full of Novocain. Not that I want to put much focus on the conversation, my mind is still in the studio, laying the groundwork for a masterpiece. After my tantrum earlier, ideas started coming to me. The last thing I wanted to do was leave the studio, but I needed to pay attention to my family as well. All work and no play makes Jack a dull boy, and all.

"How was school?" I ask Paul.

He shrugs his shoulders, the universal sign language of a twelve-year-old boy. Why do I even bother? Tiffany sits next to me after placing a large salad bowl in the center of the table. *Lovely, this should get the creative juices flowing... a plate of grass.*

"How's the cover coming?" Tiffany asks.

"Getting there. I have a meeting with the publisher tomorrow. So it'll be a long night for me. Need to get this just right," I say, biting into a forkful of bland vegetables.

"I was thinking, maybe I'll take Paul away tonight for a few days so you can focus solely on the project. How's that sound?"

"That... that sounds *great*. It's not fair to you guys that I take my stress out on you. I promise, once this is out of the way, things will get back to normal."

Tiffany stares at me, and I can see the doubt in her eyes. She's worried. She can see through my lies. In her defense, she knows of my past. She was one of the nurses treating me during my stay at the hospital. We hit it off, and against her better judgment, she gave me a shot. She saw the improvement from Seroquel. The work I put in with doctors and therapists. Tiffany was the only person who treated me like a human being after the news of Lilly's death. At first, I thought maybe she just had a fetish for murderers, like you see in all of those serial killer documentaries. But it was clear her feelings were genuine. She loved me enough to trust me around her son, and after promising myself I'd never let another person close to me, I fell in love. Tiffany gets me.

"Okay. After dinner, Paul and I will pack up and have a nice long weekend together, mother and son. How's that sound, Paul?" Tiffany asks.

"Cool. I get to skip school tomorrow then?"

No, you fucking moron. You're going to do remote learning from a hotel.

"Yep! Just you and me. You can hang out at the pool. It'll be fun."

"I appreciate you doing this, babe. It means a lot that you see how important this project is."

"Of course."

"Gross... Can you not call each other babe in front of me? Especially at the dinner table. I want to keep my food down," Paul says.

I want to slap him in his obnoxious little mouth, but I fake a smile. In a perfect world, it would have just been Tiff and me. But someone like me doesn't get to dictate what baggage a companion brings into a relationship. Especially when they are a catch like she is. I eat the rest of my dinner in silence, picturing the groundwork for the painting and ways to improve it.

When I snap out of my daydream, I'm alone at the table. I hear Tiffany packing a suitcase in our bedroom. This has been happening too often. How much time did I just let slip by without even realizing it? After I rinse my plate and stuff it in the dishwasher, I help Tiffany finish packing and walk her and Paul to the door. She kisses me, but her lips are stiff as a mannequin's, not that I've ever kissed one before. When I pull away, I see it again. The concern in her eyes. She's not leaving to give me space; she's leaving because she's scared of me. Maybe she won't ever come back.

Can you blame her? You're showing signs of cracking again. If you can see it, surely she can as well. Don't let her go.

If I'm having a breakdown, I'd rather have her gone. Plus, that's not going to happen again. I've gone through measures to make sure of it.

"You guys have fun."

"We will. And Seth, don't push yourself too much, okay? I'm worried about you. We'll get through this no matter what. And don't forget to take your Seroquel. I know how you forget if I don't remind you. The pill organizer is on the kitchen counter," Tiffany says.

I don't say anything. I can't. Instead of telling her how stupid that sounds, I nod and wave goodbye. As soon as they step into the elevator in the hall, I shut the door and lock the deadbolt. It's as if them leaving instantly relieves half the stress I was feeling. I grab a beer from the fridge and head back to my studio. Back to the canvas and my tools. It's going to be a long night.

I WAKE UP TO A SHARP PAIN SHOOTING THROUGH MY NECK. Daylight shines in through the window, forcing me to squint. I worked all night, blending the red and black into the cover that will truly give the art department at the publisher the chills. I glance at the clock and jump out of the chair, sending another jolt of pain down my stiff back. I'm supposed to be at their office in an hour and still need to shower, pack up the art, and catch an Uber. As I grab the corner of the painting, I freeze. I don't remember painting this. I was in a trance; the demons inside my head took control. It's depraving, horrible, disgusting. It's *perfect*.

The office told me to just scan the art and email it, but I refused. Told them they had to see it in person to take in its true beauty. This shit will blow their minds and will make it impossible to turn down.

After a quick shower, I throw a dress shirt on and a clean pair of jeans, then open the Uber app and request a ride. By the time I get down the elevator and onto the sidewalk, the car is already waiting. My heart pounds in my chest as we get closer to the headquarters, planning out everything I'm going to say when I get inside. The driver tries to start up small talk, but after a few one-word answers, he gets the hint that I'm not here to make friends and shuts his fucking mouth.

I get out of the car and enter the building, a towering skyscraper with the publisher's name displayed on a massive sign above the front door. The canvas remains secure in bubble wrap and a 12x16 hard case. Countless people with business suits and punchable faces shuffle in and out of the building, going about their day. I spot the front desk in the corner of the main lobby and push through a crowd of people chitchatting about politics. I'm pretty sure one lady even swears at me as I bump past her but *fuck* her. She can talk about this wherever she wants, blocking me from my destination deserves far more than an accidental nudge.

The man sitting behind the counter looks up at me and smiles. His black hair is slicked back with too much gel, and his teeth are sparkling white. "Can I help you?"

"Hi, yes. I'm here to see the art development team in regards to a cover I've been commissioned for," I say, holding up the case as if he can see through it.

"Let me take a look... Typically they don't do in-person meetings. Are you sure they didn't just want you to email them?"

"I'm sure. They said to email, but I told them I wanted to meet in person, and we have something set for right now," I say, double-checking my watch.

"And what's your name?"

"Seth Bennet. They're expecting me," I say, reading the man's name tag. "Rick."

As gel-head types away at the computer, I observe the lobby. These people are so content meandering around, going about their dead-end jobs. The world needs more people like me, with creative juices that can inspire the masses.

"I'm sorry, Mr. Bennet. I don't show any appointments on the calendar today. There must have been a mix-up."

"Check again. That's Bennet with one 't.' I just came all the way down here from across town, rushed around to make sure I was on time. This is important, a cover for a prestigious author."

"There's nowhere else to check again. They're in a board meeting right now, and none of them would be able to meet you one-on-one anyway. I can take a message for them."

"A message..."

"That's right."

"Tell them Seth Bennet is here, and he's waiting in the lobby until they *are* ready for him. I marked off my whole morning, so I'm okay waiting."

"Sir—"

"Just tell them. This job's important to me. To my family. I can't afford to be dicked around."

"Please, no need to talk that way. If you'll have a seat, I'll reach out to them right now. I can't promise they will see you today, but I'll at least get a resolution."

"They'll see me. Thank you," I say, then walk over to the waiting area and sit in a chair stiffer than the prick behind the counter. *A resolution*. The only resolution is me leaving here with a signed contract and a check. If we don't get this, we'll lose everything. I won't let that happen. I admire the art on the wall and think if the people in charge actually like this shit hanging in here, they'll drool over this cover.

The man behind the front desk is giving me a strange look as he talks on the phone, saying something too quiet for me to hear from my seat. He nods, blocking his mouth as if he's telling the world's most important secret. When he sees me staring back, his eyes flit to the side, but it's too late.

I already saw you, buddy.

Slick Rick hangs up the phone and flags me over. I can see him swallowing the nerves from here. As I get closer, those nerves turn to something else... *Fear.* This prick is scared of me. I try to smile to ease his nerves, but it's not easy. I want to strangle him for treating me like some bum off the streets.

"Sir—Mr. Bennet. The art team assures me they have no meeting scheduled today with you. Furthermore, they state that when you demanded to meet in person, they specifically told you that wasn't something we do. And my boss tells me to remind you that they have passed on your project. Deadlines are important in this industry, and you missed yours—"

"Whoa, whoa, whoa. Settle down. There's got to be some confusion. I'll show you my email exchange with them. They gave me two more weeks to get it done," I say, pulling out my phone and opening the email app.

I quickly scroll through my inbox, searching for the conversation with the art team about coming in and presenting the cover.

Where the fuck is it? Please don't tell me I accidentally deleted it.

"Mr. Bennet, I'm the one that emails for them. That email was never sent. You must be mistaken."

"*Rick?* I'm not fucking crazy. Let me find it."

It's not there. I grind my teeth behind closed lips. Slick Rick clears his throat, his hand resting on the phone like it's a gun and we're about to have a quick-draw shootout. What does he think I'm going to do exactly?

"I'm sorry. Whether you think the email is there or not, they're busy at the moment. And they will be all day. There's no point waiting around, Mr. Bennet. If you don't leave, I'm afraid I'll have to call security."

"*Security?* I'm a fucking artist, not a terrorist. What the hell do you think I'll do?"

"No offense, but you're a bit unhinged, sir. Nothing you have told me is true, yet you insist that it is. Did you find that email yet? If someone else responded to you besides me, I'd love to see it."

Smug prick. He knows I can't find it. I bet they found a way to rescind the email. That's why I'm not seeing it.

"Fine. I'll leave. But you should be really careful how you talk to people, Rick. I'll be seeing you."

I have no intention of leaving. But if I can get this pest's atten-tion off me, I know exactly where to go for the art department. The sign at the front of the lobby said it was on the second floor. If they were busy, I'd just have to force my way in and give them no choice but to say yes to me. Still, I have to be careful. Slick Rick doesn't believe me and continues to watch my every move as I head toward the exit. The elevator sits to my right, and I focus on it out of my peripheral as I near the main doors.

Just when I need to make a final decision, the elevator dings open. I glance back at the front desk, and Rick is back on his computer typing away, probably emailing coworkers about his experience with the rude guy. I slide into the elevator and hit the button for the second floor, relieved to be the only one in here. I'm not in the mood for small talk. The ride up is too fast; I didn't even have time to go over my presentation in my head before the door slides open.

When I step out, it's not what I expected. Instead of big confer-ence rooms with giant mahogany desks surrounded by a bunch of suit-wearing snobs, I see floor-to-ceiling glass walls and a group of kids who looked barely out of college wearing t-shirts and jeans. They're all focused on some PowerPoint presentation up on a big screen with their backs to me. I don't waste any time, walking straight toward the office door and knocking. The man presenting, a thirty-something douche who looked as if he enjoyed the glory days of his frat house, where they'd slip roofies into girls' drinks, stops talking and looks at me with confusion. I open the door and enter.

"I'm sorry, may we help you?" Douche Boy asks.

"Yeah. I'm here for my meeting. I'm Seth Bennet. You guys hired me for the cover on McQueen's new book?"

Instead of recognition, it's confusion I notice on their faces as they exchange looks with one another. I feel the rage boiling inside again, something I've tried to keep at bay since my outburst with Tiffany last night. But these assholes acting like they have no idea who I am is pissing me off.

"Mr. Bennet, we weren't expecting you," Frat Boy says.

"I keep hearing that from you people. Why is it so hard for you to remember we had a meeting scheduled today?"

Again, Frat Boy appears confused, scanning his coworkers for help. I notice him glance briefly at the screen where he was in the middle of presenting before I interrupted. My eyes follow, and that's when I notice what they were in here talking about. Some generic cover art for the new McQueen book. The book I was being commissioned to do the cover for. Frat Boy quickly powers down the screen like he's protecting the country's nuclear codes and clears his throat.

"We don't have a reason to meet, Mr. Bennet. You know we've moved on for the cover. We've discussed this with you on multiple occasions through email and over the phone."

"No... I need this. You told me I had two extra weeks, and... and I've finished it. I scheduled this time to bring it in and show you in person."

Frat Boy raises his hand to stop me, and I want to snap every one of his fingers.

"I'm sorry, truly. But we've already submitted the new cover. The book is moving forward with it. You need to leave, please."

"For that piece of shit up on the screen? You haven't even seen my work yet. At least let me show you—"

"Mr. Bennet. You're wasting your time. Please leave."

"At least tell me who you got to replace me? My family is about to be on the streets because of this... I-I need this," I say. Maybe I can reach out to the other artist, explain my situation, and they'll tell the publisher to go with me instead. I can't just take no for an answer.

"When I say we're going in a different direction, I wasn't referring to another artist. Far too often we run into situations like we did with you, where we are waiting for work, contracts breached. A deadline is there for a reason, Mr. Bennet. We're going with a top-of-the-line AI technology. It's not stealing art from real artists. We've developed an application that builds covers from scratch and avoids the backlash publishers keep receiving while trying to evolve with technology."

"AI? I'm losing a job because of fucking AI?"

I don't hear his response. Red filters over my sight, and it's all I can do not to jump across the table and strangle this cocksucker in front of his coworkers.

"Whose decision was this? There's no heart. No blood, sweat, and tears put into it. It defeats the fucking purpose of art, don't you get that? Why not just release books prompted from a computer too?"

"The final decision is mine. I run the art department, and the publisher has already agreed to it. So please leave before I call security. You're interrupting our meeting, Mr. Bennet."

"I don't give a fuck about your meeting. You should be ashamed. I hope you all rot in hell!"

I storm out of the office, slamming the door shut on the way out. It's too bad the glass doesn't shatter on impact. When I reach the first floor, Slick Rick at the front desk tries to stop me, but I give him the finger and march out the front doors. I'm not done with this place. People like Slick Rick and Frat Boy don't get it.

I have some work ahead of me. They will regret passing on my cover, but the true masterpiece has yet to come.

BY THE TIME I GET BACK TO THE APARTMENT, IT'S PAST LUNCH time. I grab a bagel and load it with cream cheese, then pull open my laptop. It doesn't take long to find information about the employees of the art team, nor the receptionist. I knew that pretty boy would have too much of an ego to hide his personal page. A few minutes scrolling through Instagram and I know all I need to about him as well as Frat Boy. Frat Boy's name is as fratty as you can get. Brody Hightower. He's single and posts countless pictures of himself at the Bullseye Sports Bar on the main strip. Slick Rick, however, spends a lot of his time at the huge indie bookstore downtown. Wonder if he judges a book by its cover?

I glance at my phone, wondering why I haven't heard from Tiffany and Paul yet. I assumed they would want to at least check in to see how the meeting went. Not that I'm upset to hold off on giving that news. Still, it's not like my wife. I shrug it off and shut my laptop, then head back into my studio and set the cover art on the easel. I gather supplies into a bag and grab a blank canvas as well. There isn't much time, as I want to make sure I get back to the city before everyone leaves work for the day. As I head back to the front door and prepare to leave, I spot my pill organizer that has slots for every day of the week and realize I haven't taken my meds in three days.

There's no time for that right now. Worry about it when you get back.

This agitation, it's not me. I want to hurt everyone and everything in front of me right now.

So... do it.

I HAVEN'T BEEN IN A BOOKSTORE IN YEARS. I STOPPED READING after Lilly died, as every time I read I hear it in her voice. It hurts too much. But right now, I make an exception to my rule, browsing through a book while keeping my distance from Slick Rick. I sit in one of the leather chairs in the corner of the store, holding the book up high enough to block most of my face. Rick finishes paying for his latte and heads toward the romance section. Not what I expected for his genre of choice, but I'm not here to judge. I watch him read the back cover synopsis of a few books before he finally grabs one and heads toward the register.

With his back to me, I set the book I'm holding on the small table next to the chair and get up, exiting the store before he sees me. He's going on living his life as if nothing bad happened today. As if his employer didn't ruin my life, all so they could use AI. My mouth starts to hurt as I grit my teeth too hard, but I ignore the pain when he exits the bookstore. His gel-smothered hair shines in the late afternoon sun. The sidewalks are busy, and I use it to my advantage, staying a good twenty feet back as I tail him.

Eventually, he hops on the subway, and I follow suit. After a few stops, he gets off, and I do the same, making sure nobody thinks I'm out of place. He answers a call on his ear pods as he makes a left turn down a side street, which I already know is where his apartment building is located. I'm thankful for his distraction, as the crowd thins when we go down this street, and if he was paying attention, he'd likely spot me.

Rick greets his doorman who half pays attention to him and continues talking with someone else. After slipping through the turn-stile sliding glass door, I stay back and watch the light above the elevator that tells me which floor Rick stops on, then rush over to the next elevator and hop in, pressing 4.

When I step off the elevator, I'm lucky enough to spot Rick down the hall heading toward his apartment, still chatting with someone on the phone. I pick up some of his conversation.

"Yeah, man. Guy was a fucking lunatic. I thought he was going to go postal on us right there in the lobby. Yeah... Funny thing is, he was never even contracted. I just had to play it off like he was because I didn't want him pulling a gun on me. Looked like a rabid animal, or some nutjob high on bath salt—"

Rick entered his apartment, and with it ended what I could hear of the conversation. But I had heard enough. He was talking about me. Mocking me. I'm an artist, not a terrorist. Hell, I don't even own a gun.

Time to show him what true art really is.

I knock on the door and immediately move away so Rick won't see me through the peep hole. I hear him say bye on the phone as he approaches the door. I wonder if he's too much of a pussy to open the door, but then he surprises me and opens it. He pops his head out and says, "Hello?"

He sees me as soon as he asks the question, but it's too late. I push the door open with my boot, sending Slick Rick stumbling back into his apartment, then enter right behind him and slam the door shut. Rick's still trying to comprehend what the hell is happening.

"Wha-what the hell do you want?"

"To make art."

Short and sweet. No need to overexplain the situation. He knows I'm not here to make friends. I notice his eyes stray toward his kitchen counter, where I see a butcher's block full of knives. Can't let him get there first.

We both take off at the same time, but I'm faster. I tackle him to the floor and hear his head crack off the kitchen island on the way down. When I turn him over, he's delirious.

"Please... I didn't do anything. I only work for them."

"You weren't very nice to me. You laughed at me. All I ever wanted was to provide for my family, and you took that from me. But that's okay. We all get what's coming to us."

I no longer have control of my actions. The demons that had infected Lilly are inside me, telling me to do awful things.

It's not awful. It's deserved. And you're just getting started...

Slick Rick's eyes roll in his head. I think he got concussed on the way down. It's a shame, really; I'd prefer he feels everything that's about to happen. I mount him and take my backpack off. I carefully take out the supplies I packed, and concussed or not, Rick stares back in confusion and fear.

"Wha... what are you doing?"

"I told you, Slick Rick. I'm making art."

First, I zip-tie his hands behind his back and lift him from the floor and force him to sit in one of the island chairs, then I zip-tie his ankles to the chair legs. I consider gagging him so he won't yell for help, but I want to hear him scream. Instead, I notice the remote to his sound system on the counter and turn on some music. The first song that plays is "Espresso" by Sabrina Carpenter. Not my preferred music of choice, but it will have to do.

Rick's head sags forward, but he tries to lift it and watch me as I set up. I pull out the small easel and place it on the counter, then set the blank canvas on it. I can see the confusion behind his dazed eyes, and I love every second of it. When I pull out the utensils and brushes, his expression changes to one of abject horror.

"Please. They'll suspect you. They saw the way you acted in the lobby today."

"This isn't about getting away with it, Slick Rick. This is about proving a point."

His crotch darkens as he pisses himself. He knows this can only end one way. Once he realizes that begging won't do him any good, he starts thrashing around in the chair, as if his weak ass could break free of the zip-ties.

"You crazy motherfucker! Let me go!" he yells, drool sliding down his chin.

"What's wrong? We're just creating art. Want to start with a watercolor?"

I take a paint brush and slide the bristles along his mouth, dabbing it with his drool. He jerks his head back, but there's nowhere for him to go.

"No peeking. You have to wait until I'm done to see it."

Again, he attempts to break free, slamming the legs of the chairs off the floor. While I'm not worried about anyone hearing over the music, I can't take any chances. He opens his mouth to scream, and before he can let one out, I drive the back end of my paint brush into his mouth, pushing through the resistance until it reaches the back of his throat. His eyes go wide. He gags, choking on the handle, but it shuts him up. Now, the only sounds coming from him are moans as he tries to gag the brush from his mouth.

"Sorry. That's not coming out anytime soon. Maybe now you'll shut the fuck up."

Rick cries, and with each hitch in his chest, I can see the pain in his eyes as the brush handle presses into his throat. Hopefully he won't choke to death before I'm done. That would take away most of the fun. I grab a second paintbrush and point it at him.

"Now, time to get to work. But I have one problem. I forgot my paint. Do you have any here?"

His head shakes slowly as his crying intensifies.

"I didn't think you would. No need when you can just use an app to generate art for you, right? Except that's not real art, Ricky. I'll show you what real art is."

He doesn't see the boxcutter in my hand until the blade punctures into the top of his chest. He screams, opening his mouth so wide that the paint brush dislodges and falls in his lap, covered in a bloody spit. Now he's screaming at the top of his lungs, and I can't have that. I leave the box cutter hanging out of his chest and reach into my bag to grab a small towel. After balling it up, I force it into his mouth, deep enough that it won't fall out like the paintbrush. His cries are muffled, and now I can get back to work.

I grab the boxcutter and slice, starting at his chest and slowly forcing the blade through the muscle beneath the skin, down to his stomach. Rick's breathing intensifies, and his chest heaves up and down, making it difficult to keep the blade steady. But the pain is part of the art. The blade meets resistance, but I force it through, now sliding it below his belly button and back up around to the other side of his chest. I think he's about to faint.

"Stay with me, Rick. The worst part's almost over."

I'm lying. It's far from over.

Once the blade reaches the place I started, I pull it free. Rick sighs in relief, but it's going to be short lived. I wedge my fingers into the top of the fresh gash and his eyes go wide. He's got some life left in him after all. I think he knows what I'm about to do, but even I don't know if it will work. It's not like I'm a surgeon who cut open countless patients. When I begin to pull, it's much easier than I expected. I tear the skin free, pulling harder when I'm met with resistance. It reminds me of when I used to buy a copy of books with my cover art and the store put a price sticker over my work. I'd try to peel it off only to have some of the sticker remain stuck. I'd have to really work at it to get it free, just like Slick Rick's skin.

The skin rips from his torso, displaying the tissue and red muscle below. Blood pours from his chest, drenching his pants. Sweat drips from Rick's forehead as he shows signs of fading. It's clear he's about to pass out from the pain, a real bummer. I want him to watch as I create.

I grab my paintbrush and dab it into his bloody flesh, then get to work.

I slap Rick in the face, and when once doesn't wake him, I think he might have actually bled out, but then I slap him again, this time harder, and his eyes lazily flutter open. The towel rests on top of his open torso to hide the mess from his view. Don't need him passing out from the sight of it.

"Wha... *Elllp* me..."

He's just going through the motions, pretending to fight for his life. I should have just left the towel in his mouth, but I needed it to fix a smudge on the canvas while he was unconscious. I can't help the smile spreading on my face like the blood, *his* blood, spreading on the canvas.

"You ready to see my masterpiece? I assure you, no AI program could imitate this. Blood, sweat, and tears went into this—literally—and that's something no machine can replicate. Does your fancy program have a wife and kid to support? Does it have to live on the streets if it can't pay its bills? No... No, it doesn't. Yet you talentless dirtbags decide it's worth ruining the integrity of artistic creativity, typing words into a prompt and stealing art, to save some *money*? Should I go into the grocery store and steal food for my kid because it saves money?"

Rick closes his eyes, and I fear they may never open again. I can't let him die before he sees the finished product. I turn the easel around to face him, and he opens his eyes again in response to the wood legs scraping across his floor. His droopy eyes lock on the painting, and I can't tell if he's amazed or terrified. Probably a mix of both.

"Beautiful, isn't it?"

Tears drop from his eyes, diluting the blood on the towel in his lap. The painting is a portrait of him, created with his blood, his tears, and whatever the fuck ever strange fluids I could extract from his insides. It's perfect. But there's something else in the painting I can't identify. I swear there's multiple sets of eyes hidden in the back-ground staring back at me. I realize I don't remember creating most of this, as if I blacked out. Just like with the book cover. It's not something I plan to question right now, as it's led to some of the best work of my career.

"I think it's time to clean up my station. What do you say, Rick? I have another project waiting for me, deadlines to hit and all."

At this point, it's like talking to a strung-out meth head. I pull the cloth away from his lap, revealing his shredded insides. That brings him alert, ever so slightly. He moans in agony, but he's dying. I can see the life fading from his eyes. Still, I can't risk him surviving. My point is made, no more need for theatrics. I grab the same boxcutter I cut his chest with and make one swift slice across his jugular. His eyes go wide, one last time as he chokes on his own blood. He tries bringing his hands to his throat out of instinct to stop the bleeding, but the zip-ties hold firm, more than enough for his weakened state. And then his eyes fade to nothing, dead to the world.

I quickly pack up my supplies and use Slick Rick's bathroom to clean myself up. Where I'm headed, I need to look nice. I hear the Bullseye Sports Bar serves a killer drink.

I ENTER THE BAR AND AM PLEASANTLY SURPRISED TO SEE IT'S BUSY enough to remain hidden, but not so busy that I worry my plan won't work. Unlike Slick Rick, I've thought this through a bit more. Brody Hightower sits at the bar with his back to me, and I plan to remain out of his line of sight until the time is right. I order a drink at the opposite end, sitting back enough so the other patrons block me if he turns in my direction.

This smug dickhead probably wouldn't remember me anyway. It was just another day in the life of hot-shot Brody Hightower. It meant nothing for him to tell me I lost a job to a fucking app. I don't plan on drinking, but I need to play the part. After scrolling through Brody's Instagram, I discovered his favorite drink. I order one, an Old Fashioned with extra bitters.

Fucking disgusting.

I seat myself at a table in the corner and reach in my bag. Once I know I'm not being watched, I open the little container that I'd mixed my own little concoction in and dump it in my drink. After stirring it for a few minutes to try and hide the smell as best I can, I make my move to the bar. The bartender glances my way but averts his attention back to new customers, taking some annoying college girl's drink order, focused on her prostitute-level cleavage.

Perfect. Keep him distracted like a good little whore.

Brody is facing someone to his right, his body fully turned at the bar. My heart slams into my chest as I close in, as one wrong move, one second too soon, and Brody will spot me. I sit two stools down from him on his left, quietly enough that he doesn't notice. The drunk asshole won't take his hand off his glass. The guy on the other side of him listens while Brody tells a story that he surely thinks is more entertaining than it really is.

Finally, he raises his hands to animate something in his tale, and I quickly make the switch. My hands are clammy, my throat so dry I consider drinking from fuckface Brody's old drink sitting in front of me. The craving quickly passes. I don't want to catch his douchebag disease. Nobody saw me do it. Now, I just need him to drink it and hope the taste isn't so bad that he refuses to finish it.

Before he sees me, I decide to retreat from the bar and observe from a distance.

Drink it, you son of a bitch.

Finally, he raises the glass and takes a big swig. Even from the other end of the bar, I see him cringe.

"Whew! You made this one nice and strong, Monty!"

The bartender laughs, and Brody tosses back another mouthful, scrunching his eyes. The drink is gone within five minutes, and Brody orders another. I wait. I'll wait all damn night if I need to. Eventually, I hear Monty the bartender comment on Brody's slurring and he cuts him off. Brody obviously isn't used to being told no and argues, raising his voice and causing a scene. I see my opening.

As I reach the bar again, Brody goes to stand, telling Monty he's making a huge mistake when he loses his balance and falls into another customer. I swoop in for the rescue.

"Easy does it, Brody. I got you," I say.

"Huuuh? Wha..."

He's confused, finally turning to see me, and his eyes go wide with an understanding of what's happening. Monty thanks me for getting him away from the bar, and I tell him it's no problem at all, but Brody isn't going out without a fight.

"Heee did this! It's his fauuult!"

He fights me, but my concoction is working its magic, depleting any strength he has left.

"Brody, you did this to yourself, man. I'll be sure to make the drinks weaker next time. No hard feelings, bud," Monty says with a laugh.

I pull Brody toward the exit, and he continues to slur, but thankfully his volume fades the longer the drink works inside him. The bouncer opens the door for me and nods with a face that looks like someone just fisted him.

Once we're outside, I pull Brody toward the alley at the side of the building.

"Uhh."

"What's that, Brody? You want to have a chat? Right back here."

He has no fight left. This is going to be easy. I drag him by the dumpster, hidden enough from the road. I push him against the brick wall, and his head smacks off with a *CRACK!*

Blood smears down the wall behind him as he slides down to his ass, leaning against the dumpster to hold himself upright.

"I hope saving a few dollars was worth it. If you're wondering what made you feel all loopy, I gave you a special drink. Straight from an artist's heart. A bit of paint thinner never hurt anyone, right? The body can shut down if you ingest too much, but a tablespoon worth is just enough to make you act like a sloshed soccer mom watching a *Desperate Housewives* marathon. So, when you blamed me, you were right. I did this to you. But you also kinda did it to yourself, didn't you? I mean, you left me no choice, Brody."

Drool pooled at the edge of his mouth, but he couldn't talk. He could barely move. I open my bag, finding the boxcutter again. It's time to do a little graffiti on the side of Bullseye Sports Bar.

"Hey! What's going on down there?"

I almost drop the boxcutter in a panic. Someone is at the mouth of the alleyway, staring at us. Can he see what I'm doing?

Think quickly, Seth. Your work isn't done here.

"Give us some privacy. Can't someone get a blowjob in peace?"

I make sure to keep my back facing the man and pull Brody's face close to my crotch. Hopefully he's still so far gone that he won't do anything stupid. I moan, disgusted with myself for even pretending I'd let this scumbag suck me off.

"Get a fucking room!"

I glance over my shoulder as the guy mutters something else under his breath, then shakes his head and leaves. My entire body is shaking with adrenaline. Brody lifts an arm and tries to slap me away, but he's too weak. I shove him back against the wall, and he groans again.

Time to get to work.

I shove the boxcutter into his midsection repeatedly, the sound of the blade penetrating his skin almost orgasmic. He tries to fight me away, but he's useless. Darkness borders my vision, and I feel myself getting woozy. Did I accidentally drink some of the poison? No, I know that's not it. Something is happening to my body. I recall blacking out every time the demons take over. That has to be what's happening right now, but I don't remember feeling this last time.

The darkness closes in, and then it completely consumes me.

When I come to, I'm still in the alley, standing over Brody Hightower. Only he's no longer alive. He couldn't be with how his body is torn apart. What the fuck did I do to him? His limp corpse remains leaning against the dumpster, but his insides are hanging out of his stomach. The brick wall behind him is covered in his blood and viscera in a haunting abstract mural. The brick is defaced with so much gore that I can't even imagine how all of it came from one body. But it did, and it's beautiful. Mixed in the abstract painting, I see those eyes again. Staring at me. A face smiling at me.

Unlike the painting of Slick Rick, this one is not a portrait of Brody, but a symbol. The publisher's logo sits in the middle of the bloody mess, molded from a substance I can't identify. I need to get out of here, and now. For the first time through all of this, I start to wonder what the fuck I've done. These people needed to pay, but part of the real me is coming back now. Lilly's demons have had full control for weeks. I realize that now. I need to get home, call Tiffany, and tell her to come back. I've made a terrible mistake.

But it's so beautiful, isn't it?

Stop it! Get out of my head!

I take one last look at what remains of Brody Hightower, then exit the alley, covered in his blood. I get some looks, but this is the city. It's just another day of the week for them and I'm just some crazy person living on the streets. I need to talk with Tiffany. She'll make me feel better.

WHEN I WALK INTO THE APARTMENT, I'M DISAPPOINTED TO SEE that Tiffany and Paul aren't there yet. They were only supposed to be gone for a few days, so where are they? I can't help the creeping feeling that she knew I was about to crack and left for good. She knows my past better than anyone, and she helped mold me back into a functional human being. But she knows the demons Lilly left me with. She knows they can come back, and stress is their friend.

I walk into my studio and plop down in my chair, taking a deep breath. I left my cellphone charging by the window when I left to head to the bookstore. It's as if my dark side knew to leave it here so it didn't leave a trail of evidence the authorities could track. I check the phone for any missed calls or texts from Tiffany, but the only calls I missed were from unknown numbers, likely telemarketers.

"Damn it, Tiff."

As I contemplate calling her, deciding on what exactly to tell her over the phone, I focus on the canvas resting on the easel in front of me. The book cover that I thought was so beautiful. For the first time, I notice those same eyes hidden in the background staring at me. I dial Tiffany and continue observing the painting, hit with a sudden realization of who the figures are in the painting.

Tiffany's phone rings.

I hear it in my ear... but also somewhere else in the apartment. Each ring hits me like a knife to the gut. It goes to voicemail. I don't bother leaving a message. Instead, I end the call and drop my phone to the floor. I hear the screen crack, but my attention is elsewhere. On my masterpiece. The faces looking back at me...

...I get up and numbly walk down the hall, trying to force down the lump in my throat. I pass our bedroom and head for the closed door of Paul's room. Where I heard the ringing come from. As I turn the doorknob, I hear the faint sound of buzzing. The suffocating scent of death and decay greets me.

I push the door open.

Sprawled out on Paul's bed, I stare at the corpses of my wife and stepson. They both stare back at me, only their eyes are clouded, two stones resting in their sagging eye sockets.

"No..."

I charge toward the bed and trip over their suitcases, falling face first into Tiffany's shredded torso. Her insides hang out like a bomb went off in the pit of her stomach.

"NO! Tiff! Wake up!"

I wipe the rot away from my eyes and see Paul, his body rigid, his face turned in my direction.

Is he looking at me? No. He's dead. Long dead. You killed him. You killed Tiffany, just like you killed Lilly.

Tears pour down my face; my body trembles. I resist the urge to vomit as flies buzz around my head. I can't stop staring at them. But then the demons are back. I feel my lips curve upward in a grin.

This is your masterpiece.

ABOUT THE AUTHORS

Nick Roberts is the award-winning author of *Anathema*, *The Exorcist's House*, *It Haunts the Mind & Other Stories*, *Mean Spirited*, *Dead End Tunnel*, and *The Exorcist's House: Genesis*. He's a member of the HWA and a doctoral graduate from Marshall University. Find out more about Nick at nickrobertsauthor.com.

Ben Young lives in the Cincinnati, OH, area with his family and dogs, where he is currently working on more stories that may or may not ever see the light of day. He does not enjoy writing about himself, especially in the third person like this. Find out more about Ben at benyoungstories.com.

Leigh Kenny was born and raised in the garden county of Wicklow, Ireland. She lives by the Irish Sea with the love of her life, two wonderful boys, a black Labrador, and a three-legged cat that hates people. You can find out more about Leigh's work and any upcoming releases on her social media: LeighKennyWrites.

Megan Stockton is an indie author who lives in Grimsley Tennessee with her two children and her husband, who is an indie filmmaker. She writes in a variety of genres that all have dark/horror elements, and all of her work is character-driven and immersive. She is known for delivering works that are raw, thought-provoking, brutal, and cinematic. She has been writing since she was a child and was always obsessed with horror and the macabre. When she isn't writing (or working her day job) she likes to work with the animals on their farm, read, play video games, and watch movies. Find out more about Megan at meganstocktonbooks.com.

R.E. Sargent is an editor, publisher, and author whose works delve into the sinister depths of horror, suspense, and the supernatural. His story "Lucy," featured in the Splatterpunk Award–nominated anthology *If I Die Before I Wake Volume 3 – Tales of Deadly Women and Retribution*, also resides among the dark tales in his collection, *Everything Went to Shit*.

Nestled in the hauntingly beautiful Pacific Northwest, R.E. lives with his wife, their two grand dogs, and the unyielding rain—a perfect companion for someone who revels in the eerie. Beneath the perpetual gray skies, he crafts stories that reach beyond the ordinary into realms best left undisturbed. Find out more about R.E. at resargent.com.

MJ Mars is a horror enthusiast living in Lancaster, UK. Her debut novel, *The Suffering*, was published by Wicked House in 2023. You can read more of MJ's short stories in her award-winning collection, *We've Already Gone Too Far*. Find out more about MJ at mjmarsauthor.com.

Devin Cabrera, a former filmmaker turned author, brings a cinematic edge to his gripping novels. Drawing from his experience in the film industry, Cabrera infuses his narratives with immersive scenes and dynamic characters. Through his transition to literature, he continues to showcase his talent for crafting compelling stories that linger in the imagination.

Devin lives in upstate New York. When he's not writing, you can find him hiking through the mountains, exploring caves, and trying to find the perfect slice of pizza.

Gage Greenwood is the best-selling author of the Winter's Myths Saga, and *Bunker Dogs*. He's a proud member of the Horror Writers Association and Science Fiction and Fantasy Writers Association.

He's been an actor, comedian, podcaster, and even the vice president of an escape room company. Since childhood, he's been a big fan of comic books, horror movies, and depressing music that fills him with existential dread.

He lives in New England with his girlfriend and son, and he

spends his time writing, hiking, and decorating for various holidays. Find out more about Gage at gagegreenwood.com.

Clay McLeod Chapman writes books, comic books, YA/middle-grade books, as well as for film and television. *Wake Up and Open Your Eyes* is his most recent novel. Find out more about Clay at claymcleodchapman.com.

M.L. Rayner Born and bred in the county of Staffordshire, Matt is a keen reader of classical, horror, and fantasy literature and enjoys writing in the style of traditional ghost stories. During his working life, Matt joined the ambulance service in 2009, transporting critically ill patients all over the UK. After writing several novels, Matt now dedicates his time on future releases. His hobbies include genealogy and hiking, and he enjoys spending time with his wife, Emma, his children, and his family. Find out more about Matt at https://m-l-rayner-author.sumupstore.com.

Steven Pajak, a Chicago-based author, crafts stories that explore the depths of horror and the human psyche. With a pen that dances on the edges of darkness, Steven brings to life tales that challenge, terrify, and linger in the minds of readers. Drawing inspiration from the urban tapestry of Chicago, his work merges the pulse of city life with the eerie quiet of the shadows lurking within the darkest corners of our minds. Steven invites you into a world where fear meets courage, and the journey through his imagination proves as haunting as it is unforgettable. Find out more about Steven at stevenpajak.com.

Jay Bower is a horror author living outside St. Louis, MO, in the forest of Southern Illinois. He spends his time reading, writing, and convincing his wife the dark stories he writes do not involve her.

One time punk-rock skateboarder and heavy metal kid of the '80s, Jay approaches his work with the same indie attitude as those early punk bands.

He's the author of several dark novels and short stories. Find out more about Jay at jaybowerauthor.com.

LM Kaplin is an author from Albany, NY, who has been a horror enthusiast his entire life. His books include the psychological horror *Mine*, the cosmic occult horror *Usher of the Fallen*, and a collection of vampire stories, *Fang Fiction*. In addition to his own books, he publishes a series of anthologies through his publishing company, Broken Brain Books. Find out more about LM and Broken Brain Books at brokenbrainbooks.com.

RJ Roles grew up in the mountains of West Virginia. His love for horror and all things macabre was instilled in him at a young age, as was reading when he discovered the Goosebumps series. He currently works as a private security guard when he's not trying to peck out stories on the computer. He spends the majority of his time at home with his wife Jessica and their spoiled-rotten cats. Find out more about RJ at rjroles.com.

Lance Dale was born and raised in Wisconsin and is the author of *Title Pending: A Collection of Short Fiction*. His stories have been included in several anthologies, and he is an avid fan of extreme metal music, horror movies, and books of all genres. Although he loves writing, he enjoys spending most of his time hanging out with his amazing wife and two children, dog, and two psychotic cats near La Crosse, Wisconsin.

John Durgin is a proud active HWA member and lifelong horror fan. Growing up in New Hampshire, he discovered Stephen King much younger than most probably should have, reading *IT* before he reached high school—and knew from that moment on he wanted to write horror. He had his first story accepted in the summer of 2021. His debut novel, *The Cursed Among Us*, was released June 3, 2022, and went on to become an Amazon bestseller. Next up, his sophomore novel titled *Inside The Devil's Nest*, released in January of 2023, followed by his debut collection, *Sleeping In The Fire* in June of 2023. In 2024 he released two more novels, starting with *Kosa*, which released to stellar reviews, and *Consumed by Evil* through Crystal Lake Publishing. Find out more about John at johndurginauthor.com.

Join the Crystal Lake community today!

Subscribe to our Newsletter!
(Scan the QR code or click if eBook)

Subscribe to our Patreon!
(Scan the QR code or click if eBook)

**Visit our Linktree for
all social media sites!**
(Scan the QR code or click if eBook)

Download our catalog!
(Scan the QR code or click if eBook)

www.ingramcontent.com/pod-product-compliance
Lightning Source LLC
Chambersburg PA
CBHW021028310726
48969CB00006B/1591